Railed By The Alpha

Mia Kerr

Copyright © 2023 by Mia Kerr

All rights reserved.

No portion of this book may be reproduced in any form without written permission from the publisher or author, except as permitted by U.S. copyright law.

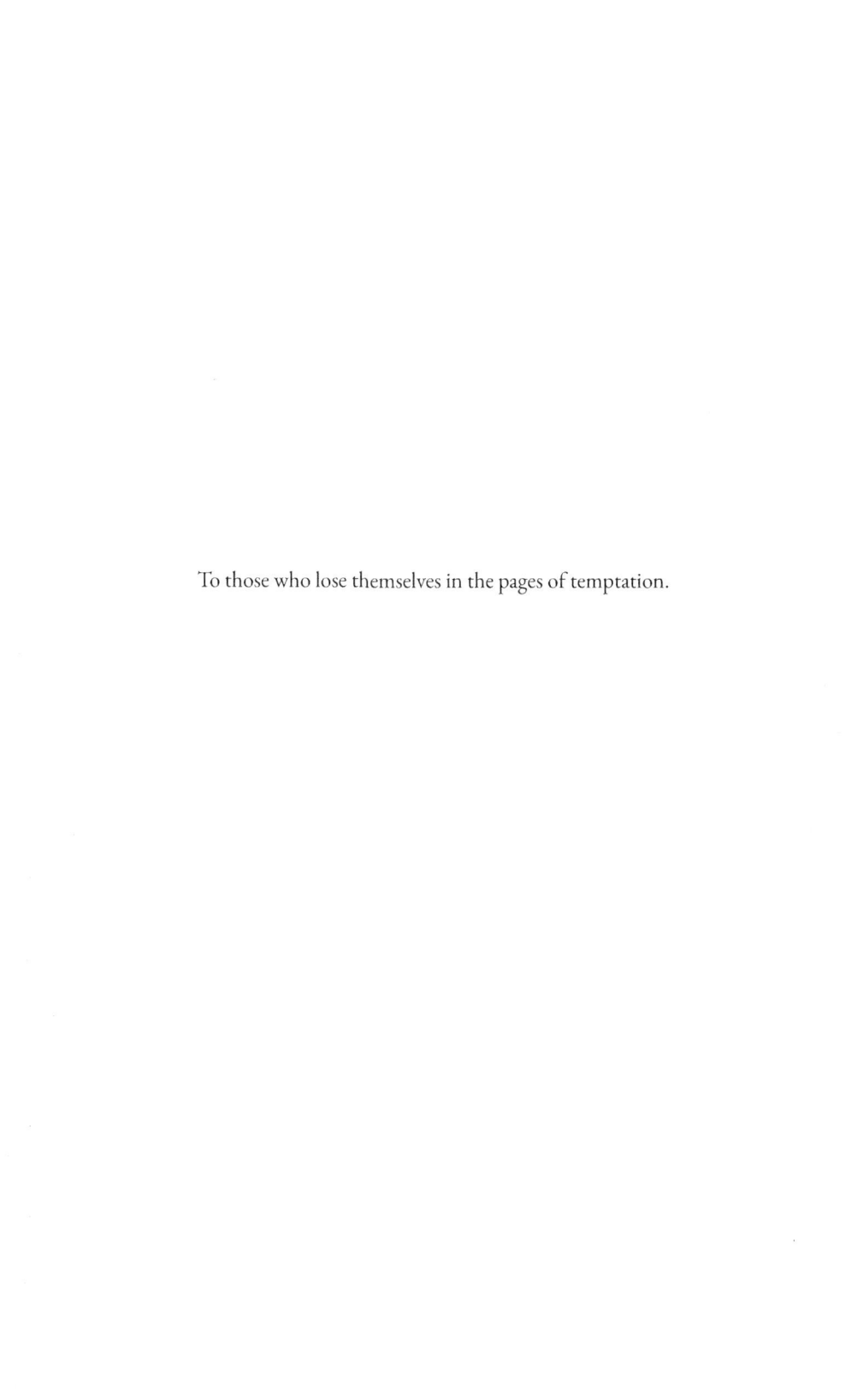

To those who lose themselves in the pages of temptation.

Contents

1. Chapter 1 — 1
2. Chapter 2 — 7
3. Chapter 3 — 12
4. Chapter 4 — 18
5. Chapter 5 — 24
6. Chapter 6 — 29
7. Chapter 7 — 33
8. Chapter 8 — 38
9. Chapter 9 — 43
10. Chapter 10 — 48
11. Chapter 11 — 53
12. Chapter 12 — 58
13. Chapter 13 — 63
14. Chapter 14 — 68

15. Chapter 15   73
16. Chapter 16   79
17. Chapter 17   84
18. Chapter 18   91
19. Chapter 19   96
20. Chapter 20   101
21. Chapter 21   107
22. Chapter 22   113
23. Chapter 23   119
24. Chapter 24   125
25. Chapter 25   131
26. Chapter 26   137
27. Chapter 27   142
28. Chapter 28   148
29. Chapter 29   154
30. Chapter 30   159
31. Chapter 31   164
32. Chapter 32   170
33. Chapter 33   175
34. Chapter 34   181
35. Chapter 35   185
36. Chapter 36   190
37. Chapter 37   196
38. Chapter 38   201

39.	Chapter 39	206
40.	Chapter 40	213
41.	Chapter 41	218
42.	Chapter 42	223
43.	Chapter 43	228
44.	Chapter 44	233
45.	Chapter 45	239
46.	Chapter 46	243
47.	Chapter 47	248
48.	Chapter 48	255
49.	Chapter 49	261
50.	Chapter 50	266
51.	Chapter 51	272
52.	Chapter 52	277
53.	Chapter 53	282
54.	Chapter 54	287
55.	Chapter 55	292
56.	Chapter 56	298
57.	Chapter 57	302
58.	Chapter 58	308
59.	Chapter 59	313
60.	Chapter 60	319
61.	Chapter 61	323
62.	Chapter 62	328

63.	Chapter 63	333
64.	Chapter 64	338
65.	Chapter 65	343
66.	Chapter 66	347
67.	Chapter 67	353
68.	Chapter 68	357
About Author		361
Also By Author		362
Newsletter		364

1

REBEKAH

"Yeah, it's pretty messed up here. I mean, they're arguing again. It hasn't even been twenty-four hours. I just locked myself in my room and put some headphones on. You might want to stay out or crash somewhere else. This is exhausting!" Rose said, her voice dripping with frustration, and I could practically see her rolling her eyes.

"Thanks for informing me. I might consider sleeping elsewhere," I quickly replied, my voice echoing in the empty subway station as I watched my steps, descending the stairs. It was the middle of the night, and my shift had just ended twenty minutes ago. I was bone tired.

I didn't have the energy to endure my parents' arguments, nor did I want to worry about my poor little sister's mental health, like a weight hanging over my head.

"Take me, too!" she exclaimed, her voice sounding like a plea.

"Not tonight. I'll take you on the weekend for a sleepover at Faye's. Just get some sleep, and if you can't, call me. Don't listen to them arguing, please," I told her, my footsteps quickening as I reached the station just before the train could arrive. There was still plenty of time left, but I craved the sanctuary of the silent subway, a welcome reprieve from the chaos at home.

At this time of night, the subway was deserted, not a soul in sight. The last train was scheduled to leave at one sharp, after which the station would close until morning.

I spoke with Rose for another minute, calming her nerves before ending the call. As soon as the call ended, I put on my earphones and sat on one of the benches, waiting for the train to arrive.

Glancing up at the monitor, I noticed I still had a few minutes to spare—eight, to be exact. I scrolled through the photos Faye had sent me from the party she threw last weekend. In some of the pictures, I appeared a little tipsy, striking poses all by myself.

The music pulsed in my ears until I felt the ground beneath me tremble. Startled, my gaze snapped away from the phone, scanning my surroundings. Finding nothing, I glanced over my shoulder and heard a faint, mysterious sound.

Initially, I assumed it was just the song playing in my earphones, but when I removed my noise-cancellation headphones, the sound grew louder.

My brows furrowed.

A *grumble*.

A very loud grumble that reverberated through the subway station. Cautiously, I switched off my phone, removed my headphones completely, and rose from the bench.

Checking the time, it was almost one, but there was no sign of the train arriving. Another loud thud echoed, making me flinch.

Suddenly, I heard several men arguing in a language I couldn't understand. My curiosity piqued, I followed the voices to the back of the waiting area, where a long, white door led to a small office.

The room was situated near the staircase and escalator and was usually locked, but not today.

Curiosity piqued, the voices punctuating the silence of the deserted subway station. I tucked all my loose belongings into my bag before cautiously grasping the door handle and cracking it open just a bit.

Just as I opened it, I heard another loud thud, as if someone had been thrown across the room. A couple of groans and grumbles followed before someone spoke in what sounded like Italian or German. I couldn't be sure.

"*Non scopare con me, cagna!*" The man yelled with a thick accent, his voice shifting abruptly as he addressed someone else. "Are you going to fucking kill him? Or should I rip out his *cranio*?"

Oh, shit.

I gasped quietly, turning away from the door and pressing my back against the wall. My breath quickened, and goosebumps rose on my skin as I swallowed hard. It was the first time in twenty years that I had actually witnessed a fight in the subway station, in the dead of night, just before closing time.

I stretched my right arm, searching for the pepper spray buried deep inside my bag. After a bit of rummaging, I pulled it out, gripping it tightly between my fingers.

Peering through the gap again, the scene became clearer. A man lay on the floor, his brains seemingly scrambled, yet he continued to laugh at the two other men standing before him.

The two men standing side by side appeared far from pleased. One wore a look of disgust, while the other, older man's face burned red with anger, his nostrils flaring and his eyes bloodshot.

It seemed as if someone might die tonight.

All of them were neatly dressed, not in suits but in crisply ironed black and gray shirts. They wore glimmering watches under the white light of the room, and one sported a gold chain around his neck.

Glancing back at the monitor, I saw it flashing. The train was on its way—arriving in less than a minute.

A flurry of thoughts raced through my mind: *Should I call the police? Or leave it be?* I wasn't one to intervene between men and their fights, especially knowing they were stronger than someone like me.

So, I turned around and began walking away from the door. As I stepped away, the door slammed shut by itself, followed by a sudden, eerie silence that enveloped the entire subway station. My heart dropped, and I froze mid-step.

"What the fuck was that?" one of the men inside the room yelled, and then another began stomping towards the door.

Everything happened so quickly. I didn't have a second to move or run. The door flung open, and one of them emerged, his gaze piercing straight into my soul. I placed one hand over my chest, feeling my heart pounding beneath my fingertips.

Taking a deep breath, I raised my arm, aiming the pepper spray at his face. Without hesitation, I pressed the red button, releasing a stream of burning liquid into his eyes. The man immediately screamed and doubled over, the pepper spray taking effect.

Out of the corner of my eye, I saw the train approaching the station, a couple of minutes late but finally here. Just as I readied myself to leave, the second man stormed out of the room, his face twisted with rage. He was larger and clearly stronger than the other one, a growl escaping his throat as he advanced toward me.

I shook the pepper spray again, taking a few steps back. Raising my hand, I sprayed the second man's face without wasting any time. Over the years, I had learned to protect and defend myself, never thinking I would need to use that training.

Until tonight.

"Fuck!" The man growled again, the sound animalistic and chilling me to the core. My heart hammered in my chest, and I clung to my bag as I retreated a few steps.

The battered man remained inside the room, tending to his injuries, while the other two continued screaming at each other. One of them cursed in Italian, pacing back and forth.

The larger man closed the distance, sensing my presence somehow and seizing my wrist. "You fucking *cagna*. You're dead!" he snarled while rubbing his other hand over his eyes, blinded by the pepper spray.

My breaths came in rapid gasps as I tried to wrest my hand from his grasp. He dug his fingernails into my flesh, leaving bruises while trying to clear his eyes of the burning spray.

Fuck.

"Not so tough now, are you?" He yanked on my wrist, reeling me in.

I dragged my nails across his arm, cutting deep enough to injure him. Suddenly, a scent—something—captivated me, causing me to lose focus for a moment. As I regained my senses, I realized his grip on my hand had weakened, and the train had arrived.

I smiled to myself, wrenching my hand free. "Goodbye," I whispered, about to turn away when another idea struck me.

The man spat out a string of Italian curses as he tried to grab me again, failing each time. Seizing the opportunity, I reached into his pocket, swiped his wallet, and sprinted towards the train.

I barely made it, slipping through the doors just as they began to close and the train started moving. The ground trembled beneath me, and an eerie sound reverberated while I waited for the train to depart the station. As it finally pulled away, I exhaled in relief and sank into the nearest seat, still clutching the pepper spray and stolen wallet in my hand.

2

Rebekah

I took a moment to catch my breath and process the harrowing event that had just unfolded. Fights between men were common in the city, but the police usually intervened within minutes, bringing them to a halt. This was the first time I had witnessed a fight with my own eyes. Whoever those men were, they appeared to be dangerous.

A handful of people occupied the train, as it was the last one to traverse the city that night. Lights flickered in nearly every compartment, accompanied by a small screen in the right-hand corner.

No one else was in my compartment, so I took my time to breathe deeply and steady my frayed nerves.

I could have been killed.

Questions raced through my mind: *Who were those men? What were they doing in the subway? Who was the other man on the ground, beaten and battered?*

I didn't dwell on it for long. Once calm, I returned my trusty pepper spray to my purse and picked up the stolen wallet from the seat. Time was short, and I desperately needed money.

I always needed money.

I opened the black, expensive leather wallet, noticing an initial in the corner, studded with diamonds.

CD.

Hmm.

I extracted the warm banknotes tucked inside the wallet. There weren't many, just a few hundred-dollar bills, but it was enough for me. After counting them, I stashed the cash in my bag, a wide smile lingering on my face. This wasn't my first theft.

I had shoplifted a few times over the past year, typically taking items I needed from grocery stores. I had always fantasized about swiping a wealthy man's wallet and finding it filled with hundreds or even thousands of dollars, but this haul was underwhelming. Besides the cash, the wallet contained cards.

Bank cards.

ID cards.

Hotel cards.

And other cards I couldn't recognize.

Regardless, I now had enough money to cover my immediate needs. Stealing the wallet was a thrill, but I wasn't sure I would attempt it again. My heart still pounded as I considered the myriad gruesome ways I could have met my end. They might have killed me if I hadn't temporarily blinded them.

I glanced at the monitor and realized the train was still six stops from my destination. It dawned on me that I wasn't heading home; I needed to go somewhere else, far from the chaos at home.

It was shaping up to be a long night. Each time the train halted, I checked the compartments, ensuring the men hadn't pursued me, although it seemed unlikely.

My nerves were shot. I needed to leave the train station as quickly as possible.

I tucked the leather wallet into my bag, intending to examine the cards later. I knew I couldn't use them at ATMs due to CCTV cameras, but perhaps I could utilize them online.

Clutching my belongings close, I exited the train at the next station. I surveyed my surroundings before leaving the subway and entering the dimly lit city.

The air was humid, neither too cold nor too hot, but I could see fog accumulating in the sky, shrouding the city's towering structures. I inhaled sharply and started walking along the deserted streets, making my way to Adam's house.

His place was just a short walk from the station, situated on a street corner near an amazing coffee shop. As I arrived at his building, I hesitated, reconsidering the idea of staying with him overnight.

After all, he was my ex-boyfriend.

Memories of our breakup flashed through my mind, and for a moment, I decided to turn around and leave. But that moment passed, and I entered the code he'd given me to unlock the building's doors. I proceeded to the elevator, heading to the fourth floor where Adam lived.

This wasn't my first visit to his apartment after our breakup; in fact, it was probably the hundredth time. I couldn't help myself. Whenever trouble arose at home, I found myself standing in front of his building, sometimes calling him, sometimes letting myself into his place.

I always told myself it would be the last time.

But it never really was.

"Hey, I'm sorry for showing up so late!" I said as Adam opened the door to his apartment. Seeing his face, my mood lifted, and I smiled.

"My parents were arguing, and I don't want to go home. Is it okay if I crash here for the night? I'm really sorry—"

"Nah. It's cool. Come in. I was feeling lonely myself," he replied, opening the door wider and inviting me in, as he always did. He held a bag of chips in his left hand while the TV played in the living room. "What's up? You look like you saw a ghost. Everything good?" he asked as he sat on the couch.

I set my bag on the floor and joined him. "Yeah. It's cool. I just saw a couple of men fighting in the subway station, and it was terrifying." I recounted parts of the story, leaving out the details of their intent to harm me and my theft of the wallet for my own selfish reasons.

I figured bad men didn't need money, and since they were fighting, they couldn't report the theft to the police. This meant they wouldn't be able to find me or the wallet ever again.

"Wow. That's messed up. You okay?" His concern grew, and he placed a hand on my thigh.

"Yeah," I nodded and exhaled. Being here felt safe. Adam's apartment was my sanctuary, a place free from worry. "It's fine."

"What happened at your home?"

I shrugged. "The usual, but it's getting worse. Mom's receiving emails from the bank to clear the payments by the end of the month, or they'll take her to court. She's arguing with Dad day and night, and I think she wants to leave him." My heart ached at the thought of my parents living separate lives.

Adam ran his fingers through his hair, sighing in frustration. "I hope things get better!" he said, devoid of emotion. He wasn't my boyfriend anymore; he didn't need to worry about me.

Not that he ever did.

His hand moved to my inner thigh as I kept my eyes fixed on the TV screen, watching an old '90s movie featuring a man smoking a cigar while talking to his wife about something.

"Come here," he said, extending his arm to invite me into his embrace. I knew what each of his moves meant.

First, it was *'come here,'* and then it was *'get undressed.'*

Still, I scooted closer to him, and he wrapped his arms around me as I rested my head on his chest, breathing a sigh of relief. It had been a terrifying night, and the only way to take my mind off it was to let Adam undress me and repeat history for the hundredth time.

3

Rebekah

"Oh, fuck, baby, I love being inside you," he groaned as I pressed my hips harder against his, taking his entire length. He moved his strong hand over my breasts, rubbing his fingers over my hard nipples while I rode him.

Panting heavily, I lifted my head and my eyes rolled as I neared orgasm. The tip of his cock brushed my insides, forming the perfect sensation I needed to finish. I leaned in and wrapped my arms around him before kissing him. My thighs tightened along with my insides that clenched onto his cock, milking him. He thrust his hips forward, hitting my spot and I moaned into his mouth.

"Fuck. I can't hold it anymore," he whispered, parting his mouth from mine. His face shone with sweat and redness covered his cheeks as he held himself from finishing before I did.

I grabbed his hand and placed it over my chest while a silent moan escaped my throat. Biting down on my lip hard, I rode him deeper and came to a release in a few seconds. Warm liquid gushed out of me and covered his cock. My knees weakened and I trembled a little, while continuing to ride him till he was done.

His shaft was buried deep inside me when he finished into the condom. I felt his warmth exploding and as soon as he was done, he pulled out his cock and removed the condom as I jumped over to the other side of the bed.

"Ugh. That was so good!" He was still groaning a little and fisting his cock.

I gave him a little smile before getting off the bed and going to the washroom to clean myself up. It was usual of Adam to remain on the bed for a few minutes after he had finished. He didn't have the energy to come with me, so I took a quick shower alone.

Once I was done, he hopped in the shower, and I put on a t-shirt before tucking myself into bed. We had been having break-up sex for over the past three months. It was the only thing we had ever desired from each other.

Adam and I had been together for over a year before we broke up and we only broke up because he decided to cheat on me with a hooker at his graduation party. I no longer wanted to commit myself to him after learning he had cheated on me but leaving him was hard. He was the only male friend I had in my life and sometimes, I *needed* him.

When he came out of the bathroom, the night had nearly ended. It was three in the morning, and I needed to sleep quick so I could wake up in the morning and head back home to grab a couple of things.

"This is probably the last time I am having sex with you," I told him while pulling the sheets higher to cover my clothed chest.

He chuckled and wrapped his arms around me from behind. "Liar," he whispered in my ears as I began closing my eyes.

"Whatever..." I trailed off.

Almost as I began sleeping, I realized what had happened tonight. *The men. The wallet. The money. Fuck.* My eyes snapped wide open, and sleep drifted away from me just that easily.

"What's wrong? Not sleepy? We could grab something to eat and do it again," he suggested, grinning behind me.

"No. I'm trying to sleep. I have to be at work by ten," I reminded him.

"You're boring."

"I need money, Adam." I snapped my head to him, and he silenced immediately after that. "I need to pay you back and I have to give something to my mother before she disowns me. I have a lot going on in my head. Don't call me boring." I rolled my eyes and huffed out another long breath before ripping the plush pillow from underneath his head.

At least he had a stable job.

While we were in a relationship, I had borrowed over ten grand from him, to pay Mom's debts and also cover some expenses. I had started repaying him, but it had barely reduced.

"Just give me a hundred this month and a few times more of that." He traced his fingers over my bare legs and I shuddered.

"Goodnight." I turned over and pressed my hands underneath my head before shutting my eyes again, hoping to actually sleep this time.

Maybe I could use one of the bank cards or sell the ID for something.

That would be terrible! a voice echoed in my head.

I wasn't this person, not until after my dad got cancer. He had a cancerous tumor in his chest. *Not anymore.* But his entire treatment left everyone in my family broke and in debt, especially my mom. She had to give up everything, her life, her hobbies, her time, and her mental health for my dad.

There were a hundred medical bills raked up, house bills, school bills and a couple of more bills that still needed to be sorted.

Mom had taken debt from several people and places. Some of them were threatening her at this point to return it or go to court or worse, jail.

Fucking hospitals.

I shifted on the bed, making myself comfortable before I dozed off.

When I woke up the next morning, my mind was scattered in a thousand places. I shot straight up from the bed with a painful headache and headed straight to the washroom while a few quick gasps escaped my throat. It was already late. *I was late.* It was eleven in the morning. *Fuck.* I splattered some warm water over my face and rushed outside to grab my things and leave.

I didn't bother glancing at Adam as I knew he would be in a deep sleep. He wouldn't wake any earlier that three or four o'clock and I didn't want to disturb him.

I quietly parted from the apartment, leaving a little note on the fridge, thanking him for the sex and letting me in. Once I was downstairs, I stepped out of the building and made my way to the subway station. The place was bustling and a coffee shop on the corner of the street smelled nice, but I didn't have time on my hands to go get something.

After tagging into the subway station, I went down the stairs and stared at the monitor. The train was going to arrive after twenty minutes. *Fuck.*

I gritted my teeth and stood by a wall. The place was crowded with people rushing in and out.

Minutes passed and I found my eyelids slowly closing. I yawned for the third time and pulled out my phone to check if my manager had called me and surprisingly, he had. *Three times.* My heart leapt to my chest as I dialed his phone and called him back. I was already an hour late and I had missed three of his calls.

Mr. Anderson was going to kill me.

"Hey, I'm so sorry, I didn't see your calls. I just woke up late..." I pressed my hand to my forehead, rubbing the sides and trying to find relief from the headache. "And I lost track of time. I'm sorry," I quickly said as he picked up the phone.

"You're fired, Rebekah!" he exclaimed, his tone loud and furious.

"But—"

Before I even had the chance to speak, he cut me off, "This is the third time you've been late. I gave you warnings already. You're fired. Come pick your last cheque by the end of the week and after that, don't come again," he screamed down the phone.

I felt as if I had just struck my head against the wall and broken it. Mr. Anderson didn't bother waiting for me to speak. He cut the call right immediately.

I groaned and threw my head back against the wall while melting down on the ground. It was one of the best jobs I had gotten in a while, and I was already fired.

Dammit.

I kicked the wall behind me and by the time I was done groaning and crying, the train arrived, and I stepped inside to go back home.

I sat at the end of the compartment, fiddling with my fingers while trying to figure something out. I needed money by the end of the month. I had some. I had *stolen* some, but I needed more than that. I couldn't find another job on such short notice.

I grabbed the same black leather wallet from my bag and opened it once more. To kill time and my intrusive thoughts, I decided on going through the cards and whatever else was inside it. I needed to dump it somewhere soon, but I didn't know where as this was my first robbery.

The train continued to ride through the city, passengers slipped in and slipped out while I remained on my seat, waiting for the train to reach the station nearby my home.

Slipping my fingers underneath the ID card, I pulled it out and took a quick glance at it.

Christopher Delfino.

CD.

4

Rebekah

C.D.

The initials that were on the wallet. It belonged to a thirty-year-old man named Christopher Delfino. Just as I expected, he was Italian. There was nothing more on his ID card except for his name, date of birth and his address. When I looked at the address, it was downtown Laford, where the richest of the rich lived.

This just got a bit more interesting.

I glanced over at the photo on the side of the ID card, finding a handsome man staring back at me. Grinning to myself, I placed the ID card back into the wallet and pulled out the other bank cards. There were at least six of them, different banks and three that matched the name on the ID, while others sported other names.

One of the names on the cards was Pietro Delfino, which I assumed would be the brother I had seen last night. They ought to be brothers. One was older, Christopher, while the other one was younger.

It was hard to wrap my mind around the fact that I had just stolen from someone, someone rich. *What if it was going to come back and bite me in the ass?*

I stood up from my seat when the train stopped at the station near my home. After tagging out, I began walking and reached my home in just a couple of minutes. My family and I lived in the rural part of the city, away from everything. Mom had a mortgage she had been paying for the past ten years, there were only a couple more years left but she wasn't able to cover the payments anymore.

We feared what would happen if we held it off for a couple of months.

When I stepped inside my house, I noticed the odd silence and figured one of my parents weren't home—it was either Dad or Mom.

"You're home early," Mom said, stepping out of her bedroom. Her hair was wrapped in a towel like she had just taken a shower. The scent of essential oils was in the air and there was a steamer switched on in the corner of the living room.

"Yeah. I just crashed at my friend's. What happened?" I asked while removing my shoes near the door.

"Nothing." She gave me a stiff smile. "Just that your dad is being a bitch and I'm tired of taking care of his bullshit. He can't do one fucking thing right and expects me to do everything." She started in seconds, and I knew this conversation wasn't going to go anywhere.

I didn't respond to her. Instead, I walked toward her and handed her the money I had stolen. "Cover this month's expenses."

"Where did you get it from?" She gave me an odd look while holding the money.

The hundred-dollar bills added up to two grand; enough for now. "I took from a friend." When she began staring at me deeper, I sighed and continued, "You need it, Mom, and so do I. Stop arguing with

Dad over something he can't control. I'm getting a bit more by the end of the week and I'll give you that as well."

"Keep some for yourself," she whispered before turning and returning to her room.

That was all.

My family hadn't been happy in a long while, not since my dad got cancer. Everything went downhill from there. We were all in a mess that no one could fix. Without my job, I couldn't either. I needed to find something quick, anything before the end of the month.

Entering the kitchen, I grabbed my aspirin and a juice before heading to my room upstairs. When I passed Rose's room, she quickly jumped up from her bed and followed me inside mine.

"I thought you were at work!" she exclaimed, hopping on my bed.

I laid down and took a breath. "I got fired."

"Really? That's terrible. Where were you for the night? At Faye's?" She began with her hundred questions. I didn't blame her. She didn't really have much to do. Her friends were always here and there, shopping and dining, while she was left alone as Mom barely gave her anything.

"No."

"Adam's?" His name came to her mouth quickly, as she always knew about my whereabouts.

"Yes." I looked away from her.

"Why you always go back to him? He's a terrible person, Rebekah. He cheated on you, twice, and you two aren't even together. He's just using you for as long as he can!" she exclaimed, giving me a scolding. "You can find so many other guys, hot ones and cute ones." Her hand reached into my bag, searching for any junk I had bought during the night, but she found nothing except for the wallet I had stolen. She pulled it open and before I could even reach for it, she removed the ID card and stared at it.

Fuck.

"Rose. Give that back to me," I said, reaching my hand out, but she moved back and stood up from the bed.

"Who's he?" she asked, jumping for joy. "Oh, you're seeing someone!"

"No, no!" I exclaimed, my eyes widening as I tried to grab the wallet and ID from her hand. "Give it to me, Rose!" For a moment, I found myself snapping at her in anger.

She quietly handed the wallet to me along with the ID and then rushed out of room. I opened my mouth to call her name but instead, I let her go.

Instead of putting the wallet in my bag, I tucked it in somewhere else, somewhere Rose or my mom couldn't find it—or anyone else. Picking up the mattress, I tossed it in and threw the mattress back down. A sudden pain rose in my wrist, and I hissed at it before bringing up my hand and finding an ugly bruise where the man had grabbed me late last night.

There was a tiny gash from a nail and the rest of my wrist was covered in blue and red. My face scrunched up in disgust and I pulled my sleeves back down before grabbing my phone and returning to the bed.

I dialed Faye's number and gave her a call to spill the details of the last night. If there was anyone I could talk to, it was her, my best friend—my only friend.

Instead of telling everything to her on phone, I called her out to the nearest coffee shop—Salty Lodge Café.

She pulled up at the café twenty minutes later in her blue Mini Cooper and walked out with a smile on her face. Faye was a natural redhead, she had brown eyes and very pale skin, almost as if she didn't have any melanin. Whenever she walked, her crystal bangles cackled, and her heels echoed. She forced me to wear some of the crystal bracelets and I had one on.

A pink one.

"One iced frappé for me, no whip and low-fat milk." She ordered as she sat down. As the waiter noted her order down, she silently waved at me, all excited to see me after a day of not meeting each other.

Once the waiter left with our orders, I began. "I stole someone's wallet."

Her eyes widened. "You did what?"

"Shh," I placed a finger over my mouth while glancing at my surroundings. The café was filled with people, and I didn't want any of them to hear what I had done. "There was a fight at the subway station last night. Three men. I saw a bit of it and as I was about to leave, they came behind me to attack me. I pepper sprayed them, stole one of their wallets and left, and now the guilt it eating me up and I need someone to talk to." I quickly whispered all the details to her and she listened to me with her mouth shut.

"What the fuck?" She mouthed, her eyes still wide open. "Why?"

"I needed money. Plus, they looked like they had done some terrible things." I shrugged. "I mean, it's fine, right? Tell me it's fine." I grabbed her hand on the table and placed mine above it.

"Yes. It's completely fine. I just need a moment to take it in." She nodded and for the next couple of seconds, we sat in absolute silence as she took in the information. "Okay. Did you throw the wallet?" she asked.

I shook my head. "I don't know where to throw it."

"Who's wallet was it?" she asked out of curiosity.

I reached into my bag and removed it for the third time. After hiding it under my bed, I decided it would be better if I kept it with me so I could find a place to throw it somewhere during the day.

"I don't know." I passed the wallet to her, and she opened it.

"Hmm..." A little voice escaped her throat before she began going through the cards just as I did. When she pulled out the ID and read it, a wave of shock spread over her face as if she had just seen a ghost. "Fuck," she whispered and then placed her hand on her head. "Oh, fuck. No!"

"What?"

"You're dead, Bek," she said slowly, and with terror in her tone.

5

CHRISTOPHER

Pietro was laughing in the corner, a bit too loudly, as if he wasn't the one who had been defeated as well—by a girl. I sat on the couch, staring at the scratches on my arm. The first ones I had gotten in a while.

"You got beaten up by a *girl*!" he chuckled, coming over to me and looking at the scratches himself. "Wow."

"I'll fuck that *puttana*." A low growl escaped my mouth as I rolled my hands into fists. It had been an hour since that woman—*animal*—had attacked us while we did nothing to her. My eyes were still burning from whatever was inside that spray. Even after washing my face for an hour straight, the burning sensation hadn't gone.

"I'm still in recovery. What was she even doing there? I thought the subway was closed." Pietro placed his hand on his stomach and laughed once more. "You know what the best part was. Like she blinded me, okay, but when you went to her, you let her blind you as well!"

"Another laugh and I'll bury you, Pietro. Shut your mouth," I snapped at him.

He didn't care. He walked to the other side of the room and continued to laugh while I tended to my wounds. No one had dared to ever hurt me, not even my worst enemies. The subway station was supposed to be empty at that time of night, but it wasn't. We didn't have any intentions of harming the woman. I only sent Pietro out to handle her, not kill her, and I was hesitating to even go out myself until I heard my brother's scream.

She fucking *blinded* me.

What the fuck was I even doing? Did I rip her head off? No. Nothing at all. I hadn't even touched her and she clawed me, for no reason.

We were at the station, handling our own business and it was all fine until she came. After she was gone, we returned to our business, killed the man we needed to kill and then headed home as my eyes were burning. I couldn't chase the woman—even though I wanted to—but then it was going to be a stretched out night and I didn't want to waste any more time.

"Walter is calling. He's asking if you need any help hunting down that girl. He could look into the CCTV outside the stations if you want." Pietro returned after a moment of being on a phone call. He had stopped laughing at least.

"No. Let her go but if she comes in front of me again, I'll kill her." That woman was the least of my worries.

"Fine. Whatever." He rolled his eyes and began walking away.

I reach into my pockets, grabbing my keys and wallet from the table and return to my room to take a shower. The only thing I grabbed were the keys. There was no wallet. I stood up straight and placed my hand into my other pocket, finding nothing else.

"Cazzo! Where is my wallet?" I raised my voice loud enough for it to echo across the house. My hands turned into fists as I looked behind me, on the couch, hoping it to find somewhere. I thrashed the cushions left and right but was unable to find anything.

Fury stormed into my head like never before.

Pietro froze in his steps and gave me a wild look. "Did she steal it?"

"Did she fucking steal—how am I supposed to know?" I stormed around the couches, glancing at every corner of the room. "Fuck. She fucking stole it," I growled, rubbing the back of my neck in anger. My blood boiled and my nostrils flared. "Call Walter back. Tell him to check the CCTV. I want her, alive or dead, I want her."

His shoulders hunched as he dialed Walter's number and called him back. I stood near Pietro, waiting for him to tell him.

"Yeah, he wants you to look into the CCTV and figure out who the girl is and where she went," Pietro said on the call.

I placed a hand on my hip while my head grew hot as the seconds began passing by. First, the unnecessary attack and then the robbery. I wasn't going to let that woman live for another day. She had fucked with the wrong person.

I grabbed the phone from Pietro and placed it against my ears. "Twenty-four hours, Walter, or I'll feed you to the rogues," I warned him before cutting the call and handing my phone back to my younger brother who seemed to be in a trance.

"Why are angry?" he asked in a low voice.

"I'm *enraged* and I need a moment. Leave me alone for the night. I'll talk to you in the morning," I told him while seizing my jacket from the couch and headed upstairs into my room.

I needed a minute alone before I was going to rip everyone's head off, left and right. My wolf was in need of taking a run, but I didn't have the strength to unleash him or let him free tonight.

The next morning, I woke to the sound of Claudia walking into my room and placing breakfast on the side table. She pulled open the curtains and I rolled onto the other side of the bed. My head was still hot. I hadn't gotten much sleep as I had been thinking of ways to kill *someone.* The woman's face wasn't clear in my head as she had blinded me before I even caught a glimpse of her. I couldn't catch her scent either as the pepper spray was strong enough to shake my senses.

"Good morning, Mr. Delfino," Claudia said as she stood beside the bed, waiting for me to rise and shine. "Is there anything I can get you today?"

"Put Walter on a call," I replied while my head was still covered with a pillow and a blanket. The windows lightened the room, and I couldn't bear it all.

Claudia dialed Walter's number on the telephone beside my bed. After the second ring, he picked up and she put him on speaker.

"Did you check the CCTV?" I immediately asked him without wasting any time. Everything inside me was rattled by that woman and I couldn't do anything unless I had her severed head.

"Yes, Alpha. We got the location of where she went last night. Retro residences. I'm not sure about the apartment or hotel number but I'm checking into that right now and I'll update you in a few minutes," he replied with clear words.

My fury washed off a little. "Great. Send Pietro the details."

I slammed the phone shut and waved my hand at Claudia, telling her to leave me alone. She nodded and walked out of the room whilst I removed the pillow from my head and stared at the sun burning outside of the window. I remained on the bed for the next couple of minutes, hoping to fall asleep for another hour but just as my eyes began drifting shut, I heard a loud ping from my phone.

'Got the deets. She's hot. You sure you want to kill her?' Pietro forwarded me the same message Walter had sent him.

I groaned and sat up straight while going through the details. She had left from the station at one-forty and went to the Retro residences. From there, she had spent the night and then was seen again at the station by the afternoon. Unfortunately, Walter couldn't get her ID'd, but he took snapshots of the CCTV and forwarded them to Pietro just to confirm if it was the same woman.

And it was.

The snapshots weren't clear, but I could tell she was young with auburn hair, slightly tanned, wearing a blouse and black pants along with an ugly brown bag that she clutched to her right side the entire time.

'This isn't enough. I want more details. Have someone follow her.' I texted Pietro.

'That's straight up creepy, bro.' He replied in a minute with an emoji I didn't bother to look at.

She had my wallet, everything inside of it. I was attacked, I couldn't let this go easily, not without ensuring she wasn't dangerous.

'So? I'm the Alpha. I want more details. I want to know everything. Where did she come from? Is she a werewolf? Is she one of us? Which pack? Everything. This could easily be a threat, Pietro and you know how much I hate threats.' I wrote back to him.

6

REBEKAH

"What's the problem?" I asked Faye as she carefully placed the ID back into the wallet. It seemed like she knew the man, maybe more than that, as her expression was *loud*.

Shock covered her face and then fear lingered in her eyes as she placed the wallet back on the table. "You stole this?" she asked again, as if I wasn't clear the first time. I nodded, waiting for her to continue. Her voice lowered and her words became a whisper, "Remember when I told you about the cult I am in?"

My eyes clicked away, and I stared at the brown wall to my side while a few thoughts crossed my mind. Crinkles appeared on my forehead as I furrowed my brows and remembered the time Faye had told me about this cult her and her family belonged to. It was a long while ago. We had been friends since we were children in second grade, she took me to a corner and told me about the cult.

It was called the Wolf Creed.

I didn't remember much except for a few details. They had different religious beliefs and being in the *cult* gave them duties and tasks to fulfill every month. Faye and her entire family usually disappeared on the fifteen or sixteen day of the month, sometimes earlier and sometimes later, but they were all gone.

It was certainly odd, but I never questioned it as she was brought up in the cult and I had nothing to do with it. It was her family and her *other* life. I wasn't bothered with it. There were cults everywhere in the world.

"Oh, yeah, you told me about that cult that's not a cult but you call it a cult, right?" I spoke to her after a moment, figuring out what she had meant.

A couple of months ago, she told me it wasn't a cult, but instead, it was something else, but she couldn't tell me what it was as they all lived in secrecy and sharing information with someone from outside the cult would be dangerous for them.

"Yes, exactly that!" She laughed with me for a moment before the horror appeared on her face again. "Well, like every cult, we have a leader—someone who controls everything and well, I don't know how to say this to you but you stole from that man. This wallet belongs to the leader."

A chill ran through my blood, though I didn't show my fear. "So?" I shrugged, still slightly confused.

"Simple words, Bek. He's very, very, very dangerous!" she stated, raising her voice. "And you should probably start packing and looking elsewhere to live."

I threw my head back and chuckled. "You're not serious, are you?" It wouldn't be the first time Faye would have joked with me on a serious matter. She had great humor and I always enjoyed it.

"I'm not joking, Bek." Her lips were straight, and she looked dead into my eyes.

"Oh..." I trailed off while silencing my chuckles. *Wait.* She wasn't joking. *Did that mean I was in trouble?* "I don't think it's that big of a deal. I mean, he didn't even look at me, so he doesn't know who I am."

"He smelled you. That's more than enough."

"I'm sure he didn't even do that because the pepper spray probably fucked up his all senses." I reminded her of what I had done.

"That's good. So, he doesn't know you." Faye smiled at last. The fear had finally dissipated from her face. She grabbed the wallet and clutched onto it. "I'll give this to someone and he'll return it to him so there is nothing to worry about!" she exclaimed, a hint of excitement in her tone.

Phew.

"There wasn't much inside. Just a couple hundred." I shrugged, easing the tension she had caused. There was truly nothing to worry about. "But are you sure you can do it? I'll just throw it somewhere. It's easier," I suggested.

"No!" Her eyes widened. "You can't throw it. It's fine. I know someone who can get this to him without any questions. Just don't tell this to anyone or mention his name anywhere. You don't want to get tracked by him." There was a warning in her words, a strict one.

Faye was never serious in anything but watching her tighten up today and get all concerned was a new look. It made me suspicious about the cult talks we'd had as children. "Who is this man?" I asked her again.

"You don't need to know, Bek. It's better if you don't," she murmured, her words barely reaching my ears.

I nodded, and we closed the chapter then and there. We sat with each other for a while in the coffee shop, talking about everything except for the man and the cult she supposedly belonged to. I didn't think about the man, the wallet, or the money anymore. After finishing our drinks, we left the café and Faye headed downtown to drop off the wallet to someone she knew while I returned to the subway to go back home.

As I waited at the station for the train, my phone began ringing. I glanced at it, finding Adam calling me. I cut the call and rolled my eyes, but my phone rang again and again. It didn't stop, not even when I cut the call three times. He repeatedly called me as if I was still his girlfriend.

Grunting out loud, I picked up his fourth call and slammed my phone against my ears. "What, Adam?" I snapped.

There was silence, lasting a whole minute. My heart thudded and I waited to hear his voice. *Was everything okay?* "I need you to come here, Rebekah. As fast as you can. Come here," he spoke slowly, stuttering on his words.

I opened my mouth to ask him why, but the line went dead before I could even say anything. My throat tightened and I wrapped my fingers around my phone while looking around myself. Something was wrong. Adam wouldn't just call me like that. He barely ever called me. It was usual of me to call him first, beg for his time and his attention, even after the breakup.

As his words registered in my head, I called him back and waited for him to pick up. He didn't. I called him again, and still, no answer.

I hopped onto the next train heading to his area and waited while imagining the worst. *Could he be hurt? Was he dying? Did he get sick? Did he overdose on something?*

7

REBEKAH

I kept dialing Adam's number while waiting for the train to stop at his station. It was still a couple of stations away, and the fear was growing and eating me alive. Whenever I called him, the call was either declined or ignored. Numerous thoughts formed in my head and for a brief moment, I thought he was either dead or in trouble. *No.* I stayed calm until I reached the station near his building.

I tapped out of the subway and headed up the flight of stairs and toward his building that was on the corner of the street. Upon stepping closer, I caught a glimpse of a few black cars, some SUVs and some sedans parked at the valet of the building—the valet that no one used because it was too pricey.

My brows furrowed in confusion, and I quickly stepped into the building and took the elevator up to Adam's floor.

What trouble was he in?

I called his number again while standing inside the elevator but this time, his phone was switched off and the call went to a dead end.

"Ugh," I groaned, shoving my phone inside my pocket while waiting for the elevator to reach his floor. If this was a joke, I was going to be furious and there was probably going to be blood spilled. I had left everything and ever since his call, I was anxious and terrified.

The ding echoed in my ears, and I walked out. I didn't think of anything and headed straight to his apartment, which was at the end of the hallway. Nothing clicked in my head when I saw two suited men walking back and forth in the hallway.

Nothing.

I was too worried about Adam to think of anything else.

Shoving the door open, I entered, and my eyes widened in surprise as my jaw hung open. "*Oh fuck,*" I whispered under my breath.

It was chaotic inside the apartment. There were four suited men and Adam was shoved against a couch with a buff, tall man standing beside him. When I saw Adam's face, I found a few scratches across his jaw and a red eye. His shirt was slightly torn from the side. He seemed beaten up.

What had he done?

When my eyes moved to the side of the apartment, near the open kitchen, my question changed, and I thought—*what had I done?* The man sitting by the kitchen was familiar, almost as if I had seen him last night, in the subway, arguing and beating up the other man. When he turned his head, I confirmed it was him. The older brother I assumed.

I swallowed hard.

He looked at me with such ferocity that I felt I was going to be eaten up and killed alive without even having a chance to say goodbye.

Then and there, Faye's words rang in my mind. The little picture in the ID I had been staring at the whole night was sitting in front of me, idly playing with a butcher's knife in his fingers. He tapped the tip of the knife against the small wooden coffee table that I had gifted Adam a year ago from the flea market.

"I have been waiting for you," he said, slowly rising from his seat and straightening his suit in the process. While still holding the knife, he stepped toward me like an animal reaching for its prey. "You took a very long time to come here. Did you lose your way, or did you decide to steal from someone else?" His voice was cold, loud, and with every word, I felt my own fear eating me up.

"I—" I stepped back, hoping to escape but at the same time, I couldn't leave Adam alone. He didn't deserve this. He didn't even know what I had done. "I'm sorry. I-I don't know what got into me last night. I was scared and—" I didn't have words, nor any air left in my lungs. My heart thudded hard against my chest, and I found myself shrinking underneath his gaze.

"And-and?" He mimicked my tone.

"I'm sorry," I stuttered while my gaze travelled over to Adam. He didn't say anything, but fear was visible in his features.

Poor Adam.

I had gotten him into trouble. "I promise I'll give you the wallet back and I'm sorry again. Just don't hurt him—or me." I raise my hands in defense, hoping the man standing in front of me with a butcher's knife wouldn't hurt me.

"Meh, meh." He jumped forward and my heart dropped as my back slammed against the wall. He raised his hand, leveling the tip of the sharp knife against my face. "Where the fuck is my wallet?"

"I-I don't have it. I left it at home," I lied. I knew where it was, I had given it to Faye so she could return it. If I knew this man was here, I wouldn't have given it to her, instead I would've given it him back. "I promise, I'll return it and everything inside it." I gave him my word, but it seemed like he wasn't taking it. "Just don't hurt me." I squeezed my eyes shut and stepped further back, nearly sinking into the wall behind me. There was no more space left.

His body was closer to mine, and I took in his scent, it was dangerous and threatening. It was my luck that I had pepper sprayed him right on time or he would've killed me.

"That's just not going to work." He shook his head and grabbed my wrist. "You're a thief. I think I should cut your hand off." He gazed up and asked everyone else in the room. "Don't you all agree?"

The three men behind him murmured a quick *yes* and nodded their heads in agreement.

My voice disappeared as my heart came to my throat. He brought the knife closer to my wrist with the intentions of cutting it, but before the blade scraped against my skin, I raised my free hand and drew my fingernails across his arm, deep enough to leave another scar.

"Fucking *puttana*." He jumped back, losing a bit of his control.

I grabbed my chance and sprinted out of the door, forgetting about Adam. He was a man, he could get out by himself. *Could I?* With every step I took outside of the apartment, my heart thundered in my chest. Suddenly, I heard a guttural growl behind me before an arm came wrapping around my chest, pulling me back.

I screamed and cried for help as the same man, Christopher, dragged me back into the apartment. The two men standing outside cornered me and there was nowhere to run.

Once back inside the apartment, he slammed the door shut and one of the men locked it while I dug my fingers into the arm around my chest, hoping to free myself. I screamed at the top of my lungs, hoping anyone would hear me. Adam stood up and reached for me. The men behind grabbed him and knocked him out in a few seconds.

My eyes widened in horror as I watched his body fall limply to the ground.

Fuck.

"I'll give you your wallet. I promise!" I cried out while struggling to free myself from the man behind me.

He brought the knife up close to my throat and pressed the sharp side against my skin. I froze instantly, not even moving an inch while my voice disappeared. A cold chill ran down my spine and I pressed my lips shut.

"If you use your throat again, I will make sure you don't have one," he whispered in my ear.

8

Rebekah

I moved my head, nodding slowly and carefully while tears built up in the corners of my eyes, urging to spill out.

The man behind me was angry, furious—I could hear it in his voice and even feel the violence in his body. My breathing grew uneven as he released me from his hold, but the knife was still pressed against my throat. He moved around to the front of me, facing me. His eyes were golden and full of threat while his jaw was locked.

"Please," I mouthed as warm tears spilled on my cheeks. *Was he going to slice my throat and kill me?* I didn't even want to think or imagine it.

Adam's body laid on the side, near the couch where he was just sitting a while ago. He was still unconscious, even after a few minutes had passed. *Was he even alive?*

"Where is my wallet?" the man in front of me asked, *again*.

"It's at my house," I replied, meeting his dangerous gaze. My lower lip quivered in fright. I knew it wasn't at the house and I feared worst if I told him that I had given it to someone. "I'll get it for you. I promise."

"I don't trust you, not after all the stunts you have been pulling. It's just surprising to see a little girl like you *fight*. I could kill you if I wanted to and I could dispose of your body easily. No one would know and certainly no one would care." He pressed the knife closer and closer, almost as if he wanted to cut my skin. "Give me a good reason why I shouldn't kill you?" His eyes were burning into my mine, waiting for a response but I didn't know what reason to give him.

"I won't tell anyone anything, I promise, and I won't go to the police and I'll never do it again." I lifted my hands to my shoulders in defense while at the same time, calling defeat. There wasn't much I could do while there was a knife against my throat and four angry men in the room that I couldn't even escape from.

It was the first time I had stolen from someone, and it was also the last time. I was never going to try it again.

"I don't believe you, *amore*." The man stepped forward, towering his large frame over mine.

I barely even met with his shoulders; he was as tall as the ceiling in this apartment. My heart raced harder in my chest while the space between us disappeared. There was a sudden change in his expression. The wrinkled lines on his forehead were gone and his jaw softened before his gaze clicked away from mine. He looked at the side of my face, thinking hard before his head bent slowly and he *sniffed* me.

My brows furrowed in confusion. *What? What was he trying to do?*

I didn't move an inch as the knife was still in position, but I watched him carefully, growing confused. He leaned back in again, this time closer to my neck. The knife roughly brushed away to the side of my left shoulder and I nearly winced, but it hadn't cut me.

My chest rose and dropped, and, in that moment, I grew more terrified than ever. His nose was inches away from pressing against my neck. He *sniffed* me again, this time deeply, and his face tensed up as he moved back.

"That's odd," he murmured under his breath while moving away from me as if he had just inhaled one of the most terrible scents in the world. I remembered showering and I couldn't smell anything *bad* on myself, which only created more doubt.

"So, you'll not kill me?" I asked as I watched the knife move further away from me. A breath of relief left escaped my lips and my shoulders strained back.

His eyes suddenly clicked to mine and the anger returned to his face, turning him red. He tossed the knife onto the ground and backed me up to the same wall. "You have two hours to return my wallet or I'll make sure you won't live to see another day," he said harshly.

I held my breath back and nodded. *Two hours*. It was enough. I could get to Faye and take the wallet back from her.

The man, Christopher, didn't say anything more. He glanced over his shoulder and directed his men to leave the apartment. One by one, they all walked out of the front door, but I didn't rest until I watched them all enter the elevator and leave the building.

Once they were out of sight, I slammed the door shut and locked it from inside before placing a hand over my chest and holding myself together. My breaths came out heavy and uneven. Tears filled my eyes before I rushed back to Adam who laid unconscious on the floor.

I checked him quickly, looking for his heartbeat. Thankfully, he was still alive. I sat by the couch on the ground, just a few inches away from Adam and waited for him to regain consciousness. Every minute passed by in silence. I placed my hand against my head and whimpered quietly, trying to suppress everything I had been through.

I never imagined for it to be this terrible. This was one of the greatest lengths I had been to for the sake of taking care of my family and I couldn't do it again. I nearly lost my life and even Adam's.

But the worst part was, I knew this wasn't over.

Something in my gut warned me that this wasn't the last time I would have an encounter with that man.

When Adam grew conscious, he snapped at me, asking me a thousand questions, and yelling at me while trying to contact the police. I begged him not to call them as I had promised that man I wouldn't.

"Please. Just don't call the police. I don't know what those men are capable of doing and I don't even want to, so just let it be," I pleaded, still sitting on the ground while he hovered over me.

"What the fuck is wrong with you, Rebekah?"

I groaned and rubbed the side of my head, which hurt. "Let it go."

"No fucking way. Look at my face." He crouched down and grabbed my hand, moving it away from my eyes so I could see his face. "I'm not going to let this go. I don't care. Whoever those fuckers were, I'll fuck them up."

"Adam, stop." I held his hand while my voice cracked. "Just let it go. It won't happen again and I'm sorry I got you involved in all this. I should've known better. Please," I said, my voice cracking.

I was exhausted and I couldn't bear Adam yelling at me.

"No way." He shook his head repeatedly before walking away and disappearing into his bedroom.

I rose from the ground and dialed Faye's number. Two hours were going to pass by quickly and I needed to get the wallet to that man before he sliced my head off my shoulders. I had seen what him and his brother had done to that other man in the subway station. It made me wonder if they were in a gang, or something along those lines.

It clearly looked like that but then again, Faye had told me the man on the ID was a *cult* leader.

I spoke to Faye for a couple of minutes, explaining what had happened while still standing inside Adam's apartment. He was nowhere to be seen and I assumed he was taking care of his injuries and not calling the police.

After I had finished telling Faye everything, I asked her about the wallet and if she could drop it to me before the clock struck five, as my two hours would have passed by then.

"Oh, Bek, I already gave it to my cousin after our talk. It's going to be fine. He'll probably get the wallet soon, so he won't come after you," Faye replied, her voice calm and collected.

I closed my eyes and sighed. "Are you sure?"

"Yes. Don't worry. Let me come pick you up and don't be scared. I'm here for you. Nothing will happen. He was only threatening you. He barely harms anyone unless they have harmed him," she said, reassuring me.

9

CHRISTOPHER

Walter sat beside me, staring at me the entire ride back to the house. His eyes pierced through my soul, questioning everything I had done in the apartment. "You didn't kill her," he whispered. "Why?" He glared at me, questioningly.

I kept my eyes on the road as buildings passed by and shrugged. "I didn't feel like it."

"She pepper sprayed you, stole from you, and harmed you. I thought she'd be ripped into pieces," he stated.

I turned my face to him, giving him a death glare, so he would silence his mouth until the ride came to an end. Walter looked away immediately and stopped bothering me. His words did make sense, but I didn't have an answer for them, and I couldn't tell him the reason why I had let that girl go, even though my intentions were to kill her and the boy.

I wanted to leave that place with at least one of them dead but they both were alive and as much as it made me furious, I just couldn't, not when I could still smell her scent. A scent that was driving my wolf crazy and senseless. At our first interaction at the station, I didn't smell anything, and I didn't smell anything until I leaned into her neck. Her scent was hidden, it couldn't be smelled from far away and the reason for that was because she was a human.

Humans didn't have any scents that attracted werewolves.

Unless...

I didn't want to go there.

When the car came to a stop, I stepped out and walked into the house to see Pietro and share my worries with him. I couldn't let anyone else know about what my wolf had smelled, not even my second in command, Walter.

Composing myself, I entered the house and sought my brother. After not finding him for a few minutes, I questioned one of the drivers outside, asking him about Pietro's whereabouts and whether he had left the house without informing me.

"No, he's inside. Check the library. His girlfriend arrived an hour ago. I assume that's where they spend their time usually," the driver responded.

I nodded and returned to the house, this time heading to the library that was made by my grandfather, Niko Delfino, nearly a hundred years ago. Along with an Alpha, he was a collector, and he took it upon himself to collect every book about our world and to keep it safe inside our house. Everything about werewolves and our bloodline was secured in thousands of books inside the air-conditioned library. It was carefully constructed to avoid bringing any damage to the scripts before us, by our forefathers, by the stronger Alphas and the Oracles.

Just as I stepped inside the library, I found my younger brother pounding into his girlfriend, Elena.

They both shamelessly grabbed whatever was near them and covered their bits while frustration spread across my face. It wasn't the first time I had found my brother fucking his girlfriend in the library.

"What the fuck, Pietro? I warned you to not fuck in the library. Literally anywhere else!" I snapped at him, even though I wasn't angry. The ball of rage came from within me as I couldn't deal with the emotions I was going through at the moment.

There were a few wooden tables spread across the library and that's where they usually railed each other. I stepped closer, invading their privacy, and shame wore off their faces.

Elena placed her naked leg over the other one and smiled at me. "By now you must know I have a kink for dark and cold places," she said to me.

Wasn't the first time.

"Check out the *cellar*. It's quite dark and cold and usually, you'll find some dead bodies lying around as well. I think it will help with your kink a lot more," I replied while grabbing her clothes off the table and returning them to her. "Leave, now." My chest rumbled as I stared her dead in the eyes.

She groaned and scurried out of the library while I kept Pietro hostage inside. He wasn't leaving until I had finished ranting to him, which was going to take a while.

He watched her leave and then growled while buttoning up his shirt and getting off the wooden table. "She's going to fuck me up now. You could be nice to her, eh?"

"Nope." I clicked my tongue and shook my head. "And I've told you a thousand times, you cannot use this library as your fuck room." I frowned at him for disobeying my orders.

Again.

Once he was dressed, he stood next to me and rose his head level with my height but failed terribly. He was still younger than me, shorter and less powerful. "Fine. Whatever. Why are your panties knotted?" he asked, raising a brow at me.

"They are not."

"Did you kill that girl?"

I looked away and then shook my head. "No."

"Why? You left from here all murderous and deathly." His questioning gaze wondered all over me. "What happened?" Concern rose in his voice as he continued, "Did she scratch you again?"

I rolled my sleeves down. She did indeed scratch me again but that wasn't the problem. There was a bigger problem, a much bigger one.

"There was a moment when *my* wolf smelled her—and it was just *odd*." I didn't want the term to come out of my mouth because then it would be true, and I didn't want that right now.

"Odd... like?" Pietro stared at me. His burning gaze forcing me to answer. "Is she your mate?"

The air changed and I exhaled a breath. "I don't know."

"Oh, fuck!" His voice grew loud and echoed across the library. "Holy shit." A smile grew wide over his face, only angering me further. I expected him to react a different way, completely opposite than the clown he was slowly turning into. "You're fucking dead." He grabbed his stomach and began laughing as loud as possibly could.

"Stop it, Pietro." My nostrils flared and I growled at him.

"No way." He shook his head and planted his hand on my shoulder, shaking me roughly. "Look at you. The big bad Alpha found his mate. I'm in complete disbelief! Not in a thousand years I imagined you'd have a mate. I didn't even think it was possible for a woman to be paired with you. I mean, have you seen yourself? No offense, *fratello*, you're the most heinous, monstrous man I have ever met."

My fingernails stretched into claws out of anger, and I growled once more to bring a pause to Pietro's clown session. Hearing him cackle for another second was going to force me to kill him myself.

"I don't know if she's my mate..." I trailed off.

"What do you mean?" He held his breath back and stopped laughing. "You smelled her? What did she smell like?"

"It was a strong, sweet smell. It was pleasant and overpowering." I lost track of myself for that one second as I remembered inhaling her scent. *Oh.* My wolf weakened inside me. "But that doesn't mean she's my mate, right? She could have been wearing some good perfume."

"Yeah, no." Pietro shook his head. "She's your mate."

I didn't want to believe him. I didn't even want to believe myself. "But she's a human," I added. When I took in her scent, I realized she wasn't a werewolf but instead a mere, weak human.

I didn't want a mate to begin with, nor did I want a *human* to be my mate.

10

Rebekah

After parting from Adam, I went with Faye to her cousin's house downtown. It was dreadful to handle Adam; trying to get him to not call the police and tell them what had happened. I truly feared for his life until he finally understood and decided to listen to me for once. He promised he wouldn't go to the police but at the same time, he was going to change the locks to his house and notify the security of his building about what happened.

It was understandable. He was shaken and so was I.

I tried to seem relieved in front of Faye, but she picked up on my quivering fingers and reassured me that it would be okay. "Trust me, it's not a big deal. Once he has his wallet back, he won't bother you and you don't have to be scared about anything," she repeated while maneuvering her car into the center of the city.

"It seemed like he was going to kill me, Faye." I told her, everything, every detail of it. "I don't think he will leave me alone. What if he comes and kills me?" I imagined the worst while looking outside at the tall buildings passing by. The skyline of the city in downtown Laford was beautiful and completely different to living in the outskirts where nothing could be seen.

"He will not." She patted my right shoulder while her attention remained on the road.

I shivered involuntarily and looked away. "I made a terrible mistake," I murmured under my breath, but she caught onto my words.

"People make mistakes. It's alright. Don't beat yourself up with it. If it was anyone else's wallet, I would've applauded you, Bek. Unfortunately, it wasn't." She drove quicker and then suddenly slammed on her brakes in front of a tall white building in the middle of downtown. "Come on. My cousin has a direct contact to one of his men, she can get the wallet to him, so you don't have to and after that, *we'll* be in the clear." Her lips twitched as she cut the engine and stepped out of her car.

I went out with her and took in a sharp breath. The sun shone on my face, burning my eyes and cheeks.

"Fear not. I'm here for you." Faye walked ahead of me while lowering her sunglasses to her eyes.

I followed her into the building, and we went up the elevator, reaching the twenty-fourth floor where her cousin lived. There had been a few instances where I had met with Alicia. Once at her baby shower, at her wedding, and she often came over to Faye's house where I crashed sometimes.

During the ride here, Faye told me that her cousin and her husband were in close contact with Christopher, and she agreed to return the wallet to him on behalf of me, therefore, ridding me of ever seeing him again. Just the thought of his presence made me flinch.

I wanted this to be over with. I had other problems to handle and take care of.

Alicia stared at me for a good few seconds before looking into the wallet. Her face was full of surprise. "Wow," she whispered while placing her hand over her belly and glancing at me. She was almost four months pregnant. "Really?"

"It was just the moment. I thought he wouldn't chase after me. After all, I did see a crime scene, and I thought that was more than enough." I shrugged while telling her the truth.

In my head, I believed I could've gone to the police after seeing the crime scene in the subway station but instead, I decided to make use of the moment and draw some money from it.

Bad idea.

And it was now biting me in the ass. I wanted to hit my head for my own stupidity. Though, it would've worked out if it was some other random guy that wasn't *powerful*.

"You're confident." Alicia smiled at me and then turned around to her cousin, Faye. "I like her."

"Trust me. I was baffled when I heard it." Faye shook her head, giving me a glance from the corner of her eyes.

I folded my hands and wondered what was this all about. I still couldn't understand what the big deal was. "What is the big deal about this—man?" I asked them. "I still can't wrap my head around the whole *cult* thingy." My eyes directed to Faye.

Her face tensed and she quickly grabbed my arm.

"What cult?" Alicia rose her brows as Faye pulled me out of the apartment forcibly.

"Nothing at all. Just let me know when you have returned the wallet. Thank you so much. Love you. Send regards to Max." She quickly finished before walking out and slamming the door behind her.

I stared at her, confused, as she pulled me away from the hallway and back into the elevator. My brows puckered. I eyed her as the elevator closed and we went back downstairs.

"Faye," I called out her name. "What's wrong?"

"Nothing," She gave out a fake smile while clearly she was hiding something behind it. I stared at her for another moment, demanding the truth or at least a bit of it. "It's just that the cult—it was a story I made up, I mean it's similar, but it's a cover I told you so you could understand it without going into too many details."

"So, what's the whole story?" I folded my arms again and leaned back against the tall mirror in the elevator.

"I can't tell you that." She chewed her lips while replying to me, clearly uncomfortable even talking about it.

"Why?" I remained stern, wanting to know it all. *What was the great secret? If it wasn't a cult, what was it?* An itch rose inside me. "Just tell me. I know all your secrets so what's the problem telling me this one? I promise I won't tell anyone else," I pleaded.

She cleared her throat and shook her head. "I-I really can't, Bek. It's like a box of bees and if I open it up, you'll get stung!" She was worried about me, so was hiding whatever truth it was.

"I won't. Just tell me. I'm so curious now!" I exclaimed as my thoughts ran here and there. I knew I wasn't going to stop thinking about it, especially after this whole chaos. "Are you selling drugs? Are you a part of a mafia group?" I began with my theories.

The elevator opened, saving her, but I chased her out of the building, wanting answers.

"No, it's not a mafia group, Bek." She shook her head.

"Then what?" I hopped into the car whilst she got in from the driver's seat.

She started the engine and barely made any eye contact with me while speeding out from the valet parking. "Just something. I can't say." She lined her lips straight and kept her attention on the road. "Just not now. Maybe later."

"Promise you'll tell me the truth?" I asked her but she didn't respond for a whole minute. "I won't tell anyone. We have known each other for more than a decade, Bek. You know me. My lips are sealed." Using my hands, I placed a finger over my mouth and showed her.

"I know, I know." She sighed. "It's just that if I tell you, you could be in possible danger—worse than today and I can't do that to you." She slowed her driving and glanced at me. "I'm sorry."

I pressed my head back against the seat and remembered what she told me in the café. *Like every cult, there was a leader and Christopher was their leader.* "It's okay. Whenever you want to tell me, you can." I smiled at her and stopped myself from creating any more trouble than I was in already.

This much action was enough for me.

I didn't need more.

11

CHRISTOPHER

"Good evening, Alpha." Matthew, one of the guards at post in the house walked in and greeted me. I turned my attention away from Pietro and looked up at the guard. "There is a woman here to meet you. Should I let her in?" he asked.

My thoughts clouded instantly, and my heart skipped a beat. I rolled my leg down from the other one and leaned forward. *Was she here? With my wallet?* A different unease crippled down my spine. I inhaled a long breath and nodded my head. "Bring her here."

Matthew turned around to leave the room whilst my eyes awakened. It was late, more than three hours later, but it didn't matter. *She* was here and I was going to get my wallet back—maybe her as well.

Pietro jumped up from one couch to another, scrambling toward me like an animal. "Awe, look at you," He placed his head underneath his chin and continued, "You look like a *pussy* right now. So tensed, so weak." He spoke in a thick accent, reeling my senses.

"Get the fuck out of here, Pietro," I snapped at him.

"I'm not going anywhere. I was fucking my mate; you stopped me and threw her out of here. Now, I'm going to sit right here and watch you melt in front of that woman you claim as your mate. And I'm going to cockblock you every second of your life." He stopped breathing down my neck and sat back on the couch next to mine while holding a drink in his hand.

I looked over my shoulders, staring at him with bloodshot eyes. Pietro was a different breed, never known to us. If he wasn't my brother, my own blood brother, I would've killed him a long time ago.

"I'm not leaving you alone, *Christy*. Brothers for life?" He smiled hard while uttering the nickname I despised the most.

Shaking my head, I turned away from him and watched the door closely, waiting for *her* to come in. My nerves knotted with each other. I felt a different kind of exhilaration. My eyes remained wide as the door slowly opened and Matthew walked in with a woman.

I stood up instantly and then realized it wasn't the same girl, it was a pregnant woman.

Alicia.

"That is not your mate, Brother." Pietro spoke behind me, shocked as he rose out of his seat. "Fuck. You're going to raise a bastard?" he continued blabbering in my ears.

"Quiet, Pietro," I whispered to him. "It's Alicia, Maxwell's wife." I told him as she came into the light.

"Oh…" He trailed off for a long minute before he stopped saying anything at all.

I scrambled forward and greeted her. "You look like you're due tomorrow." My gaze lingered over her belly. It was just recently that she had gotten pregnant, there was no way her bump was as big as it seemed.

"Well, it's a baby." She chuckled and then shrugged.

"Sit, please." I took her to the sitting area and we both sat while I wondered. "Max isn't with you?"

"No, he's patrolling." She shook her head and reached into her bag. "But I'm here to return this." After fiddling inside her bag for a long minute, she pulled out my wallet and handed it over to me.

I grew surprised and a bit furious. A scowl appeared on my face and Alicia continued, "My cousin's best friend was the one who had stolen it. She was a bit scared, so I came here to return it to you. Though, it lacks a bit of cash, but that shouldn't be a problem for you."

My hand wrapped around the wallet, and I opened it. The cards were there, misplaced, but the cash was gone. The important part is what was sewed inside hadn't been touched or opened.

I blew out a hot breath, bothered with all of this. I thought it would've been that girl who would've returned the wallet to me since she was the one who had stolen it and I gave her clear instructions to hand it back to me. It would have given me another chance to inhale her scent and confirm whether she was my mate.

I wanted her to be here.

My jaw clenched and I nodded. "Thank you, Alicia."

"I know her, her name is Rebekah and she's a human, so don't go around terrifying her. It was a mistake, let it go," she spoke softly.

"I wasn't terrifying her." I rolled my eyes and groaned. This all was frustrating, and I didn't know what to think or even say. "She attacked me and you know I have a temper."

"Doesn't matter. She's a human, so hold yourself together and forgive her," she replied, waving her hand through the air.

It grew silent after that. I wanted to know more, every detail about that woman—Rebekah. Just the thought of her was reeling my senses and driving me crazy. If it was true—if she was my mate, then there was going to be a lot of trouble coming forth.

"What is wrong, Chris?" she asked, narrowing her eyes.

"Nothing." I shook my head.

Pietro appeared out of nowhere, inserting himself into the conversation. "She's his mate and he's sad because he wanted to see her again, maybe fuck her as well, but now that's not going to happen because he has his wallet back and he cannot get to that girl again." He slammed his rough hands on my shoulders from behind and I growled at him.

"You have two seconds to leave from this room before I sent an order out to kill Elena," I threatened him without a thought. His unnecessary involvement in this conversation was causing trouble.

Pietro didn't think, he sprinted out of the room after dropping the bomb. Thankfully, there was no one in the room except for Alicia, my brother, and me. Nobody else had heard what he had screamed or there would be a big mess, a mess I would need to clean.

"What?" Alicia looked at me with wide eyes. "Your mate? Is that true?" she asked and waited for me to confirm but I didn't say anything. "Christopher!" she said, leaning forward and holding her pregnant belly.

"You cannot tell anyone. Not even Maxwell," I stated.

"It's true?" Her brows rose. "Tell me. I won't utter a word about this to anyone. You can trust me."

I knew I could trust Alicia, after all, she was a part of this family. Maxwell was my first cousin and her husband. They were married for over six years and were to have children now. Both of them were a decade older than me, wiser, and the only ones in my family left alive, except for Pietro and I.

"I'm not sure about it." I shook my head, not knowing what I had to say to her. "I need to be sure first. I need to see her again and you're going to arrange that." I looked up at her, twisting this all for my own benefit.

"As long as you take an oath that you won't kill her," Alicia replied, knowing well enough. She knew that I didn't want a mate or a weakness.

I scoffed. "I wouldn't dare!"

"Please." She rolled her eyes and stood. "I'll arrange the meeting after you send me a written letter that you won't kill her," she continued, making it all the more difficult for me.

How could I possibly write that?

"Fine. I will."

Written letters didn't matter, not for me. I could kill anyone I want to, simply because I was an Alpha and there was no one greater than me.

"Good. I'll arrange a meeting for this week." She paced back and forth while rubbing her belly and taking in heavy breaths.

"No. Tonight!" I exclaimed, wanting to see that girl right away.

"Yeah, not possible." She shook her head and continued walking.

12

REBEKAH

The newspapers were splayed all over the table. A cup of warm coffee beside it. I quickly ran my eyes over the jobs and circled a few of them that were to my interest. The night had passed by with ease and while there were worries in my head, one was gone.

Faye had called me late last night, telling me that her cousin had given the wallet back to the man I had stolen from, and all was well.

I was relieved finally.

"It's too early to find jobs!" Rose jumped down from the stairs with her backpack. She ran over to me, looking at what I was doing and then sat on the chair beside mine. "Did you find anything?"

I remained focused and shook my head. "Nothing good." It was true, there was nothing good in the newspaper today. Most of the jobs were old and ones that I had already rejected.

Raising my head, I glanced at my little sister and offered the omelet I had made for myself. "Here, have some."

She finished it up quickly, in a couple of minutes, right before my mom came out of her bedroom. She was dressed in her office clothes, ready to head to work and drop Rose off to her school.

When they left, it became dead silent in the house. Dad was still asleep. He had pulled an all-nighter at the gas station, working for the entire night, and he wasn't going to wake up anytime soon.

Things were still tight.

Debt collection agencies were filling our mailbox day and night. Mom was getting endless calls, forcing her to do the payments even though we truly had nothing. Making ends meet was difficult as it was.

I stayed at home the entire morning, cold-calling and searching for something for this month. It was impossible to get my old job at the café as Mr. Anderson, my manager, was the definition of a bitch. He would die a thousand times before hiring me again. I literally walked on eggshells around him the entire time I worked at the café.

It was a relief to know that I didn't have to do it anymore, but I needed to do *something*.

I pressed my shoulders against the window of my bedroom and relaxed for a minute after spending hours searching for a job. The sound of an engine revving flowed into my ears and my eyes opened wide. Glancing outside from the window, I found a black sedan parked at the entrance of my house.

With a little grunt, I rose and rushed downstairs with only my phone in my hands.

I quickly grabbed a jacket and walked outside before opening the door to Faye's car and climbing in.

"Don't you have classes?" I asked her with one of my brows cocked at her appearance. It was afternoon and I remembered that her classes didn't finish until later at four.

"I do but I skipped. I knew you'd be home alone, and I don't like leaving my bestie alone." She shot me a wink before driving away from my house and heading toward her own.

"I just need to find a new job." I pursued my lips and looked out the car window, staring at the houses passing by.

"And you will. Stop stressing about it!" she exclaimed.

Faye and I were quite different people. To begin with, she was a redhead while I was a blonde. Her family was rich, brimming with money and she was getting a degree in law whilst I was doing small jobs, trying to make ends meet. I hadn't even thought about going to college. The moment I left high school, I started working at small restaurants and cafés while my dad was getting his cancer treatment. It was just last year, and he had been cancer free for only six months so far.

Somehow, even after everything, Faye and I were best friends, and it was the only relationship I cherished. Without her, I would've been the loneliest person in the world.

"I heard about this opening at one of the grand hotels. It is a waitressing job if you'd like it," she began, and my head snapped in her direction. "I know the manager so I could get it for you."

"Yes, please," I begged, hands clasped.

"But the hours are quite long."

"It's fine. I'll manage. I just need something better than my old one." I didn't care about anything except for the money.

"Fine." She glanced and smiled at me. "You'll get it. Don't worry."

That was settled.

When Faye drove me to her home, I found something odd in the air. It wasn't often that we went to her home at this time of the day. She preferred blowing up her dad's card at shopping malls instead of staying low-key inside her bedroom.

She parked the car on her driveway and hopped out. I followed her into her beautiful two-story villa close to the beach and we headed straight up to her bedroom.

"You seem *fishy*. What's up?" I asked her as I stepped up on the spiral staircase that led into her bedroom.

"Nothing…" She looked ahead, not making eye contact with me. When she began scurrying up the stairs, I instantly figured out something was wrong. I followed her into her bedroom, waiting for her to drop whatever bomb she was holding within herself. "Fine. I wanted to talk to you about something."

Her bed bounced as I jumped on it. "What?"

Faye stood in front of me, fiddling with her fingers while her eyes went back and forth. Worry was smeared across her face.

"What is it?" I asked again, my smile fading as I silently hoped it wasn't what I thought it would be.

She cleared her throat and said, "*He* wants to see you."

"What?" I laughed a little, unable to make sense of her words. "Who?" My lashes fluttered, and for a moment, I forgot about everything that happened yesterday.

Faye gestured with her eyes, forcing me to remember the man I had stolen from. "*He* wants to see you," she repeated.

"No," I stated. "No way!" My eyes widened a little in disbelief.

"Alicia spoke to him yesterday and she returned the wallet but he told her to arrange a meeting with you," she explained, but it still didn't make any sense.

I jumped up from the bed while rubbing my sore forehead. *Why?* "I gave the wallet back. So, why? What does he want? I even apologized, even though he should've been the one apologizing to me for breaking into Adam's apartment and threatening us both." My voice rose louder than ever, and I felt a ball of rage folding inside me.

I thought the chapter was closed.

"Bek, listen, it's just for a while and he'll let you go. He doesn't want to hurt you. He simply wants to see you." Faye tried to convince me but none of it was going to work because I didn't want to see him or even be in the same room as him.

"No, I don't want to see him!" I exclaimed, throwing my hands in the air.

Faye fell quiet and she nodded her head, taking in my decision. "I'll tell Alicia that you declined and she'll tell him."

I placed my hand on my hip, shaking my head. *Why would he want to see me again? Did he want to threaten me? Or maybe kill me this time?* I blew out a breath and looked away, considering seeing him once more as I didn't want to endanger myself. Maybe he'd appear at my home next time. If it was possible for that man to figure out Adam's location, he could figure out where I lived and barge into my house.

"No, wait. I'll see him." I stopped Faye from calling her cousin. My lips twitched and I continued, "But I'm going to take a knife with me and it's going to be somewhere in public or else I'm not going."

"Okay." Faye sighed and texted her cousin from her phone. "I don't understand why but I think he wants to talk to you about something. Alicia didn't tell me much." She shrugged.

I heard a little ting that meant she had sent the message and it had been received.

I sank back into the bed, splaying my arms over it while my eyes stared up at the golden light shining on my face. "Can't wait!"

13

REBEKAH

The next evening, Faye picked me up from the house and drove me to the subway station in her Mustang. It was around eight and everything in my body was trembling with fear of the unknown—of the man I was going to meet. *Why me?* I thought hard and came up with several assumptions to why this *arrangement* was taking place but none of them made sense—I had returned the wallet and I wanted to go on my way.

"Don't be scared," Faye whispered as she glanced at me from the corner of her eyes.

"I'm meeting someone who assaulted me, broke into my ex-boyfriend's house and threatened us both." I paused to take a sharp breath. "I'm definitely scared!"

I turned my head back to the window, watching the tall building flash by me. We were meeting at the station, as I wanted, since there were going to be people surrounding me at all times. He couldn't hurt me, even if he wanted to and whatever *civil* conversation we were going to have, we would.

"Well, that does make sense…" she trailed off before slamming on her brakes near the entrance of the subway station.

"Do you know this guy?" I asked her as she rolled her car back and parked.

"Yes. I told you; I've known him for quite a long time, not personally, but my cousin knows him personally," she responded while removing her keys and cutting off the ignition.

I took another sharp breath. "And?"

She stepped out of the car and came over to my side. I opened the passenger door, one leg hovered out of the car while the rest of my body remained glued to the seat. I didn't want to see him, not again.

"There is nothing to be scared of because Alicia is here." Faye directed my attention to the car parked in front of us.

Her pregnant cousin stepped out, holding her belly, while a smile spread across her face. She waved her hand at Faye and me and I smiled back at her. The creases of worry were clear in my face, and it didn't matter how much makeup I applied, it was still visible.

I was terrified.

"How are you feeling?" Alicia asked, walking over to me. She held an umbrella over her head, avoiding getting wet from the slight rain.

"Nervous."

"Come on." She offered her hand, and I took it before stepping out of the car and going along with her into the subway station. "That man needs to figure something out and he can only do it if he sees you again," she said, holding my arm tight.

Faye, my best friend, was a few meters away from us. We took the stairs and went down, underground.

"Figure what out?" I asked Alicia with a strained voice.

"Just something. I can't tell you now, but I hope you'll know soon. And don't be scared. That man can barely harm anyone." She scoffed and shook her head.

I froze in my steps. "He nearly killed a man in front of me. I watched it." I told her about the night in the station where I had watched him beat up a man till he was bleeding, and he had no intentions to stop until I'd interrupted him.

I still wondered if that man survived.

"Oh..." Alicia wasn't surprised. It seemed like she was trying to make me feel better about all of this, but I saw what I saw, and my judgement was correct. "Well, he does have a little bit of anger." She shrugged and we strolled past the crowd leaving the station. "But don't worry, he won't hurt you."

I doubted that.

The station was packed, just as I expected it to be. My boots were soaked in rainwater by the time I reached downstairs. Alicia closed her umbrella and Faye came forward, pressing my shoulders hard, soothing my tensions.

My eyes wandered all over the station, I saw faces—hundreds of them—and then I saw him, standing by the same room where he had nearly murdered someone. It was the technical room of the station and was usually locked but somehow, that man had the key to it. It made me wonder a lot more about other things.

My heart thumped hard and fast. Hair rose over my skin and a hot breath flew from my throat when his eyes bore into mine. There was something hidden behind them but I couldn't see anything beyond the violence and devilry. Just beside him, there was another man, the younger one—his brother, as I had assumed. He seemed less threatening but his eyes shared the devilry as well.

There was no one else, just him and his brother, waiting for *me*. I no longer felt as scared as I was earlier. Seeing his men, suited and with sharp weapons in their hands while they were in Adam's house scarred me for life.

I couldn't see beyond that.

"We will be here, Rebekah," Faye whispered as we approached them.

It somehow relieving that there were a hundred passengers going in and out of the subway. He couldn't possibly attack me in front of the public.

I moved one arm to my back, and the knife I had sewn to my sleeve pressed against my skin. It didn't matter how safe this all was. I couldn't get comfortable unless I had a knife or some sort of weapon with me. Faye nor Alicia were aware of what I was carrying, and I didn't want to tell him either.

When I got close, he walked straight toward me, inching a lot closer than I expected. Alicia quickly stepped in and stretched out her arm, stopping him from getting any closer.

"Be nice," she said in a low, warning tone.

"Fine," he grunted, and walked away from me, heading toward the technical room in the station. It was loud, and I wasn't able to hear much except for people chattering and footsteps rushing in and out of the station. He opened the door and held it for me. "Please?"

My fingers tightened around my phone, and I headed into the room, the same room where I had watched someone injured—or die. The walls had been repainted and the blood was gone. It seemed like no one had been in here for a while.

The man stepped into the room and the door closed behind him. Alicia and Faye both remained outside and just when I realized that, I headed straight to the door to leave. I couldn't be alone with this man. *I didn't want to be.*

His large frame towered mine and he grabbed my hands before I could reach for the door. Instead of taking steps forward, I took steps back as my heart thudded hard in my chest and my throat began closing up. Raising my head, I looked into his eyes that were filled with mischief. The corner of his mouth turned into a grin before he wrapped his hands around my elbows tighter.

"I'm not going to hurt you." He bent his head slightly forward, and the words he spoke didn't exactly match his actions. "But you have seen what I can do, right?" he asked.

I nodded and swallowed hard.

"Then be a good girl and sit," he instructed while guiding me back to the chair near the scrappy monitors.

14

REBEKAH

I was alone. *Entirely. Alone.* For the first time in a while, I felt completely alone, even when Alicia and Faye were right outside, on the other end of the locked door. Somehow, it was still threatening to be in the same room as the violent person named Christopher.

Pulling my sleeves up, I rolled my hands into a fist and questioned, "What do you want from me?"

A second passed and then another. His attention was elsewhere, on his phone. I took that chance to study him closely as he turned a deafened ear toward me and my presence. His brows were furrowed, a frown on his face as his eyes ran back and forth over some message he had received.

I cleared my throat, grabbing his attention. I didn't want to be in this room, nor did I want to stay here for any longer than needed.

He looked up and my heart suddenly jumped in fear. His frown was soon replaced with a smile as he placed his phone on the side of the table and leaned back. "So many things."

"You have your wallet." I cocked a brow at him.

"Yes, but that's not what this is about. This goes much deeper than the thief you are." I waited for him to explain to me in clearer terms, something I could understand, as I was confused and wasn't sure where this was heading. "You crossed my path, you should've been more careful."

"What do you mean?" I asked him. "Is there something you want from me or are you just wasting my time? I have other things to do than to meet some *mob*." That's what I had named him in my head.

A mob. I mean, he did look like one. Suited, walked rigidly and with every breath he took, he threatened people. Either he was in a gang or much deeper into the underworld.

"I'm not a mob," he clarified, sounding a bit hurt. "Was that your boyfriend? That boy?" He stepped away from the table and approached me with a questioning look. His posture firm as he stood above me while I was seated.

Quickly, I replied, "Yes. No. What's your problem?" My lashes flickered at him, and I smiled.

"Is he?" He repeated his question, this time in a stern voice, demanding an answer—a clear answer.

"Yes. Do you have a problem?"

"That's going to change. I don't want you going anywhere near that boy or that place. Do you understand me?" He paced in the small room while his face changed colors, turning into a bright shade of red, almost as if he was packing fury instead of anything else.

My lips parted at his demands. *For what reason? Who was he?* I laughed a little and then shook my head. "In your dreams. This is the last time I'm seeing you. You have your wallet. Leave me the hell alone," I stated before getting up.

Just as I started to move from the seat, his threatening eyes met with mine. He neared me and lowered his face, forcing me back down. "You will not move unless I want you to move." The intensity in his eyes and his voice demanded me to obey.

Fear spread on my face quickly, and I swallowed hard. "I-I just want to go. I don't know what you want with me. I apologized for stealing your wallet, and pepper spraying you but there is nothing else I can do!" I replied to him in a slow, shaky voice. Every word pouring out of me showed the terror I was holding inside me.

He stomped a foot forward. "You're not going to see that boy again," he repeated, staying on that topic that didn't make any sense.

My nostrils flared. "I will," I said. "Do you have a problem?"

"Not yet but if you do then I'll have one," he replied, his hands were now wrapped around the armrest of the chair I sat on.

When he looked at me, I stared back into his eyes. His face was now only inches away from mine. A strong, pungent smell diffused around me, and I took an inhale of it. It was the same scent from the night where I had seen him and attacked him with my little bottle of pepper spray.

"Am I done here?" I asked, sitting back.

Was that all he wanted from me? To threaten me a bit more? I wasn't scared of his threats—not anymore. I didn't even know the man nor had any idea who he was. This was all getting a bit stretched and I just wanted to return to my normal life, worry about other things than this stranger.

His eyes lowered to my arm and before I could even think, he grabbed it and turned it around. My heart sank. The sharp tip of the knife pressed against my wrist and became slightly visible. He caught a glimpse of it and his face hardened with anger.

"Really?" He held my arm tighter.

"I have to protect myself." I gave him a quick smile before tugging my arm away from his hold.

He grew defensive. "A knife? What do you think that's going to do to me?" Something unleashed in his eyes as he spoke.

The handle of the knife was now wrapped around my fingers. I was being cautious, nothing more, as he closed in on me. He was a lot taller and *heavier* than me. The door was locked and barely any noise came from inside the room, which forced me to think the walls were soundproofed and that even if I would scream and yell, Faye or Alicia wouldn't hear me.

"Hurt you," I whispered back as my expression filled with fear.

It was alright when he was standing on the other end of the room, not threatening me, but he was right in front of me, while I was stuck on the chair he had forced me to sit on.

"You did not need to bring a knife to this conversation. I was being *nice, amore*. You have provoked me." His golden eyes turned darker and deadlier as he responded to me. The corners of his jaw tightened, and I took in a quick breath. "Give it to me," he demanded while flattening his outstretched hand.

I hesitated and then shook my head. "No."

"Give it to me. I won't repeat myself again." His eyes darted to my hand where I clutched onto the knife with my life. The last time he was holding one, it was against my neck, and I didn't want that to happen again.

"No."

"You're a difficult one, aren't you?" He leaned back and took a deep breath. He folded his sleeves, pushing them up to his elbow and for a moment, I believed he was certainly going to attack me again to get the knife but instead, he said, "Fine. Go on your way."

He tossed the keys over to the table beside the door and I quickly jumped up from the seat and grabbed it.

"But remember, if I see you around that boy ever again, it will get deadly for both of you," he quickly whispered down my neck before I could move. "I have eyes everywhere. Be careful."

With a last warning, I sprinted out of the room while his words echoed in my head.

15

REBEKAH

"I can talk to whoever I wish and Adam was my boyfriend. Why should I stop seeing him?" I raised my hands in frustration and furrowed my brows together as Faye drove her Mustang back to my home.

"Emphasis on *was*," she clarified, holding the steering wheel loosely between her fingers.

I gave her a deadly look and lined my lips straight. "Really?"

"Come on. We both know that Adam was toxic and a terrible boyfriend. I have been trying to stop you from going there every day and night. I hated him then and I hate him now. It's not going to hurt you if you stop seeing him," she said, her voice loud and clear while her words were throwing shade. It wasn't the first time she had begged me to stop seeing Adam. During our entire relationship, she tried hard to show me the red flags that I couldn't see.

I avoided them altogether and still fell for Adam. My love for him was great, even though he was a terrible boyfriend who had slept with another girl. I even went ahead and forgave him for that. Nothing truly mattered because I was attached to him and the comfort he gave me.

I shook my head. It made no sense to stop seeing Adam. "It's my wish, Faye. If I want to see him, I will and if I don't, I won't," I stated.

She sighed and nodded her head. "Alright."

After just a couple of minutes, she pulled up to the driveway of my house and parked the car. I gave my goodbyes and left while grabbing my bag from the backseat and stuffing the knife I had taken inside. It was hurting me to keep it in my sleeve for another minute more.

"Goodbye. I'll see you soon!" She waved her hand while rolling her windows up and driving away.

"Goodbye." I smiled back at her and once her car was out of the street, I turned and went into my house.

It took me a moment to find my keys inside the bag but once I found them, I opened the door and stepped in. Immediately, I clashed with Mom who was reaching to open the door as well.

"You're early today." She had a questioning look on her face.

"Yeah..." I trailed off. "I was just looking at some jobs and sorting things." None of what had happened over the past week had been repeated to Mom. I didn't want to tell her anything or have her worry about me.

She had enough on her plate.

"Adam came by," she said, following me into the living room. "He dropped off a couple of things of yours," she added.

My eyes turned quickly, and my heart jumped a beat. *What things?* Mom directed her gaze to the box on the side of the room labelled with my name. My brows furrowed and I opened the box to find some of my clothes, my bags and a few more things that I had left in his apartment, all this while we had been seeing each other.

"Did he say anything?" I asked Mom.

She shook her head. "No. I thought you two were broken up."

I stared at my clothes for a long minute before nodding my head. "Yes—we still are." It had been confusing. I didn't want to date Adam after what he had done but I still wanted to be comforted and loved by him. We were in a *very* casual relationship. That was no one's business.

I kneeled and picked up the box, carrying it upstairs to my room while a couple of thoughts ran through my head: *Why had he dropped off these things now? Did that mean we were done, done?*

I placed the box on the side of my bedroom and dialed Adam's number. He picked up my call after a few rings and said, "Hey!"

"Hey. Adam. I just came home, and Mom told me about the box you dropped off," I said while placing a hand on my hip and pacing around my room.

"Yeah. It was getting crowded in here and plus, I'm thinking of changing my apartment after the whole—*thing*. I don't think I'm safe here," he responded, a bit of worry lacing in his words.

"Really? I'm sorry about that." It was my fault that man and his people had broken into Adam's apartment for no apparent reason. I wondered how that man had even gotten the information to where Adam's apartment was.

"It's okay. And I think it's better we keep our distance from each other for a while. I mean—I don't know what company you're running with but it's dangerous and I don't want to be involved in all that." He sounded a bit more than nervous.

I placed my hand on my head and sat on the edge of the bed. "No, no, it's not like that. I don't know those people, Adam. I told you; it was an accident and—" I stopped blabbering and held back my words. *What was I even trying to say?* "Well, it's okay if you don't want to see me again."

"Yeah. Sorry for that. Goodbye."

I opened my mouth to say something but before the words even escaped my throat, he cut the call and the line went dead. Just then and there, Adam was out of my life, just like what that man wanted.

I pushed my phone over the bed and groaned.

"So, what is the theme of your Halloween party this year?" I asked while covering my toes with the brightest red I could find. It had been a boring day and the only option I had was to either sleep through it or take care of myself. I went ahead with the second option, finding it much better.

Rose tapped on her iPad, playing some game while she replied to me, "It's really weird. None of us like it. It's based on lore and this legend where a massacre happened hundreds of years ago by this group of witches that killed everyone who had sin in their blood."

I quickly looked up in disgust. "Isn't that a bit too dark for high schoolers?"

She shrugged and kept tapping on her iPad. "Yeah. But we can't really change it." For a moment, she looked up at me and exclaimed, "You should come!"

"No." I immediately shook my head in response. "I can't. I need to get a job, so I'll be probably busy by Halloween." There was still a week left to Halloween, plenty of time to find a job, something or other I could stick to.

My head lowered back down, and I dipped the brush into the nail polish again before covering another one of my toes.

"Okay, but if you don't have a job by Halloween, then you have to come!" She jumped up on the bed, trying to hold my attention.

"Yes, yes, okay!" I dragged myself away from her before she ruined my entire nail polish. "What are you going to dress as? A witch?" I asked her.

The high school she went to was one of the top ones in the area and they held amazing Halloween parties every year. Old students could visit, along with parents and siblings. It was something I needed to consider with Faye as I was only going to go if she was.

Rose shrugged again, not knowing what she was going to go as for Halloween. "Maybe." Her attention diverted back to her iPad and mine to my toes.

Suddenly, my phone began buzzing and I turned my head around to get a glimpse of the caller ID. *There was none.* I closed the nail polish and grabbed my phone from the table, picking it up and hoping for it to be one of the hundred jobs I had sent my CV to.

"Hello!" I said, accepting the call.

"Glad to find out the number was correct."

The smile and the moment of peace was ripped off from my face when I recognized the voice on the other end of the call. It was that man—Christopher.

I drew my phone away from my ears and tapped on Rose's shoulder before quietly whispering for her to leave the room. I didn't want to have any conversation with that man in front of my little sister. She took my order and sprinted out, closing the door behind her.

"What do you want from me?" I asked, frustration clear in my voice. "Are you so obsessed with me that you found my number? What, did you pay someone to get it?" Words blew straight out of my mouth. I held nothing in anymore.

It had been a good two days without hearing his voice or his threats. I had gathered enough courage to face him again if he forced me to.

"Yes, and no," he replied, cheekily.

My nostrils flared. "What now?"

"Don't be hard on me, *amore*. I have done nothing yet and there are many things I can do," he began. "I'm still being very *nice* and to be honest, I don't need to be."

"You were not nice when you broke into my *boyfriend's* house and then proceeded to assault me with a knife and then threaten me to see you again. That's not nice," I reminded him.

The ache began in my head soon after hearing his voice. I pressed my fingers between the bridge of my nose and held my head low while the phone was pressed against my ear.

"And I would do it all over again because I can and I will. And I thought we were clear the last time we spoke. That boy is not your boyfriend, nor will he ever be," he spat out, his words hot.

The only reason I had mentioned Adam was my boyfriend was to see his reaction and it was just what I expected it to be.

This man, Christopher, he had a *liking* for me, and I wasn't sure why.

16

REBEKAH

What did this man even see in me?

I was in disbelief, and I couldn't come to terms with the fact that this man *liked* me for whatever reason. We had terrible encounters. He couldn't like me.

"He's my ex-boyfriend. Not that it should concern you." I leaned back against the headboard of the bed while the nail polish on my toes dried. "And why are you even calling me? I still don't understand. Is-is there something you want from me?" This time, I asked him in a gentler tone, hoping it would be something he would respond to.

"I want to talk to you, so I talk to you." He took in a sharp breath. "Is it hard for you to respond to me?" One moment, he was *trying* to be a normal person and the other moment, he was snapping, and his voice was changing.

"If you keep talking to me like that, I will cut the call right away..." I trailed off.

"I dare you to cut it, *amore*. I will be at your front door, and you will be over my fucking shoulders, passed out as I carry you away from your house and trust me when I say there will be no one to save you from me." At this point, threats were pouring right out of him, and he didn't even have to try.

I lined my lips straight and looked over to the window. It was dark outside; the trees were slamming left and right with the strong wind and the sounds of cars passing down the street could be heard.

A part of me wanted to laugh at his *threats,* as they were quite unreliable and irrational. He couldn't possibly get away with kidnapping me but then again, my head flashed back to the night in the station where I first saw him. *Could it be possible? Was he a mobster or was my head running wild?*

"Okay," I whispered, still holding the phone and the call instead of cutting it. "I won't cut it."

"Good. Don't be hard on me. I'm really trying here." Excitement grew at the back of his tone. "Anyway, I have heard things about you."

My brows furrowed. "What things?" I asked.

"I heard about your daddy's medical bills and the issues within your family..." I knew where this was going. *Exactly* where this conversation was heading to. "I can help you."

"Mhm. Keep talking," I coaxed him to continue.

"I can arrange whatever amount you need and in return—"

"Let me guess, I have to sleep with you?" I asked him, rising from the bed. Something curled inside me, and my head grew hot. "That's not happening."

"You have *very* dirty thinking, *amore.*" He sounded disappointed at what I had said. "I don't want to fuck you, not right now at least." He paused, clearly changing his demands in those few seconds. "I would arrange whatever you want and in return, you'll have a date with me."

"Pfft." I laughed it off and ran my fingers through my hair.

Was this man even real?

"My place, my conditions, and you'll wear what I want you to wear," he continued, his words becoming wilder each second.

"I'm not a whore," I reminded him.

"And you won't be," he stated and took a deep breath. "Unless *you* want to be."

Suddenly, I was considering it out of nowhere. There was someone offering me money in exchange for a simple date that wouldn't lead to fucking, as promised. But there was a drawback to it all, *someone* was the same man I had seen become violent and I wasn't sure if I even wanted to talk to him for another minute.

"I need time to think," I said, clearing my throat.

"I can work with that. Call me when you've made a decision. The offer won't be on the table for long," he quickly replied before cutting the cull.

I drew my phone away from my ear and switched it off for the moment. My fingers raced across my throbbing head, and I sighed heavily before curling myself forward and pulling my knees to my chest.

I felt terrible that I was even considering his offer. He had threatened me, not once but repeatedly, he had a knife to my throat and nearly killed me. I hated how I was trying to make excuses for it even when the red flags were clear and in front of me. The flags weren't even red, they were crimson—with blood pouring down them.

I could not go on a date with him but at the same time, he was offering me whatever amount I needed to clear my dad's hospital bills for the time being. The relief it was going to bring me and my family was greater than anything else.

But what if he wanted more?

I didn't have the courage to put a price on my body nor did I ever want to do that. It didn't matter if times became worse or not—I'd never sold my body for money and I still didn't want to.

Christopher

My hand was covered with blood. It soaked into the white sleeve of the shirt I had accidentally wore. On nights like these, it was usually black, but I was firm I wouldn't be killing anyone tonight until Walter brought me a rogue who was stranded on the road surrounding the city.

"Tell me the truth." I rolled my eyes and looked back at the man staring at me. His face was bluish red, his life was draining in front of him and there was nothing he was doing about it. "Who sent you here?"

"No-no one," he choked out, shaking his head on the ground. "I lost my way. No one sent me here." His voice echoed across the empty, dark hallway of the house. Struggling, he reached for my hand that was buried deep into his chest, wrapped around his beating heart.

"I don't believe you and because I don't believe you, I'm going to kill you." I moved my fingers a little and they ached. It had been a while, probably an hour that I had been forcing a rogue to tell me where he had come from.

He just wouldn't answer.

His eyes lightened up with horror and he saw his end coming when I withdrew my hand from his chest, also drawing out his heart at the same time. Blood poured left and right, spilling everywhere, and leaking across the hallway. My claws tugged back into my skin, and I tossed away the dead heart to the side, right beside his body.

The rogue's eyes were still wide open, but he was dead. It was only a matter of time before his scent would disperse into the hallway and spread across the house.

I didn't want that.

"Take care of the body. Fast." I tapped on Walter's shoulders. "This was a fail of an evening."

"True." Walter agreed as he kneeled and collected the legs of the dead man.

It wasn't the first time I had killed, and it wasn't going to be the last time. I intended to only *rest* after ensuring every living rogue was dead and not entering my territory.

17

CHRISTOPHER

It was late, almost time to fall asleep, but my mind was occupied. The warm water ran over my fingers as I cleansed them of the blood I had spilled earlier. The scent was rising in the house, which meant Walter hadn't taken care of the body *yet*.

"Walter!" I yelled while rushing out of my room. "I have guests coming in an hour. Take care of the body before I take care of yours!" I coursed through the hallway, searching for him, finding him moments later, still standing beside the body with two other men by his side. Giving him a death glare, I said, "Quick."

"Sam just brought the truck. We are going to take it in and throw it in the dumpster," Walter replied, quivering a little.

"Good." I sighed and drifted downstairs, ensuring everything was in place, including the food that was being prepared for tonight.

Alicia was coming over with her husband, Maxwell, my first cousin. It was going to be a small family dinner, even though the last time I had one of those, I nearly killed Pietro for his remarks at the table. But things were different now, Alicia was *my* direct contact to my *mate* and I couldn't ruin it.

I needed to be in her favor.

When I walked out of the kitchen, I nearly slammed against Pietro who stood around, lurking in the hallways while holding a bag of chips.

"I heard screams..." he trailed off, chewing a large chip so loudly—to the point where I could even hear him swallow.

"Someone died," I replied.

His eyes barely widened but a surprised expression covered his face. "Really? Who was it?"

"A rogue."

"Another one?" The bag of chips scrunched in his hand as he went in for another bite.

I snatched it away and discarded it. "You know that irritates me."

"What doesn't?" He rolled his eyes and clicked his tongue in his mouth, only worsening it all the more. The sounds he made were torture for my ears. I still wasn't sure how I was *living* with him, as I was barely able to hold my wrath. "Do you know it's all going to change when your preppy little *princess* walks through those doors? She's going to be chewing in your ears and it's going to be a melody for you." He leaned down and grabbed the packet of chips. "Sometimes, you just have to make sacrifices for those you love. Including me."

I stood sternly in my spot as he gave me a wide smile before walking away and retiring to his room. A sigh of relief passed my lips as I realized he wasn't going to be at dinner since he would be sleeping. I could not have him commenting on every little aspect of my life, especially something as sensitive as *mates*.

It was diffcrent for an Alpha to have one.

Much more different for me to have one.

My face lightened for a moment as my phone buzzed in my pants. I grabbed it and quickly attended it before wasting a precious second of my *preppy little princess*.

"Hello, *Amore*."

"Stop calling me that!" Her voice roared in my ears, setting fire to every emotion I had in my body and leaving it to burn.

It had been a few hours since I had heard her voice and more than just a couple of days since I had seen her. My eyes were yearning to get another glimpse of her face, once more or maybe more than once. It was getting uncontrollable. The mate bond was *raw*. The last time I saw her, I confirmed that she was bonded with me, sewn to my soul, sculpted for only me and truly nothing mattered beyond her. In those few minutes, everything fell from my hands, my whole entire world—and I only snapped out of it when she left the room.

Until then, I was drunk and under a heavy love spell.

"Tough. I can call you whatever I want to call you." I turned around, moving toward the seating area in the house. "Have you made a decision? I suppose it is a yes." The smile grew wider on my face and if Pietro had seen me, he would laugh for the rest of his little life and even die while laughing.

"Well—" She cleared her throat and then remained silent for a few seconds. I knew the offer was alluring and there was no reason she would decline it. She needed the money, and I needed her. "I-I need to be sure there is no sexual activity involved in this." She spoke slowly but with every word falling out of her mouth, I felt my cock restraining in my pants.

If only she knew.

"No sex, no anything, no kissing—nothing!" she stated.

I pressed my eyes shut. A warm breath left my mouth. *Oh, Amore.* If she could only see the things I had planned for her.

"No sex..." I whispered. "Nothing—unless of course, you want it."

"I don't," she quickly responded.

I sat back on one of the leather couches while pushing my hips forward and adjusting my pants. It was going to be hard to manage my *feelings* when her voice alone brought a rise out of me. But I was going to control it—for the time being. It wasn't going to be long till her knees would be bruised for me and she would be begging for more.

"Fine. Friday night. I'll arrange whatever is necessary. Goodnight, *Amore*." I grinned, resting my back against the couch with my arm spread over it.

I drew the phone away from my ears and canceled the call. The smile grew wider on my face as my leg slowly swung back and forth. Everything was going to go the way I planned and there was nothing that was going to stop me from having her, *my way*.

The silence enveloped around me and remained for a couple of minutes before Alicia and Maxwell came rushing in through the front door. I rose from my seat and went to greet them into the house, the house where a dead body still hadn't been moved.

Walter was doomed.

"Good evening, Christopher!" Maxwell shook his hands with me. "It's been a while. How's everything?"

"Good, good. Please take a seat."

We all returned to the living room while dinner was being arranged in the dining area. The lights were dimmed to create the mood for the evening.

I spoke with Maxwell about him patrolling the borders and handling whatever was coming into the city, anything that was related to werewolves. He was my eyes and ears in that part of the pack. A job I had given him when his father, my uncle, passed away.

Though we spoke on the phone, we'd barely met over the past couple of months as I had been occupied with other matters.

"Alicia told me something earlier..." he trailed off while glancing in her direction. She gave him a worrisome look, which only forced me to think that she couldn't keep a secret in her huge belly. "Don't blame her. I forced it out her."

My arms splayed over the couch, and I sighed. "No one can know yet."

"Why is that?" He leaned forward while holding a glass of wine in one hand.

"Because it's a human and Christopher is terrified his name will be tarnished the moment his people realize that their mighty Alpha has mated with a human." Alicia slimed her way into the conversation, taking every moment to enjoy this just as everyone else was. She moved her attention to me and continued, "But, I don't agree. So what if she's a human? She has been paired with you."

I nodded and agreed. "I know—which is why I'm pursuing her."

An amused look crossed her face. "Really?"

"Yes. In fact, we are set on a date on Friday."

"Oh..." She leaned back on the couch and placed a hand over her pregnant belly. "That was quick. Are you going to tell her the truth? I mean, she's a human after all and to come into your world, she needs to know."

"I will," I responded.

Maxwell stayed quiet during the entire conversation. I supposed he was still surprised with the fact that *I* had a mate. No one truly expected it—neither did I.

"I can talk to her if you want," Alicia suggested with a shrug. "My cousin, Faye, twisted a story to her about the whole thing since they were children. It's not going to be hard to twist the story back to the truth."

What twisted story?

"What did your cousin say?" I asked her, furrowing my brows. If my mate even had an inkling of what we were, it was going to be a lot easier to convince her rather than force her into my world.

Perfect.

"Something along that lines that you're a cult leader and people follow you..." she trailed off, leaving the bits I wanted to hear out.

I forced out a chuckle and shook my head. "It's fine. I'll manage it. She will be my mate after all, sitting right beside me." A smile crept across my lips, and I looked away.

I could not wait to have her.

"What will you do next?" Alicia asked, shifting in her seat. I watched her eyes as she glanced over at Maxwell with concern and then back over to me.

As much as I didn't want to spill every part of my decisive plan, it came out of me by itself. "*Turn* her."

"Into one of you? That's not possible." Max interrupted, his eyes wider than ever. Dread washed over their faces as they took in my words.

"Everything is possible when you're the Alpha and—well, I am," I scoffed, pushing my shoulders back.

"She wouldn't want to change, Christopher!" Alicia snapped.

"Doesn't matter. She's destined to be with me, so she has to become one of us." I kept my pose. There wasn't anyone who was going to stop me from doing whatever I wanted as I was the Alpha and there was no one greater than me.

They both looked at me after exchanging looks with each other.

Maxwell's arm stretched over to his wife, while Alicia's head lowered. Clearing his throat, he asked, "You'll bite her?"

"Yes."

"The full moon doesn't occur until later next month," he pointed out.

It was true. The full moon had just passed by recently but that didn't matter. "Who's talking about the full moon?" I glanced away from them, my attention diverting to the sky outside. It was cloudy but the fading crescent could be still seen. "It's the new moon that matters," I whispered.

The moon was going to disappear tomorrow at dusk and the crescent of the new moon would be appear later at Saturday evening, which meant I had plenty of time on my hands to turn her on Friday, exactly when our date was set to be.

18

Rebekah

When the bell rang, I rushed downstairs and opened the door as my fingers quivered. Faye pushed herself in, worried sick for me. "What happened?"

"I'm terrified!" I exclaimed, closing the door behind her and locking it.

It was still early in the morning, and no one was going to be home until later in the afternoon. Rose was at school, Mom was handling a couple of chores and Dad was outside working. I was alone at home, sleeping and dreaming when the bell first rang. It was a delivery, by Christopher Delfino.

I set the delivery aside and went on with my day, having breakfast and showering. The minute I was free, I tore through the delivery and found clothes, along with a card that gave me strict instructions to wear only those and nothing else.

"I'm not going to wear this!" I picked up the thong between my fingers. "He clearly wants to fuck me." We had agreed on not having any sexual activity during the entire date but now I was assuming otherwise.

Faye glanced over at the dress in the package. It was a burgundy strappy stain dress, long enough to go beyond my knees.

"I mean, the dress looks nice," she said cheekily before picking it up and feeling the satin brush against her fingertips. "Maybe he just wanted you to wear something underneath and not come *bare*." Her explanation was far worse than I imagined.

"No, he wants to fuck me. I know guys like him..." I groaned, shoving the thong back into the box. Like hell was I going to wear that tonight. It was far more than enough that I actually agreed to it.

"Just wear the thong. It's gonna be fine." She patted my shoulder while glancing at the thong I had shoved into the box. I had already made my decision; I wasn't going to wear it.

I turned to Faye with a worried look and asked her once more, "Do you really think I should go?" My hands laid flat over my thudding chest, and I chewed on my lower lip as anxiety spread through me. I had reconsidered it last night and stayed up late, thinking and thinking whether I'd made the right choice.

I *truly* feared that man and going on a date with him was terrifying. *What if he killed me? What if he hurt me?* There wasn't going to be anyone else—I would be alone with him. I didn't even know where he was going to take me or if he would ever let me go back home. My eyes widened at the thought of him kidnapping me and holding me hostage for reasons I couldn't think of.

"It's okay, Bek. If you don't feel like going, just tell him you don't want to. You don't have to listen to him and everything he says." She shrugged and sat down.

I took the couch beside her and fell back against it as a sigh passed my lips. "But the money..." I trailed off, pouting. "It's enticing and he's offering it to me without any strings attached—just one date." I couldn't imagine making that much money even after years of working. There was an offer falling straight into my lap and I was still reconsidering it.

And ethically, it was correct. He had promised that there wouldn't be anything sexual involved and it would just be a one-time date. He wouldn't hassle me again.

I could use that money to clear most of my dad's hospital bills. My parents wouldn't have to argue about money anymore and they wouldn't be cornering to divorce every night.

It was good.

"Look, Bek, if you know him, he's a nice person with a little bit of temper. And it's just going to be a few hours. You'll go and come back and forget it ever happened!" Faye said, cheer on her face as she tried hard to excite me.

I looked over at her and we both fell into laughter. "I'm definitely not going to wear that thong!" I exclaimed, my finger hovering over the box.

"Don't." She shook her head and laughed deeper. "Wear your cotton underwear and enjoy it. Trust me, you'll come back in one piece." She reassured me about my decision, and I felt less anxious about it all. "Plus, it's been a while since you have gone on a date. Forget everything he did and just enjoy it."

Just one date

"Yeah, that sounds better." I faded back into the couch, resting for a while after panicking the entire morning. I came up with the worst situations that could possibly happen tonight, but it was just my mind overworking and thinking too hard.

Time passed quickly. Morning faded into evening and the skies grew dark and cloudy. Faye left after having lunch with me and I went for a shower. By exactly seven, I was ready, wearing the strappy burgundy dress that fitted me perfectly. The thong was out of my sight, far away, buried inside my closet.

My brown hair, blown out, fell over my shoulders with ease. I smeared on dark red lipstick while keeping the rest of the make-up minimal and matching with the dress.

By 19:01, there was a black car parked down the street. Tinted windows and complete silence. The engine barely roared or vibrated when passing my house. The car remained at its spot as I hurried downstairs with a black coat hanging off my shoulders.

It was going to be a cold night and I needed to be prepared.

"Going on a date?" Rose asked as she stayed underneath the lamplight, studying and finishing her homework.

I glanced over my shoulders, looking at the closed rooms and the deafening silence from the kitchen. Dad had fallen asleep after he came home from work and Mom was in the kitchen, clearing the dinner.

"Don't tell Mom. Just tell her I'm going to see Faye," I whispered to my little sister while pushing a key into the knob and opening the door.

I couldn't let Mom see how I was dressed. It would take her seconds to put two and two together. I wanted her to be absolutely clueless when I offered her the money to take care of Dad's hospital bills. She didn't need to know that I was going on a date with a complete stranger for money.

My heart beat hard the entire time as I slipped out of the house. The heels I wore cackled as I moved across the pavement, nearing the parked car.

An unfamiliar man stepped out of the car and came over to me. For a minute, I thought he was going to jump at me until he said, "Good evening, Ms. Anderson."

My last name. *How did he know?*

"Oh, good evening." I smiled at him as he drew the door open for me. I pulled my coat tighter over my shoulders, stopping myself from freezing before I slipped into the car.

Just as I sat, I moved my head, tilting it only a few inches before my gaze connected with the alluring golden eyes of my *death*.

19

Rebekah

My stomach twisted and turned as my heart rate jumped to its peak. Goosebumps spread over my skin as winter was spreading in Laford. The wheels moved and I barely heard them as they drove farther away from my house and the little community we lived in.

My knees were touching each other as my hands were buried between them. I glanced outside, never looking back or over my shoulders. My head remained in one position, and I didn't dare make a sound.

"You're not in a movie, *amore*. There are no cameras. Turn and look at me." His voice came from behind, alluring, and dark and I found my heart quickening.

Swallowing hard, I turned to look at him. His golden eyes pierced mine effortlessly. He was suited in a black coat, the first few buttons opened, showing his bare chest that I *tried* not to look at. A chain fell from his neck, a thin golden chain that resembled the color of his eyes.

Mesmerizing.

I took another breath. "Do you want something?" I asked, stiffening my shoulders.

"Yes." He pushed his elbow against the car seat and rested his hand underneath his head. "Your attention." When he spoke, it was clear, and he was loud even when there was no one around.

There was a barrier between the driver and us that stretched from the roof of the car to the seats. I couldn't see him, nor could he see me. Starlight flickered over me, providing me with a little light. With the tinted windows, I could barely see anything outside, but I could feel we were going fast.

"You have my attention." I tried to be *sweet*, though it wasn't my favorite quality. There were a couple of guys I had flings with but that was all in my high school year.

Aside from Adam, I hadn't dated anyone recently nor ever spoken to a man with such little distance.

"Are you panicking?" he asked, his gaze racing all over me and cornering me.

"No," I scoffed, keeping my pose. "Why would I? It's just one date, probably a few hours and then I'll be rid of you for the rest of my life. I don't need to panic," I spilled out, without a single thought. It was like the words fell on my tongue and before they could register in my head, they came out.

His face changed, eyes suddenly turned dark and misty. For a moment, I felt as if I was going to be attacked by *something*. "I don't like when you talk to me in such a terrible way." His voice became cruel, and it was the same voice I had heard for the first time at the subway station.

"Oh, my Lord." I placed my hand over my chest and battled my lashes. "Do you want me to bow to you?" My head lowered a little. A little gasp escaped my throat, and I kept up with the act. "Do you want me to kiss your feet?"

His long muscular leg shifted, moving over his lap. He chuckled and then shook his head. "Not tonight."

My lips lined straight. "Never!" I tried to look away but when I glanced at the window, I saw nothing except for my reflection staring back at me. With a huff, I leaned back and folded my arms, waiting for this journey to come to an end.

"Why do you have to be so hard? You're merely just a boring girl and oftentimes, girls like you are on their knees for me, *amore*." He tried to get my attention with his words, but I didn't give in. "You should be lucky that I *want* you."

My head cocked in his direction. "I'm not a boring girl and I wasn't gifted with knees to submit to a man who has the same worth as me at the end of the day and you—" I stared into his eyes like a hawk. "—should be lucky that I'm sitting here, with you. And I doubt any woman would want to go with such a *narcissistic* man."

The smile over his face faded before he shifted in his seat and invaded my comfort. Taking in a breath, I moved back, distancing myself from him. His hands were inches away from coming at me, grabbing me, but he didn't.

Instead, he smiled.

"You—you tempt me," he whispered, shaking his head. "But beware of your words, *Rebekah*. Don't speak of what you don't know. I'm trying here, I want to *like* you but if you become hard for me, I'll ruin you in ways you cannot even imagine. You don't know me. Let's keep it that way." His words were a warning.

The car came to an halt at an unknown residence. I only caught a glimpse of it when he opened the door to his side and stepped out of the car. Swallowing hard, I began realizing the mistake I had made.

What if I had tripped his anger switch? Was he going to kill me?

The door to my side was drawn open and he offered his hand. I hesitated for a few seconds before placing my hand over his cold one. He tightened his fingers and clasped it whilst I managed to step out of the car without falling on my face and striking my jaw against the hard ground beneath me.

When the door closed, the driver drove out of the driveway. Too lost in my thoughts, I didn't look at the house in front of me until a few seconds later when I snapped into reality. My head rose and I contained a gasp as my gaze rushed over the awfully big residence that stretched to the sky with acres of bare land and surrounding trees.

Fingers fell over my hair, drawing them over my shoulder before Christopher moved behind me, inching closer. I felt his body heat against mine as he sniffed and took another whiff of my scent. It wasn't anything interesting, just a Victoria Secret perfume that I finally found in Rose's room.

The hair over the back of my neck rose as his head moved, reaching closer to my neck. "I'll be civil tonight and I'll remember my manners, *amore*, but don't *hate* me." It was another warning, much deeper than the last one.

I pressed my lips shut and nodded. It wasn't going to be hard to shut my commentary and insults for a couple of hours, even though I wanted to tear this man from the top to the bottom with *only—only* my words and pepper spray him once more before taking all his money and fleeing.

If only.

I sighed and whispered, "I apologize."

"Don't. That's the last thing I want to hear from your mouth." He held my hand tight before dragging me into the unknown residence.

In the darkness, my eyes remained wide open, straining to see through the gloom as the sound of my heartbeat reverberated in my ears. My chest vibrated with each thud and my breaths were short and shallow, making it difficult to keep pace with Christopher, who strode ahead of me. His grip on my hand was firm, yet his touch made me uneasy.

Silence enveloped us, thick and impenetrable. I scanned my surroundings, searching for any signs of life, but the emptiness was absolute. Then, at last, a glimmer of light appeared, casting a warm, golden glow that flickered against the high ceiling of the residence. Candles were scattered throughout the area, their light dancing and playing against the walls.

Suppressing a gasp, I took in the scene before me, trying to remain composed as Christopher watched my reaction intently. My hand slipped from his grasp as I settled into a seat at the opposite end of the long table that was nestled against the brick wall, which seemed to be a part of an indoor waterfall.

Christopher took his place across from me, his eyes locked onto mine, a piercing gold that seemed to see right through me. I tried to make small talk, hoping to ease my nerves. "This is a really interesting place you've got here," I said, forcing a smile.

He smirked, his eyes narrowing with a dangerous edge. "My room is even better."

I rolled my eyes, trying to hide my fear. "I'd rather die."

"Maybe you will," he replied with a shrug, his smile growing wider as a dark cloud seemed to overshadow his gaze.

20

CHRISTOPHER

My cock was *throbbing*.

She was sitting right in front of me, taking food down her throat while I merely sat inches away from her, unable to get my hands on her. It was *pure torture*. I imagined thrashing the whole dinner away and taking her on the table over and over again till her mouth would run dry from screaming and moaning my name.

I ran my fingers through my hair, sighing heavily, before my head turned to one of the servers. "Bring the cocktails. I need a drink," I said quickly. My hand lowered to my pants where I adjusted my cock, tucking it aside.

I had always controlled myself in front of women. Women barely ever enticed me, and they usually worked hard to get me in bed. But here I was, tonight, willing to bed the woman sitting in front of me.

The feelings came out of nowhere and at random times. I blamed my wolf for it all. He was eager to mate, meanwhile, I was eager to casually fuck her. *At least once.*

There was nothing interesting about her. Her features were normal, *common* except for her neck, it was bright and pale, waiting to be marked. There was more I wanted to do to her neck than just mark it. I wanted my hand wrapped around it, I wanted to leave marks of my own, bites and bruises.

My cock stiffened in my pants, at this point aching terribly and watching her didn't help at all.

The server returned with the drinks. *Alcohol.* Just what I needed right now. I waited for Rebekah to take hers and drink it before I did the same, but for the next few seconds, she only eyed the drink at her side.

"Yeah, I'm not going to drink that." She shook her head.

"Why not?" My face went tight. "Are you pregnant?" I slammed her with the question immediately as I hadn't seen her drink wine nor anything else except for water.

Her eyes widened. "No!"

"Then drink. One is not going to hurt and maybe you'll enjoy this more." I smiled at her, patiently waiting for her to drink it. "Unless you're pregnant." I leaned forward, catching her weary look. "If you are, you can tell me. From the looks of it, you seemed pretty comfortable in that apartment of your ex-boyfriend." My brows rose.

It wasn't going to be a problem *if* she was pregnant. I didn't care much as that child would be given up for adoption the moment they stepped out of her womb. I would never care for a bastard child.

She stared me back in disbelief. "I'm not pregnant. *Fuck.*" She rolled her eyes and cursed under her breath. "How do I know there isn't anything inside this? Maybe you'll roofie me and then rape and kill me."

That was at least better than being pregnant. I needed to be sure of everything before biting her and turning her before midnight. Small details mattered.

"I prefer consent, *amore*."

Stretching my arm, I grabbed her drink and brought it to my mouth. After taking a sip of it, I placed it back and then waited for her to drink.

She sighed and picked up the glass at last, drinking from the cocktail while finishing up her dinner. I was long finished with sitting on this seat. Nothing went down my throat. I didn't want to eat. I didn't want to do anything except watch her and wait.

When she wiped her lips with the cloth, her eyes moved over to the wall clock behind me, and she gazed at it for a long minute.

"The date ends when I want it to." I rose from my seat and moved toward her. Her eyes stared back at me and in that moment, I noticed how wide and full they were. "Get up." I didn't know what else to say.

A frown appeared on her lips. "I thought you were keeping your manners." She rolled her eyes at me and stood up, farther away from me.

Like a game, she was playing me over and over again, denying me and rejecting me. It began pissing me off. I displayed my *need;* I approached her like a gentleman and asked her on a date but the entire time, she acted as if she was forced to be here.

I suppose she was.

"*Vaffanculo,*" I growled silently and offered her my hand. "Give me your hand, please." My voice shifted just like my internal emotions. It was fortunate that she could not understand Italian.

"What did you say?" she asked, folding her arms as her brows bunched.

"I said, you look beautiful." My smile widened more and the sweet words that I despised ever saying came out by themselves. "I want to take you somewhere."

She lowered her gaze to my hand and then looked up at me. "Where?"

"Just outside."

Why was it hard for her to just obey me for once? Why couldn't she just shut up? I imposed control over myself before I went wild on her, *again*. I needed to be calm and collected in front of my mate, in front of someone I was going spend the rest of my life with, whether she knew it or not.

She was my destiny—*my* destiny.

After a few seconds, she placed her hand in mine, *finally,* and agreed to let me take her outside the house. There was nothing much interesting outside, but I preferred making my move there, away from all the servants. They wouldn't hear her screams when I'd bite her and turn her into a werewolf.

Of course, she wouldn't be one until my bite sank into her blood stream and changed it—which could take days.

In the dark, I held her soft hand and felt her skin rubbing against my rough hand. She was warm, even though it was cold. I gazed at her fingers that were small and barely wrapped around mine. Her nails weren't sharp, in fact they were clean and without any polish on them.

There was a bruise underneath her pinky finger, a cut. It was old and seemed more like a scar that had been there for a while. My brows furrowed as I traced my thumb across the scar.

It was a deep one.

"What happened here?" I asked, concern in my voice.

She glanced at her own hand and replied, "Nothing. I just broke something, and it cut me."

"What did you break?"

"I don't know. *A vase.*" She shrugged, clearly lying.

"Don't lie."

"Don't be a creep." She pulled her hand away from mine and hid it behind her hip, taking it a bit too seriously.

My jaw clenched when I saw my hand bare, without hers. It was merely a fucking question, nothing more. She didn't need to snap and because she did, it angered me. I stepped forward as my face turned red. "I don't like the way you respond to me, *amore.* That's going to change."

"Nothing is going to change because this is the last time I'm ever going to see you." She paused to take a breath while considering something. "You told me, just one date." Her straight, index finger rose to my eye-level. "Nothing more. So stop acting like I'll fall for you or something because I will *never* fall for you!"

Her mouth. The way it ran wild, it only urged me further to take her right then and there. Silence her.

I took a step closer, close enough to *smell* her. Her scent was far more than enough to calm me down, to tuck away all the rage bubbling in my head. She gasped when I laid my hand over her shoulder and drew it closer to her neck. Color drained from her face, and she stood surprised as I broke the *promise* I had given her—to not touch her.

My fingers brushed past her soft neck, moving to the back of her head where her hair tangled. She held her breath and placed her hands against my stomach in fear as I closed the distance.

I didn't want to do anything wrong to her.

Just everything right.

"Wh—what are you doing?" she asked, her voice trembling.

I smelled her fear, it was strong. My eyes lowered to her mouth; her full lips that were formed to be only kissed. Finally, I had seen her close enough and she was beyond *perfect*.

"Nothing," I whispered while her hair was still wrapped around my fingers. "Do you want me to do something?" I moved closer and closer till her face was only a few inches away from mine. Her glazed eyes looked at me with such curiosity and confusion that I had never seen before. "Tell me. *What do you want me to do?*"

21

Rebekah

"*What do you want me to do?*" he asked me, and for that moment, his voice was heavenly in my ears. My heart thudded hard in my chest. Chills raced down my spine and over my skin as I looked at him. There was barely any distance between us. "Do you want me kiss you?"

My eyes shifted from his. "I—"

His hand pressed firmer against the back of my head while the other one came wrapping around my wrist. "Do you want me to touch you? I can show you things that you have never seen or done," he whispered, tracing his hand over my arm. "I can give you that *pleasure* that you have never even come close to..." My insides throbbed and my legs began trembling at his words. "Look at me." He curled his fingers underneath my chin, raising my head and forcing me to look at him.

He pinned me down with a stare and I barely moved from whatever spell he had me in. It was a *spell!* I couldn't snap out of it, and I couldn't move.

"Oh, *amore*, you're going to remember nothing but my *name* by the time I'm done with you. Tell me if that's what you want, and I swear that's exactly what I'll do." He waited for my response.

I didn't know what to say. I didn't know what the question was. My mind was running wild. *Was I imaging this or was this reality?*

I tried to think of anything else except for the man standing in front of me. I couldn't think of him *like* that. *Never!* God! I hated this man. I couldn't let him win and *have* me.

I restrained myself, pushing away those thoughts and thinking of anything else that mattered but it was a struggle. After a minute of silence, I ran my tongue over my lips before moving back from him. "Don't touch me," I snapped.

"Your wish." He shrugged and quickly moved his hands away from me, though that left a longing on my skin.

My heart dulled a little, but I tried not to show it. "Am I done being here?" I asked him, sounding a little rough.

"You're done." He didn't argue with me, for the first time. *Did I hurt his feelings?* He looked away from me, and glanced over at the door, waiting for someone to appear.

Moments later, a man walked out and approached Christopher. He handed him a book, a cheque book, and that's when he wrote a cheque for me, enough to clear most of Dad's medical bills and the debts Mom had taken for it.

It was plenty!

I was a bit surprised that he had actually given it to me—the money. I assumed he was going to force me to do something or—I didn't know, but he easily gave me the cheque, asking for nothing more.

Was I done?

We were just outside the residence, which overlooked the breathtaking courtyard. The wind was cold and chilly. I barely remained warm even with the coat over my shoulders. When I looked up at the sky, I found it dark and cloudy with the moon *lost.*

I folded the cheque and placed it inside the pocket of my coat before my attention turned back to Christopher, who stood alongside a man I hadn't seen before.

"Michael here—" He glanced at the man and continued, "—will drop you home. Thank you for spending your time with me. Goodnight, Rebekah." He offered me a warm smile before walking past me and returning to the residence.

"Goodnight," I mumbled, watching him drift into the house.

I couldn't tell if he was pissed or not—or sad, or angry. All I had done was simply rejected his moves toward me. He had promised no sexual activity, and he *did* keep his promise. Those few minutes when he was close, it was tempting, and I had almost let it slip while forgetting all the terrible things he had done. I only agreed to a date because I wanted the money, nothing more, and he knew it.

I didn't ever want to see him again and it wasn't my concern.

"Please drop me home, Michael." I smiled at the man before tightening the coat around my body.

The next morning was welcoming and also torturous. Rose threw a pillow at my head, forcing me up from the sweet dream I was having. I jolted up from the bed and stared at her with rage covering every inch of my face.

"What is wrong with you?" I snapped while clenching the sheets underneath me.

"It's literally two in the afternoon and you're still sleeping!" she exclaimed, grabbing another pillow from the side. "Mom told me to wake you up so you could have some food."

Shit.

I drew the covers from myself and quickly stood up, wide awake, while rubbing my burning eyes. It was two in the afternoon. I had slept for way too long and somehow, not once had I woken up. Groaning, I went back and forth before rushing into the washroom and splattering some ice-cold water over my face.

"When did you come home last night?" Rose asked, standing by the door. Her voice was full of sneakiness. "Midnight? One?"

"Midnight," I replied. "Why do you care?"

"How was the date? Hmm?" She winked at me from her left eye, and I looked back at my reflection in the mirror. I couldn't believe my own little sister was questioning me. "Was it a nice guy? You were gone pretty late. If you don't want me to tell Mom, you need to give me some details." She stretched her arm, placing it against the doorway while her other hand rested on her hip.

"You need to go and focus on your homework and boys your own age!" I exclaimed, walking out of the bathroom, and drying my face. "If you must know, it was a terrible date and I hated it. The guy—he was like this terrible man that I can't tell you about, Rose, but it's very eye opening to know what kind of men you can find in this world," I blurted out, ranting to my little sister about last night.

I had tossed and turned the entire night after spending time with Christopher. His face was an image glued in my head that I couldn't possibly get rid of. He sat in my every thought, and it felt like he was breathing down my neck the entire time I was sleeping.

Mixed emotions coursed through me. There was guilt for taking the money, talking to him rudely and rejecting his advances and then there was anger for what he *wanted* to do.

Pleasure.

I took a deep breath and brushed off his voice that kept echoing in my head. I imagined repeatedly what he would do if I had let him *touch* me. I imagined his hands roaming all over my body, his vile mouth against mine and my hands against his rock-hard chest.

"Bek?" Rose called out my name while snapping her little fingers in front of me to grab my attention.

"What?"

"Did—were you day dreaming?" she asked.

I shook my head slightly. "No," I scoffed before grabbing the cheque off the table and heading downstairs to give it to my mom.

Yesterday, Faye and I had agreed that we would tell my mom that the money came from her family, a couple of her cousins pooled in and agreed to help me and that it didn't need to be paid back.

"Good lord, you slept for long today!" Mom exclaimed as I stepped downstairs with Rose trailing behind me. "Are you okay?" she asked with concern in her voice.

"Yes, it was just a long night." I approached her and unfolded the cheque before handing it to her. "Some of Faye's cousins helped and they came up with this amount. They wanted to help me, and of course, my family."

Mom was surprised. "I cannot take this, Rebekah," she whispered before taking my arm and pulling me into the kitchen, farther away from Rose who took her seat near the TV and began watching a movie.

She was still too young to understand anything.

"It's a lot!" Mom exclaimed, her eyes stretching wide. "No way." She shook her head and blinked crazily.

"Mom, it's okay. They wanted to help." I gave her a warm smile. "And plus, they are rich people, they have plenty of money to spare. It's alright," I quickly added.

Unfortunately, Christopher's name was bluntly displayed on the cheque, along with his signature. I hoped Mom wouldn't question me about who this man was. She glanced over the cheque once more, this time her brows drew together as she registered it.

"Are you sure?"

"Yes." I curled my fingers around her arm, reassuring her. "It's fine. *They* wanted to help, and I couldn't say no. And this is far more than enough to cover all the debts you had taken for Dad's medical bills. You no longer have to worry about it and fight with Dad day and night." I looked up at her, waiting for her to accept it.

I blinked frantically, waiting, and waiting. Mom pressed her fingers against her forehead, easing the tensions in her mind.

"Thank you, Rebekah, and tell Faye that I'm grateful for what she and her family has done," she finally said, taking the money.

"I will!" Excited, I nearly jumped. "I'll call her over later for dinner and you can meet her." My voice boomed and warmth spread all over my body.

Just like that, one worry was out of my life forever.

22

REBEKAH

The sun shone straight at my bed, stronger than ever. It was about to set in an hour. I had opened the curtains to let the golden hour slip in before the night came and the never-ending darkness and gloom.

I curled my fingers around the phone and laid back on my bed. "Yeah, just lie or something. I know you're great at lying!" I said to Faye, talking to her on the call and telling her the details I had given Mom. "And be here by eight."

"Yes, I will be! But I'm so glad you got this all worked out. Finally..." She sighed, feeling happier for me than I was.

Watching my mom sink deeper and deeper into debt took a toll on my mental wellness and since Faye was my best friend, she had watched me all those days I was struggling to make ends meet. Unfortunately, Faye couldn't help me much as her funds were limited. Her family did try to help, but I couldn't take money from them.

I surely could take money from a stranger that I had gone on one date with. That was different and it didn't really matter anymore.

He was out of my head.

A knock sounded on the door, and I quickly rose from the bed. My hair scattered over my shoulders and face as I pressed the phone against my ears. "I'll call you back," I mumbled under my breath before cutting the call with Faye.

Mom walked into the room with my laundry done. She placed it near my dresser and then closed the door behind her. Her face remained dull and down, which made me nervous of what was going to come next.

"Mom." I moved my legs, placing my feet on the ground. "Is everything okay?"

"Yeah. I wanted to talk to you about something…" She trailed off before sitting beside me on the bed.

With the silence, I grew worried. "Yes?" There was nothing that we needed to worry about. Once the debts were paid, we were free to live peacefully, and it wasn't going to be hard to make ends meet. The debt collectors would finally be gone, and we could actually, for once, be happy again.

Right?

My brows rose as I silently questioned Mom. She tried to cover the worry smeared on her face, but I could see right through it. *Something wasn't good.* This was beyond money and debts.

"Your Dad and I have agreed on a divorce," she said, and suddenly, I felt my heart being crushed.

"What?" I shook my head and laughed a little while taking in her words. *What did she mean? What divorce?* "Why? Is—everything is good, isn't it? I mean, you can pay the debt and you don't have to stress about money anymore," I began stuttering, losing my voice for the first time ever.

"It's not just about money, Rebekah." She lowered her gaze and swallowed hard. "It's beyond that. Your dad and I aren't on good terms, and we are both quite unhappy with each other. And at this point, it is affecting you and Rose, and we do not want that."

"Isn't that normal?" I cocked a brow at her explanation. "I mean—people fight every day and that's normal, Mom."

"No, it's not normal. It's affecting you and Rose; it's getting more violent day by day and it's eating us both alive. We cannot live like this. And it's not about the money or the debts. Your dad is different, and his sickness made me different as well. We are both different people now, and we don't share the same feelings as we did before," Mom explained, pain rising in her voice as her eyes flooded with tears. "We agreed last night that he'd divorce me and move out, hopefully by next month."

"But what about us?" My heart ached with pain that I never imagined. "Rose is still in high school!" I exclaimed, reminding her that she still had a young child who would be wrecked with this knowledge.

"Till Rose finishes school, she will stay here with me, during summer she can go be with your dad and as for you, it's your choice where you want to stay or who you want to stay with. Your dad will move to a town three hours away from here, he will crash with his family for a while till everything is sorted out," she continued, and by the time she finished, tears were dripping down my cheeks.

I didn't know what to think anymore. My head was clouded. I was losing control of myself. I wanted to snap at my parents for the decision they had made. *How could they? How could they leave each other? Why were they getting a divorce?*

I was irrational, not thinking much.

Pressing my eyes, I took in a few steady breaths, holding myself together before I opened them and looked at Mom. "Are you going to be okay, Mom?" I asked her.

"I will be, eventually." She placed her hand on my shoulder. "It's going to be hard, Rebekah, but it's a decision that took plenty of time and thought to make. Try to understand us. Love, marriage—it's not forever. I'm sorry for taking you through—"

"No, Mom, don't apologize!" I exclaimed, shaking my head, and wrapping my arms around her. "I understand." *I think I did.* A part of it at least.

I knew something like divorce was going to come soon. My parents didn't love each other, and they still had plenty of time to live, they couldn't waste the rest of their lives hating each other and being in an unhappy marriage.

"I'm here for you, Mom, if you need anything," I whispered, pulling away from her embrace.

"Love you, Rebekah."

We spoke for a minute more, talking about Rose and when she needed to know. We agreed on telling her after the divorce was finalized and, in some ways, we were going to twist it and tell her that Dad was moving out for some time and he was going to stay with his extended family.

I needed to talk to Dad as well. His heart must've been broken, just as Mom's was.

But right now, I needed to be alone. I was angry, furious at my parents for not sorting out their shit and snapping at each other day and night.

When Mom left the room, I locked it and tears poured out of my eyes, dripping like a waterfall. I closed my fists, walking back and forth while taking everything in. After nearly twenty years of marriage, they were going to divorce and all because they didn't have love for each other anymore.

It was *wild*, fucking *crazy*.

I blamed Dad's cancer for it all. If he hadn't gotten sick with that terrible thing, he wouldn't been in the hospital for a whole year and Mom wouldn't have had to over work herself and try to make ends meet. They wouldn't have been divorcing if he hadn't gotten cancer.

Before Dad was sick, my parents were happy—more than happy—with each other. They woke up every morning in the same bed, ate from the same plate and even drank from the same glass. They were obsessed and deeply in love with each other—until cancer caught up to my Dad.

Ugh.

I clenched my teeth and groaned while glancing outside of the window. My face was covered with tears and my cheeks were deep red from the flame I felt burning inside me. *Why? Why now? Why my parents?*

My brows furrowed and lines appeared on my forehead when I found a car parked on the side of the road. *A tinted car.* A hot breath left my throat before I grabbed my phone and headed downstairs. There was only one person with a tinted car, someone who was a little too obsessed with me.

I grabbed my coat from the hanger near the door and buttoned it up before unlocking the main door and stepping out.

"Where are you going?" Mom's voice stopped me.

I turned to look at her with my eyes red and puffy. "Faye wanted me to drop something off. It will be just a minute!" I quickly lied, coming up with anything before I turned my head around and rushed outside.

Mom closed the door behind me as I made my way through the driveway and towards the road. A car sprinted and I gasped, taking a step, and holding myself calm. The cold air slammed against me, and I shivered before carefully stepping on the road. Looking left and right, I made sure there was no car coming my way before I approached the tinted car.

I was going to kill him!

In fact, it was the perfect time to kill him. I was furious and sad at the same time. Nothing was going to stop me from tearing this man limb from limb.

23

REBEKAH

Tightening the coat around my body, I stepped forward and stood beside the tinted car. I tapped my phone against the window, waiting for it to be rolled down. My patience was thinning. A couple of moments later, the window came down and to my surprise, I didn't find Christopher *stalking* me. It wasn't him.

It was his driver, Michael—as far as I remembered his name.

My brows furrowed in confusion, but my anger only furthered from there. "What are you doing here?" I questioned while placing a hand on my hip.

"I have been ordered to watch you."

I blinked, hard. "What?"

The driver shrugged. "I have to keep my eyes on you for the next couple of days, ensuring you don't visit that boy you have on your side." He told me in words I couldn't understand.

When I realized what he meant, my face turned red, and rage coursed through my veins. He was talking about Adam. *Fucking hell.* Clenching my fists, I turned around and grunted.

I grabbed my phone and dialed Christopher's number that was still on my call log, I hadn't saved it yet, but next on my list was to save it under the name of *'creep.'*

Complete disbelief struck me. There was something clearly unwell with this man who couldn't stop bothering me. It had barely been a week since I had stolen his wallet and he was driving me crazy with his actions—all of them. *Who would send someone to watch me?*

Only a creep.

Maybe if it was any other night, I would've ignored it and locked the doors in the house but tonight was terrible timing. My Mom had just told me about the decision she was going to take over the next few weeks and I was *wrecked* from within. My mind was barely working. I was heartbroken over the fact that my parents were going to divorce and now this.

I was done.

"What the fuck is wrong with you? You fucking sent your guy to my fucking house—to keep an eye on me. Are you delusional or what?" My frown deepened as the call was picked up. I didn't stop there. Like vomit, words flooded out of my mouth. "You're so fucking obsessed with me. Take your sicko driver and tell him to get the fuck out of here before I hit him. You can take your threats and shove them up your ass. And I swear, if I see you or your people again, I'll literally fuck you up."

It was like a weight had been lifted off my chest. Suddenly, I felt as if I had been reborn and was carefree once more.

On the other end of the call, there was silence for a long minute before Christopher said, "Fine." His voice was barely above a whisper.

Just one word and the call went dead. I stared at the phone for a moment before turning around and glancing at the driver who still sat in his car. His terrifying gaze was upon me as he heard every word leaving my mouth.

I rolled my eyes at him and just then, a ringtone could be heard. The driver's phone rang, and a smile spread across my face.

"Tell your boss to suck his dick." Grinning, I turned around to leave as he attended Christopher's call.

That wasn't hard at all! I pushed my shoulders back and looked down either side of the street before stepping forward to cross the road. I suppose the driver was *now* being told to get out of here and hopefully, I wouldn't have to see his car again.

A corner of my mouth remained up as I smiled at myself for what I had done. Wind flew over my face, and I pushed my hands inside my pockets as my fingertips had begun freezing in the cold.

A sickening feeling wrapped around my stomach, and I drew my eyebrows together while scanning the streets again. *Something was wrong.* The feeling rose up to my chest, my heart tightened as if someone was clutching it.

Moments later, I felt fingers pressed on either side of my head before the driver whispered in my ears, *"Morpherous."*

Everything came pounding in my head. My heart thudded quicker and suddenly, I lost sensation in my hands and then the rest of my body. When my limbs faltered, my eyes rolled back before they shut completely. Then and there, I fell, losing conscious, not knowing what had come over me.

Christopher

I knocked on the door before I scanned the open bedroom, finding Pietro sitting on his swinging chair and using his phone. Clearing my throat, I said, "I need you to leave the house."

"Yeah, no." He shook his head, still swinging back and forth. His eyes were glued to his phone as he probably texted his girlfriend, Elena, who still had to be doomed. "Try again. Later. It's my time to sleep," he added lazily.

"I need you to leave, Pietro, so I need you to leave. Go fuck your girlfriend or something. You have other things to do than be here," I reminded him and tried hard to remove him from the house. I could not have him here, *not now*.

Finally, he lifted his head and met my eyes while lowering the phone to his stomach. Mischief swarmed over his face as he asked, "Why? Is your preppy princess coming here? Is that why you want me gone?"

I didn't lie. "Yes and yes."

The last time, I had *paid* him to leave the house while I was on a date with *her*. I knew her name yet somehow bringing it to my thoughts tendered my heart in a way I didn't want it to. She was like warmth in my head and pure fire in reality. Though I didn't care much. Her flame was easy to burn.

"Are you going to leave?" I asked him again.

"Nope." He shook his head, torturing me in every way he could. His presence was going to be a disturbance for me, but I knew how to handle that as well.

"Fine." I grabbed onto the silver handle of his door and drew it towards myself. "If I see you leaving this room in the next few hours, I'll kill you and then your girlfriend."

He laughed as I spoke to him.

Unable to hear his laughter for a moment longer, I slammed the door shut and a thud echoed in the hallway before silence spread everywhere. The house was *usually* silent until Pietro created chaos.

There was order everywhere, in this house and in this city, the order was straight from me. I despised chaos and anything that troubled my peace and serenity. One of them was Pietro and having him silenced at this time was important. I couldn't have him inserting himself in *this,* this vulnerable moment of mine.

Straightening my shoulders, I took the spiral staircase and rushed downstairs while closing the buttons of my shirt.

Michael pulled into the courtyard in minutes and the car came to a halt near the entrance of the house. As the doors drew open, I stepped out into the harsh weather and approached the car.

"She's out," Michael whispered, approaching me hurriedly. "And she will be for a while. Do you want me to extend her *sleep?*" he asked.

I shook my head while my gaze remained on the car. "No. It's fine. I'll handle it from here."

He nodded at me before walking away from the courtyard and the car. With no one around, I opened the door of the car and found Rebekah, unconscious in the back seat, her eyes shut and her heart drumming slowly as the *spell* lingered over her, keeping her knocked out for as long as I wanted.

Shouldn't have run her mouth.

Earlier, after she had called me, I instructed Michael to bring her back here instead of leaving the street. If she had spoken to me in a respectful manner, I would've listened to her and told him to leave but instead, she used nasty words, and they didn't suit her.

Those lips weren't made for such nastiness.

I looped my arms around her, pulling her toward my chest and taking her out of the car. Her head hung over my left arm while her legs were over my right arm. I watched her carefully, studying her features once more, burying myself into her beauty and getting lost over and over again.

Why her? Why was she destined to me?

24

Rebekah

Waves, spirals, and stars were the only things I could see. I tossed my head around, trying to force myself up and snap out of the state I was in. When my eyes finally peeled open, I saw a tall black ceiling above me, the sides of it carved into shapes as red light illuminated it from above. A chandelier hung over my face, a thousand pieces of glass falling onto me.

My eyes widened a little and I snapped back as a gasp escaped my throat. *Oh no. Where am I?* Quickly, I scanned the room, taking in all of it. The walls were dark brown, long and wide. My fingers ran across the deep blue duvet I laid above.

Then and there, my memory returned.

I remembered being outside, going back home after yelling at Christopher and his driver. Though his driver was about to leave, but he didn't. He came at me—he did something, something I couldn't understand. My heart beat harder. Harsh lines appeared on my forehead. I blew out a few breaths while turning my head around, looking for *help*.

I had been kidnapped.

That obsessive creep had kidnapped me and had told his driver to take me instead of sending him away from my house.

I tried to move but there wasn't much mobility in my limbs. They were still sore and numb. I barely felt my legs as I drew them to myself.

What was wrong with me?

I rose but my head throbbed terribly as if I had been drinking last night and just woke up with a hangover. There was a *little* pain everywhere in my body and it confused me. I didn't remember drinking or anything.

The door open and I tried to jump up but failed once more. Holding my breath in, I flattened my head against the bed and pressed my eyes shut. He couldn't do anything if I was asleep. And I didn't have enough strength yet to run away from here. I could barely lift my leg. I needed a minute, maybe two.

In the meantime, I acted as if I was still sleeping.

I smelled that obsessive man from a distance as he approached me. The bed creaked a little as his weight came upon it. His scent spread all over and it was *intoxicating* for some reason that I couldn't understand. He leaned closer, a little too close. I could feel his body heat against mine.

"I thought I heard something..." he trailed off in a low whisper, barely even reaching my ears. "Still sleeping, aren't you?" He shuffled a bit before his fingers came against my face.

My breathing quickened and I began panicking as his finger curled around a lock of my hair. Worry crept inside me. I began imaging the worst. *What if he was going to rape me? Or worse, kill me.* I didn't know what his issue was or what he wanted from me, but I needed to get out of here and out of this town as this all was more than threatening to me.

I moved my own finger a little, feeling my energy returning to my body. Before he could get any further, I snapped awake and bit down hard on his arm, sinking my teeth into his wrist.

Instantly, his free hand came wrapping around my throat and he pushed me back before drawing his other arm away from my mouth. A bit of pain surfaced on his face but quickly disappeared when his wicked, evil eyes clicked to mine.

"Don't fucking touch me!"

"You little *cagna*." He rubbed his wrist where I had bitten him before a sly smile spread over his face. "You impress me every time." His hold on my throat tightened as I tried to claw his other hand. "Do whatever you want. Try and kill me as well but I'll still be right here."

"Let me go, you creep!" I shouted, and as the sensation returned to my legs, I began kicking them over the bed.

"Stop screaming." His voice dropped low.

I lined my lips straight and slammed them shut. My hands pulled away from him and I stopped striking the bed with my legs. Slowly, he moved his hold from my throat, and I sucked in a sharp breath.

What is wrong with this person?

I glanced over his shoulders, getting a glance of the time by looking outside. It was still dark, which meant I must've been here for only a couple hours—unless a whole day had passed by. I wasn't sure. That man, Michael, he did something and I didn't know what it was, but it knocked me out instantly.

"I prefer you quiet and obedient." Christopher smiled at me while getting up from the bed and moving farther away from me. "And on my bed..." Standing afar, he watched me as if I was his prey. There was hunger behind his eyes, hunger for me.

"You're such a disgusting creep." I pulled my legs closer to myself while raising up from the bed. "What is your deal? Why won't you just leave me alone?" I asked, frowning.

Thankfully, none of my clothes were taken off my body. I was still wearing the pajamas I had worn at home along with the jacket. However, my phone was missing as it wasn't in my pocket. I tried to feel it by slipping a hand into my pocket but there was nothing in there. He stole my phone.

Christopher shrugged. "My wish."

His responses were bland and unhelpful. Every time I asked him something, he barely answered straight, almost as if he was trying to hide something.

"What am I doing here?" I asked, folding my hands over my chest. "You literally kidnapped me. For what?"

"I didn't like your tone, *amore*. I sent Michael to merely look out for you, it was a nice gesture, especially since where you live there is a lot of crime, but you didn't appreciate it." He paused and a strange look appeared over his face. "I got hurt."

I scoffed, "Fuck you."

Suddenly, his eyes darkened, and his demeanor shifted. In moments, he became scary and threatening as he began approaching me from the side of the bed as I insulted him. *Again.* I tossed my legs and turned around before jumping from the bed and gaining my foothold.

"I want you, *amore*," he stated.

I lifted a brow at him before fleeing. My bare feet turned cold instantly as I paved my way through the large room. He chased me. *He fucking chased me.* My heart thumped hard. Sweat dripped from my forehead. I knocked things left and right till I reached the door where drawing it open was easy.

I needed to escape.

Now.

His actions and his words didn't make any sense. He was never going to have me—I was *never* going to like a man like Christopher or even date him. He was everything I didn't want in my life and for all the terrible things he had done, I hated him. My hatred grew even deeper now that I had been kidnapped and held hostage in his residence.

God.

I kept running across the dark hallways, unable to find any clear way out. All I knew was that I was on the second floor. I needed to find a staircase, anything that led me downstairs and out of this place.

Barely any lights were switched on. During the entire time I ran, I didn't find anyone who could help me. *No one.*

My harsh, loud footsteps echoed across the walls along with Christopher's as he chased me around, hoping to catch me. Somehow, he was a little slower than me or maybe I was too terrified for my life that I needed to run quicker.

The hallway stretched to another wing of the house where the windows were bare and the moonlight slipped in, providing me with some I could see with. Panic rose and spread over my body. I continued to run as my head lashed right and left, scanning where I needed to go next.

I slipped into another hallway quickly before *he* could reach me. My back pressed against the thick wall, and I hid myself in the darkness. My chest rose and dropped. I breathed heavily and my head spun. His footsteps reached closer to me, and I moved across the wall without making a single sound.

He stopped running when he couldn't find me ahead. "Hide and seek is my favorite game, *amore*. I can smell you wherever you are. You can't hide from me." His voice echoed in the hallways. A shiver ran down my spine as I pressed my teeth a little too hard against my lower lip. "I won't hurt you. *Of course.* But I don't want you to get lost here. There are monsters hidden in these walls that I don't want you to see."

I moved horizontally against the wall and kept moving forward. His shadow stretched and appeared when I looked at the other end of the hallway. He began reaching closer. I thought I had lost him, but I was wrong.

My heart jumped once more before I scrambled to the nearest door and opened it. Without wasting another second, I slipped inside and closed the door behind, surely losing him this time.

25

Rebekah

I held my breath back while my hand moved to my chest. It was dark inside the room; I barely saw anything until my eyes adjusted. My ears remained perked, hearing every step outside of the room. He began approaching closer to the hallway and I quickly turned around, hoping to find an escape before he caught me.

"Who are you?" In the darkness, another pair of golden eyes met with mine and I nearly screamed. "Oh, wait…" he trailed off, stepping closer to me. It took a moment to recognize him in the dark, but I soon did.

Then, I scanned the room, it was a bedroom, probably his- Christopher's younger brother. The same man I had encountered at the subway station, who I also pepper sprayed. Thankfully, he wasn't chasing me like his brother.

"You're his mate, aren't you?"

Huh?

"Please—" My mouth hung wide open as panic collected in my throat. "Don't tell him I'm here. I just want to go home," I pleaded, my voice as low as a whisper knowing Christopher was right outside, shuffling through the hallway, trying to find me.

I didn't know what he wanted from me, but I was terrified. He had kidnapped me from the doorstep of my own house and had forced me here. I was *unconscious* for hours and had no memory of what had happened.

A knock landed on the door before the younger one replied to me. My heart leaped at the sound of the knock, and I quickly shifted against the nearest wall, hiding. Silence fell. It was then I noticed that the younger one had just slipped out of the shower and was only wearing a towel around his waist.

He reached the door, opened it and I dug my teeth into my lower lip, being as quiet as I could be. "Yes, brother?" the younger one asked.

"Have you seen my mate run through these corridors by any chance?" Christopher asked, talking about me. *That word again... what did he mean by mate?*

"Nope. I was in the shower," he replied while shrugging his shoulders.

When I turned a little, I could see both of their frames near the door. Christopher was *clearly* taller than his brother, and more dangerous. The way he spoke to his brother showed he was in charge, in control.

"Why? Is she running around here?" His brother said in a teasing tone, and I furrowed my brows. He knew I was inside this room yet for some reason, he wanted to know more. "Does she not want you?"

"You're a waste of time, Pietro. Goodnight," Christopher said before slamming the door shut and soon, his footsteps faded.

I took a sigh of relief and a little smile stretched over my face as the younger one walked back in. "Thank you," I whispered to him, cheerfully.

"No worries. I'd love to see him burn after all he has done with me..." he murmured before walking back into the other door he came out from. "I'll come and attend to your needs in five minutes!" He spoke with a tone that was *eager* and excited.

After a couple of minutes, he came out of the room all dressed up and his hair dried instead of wet and dripping. "So, tell me, what concerns you? Are you not interested in my brother?" he asked, folding his arms across his chest. "Usually his charms are spectacular but you seem uninterested." He paced around me in circles, questioning me.

God. Not another one.

"He kidnapped me from my own house and he's not letting me go. I want to go back home, and I can't with him *hunting* me!" I exclaimed, a little too exhausted from all the running I had done. He had chased me for a good ten minutes and yet, he hadn't stopped.

"He... what?" The younger one's voice became a bit too loud. "Wow." A grin spread over his face as he stared up at the ceiling. "Shit." He shook his head, seeming disappointed.

"Can you help me?" I asked.

"Of course, I'd love to. Anything for you, love." The smile returned to his face. I couldn't tell if he was being honest or if he was acting mischievous but either way, I needed his help to get out of his place and go back home. I couldn't run from here alone. He propositioned leaving the residence from the courtyard. At this time of the night, there wasn't going to be anyone around.

When the clock struck midnight, I realized I had been in here for the past six hours. He had kidnapped me at five or six, but I couldn't remember exactly when.

After spending a few long minutes inside the bedroom, we finally left after checking on either side of the hall, ensuring Christopher wasn't still trying to hunt me.

"It's fine. Just follow me and I'll take you straight outside," his younger brother said, sounding promising.

I stayed behind him, covering myself by his broad shoulders as we moved slowly across the hallways. There was a long distance between the room where I was being *kept* and the room I had forced entry into.

"If you don't mind, may I ask something?"

"Yes?" My thoughts diverted from being caught by Christopher.

"It seems like you have no interest in my brother. Am I right?" he asked, tilting his head a little till his eyes were searching for an answer in mine. For a moment, his face was filled with concern.

"Yes. I don't. I don't know why he's *chasing* me. Can you tell?" My voice remained low. I peered left and right into the distance ahead of us and found no one, yet my heart continued to pound in my chest as if I was going to be caught by *him* any minute now. "I think... maybe he likes me..." It was the only explanation I could find.

His younger brother chuckled lowly before brushing his hand through his hair. "Oh, dear..." He shook his head and his laughter didn't come to an end yet. "Of course he likes you."

"Why? Why me?" I sounded a bit absurd, even to myself.

"Well, we have a concept," he started, thrusting his hands in the air. "It's kind of a weird concept for you to understand but in our—*thing*—" I cocked a brow at him but let him continue. "We have a concept of soulmates. We believe that every man and woman is destined to be with someone, their other half. Finding them would complete a person. Now, Christopher believes *very* strongly in this concept, and he believes *you* are his other half, someone he didn't think he'd find. Neither did I."

The frown lines over my face tightened even more. I could not understand anything he had just said asides from *soulmates,* which was rather an ideal boyfriend or girlfriend, not a forced friend. It included love and *consent,* neither of which Christopher had shown.

"That's oddly confusing." I shrugged and continued walking.

The longer I thought about his words, the more I grew dazed. I couldn't think about all this anymore. I had better things to do in life than to worry about a stalker and a kidnapper.

We walked for another long minute in silence before the younger one stopped in the middle of nowhere. He turned around in the dark, his gaze settling over my face as he said, "Christopher *will* pursue you, Rebekah, and he will not stop at anything. I'll let you out from here, but this is not the end. He will come after you again and again because he wants you. And he's a *powerful* man." He stopped to take a breath before his eyes stretched even wider. "I'm not suggesting you submit to him but rather, for the meantime, enjoy it rather than refusing him."

"But I don't want him!" I exclaimed, folding my arms and frowning.

He sighed and then something appeared in his eyes, a questioning look. "Oh, don't lie to me or yourself."

Before I could say anything, he turned around and guided me downstairs from a staircase at the corner of the house. Dust flew around me and I nearly sneezed. While creeping down the stairs, I questioned myself.

Was I lying to myself?

No. I didn't like him. But a part of me was certainly enjoying the feeling of being *wanted*. I couldn't deny that. And the kiss we nearly had outside.

Oh.

It was something.

Suddenly, I was too nervous thinking about it all. There were too many emotions, one of the main ones being fear of what he could possibly do. He had kidnapped me, brought a knife to my throat, and threatened my ex-boyfriend, nearly forcing Adam to shit his pants.

How could I like someone like that?

How could I not?

26

Rebekah

"Yes. He fucking *kidnapped* me!" I exclaimed in a low whisper to Faye.

She sat on the edge of the bed, her fingernails between her teeth as she listened to my story of what had happened and the reason why I came home late. She had been here for a couple of hours, talking to Mom and waiting for me. They'd both contacted me, trying to reach me but failed as my phone was *lost*.

The younger brother, Pietro, guided me out from the residence and helped me get a cab home. I thanked him and quickly left while his elder brother searched the hallways, hoping he could find me.

It was an hour past midnight. I had been gone for over six tedious hours and in that time, I had been struck unconscious by an unknown force, kidnapped, threatened, harassed, and then led to freedom.

"That's so crazy. I was worried about you. I thought you'd ditched me or something. But are you okay?" Faye asked, reaching out to pat my lap.

"Yeah." I shivered involuntarily. "I think I'll be fine."

"Sure? Do you want me to stay with you for the night?" she offered.

I kindly rejected it. "No, please, don't. Go home and get rest. I'll see you in the morning and trust me, I'm fine. Actually, I'm happy I was kidnapped because I'm going to—" My hands curled into tight balls as anger surfaced. "I'm going to make that man suffer. Make him wish he had never collided with me."

Faye gave me a frightened stare. "Are you okay?"

My lips curled into a stiff smile, and I nodded my head. "Yes. Go home and thank you for lying to my mom."

I had told Faye everything, given her every detail and even asked about the *theory of soulmates* or whatever Pietro had told me. She agreed with it being a part of her *thing* and explained it to me in a bit more detail. While she explained, I began questioning what *thing* she was following or what her beliefs were.

I smelled secrets in the air, but I was unbothered by it. The problem wasn't the secrets, it was one man, and his name was Christopher. He was the only problem I needed to deal with, and I had found the perfect solution for his obsession.

Like his brother said, I didn't need to *submit* to him or his infatuation but rather enjoy it.

I was going to enjoy it.

I followed Faye outside as she was about to leave and go to her home. When I stepped into the cold, my gaze lingered over where the car was parked earlier and where that driver named Michael had knocked me unconscious in a way I didn't understand.

Something glistened on the ground, and I jumped into the road, hurrying toward it.

"My phone." I kneeled and grabbed it from the pavement on the side. After a little check, it wasn't cracked or broken, just a little too cold and dusty. "Thank God!" A sigh left my throat, and I turned back to Faye.

"Yay. Now you don't need a new phone."

"Yes. Message me when you're home." I winked at her and walked back into my house as she left the driveway.

Upon opening my phone, I checked all the calls I had received from Mom and Faye over the period of six hours. It was way too many calls. I checked my call log, finding Christopher's number at last.

The corner of my lip tugged into a grin. I stepped upstairs, returning to my room while the house was dead silent. Everyone, including Mom and Rose were asleep. Neither of them knew what had happened to me. I lied and told them that I went for some work and couldn't get out until late instead of telling them that I was kidnapped.

Slamming the door behind, I pressed Christopher's number, calling him and informing him that I was home, far *far* away from his creepy place and self.

My back pressed against the bed. I rolled a few strands of hair around my fingers while my phone was ringing against my ears, waiting for the call to be received.

When it finally did, I said, "Hello! I hope you're still not looking for me through your house of horrors because I'm already out of there and back in my secure house where you and your magician of a driver cannot reach." My grin only grew wider.

His younger brother had told me the truth and no matter how *creepy* it was, I was going to use it to my benefit and disturb him the same way he had been disturbing me.

"Yes, I'm aware of that," he replied, his voice rough and exhausted. "If you're expecting an apology, it's going to take a while." He spoke with pride in his tone and care for nothing except for himself.

Cocky, much.

I ran my tongue over my lips, tasting the orange juice I had hydrated myself with after running back home. "Oh, I don't need you to apologize. I only called you to let you know after what you did to me today, I'm not going to go to the police or press charges on you..." I trailed off before turning onto the right side of the bed. My legs dangled over the frame and my smile grew wider. "Instead, against your wishes, I'm going to text my ex-boyfriend tonight."

"You wouldn't do that, *amore*." I could *feel* his nerves tangling and his face turning red at my words.

"Oh, I would, and there is nothing you can do to stop me. Adam and I dated for a very long while and we have been great friends with each other even after breaking up. He always gave me *comfort* when I needed it and tonight, I feel like I need more than just comfort." I sighed, rubbing my forehead as my voice became thin. "And you can't do anything because I'm in my home. You cannot kidnap me again or threaten me. Hell, you can't do shit."

"You'll not communicate with him. Do you understand that?" he said, roaring.

"Nope." I chuckled lightly. "I might even throw in some illicit pictures. We used to sext a lot before you barged into our life and ruined everything for me. So, goodbye, Christopher. Have sweet, sweet dreams and don't call me again because by then, I'll probably be someone's girlfriend," I whispered in a low tone before cutting off the call without giving him a chance to speak.

I pushed my phone over my head and heard it buzz for the next several minutes. He continued to call me and in those few minutes, I hope he *burned* with anger as I did. He didn't spare me and I didn't care about his reasons. He went too far when he had me kidnapped.

What did he think? That I was going to be bought off with some money? That I would fall on my knees for him after he'd kidnapped me?

Or that I would be head over heels in love with him when he held a knife against my throat?

After tonight, he will wish he had never done anything to me.

27

Rebekah

Every time I went anywhere, I looked over my shoulders, carefully watching everyone who passed by me. There was a new panic forming itself inside me ever since that night. It had been three days—seventy-two hours—and I had heard nothing from Christopher. He hadn't called me after the twenty missed calls he gave me that night. There was no message. *Nothing*.

I wasn't sure if I needed to be scared or not.

Maybe he was out of my life forever or maybe he was scheming to murder me without a trace.

I swallowed hard and knocked on the wooden door in front of me. The hotel door opened, and Adam invited me inside his room. He had moved from the city after Christopher had barged into his apartment that day.

"Hey. How are you doing?" he asked, closing the door behind him, and locking it twice. He had been more traumatized by it all than I was.

"I'm good. How are you?" I asked him while glancing around his hotel room.

The hotel wasn't too far from the city. It was an hour's drive away and I needed to see Adam anyways, maybe one last time before we parted ways forever. I couldn't drag him into this, no matter how many times I dropped his name in front of Christopher.

The interior of the hotel room was light, and it gave a homey feeling. Adam had been crashing here for the past week, ever since he'd moved from Laford. I hadn't been in contact with him until that night when I *actually* messaged him, not for comfort but instead to return the loan I had taken from him. It only made sense that I gave his money back before cutting all ties with him.

"I've got your cash..." I trailed off while handing the envelope of cash to him.

His eyes clicked to the envelope before returning to meet with mine. "How did—how did you arrange it?" he asked with furrowed brows.

"I..." I scratched the back of my head, wondering if I should tell him the truth or lie. "Faye helped me out with it. Plus, I got a new job in the city and it's paying well." I lied, about everything.

The last thing I wanted was for Adam to judge me when he'd realize that I had accepted money from the same man who got violent with him and me. That dangerous man he was still terrified of.

"Oh. That's good." He moved his head up and down before accepting the money from me. "Thanks."

"What about you?" I tried to make some conversation even though it was now *odd* between us. I still remembered his last message when he wanted to cut off every connection with me after everything that went down in his apartment. "How's everything? You're staying here?"

"Yeah, just for now. I might move in with my dad." He shrugged and tucked his hands into his pockets.

"Well, I wish you luck, Adam, and I hope we cross paths again." I concluded our meeting quickly and left his hotel room in minutes.

There was nothing left between us. We were once a great couple but now, it was all over, and I needed to accept it and move on. I no longer missed him like I used to. He was another chapter of my life that I needed to end forever.

Whatever I had told Christopher that night was simply to piss him off, anger him, enrage him but I guess it didn't work. My phone had been dead silent after that night.

Maybe he was out of my life as well.

With a pleasant smile lingering on my face, I left the hotel room and slumped back into the mini cooper I had stolen from Mom earlier. *Three days.* And not a single man disturbing my life. I was in peace, floating like the clouds in the blue sky above me. Most of my worries were gone, Dad's bills were paid, debts were over, my obsession with Adam was gone and Christopher's obsession with me seemed like it no longer existed.

I was in peace.

The speakers of the mini blasted with classical music as I got back on the road, heading to Laford and back home with not a single worry in my head, except for the fact that I needed to get a costume for Halloween, which was two days away.

Christopher

Burning hot water ran down my shoulders, setting my skin on fire. I slammed my hand against the bricked wet wall in front of me and fisted my cock. My head rose and my back arched as a deep, menacing growl escaped my throat. My chest rumbled as my hand closed around my cock tightly, forcing a release out of myself to soothe my nerves.

When I closed my eyes, *her* face came into my head, only elevating my rage and the swell of the fury I had been packing inside myself.

But at the same time, it was the only thing helping me to *finish*. In seconds, I came when I imagined her milking my cock, her filthy little mouth taking every inch of it and gagging on it. The only minute she wouldn't be running her mouth wild.

Fuck.

With a groan, I cussed and finished before cleaning up and getting out of the steaming bathroom.

It wasn't like I could fuck anyone or any woman. Though I had plenty of times. Usually, it was women who were interested in me or wanted a favor from their *mighty Alpha*. It always helped to be higher in power and position.

The last time I had pounded a woman was eighteen days ago. After I had learned that I had a mate, I couldn't even think about fucking someone else. It was either my own fist or nothing. I couldn't even finish without thinking about my mate and all the ways she would take my cock. Unfortunately, it seemed more difficult now, especially with her running away from me day and night.

I didn't understand what her problem was. I tried to melt her in every way, but she was a cruel woman with a heart of stone that I needed to break with time.

"I could hear you from afar." Pietro stepped into my room, chuckling lowly.

"Fuck off." I rolled my eyes at him and diverted my attention to Walter. "What's the news?"

It was early in the morning, and I needed a release after I awoke. Though I was about to return to my bed and sleep for another few hours or at least till the sun went down a little but I already knew I was disturbed when I smelled Pietro from afar.

"Walter's got some very important information about your mate," Pietro said, his naughtiness etched on his features. "Your mate was found driving on Route 13."

I clenched my hand. "She left the fucking city?" My voice roared. "And I'm knowing this now?" My head snapped toward Walter who I had given the order to keep track of my mate while I figured out a new way to lure myself into her heart of stone. "I fucking told you that I *need* to know every step she takes." I reached Walter and my nostrils flared.

"It was too early, Alpha. I was informed late."

"I don't give a fuck. What is she doing on Route 13?" I asked him as I calmed myself a bit.

Route 13 was a dangerous route for werewolves. It was out of *my* city, out of my territory and I had no reach there. There were rogues settled around Route 13 and if any of them were aware of who my mate was, she was going to be doomed before I even had the chance to get inside her.

"They tracked her to some hotel far east where she was last seen about twenty minutes ago," Walter responded, his voice shaking a bit.

I turned my head away from him and ran my hand through my hair, thinking hard about what my mate was doing in a hotel. *Of course.* Meeting her fucking *carogna* of an ex-boyfriend. I pinched the bridge of my nose, taking in slow and deep breaths like the therapist in my past two therapy sessions had told me.

Deep breaths.

I hadn't been worried about her since the night she told me she would *text* her scumbag ex-boyfriend. Since then, my men had been tracking her every move and she hadn't done much except for going out for groceries. I was relieved when she didn't meet him or go over to his apartment.

Instead of troubling her, I gave her some time, hoping it would make her realize that she *wanted* me as much as I *wanted* her. It was better than forcing her to be mine.

I guess not.

"Get Michael and tell him to get my car in five minutes," I ordered while buttoning up my shirt.

Now, I was enraged.

28

Christopher

She was going to be punished in ways I couldn't even imagine. I was *mad* that she had left the city and gone to a hotel, alone, to meet her ex-boyfriend. Over the past few days, I thought she hadn't contacted him and was only fooling around with me.

And her ex-boyfriend—he was certainly dead. I secured a hit on him right after Michael drove me out of the city and onto Route 13. I could endure anything she might do but I couldn't accept one thing—another man's hand over her special body.

It was mine.

She was mine.

No one was touching her except for me. No one was fucking her except for me. Hell, no one was even allowed to look at her except for me.

The news of my mate was spreading, slowly, but it was. I wasn't sure where it spilled from, but I guessed it was Pietro. There were a few people in the pack who already knew I had uncovered a mate but none of them were acquainted with her or knew she was a human.

A very lousy human.

It was dangerous for her to be anywhere except for Laford. She couldn't leave the city, not alone at least. For her safety, I needed to drag her back and have a little conversation with her.

My men who had been tracking her had already caught her. They pulled her over to the side of the route, banning her from driving any further without protection. I instructed them to keep her positioned there and ensure she wouldn't steer into the woodland nearby or anywhere else dangerous.

Michael drove fast, reading her location in less than an hour. He pulled over along with the other cars and surrounded her car.

An intervention.

I watched her talking to one of my men, yelling as she held her keys in her hand, the sharp side upwards, preparing for an attack. I quickly stepped out of the vehicle and approached her while directing my men to leave us alone and return to their vehicles.

"Oh, of course! You!" She didn't sound surprised. "Were you following me?"

"No, I wasn't." I shook my head. "What were doing out of the city? At a hotel?" My brow quirked as I questioned her while hoping she would just answer me straight and let my wild thoughts rest for once.

"What's your deal? I can do what I want." She flicked her hair off her shoulders before folding her hands over her chest while pushing her breasts forward.

I looked away from her chest and into her eyes in broad daylight. There was no flicker of fear in them. Instead, I was surprised to find defiance and scorn in them. Seemed like the past few days had altered her emotions for me.

Better.

I leaned closer to her while keeping my control. Lowering my head, I asked her only one, "Were you meeting that fucking bastard? Is that why you went to that hotel?"

"What are you going to do?" She lifted her head up to me, mocking me in a way.

"I'm going to kill you." Rage surged through my veins, and I closed my fists.

She took another step toward me and then raised her hand, her fingers traveled over my chest through the shirt I wore, and she smiled stiffly. "What if I tell you that I fucked him as well?"

She didn't.

"Hope you enjoyed it then." I knew she hadn't fucked him, regardless of whatever she said. I didn't give her the reaction she wanted, knowing this was all a *tease*.

"I did. Certainly. It was amazing since I hadn't done it in a while. I feel *full* after having his di—"

I couldn't bear to hear her talk about it even when I knew she was just bluffing. I just couldn't. Something inside me shifted and I felt my wolf losing itself.

"Shut the fuck up," I snapped at her before she finished.

"Make me." She ran her tongue over her lips, and it drew out a different emotion from me.

She wasn't trying to make me angry; she was *playing* with me like a little toy. And I was certainly going to enjoy playing with her. Just not here.

I grabbed her arm, tugging her toward one of the black cars. Drawing the passenger door open, I told her, "Get in the car."

"No!" she yelled, quickly backing away. "I'm going to go home in my car. Stop being such a creep and leave me alone."

"Get in the car, Rebekah," I repeated once more and it was the last time before I was going to tell Michael to step in, *again,* and he had a different way to force people to listen to me.

I didn't want that for her.

For fuck's sake, she was my mate.

For the first and probably the last time, she listened to me and hopped into the vehicle. I lifted my hand and motioned to the rest of my men to leave the Route and follow us before I got inside the same vehicle as her.

"Back to Laford, Michael," I said quickly.

"Is my car going to drive by itself?" she asked, staring at me from a distance. She scooted herself to the corner of the car as if I was going to hurt her.

That was the last thing on my mind.

"No. Someone will get it," I murmured under my breath before letting out a sigh of relief.

When Michael began driving, I gazed outside, watching the forests and the unknown territory flash by me. For the first time ever, I felt a chill bolt down my spine, and just then, I came to the realization that I had formed a weakness for myself, a literal liability and she was posing right beside me with no care in the world. As long as she wasn't aware of what my world was, she wasn't safe.

Hell, she wasn't safe either way.

I was destined to be with a human, a weakling of sorts. Unfortunately, there was no such thing as changing fate or destiny. She lacked strength, even a mind, but I hoped she was more satisfactory in other *areas.*

When I turned my head and glanced into her eyes, I found a different kind of wilderness in them. Maybe she wasn't *weak* after all, maybe it was just a front, a display. After all, she did manage to stab me—*me.*

"Are you going to keep staring at me like a creep?" Her hands folded and she gave me a look filled with disgust while her eyes squinted at me.

Her mouth was wild. I wondered what else was.

"I told you something. Why didn't you listen?" I asked her as Michael drove off the Route, returning to the city.

It was going to be a long ride and she was here, alone with me, in broad daylight. I doubt I was going to let her live after what she had done today.

"Why would I ever listen to you? Are you my dad? Sadly, I already have one, so I don't need to listen to you..." She trailed off, her smile growing wide. "And stop giving me commands like I'm actually going to bother *listening* to them." Her lashes flickered, and she tossed her attitude at me.

Fucking bitch.

I kept my irritation in check and leaned back in the seat, not giving her any response. She moved her head around and I caught a glimpse of her neck as she titled it. My mouth watered. I wanted to savor it, bite it, turn her, fuck her.

"And if you do anything with my car, I'll kill you. I could have driven it back home easily until you appeared and ruined my beautiful day!" I tried to shut out her voice, but it didn't go. "And now you're acting as if I—"

Not anymore. I couldn't bear to hear her rants for another second, it was driving me crazy, senseless.

I grabbed her face and didn't think about being gentle with the brat in front of me. Delicate wrinkles spread over her temples, her eyes instantly gushed with fear and concern and her lips parted only a little. My cock grew stiff at the mental image of her lips wrapped around it.

But that was for later.

I enjoyed the momentary silence. The tires moved and rolled against the well-made roads. Michael didn't look back. He wouldn't dare to. No matter what I did.

My gaze slumped to her mouth. *Fuck.* Her frame grew dull with unease and the longings within me awaked. *Fuck.* I wanted to fucking kiss her. *Fuck.* But she didn't want it.

I hissed and looked away, hoping to gather my feelings and dump them elsewhere. My hand remained on her face, holding it tight. She didn't move.

"Kiss me," she rasped.

29

Rebekah

"Kiss me." I ran my tongue over my lips while nerves wrecked inside me. My core tightened like never before. I watched the tension on his face grow over the past couple of minutes he held me and for some reason, I just *wanted* him to kiss me.

He didn't hesitate. His mouth slammed against mine, my lips parted, and he swallowed me whole. My eyes fluttered shut. Every worry, every fear leaped from my body. Something stirred to life within me.

It wasn't a gentle kiss. Nowhere near. It was rough, hot-blooded, and kindred to slow poison, killing me. My body quivered. I kissed him back, wanting more, *needing* more. Numerous emotions gushed inside me. My head became hot and heavy. Every inch of my body tingled as if I had been kissed by firecrackers instead of a man.

My lungs emptied; I didn't bother breathing. He grabbed the back of my head while losing his hand on my face. His mouth moved deeper into mine as if it *needed* to be consumed. Like a snake, something within me curled and tightened in my core.

When his fingers tightened around my hair, I felt my insides clench and quiver with *desire,* as if my body had just found the perfect man.

I trailed my hand over the side of his face, feeling his stubble underneath my fingertips before my hand lowered to his neck, where his skin was rough yet somehow delicate.

It lasted for minutes before I returned to my consciousness and made sense of what I was doing. "Stop." I pushed him back, regretting it instantly. A frown appeared on my face, only deepening as seconds passed.

I took in lengthy and heavy breaths while my fingers brushed against my sore lips where he had just been. *I couldn't kiss him.*

When I looked over at him, I found his mouth tightening into a smile, a *grin* as if he had achieved something. My eyes rolled back. "Ugh…" I tried to find words. "You're such a creep."

"You asked me to kiss you, *amore.*" His smile deepened as he remained close to me, close enough that I could feel his heat on my own body, his warmth branding me in a way. I smelled him and found his scent rather tasteful and attractive.

My hands pushed up against his chest and I pushed him back, farther away from me, "Don't kiss me again," I said, anger in my words.

I was *vexed*. I had kissed—I had been kissed by someone I despised. *How could I have wanted that?* I didn't. Every fiber of my body didn't want him to kiss me. I couldn't understand how I could let it happen.

"Sure. Whatever you want." He continued to grin as he turned his attention away from me and leaned back on his side of the car.

My back was against the window, my head nearly touching the glass. With every little shaky movement of the car, I jumped ever so slightly. My lips curled into a sneer as I continued to gawk at him in disbelief.

He just kissed me.

Fuck him.

My head burned. I was irked and fuming. *Why? Why did I do that to myself?* He had done terrible things and was a terrible person. I didn't want him to kiss me. But I really did. *Fuck.* It felt too good to forget.

I remained quiet and looked outside while trying to forget what happened. I didn't want to imprint my head with the kiss for the rest of my life.

"You wanted me, *amore*. At least for a minute..." He spoke in a whisper behind me. I ignored him and he continued, "Deny it all you want. I could *feel* you enjoy it. You have an impure soul and no matter what you do to hide it, I'll always feel it."

I swallowed hard. Blood rushed up to my cheeks and my body warmed as the hair over my skin stiffened. I didn't believe him. He surely couldn't feel anything. *No way.* My thoughts were certainly impure—always—and the kiss was far more than enough to set a craving within me, a craving that was usually fulfilled by Adam, but it seemed like it was no longer possible.

I had never been at rest with my body. I *only* stayed with Adam after he cheated on me because he was somewhat good at fucking me.

My pulse quickened and I continued to look ahead instead of giving any attention to the man sitting beside me. It was a closed space. My body was warming further, firing up, needing to be pleased. But I forbade myself from opening my legs for someone like Christopher.

Never in a hundred years.

Looking over my shoulder, I said with a taunting smile, "And it seems like your soul is damned."

His lips lined straight, and his eyes filled with a challenge. "You're playing with fire..." A warning in his voice.

I shifted in my seat, turning fully to him as if I needed to challenge him back. With a little chuckle, I replied, "Oh, I doubt I'd get burned by you." My gaze ran over him, drifting over his body before settling on his face that had darkened with temper.

"Do you want to risk that?" he asked, merely inches away from me. His thumb brushed against my arm and an uneasy sensation trapped within me. His eyes lowered to my mouth where I *still* felt his kiss. "If you burn under my touch, you're mine... and if you don't, I'll leave you alone," he offered.

I knew what that meant. The muscles in my core clenched. I released a shaky breath while trying to contain my quivering nerves. My heart skipped a beat when his hand moved all the way to the back of my neck.

"Okay."

I didn't know what came over me, but I agreed. *Fucking hell.* I agreed to him, this man, again, for the third time. First, it was the date, then the kiss, and now this. I couldn't shut my mouth for a minute in front of him. My nerves were wrecked, I felt something I had never felt before.

It seemed like I had been bewitched and no matter how hard I tried to ignore all the feelings and desires, they weren't just going away.

"Good." He backed away from me with a smile lingering on his face.

I registered what I had done and turned my head back to the window as he informed his driver to take us to his residence instead of my house, where I needed to be dropped off. We were still far away from reaching Laford. Only some time had passed. When I glanced behind, I found my car and two other cars following us.

The highway thinned and merged into a two-way lane that went through the forest. It was an empty road that went for miles and miles before we could finally reach Laford. The forest was still green, the first snow was expected to come after Halloween, which was in two days. I pivoted my thoughts to the Halloween party I was required to attend with my little sister, Rose.

I still needed a costume, but I was thinking to go as a *clown* this Halloween instead of anything else.

Behind me, Christopher was on the phone, speaking to someone in a language I barely understood. It had to be Italian. His roots seemed to be from Italy and when he called me a bitch, it was usually in Italian. *What else did I need to know?*

I chewed the inside of my mouth while watching the forest pass by. My brow rose when something flashed in front of me. A small gasp escaped my throat when it flashed again, in front of the car.

"Oh, fuck," I whispered to myself in fear while crawling back to my seat.

Michael's face tensed when he saw what I had seen a minute ago. *A wolf*—in broad daylight, sprinting down the narrow road. I turned my head, seeing Christopher who had stopped talking on his phone, and instead, his attention was on the wolf that swerved on the road and then disappeared into the forest.

"Fucking shit." He cursed, loudly before fisting his hands and turning his neck to wherever the wolf disappeared. I followed his gaze and from a distance, I found the wolf in the forest, standing and watching us.

My heart jumped, and I gasped in fear. I hated animals. *Any kind.* All animals terrified me, even the smallest ones.

Uneasy, I swallowed hard and forbade myself from shouting at the top of my lungs for help. The wolf bounced back out from the forest, coming for the car once more, this time quicker, jerking on his paws while his eyes were directed at us.

30

Rebekah

"Oh, fuck, I'm going to die!" I cried out while shutting my eyes tight and grabbing Christopher's arm so he'd be attacked instead of me. The wolf could kill him first and by then, he'd be full so he wouldn't even need to kill me.

I waited for the impact... but there was none. My breathing became shallow, and my heart thudded quickly. I opened my eyes cautiously and found that the wolf had passed us and entered the other side of the forest. My head turned fully and I stared out of the window, seeing the wolf disappear further inside into the tall trees and the empty land beyond.

Relief struck me and I sighed. *That was too close.*

"Really?" A voice rose beside me.

I turned my head back around, finding deep nail prints on Christopher's arm, where I had just held him. "Oh..." I was a bit surprised. I barely even touched him. "Sorry. I-I got a little scared. I didn't know there were wolves living here."

"Tell me about it." He huffed out a breath before rolling his sleeve down and covering the imprints of my nails. "There are wolves everywhere around here. Don't be a fucking pussy about it."

My jaw hung. "You need to talk to me nicely."

"I don't do nice, *amore*. You should know that by now," he added before turning his attention to his driver. "Drive quicker. Don't stop for anything, Michael, not until we are in the city," he said with worry in his tone, and he was telling *me* not to be a pussy about it.

I folded my arms over my chest and shifted back in my seat. This time, I didn't look outside out of fear. I didn't know that wolves lived here. I'd heard about mountain lions and bears appearing in the winters but not wolves and I hadn't seen one before.

My blood ran cold. The wolf was terrifying, his face and his eyes, he wanted to *attack* but stopped instead.

I took a deep breath, forgetting everything that had happened. Maybe Christopher was right, maybe I shouldn't have left the city. If I was driving back alone, I would've definitely crashed the car out of fear and killed myself.

He returned to his phone, this time getting on a call with someone else. When he spoke Italian, I didn't understand a single word of it. A car swerved from behind, one of the cars his *men* were in. The car came to the front and the other black car sat only a few inches away from the car I was in.

"Who's being a pussy now?" I asked, staring at him in rage. "Are you frightened of a wolf butchering you that you need to have your men surrounding you all the time? *Pussy.*" I fluttered my lashes, taunting him the same way he had snapped at me for merely holding his arm when I was scared.

He drew his phone away from his ears and then ended the call. For a moment, I believed he was going to spit out something *more disrespectful* but instead, his mouth tightened, and he smiled.

"I didn't know you were scared. I'm sorry," he whispered. "But... there are wolves everywhere and you are probably going to see a lot of them. I don't want you to be scared of wolves." His tone altered, turning warm as he draped an arm over my shoulders. "Not when you're with me. Trust me, I'll always keep you safe, *amore*."

Really? What was he even thinking? I was only testing one thing with him, and he acted as if we were going to spend the rest of our lives in each other's embraces.

Something clicked in my mind. His younger brother's words. It had been a few days, but I remembered what Pietro had told me about his brother—he would chase me for the rest of my life and that he believed that in some crooked, creepy way, I was his soulmate.

I grew curious, about everything. *Who was Christopher Delfino? And what else was he going to do to get me? What did his driver do to me that night? How was he so powerful in the city? What went down in the station? What happened to that man he was beating up? What cult was he running? Why did he command his men to guard me? Why did I have feelings for him?*

There were a thousand questions in my head and none of them were answered. Even my own best friend knew this man but didn't dare to say anything about him. He had paid for my dad's medical bills, freed me from any worries over it, and helped my family after one date. He had me followed by his men, his driver had knocked me unconscious by whispering something into my ear and his brother had warned me about him.

Either I was doomed for the rest of my life, or it was all normal.

We reached Laford quickly after the wolf incident. The car came to a halt near the residence I had been to earlier. I still remembered running away from here through the back exit that his brother had shown me.

In minutes, we were inside a maroon bedroom with walls as dark as they could get. There was barely any light, even when the sun was shining brightly outside. The curtains blocked the light.

"You promise to leave me alone after this?" I stood in front of him, my body as cold as it could get. I needed not to show any feelings or let him even think I'd *burn* for him.

"We'll see about that." He grinned, stepping even closer to me, and pressing his body against mine. "You're mine, *amore*." He pushed all the hair off my shoulders. "You're going to want me and you'll die for me." He sounded sure.

"I will not," I replied as my body shuddered. "I'll never want you."

"You will," he whispered, placing a hand on the side of my neck. My eyes fell over his mouth, over his lips, his fucking perfect lips. *God.* "You're going to beg for more after today. I promise you that. I'll ruin you in a way you have never been ruined. I'll consume every inch of your impure soul because that's exactly what you want..." His fingers tightened around my hair, and he tugged it back. "You will break for me."

"I will not," I whispered, stern in my words.

He lifted my chin and his lip curled into a smirk. "You don't know me."

"Why do I have a feeling I'm about to?"

Heat rushed to my core when his mouth returned to mine. I closed my eyes and savored every second of it. He kissed me as I had never been kissed before, so gently yet so wickedly.

I whimpered a little when his hands raced to the back of my head and lower to my back. My body reacted differently than my mind.

It wanted to submit, spread my legs wide and let him *ruin* me.

But my mind wanted to control, to challenge, to disagree with whatever he thought he knew about me. I wanted to prove him wrong, I wanted to deem his assumptions incorrect, I wanted him to fuck me and then look into my eyes as I told him that I would rather fuck my ex-boyfriend than him.

I wanted to take pleasure in disturbing him, to make him feel unworthy, to watch his powerful mighty self crumble as I walk out of here, unsatisfied, and never see him again.

I hated him and nothing was going to change that.

31

Rebekah

He drew his mouth away from mine, trailing kisses over my cheek and jaw as I titled my head back. Every single movement was tempting but I forbade myself from being tempted. My heart started to pound rapidly when his mouth trailed down to my neck—I often found myself pooling in pleasure when touched there.

I unfurled my fingers around his hair, and opened my eyes to stare at the dark, maroon ceiling above me. Shaky, unwanted breaths left my throat. I bit the inside of my cheek, hoping I would let out a sound that would satisfy him.

I couldn't let him win *me*.

Ugh.

Oh, but it all felt too good. A deeper crease formed on my forehead when his soft and warm tongue slithered over the nape of my neck, just where my sweet spot rested. My insides twisted and turned, burning, and warming with every second passing by.

Christopher's hands moved perfectly over my body as if he was a little too skilled. I shuddered as one of his hands flattened against my chest, just underneath my collarbone.

It grew hot and heavy quick. I struggled to breathe, to get a hold of myself.

When his mouth parted from my neck, he reached to my ears and whispered, "I can smell you, *amore*."

I shook my head in denial. "You can't."

"Trust me, I can." While flashing a grin, he took a step back, only inches before meeting my eyes. I barely held the contact as my cheeks were burning with desire, but it wasn't that blunt that he could *smell* it. The sides of his mouth curled wider, he let out a little while shaking his head. "Don't fight so hard with yourself. You're the only one losing."

"I'm not even fighting," I quickly replied.

"Well, I didn't start yet." His hand wrapped on the neckline of my shirt, and he tugged me forward. A small gasp escaped my throat, and my breathing became heavy. "Are you going to keep fighting this whole time? Or will you simply accept the fact that you want me?"

"I don't." I gulped and looked straight ahead, into his glowering golden eyes.

Before I took a breath, he tossed me onto the bed and scrabbled over me. My heart jerked. His fingers came tightening around my hair and my body reacted differently to his *power*. There was one thing I enjoyed in bed, one thing Adam barely ever gave to me and the only thing I craved from him during our entire relationship.

To take control.

To dominate me.

Christopher pushed me up to the headboard of the bed before one arm came beside my head. Leaning in close, he gave me an evil smile as if he had just opened the pandora's box and knew how to shut it as well.

"I'm going to enjoy every second of this," he murmured over my mouth before moving back and drawing my pants down.

My legs parted themselves, spreading around him. I felt my body betraying me, slowly giving into him. He unbuttoned the first three buttons of my shirt, ignoring the other four of them. His gaze sprinted over my body. I watched his eyes darken with hunger and lust, his face stiffening as his hand moved over my body.

Hair rose behind my neck. I let another heavy breath out as his fingers curled around my underwear.

"It's not too late to go back on your words..." He trailed off, his fingers pressing against my hips as he waited. "I'll let you leave if you take back your words and admit that you *are* burning for me."

"I am not."

I sucked in a quick breath. Lowering his head, he trailed wet kisses along my neck and traced his tongue over my collarbone. My bones melted. He dragged my underwear down, over to my thighs before his hand moved to my sex. My eyes slammed shut. *Fuck.* He held me down firmly with his body weight, barely allowing me to shuffle as my insides pooled with desire that I hoped would subside or disappear somehow. The slow touches, the painful torture had me furling from within.

When he raised his head, I opened my eyes, meeting with his scorching, playful gaze. My heart jerked and I gasped as I felt his fingers moving lower, between my lips. I shifted a little, forcing his fingers against my pussy—my wet, throbbing entrance.

My belly tightened as his index finger brushed over my wetness before he stopped and kept the pressure in one certain spot. I was on the verge of exploding. "You're mine," he murmured against my lips.

With ragged breaths, I replied, "In your dreams."

His eyes fluttered away from mine before he thrust his finger inside my drenched pussy. I tucked my lower lip between my teeth, refraining myself from uttering a single sound of pleasure or giving him the idea that I was anywhere close to enjoying his finger inside me.

Though I was.

"In my what?" he asked, his voice rough as sandpaper. His finger curled inside, and my walls tightened around him. Agonized pleasure ran through my veins.

"Your dre—" I held my breath back as he added another finger, stretching me wide. Heat pooled and dripped from between my legs. He shoved his fingers deep before curling them. I drew my knees to myself, and moaned, "Fuck. Fuck."

My hand lowered to his but before I could touch it, he grabbed it and pulled it over my head. "Did you say something?" His mouth returned to mine.

My cheeks flushed red. Something set inside me. I curled my hands, sinking my nails into my palms as his fingers quickened inside, thrusting in and out, drenching me further. My pussy convulsed. His mouth ducked to meet with mine. He kissed me and my lungs sought for a breath.

Throaty moans left, croaking out of me. My toes curled.

Fuck.

Fuck.

"I thought I heard something, *amore*..." He moved his face to the nape of my neck. My heart beat violently. He drew out his fingers and parted my swollen lips before giving them a little pinch. My hips squirmed underneath his hand. "How does it feel? To not even know what your body wants?"

My voice trembled, "Not you."

He chuckled in my ears, and his hot breath traced down my neck. He moved his free hand under my head, yanking a fistful of my hair and sending delicious shivers down my spine. I lifted my hips, his fingers thrusting back into my sex, burying deeper and twisting, driving me right to the edge, where I had desired to be touched for so long.

"Of course it's me. Look at yourself. You want me," he rasped.

I shook my head, not giving in. "I hate you."

"That's fine." He chuckled once more before rubbing his thumb over my sensitive clit while his fingers remained inside me. I squeezed around them, and my legs shuddered, nearing an orgasm. "I don't care if you hate me, *amore*. All that matters is that you're mine and that no ones *touches* what's mine." His fingers moved back and forth roughly.

"I'm not... yours," I whispered as my pussy clenched hard. Another moan of pleasure left my throat.

He pulled his fingers out before I even had the chance to finish. The feelings submerged and a hollowness remained inside me.

"Uh, no," I cried quietly.

His hand moved from my hair and came wrapping around my throat, cutting my breath in half. I choked for air as he lowered to my face. "Tell me you're mine, *amore*. I want to hear those words from your pretty lips."

"No," I croaked out.

Never.

"Say it." His hand tightened and his leg reached between my thighs.

"No." My pussy convulsed. I shook my head, denying him any joy from me. "I'm not yours," I said. Meanwhile, my clit rubbed against the roughness of his pants.

"Do you want to finish?" he asked.

"Yes," I moaned, arching my back.

"Beg for it."

"No."

He moved his leg aside, the feeling disappeared but was soon replaced with his fingers. My insides throbbed as one finger rushed over my clit and my swollen lips. A strong ache built up inside me and twisted. I grabbed onto the sheets underneath, holding myself together.

As I writhed, he moved his hand away from both my pussy and my throat. Gasping for air, I lifted myself from the bed while maintaining eye contact with Christopher. It was clear he wasn't going to let me finish. He just wanted to tease me.

A smile spread over his face and then, I understood.

"Fuck you." I buttoned my shirt and drew my underwear up, covering my throbbing sex that drowned in my own wetness. If he had moved his fingers inside me for another minute, I would have finished.

He stood up from the bed as I gathered my clothes and fixed myself. Chuckles rose from the side; I didn't pay any attention.

"I think I believe you're *burning* for me from within. So, I'm not leaving you anytime soon. Be careful." There was a warning in his voice.

I hadn't *lost* but it was his game and his rules.

"Go fuck yourself." Frustrated, I cussed at him while putting my shoes on and hoping to flee the bedroom as soon as I could. Agreeing with him was the worst thing I had done. He had *tortured* me this whole time and it was painful.

"I don't need to since I'll be having your tight cunt squeezing around my cock soon enough," he stated, delight in his voice and face.

I remained stoic. "In your dreams."

If I could've bashed someone's head in, it would've been his, but unfortunately, there was nothing I really had with me to do so.

32

REBEKAH

I sprinted down the stairs and collided with Pietro just as I was about to leave. He seemed a bit stunned while I tried to hide the ache growing between my legs. *How could I have let that happen? Ugh. What was wrong with me?*

"And the preppy princess returns..." the younger one said, swirling around to me.

I stopped at his voice and faced him. "You're just as terrible as your brother!" I quickly said, showing no emotion, and then turned to leave the residence. Staying here for another minute was going to *kill* me.

"Be careful. Don't be dumb," he warned as I fled from the house.

I breathed in the cold, fresh air outside in the courtyard while waiting for Faye to arrive in her car. Earlier, when I asked Christopher about my car, he told me that it was stolen or something along those lines. I grew enraged and fumed. I understood his games, he didn't want me to leave.

I called Faye, hoping she could pick me up from here in less than ten minutes as she lived nearby—downtown of Laford.

My mind was reeling. I was afraid, confused, and angry at the same time. A headache was growing in the back of my head. I felt stuck, and everything felt hazy, especially after the car ride and the *playtime* in Christopher's bedroom.

It seemed like I had attracted the devil himself and he wasn't going to leave me alone, and he wanted me to go to hell with him.

Faye's car appeared from a distance, she slowly rolled forward while her windows went down. Reaching the courtyard, I heard a gasp escape from her throat as her eyes wandered over the house.

I pulled the door open and sat down. "Please. Drive," I begged her.

"Wow. This is so beautiful," she murmured under her breath while rolling out of the courtyard at a speed that wasn't going to take us anywhere. "Fuck. This is my first time here, seeing this place, and it's so... pretty." She was taken back by the residence.

I looked outside of the window. It was, in fact, pretty but there was a devil living inside and I didn't ever want to go back again.

Christopher was a devil, Satan—*something*—and he had planted himself inside my head. I felt strange emotions inside me. I had *feelings* for him. I literally pooled at his touch and if I hadn't controlled myself, I would've begged him to fuck me.

Once Faye was out on the street and driving back toward my house, I managed to take a breath of relief. She asked me what happened, and I told her the details, just skipping a few of them that involved his fingers ramming into my pussy.

"So, you made out with him?" Her eyes were wide. "Wow."

"Yeah..." I trailed off with a shrug. It was somewhat *nice* to kiss him. He was a good kisser, probably the best one I had so far. "But that's off topic. He's a creepy snake, slithering around me all the time." I moved my hands in the air, showing Faye, expressing my emotions to her and for the most part, she understood me.

Before heading home, we went to the nearest costume shop, hoping to get some costumes for Halloween.

"Do you think I should file a restraining order? I mean, it would make sense, right? I can get it, right?" I bombarded Faye with questions while looking through the masks in the costume shop. None of them were anything I liked.

I was hoping to dress up as an innocent girl killed by a devil.

"Yeah, no, it's not going to work." Faye glanced over her shoulders and shook her head. Her straight hair barely moved as she checked out another mask at the bottom of aisle. "I don't believe the police will get *involved* with a man like him…" she trailed off, hiding something.

"Why'd you say that?" I furrowed my brows.

She shrugged and got onto her knees. "Just—he's a powerful man, Bek."

I stared down at her as she reviewed a few masks. Then and there, something popped in my head, an answer. I didn't need anyone to tell me anything because Faye knew everything about that man. She chose to keep it a secret from me.

But getting it out from her wasn't going to be hard.

I kneeled beside her, my face lightening up. "You know everything, don't you?" I asked her, my eyes wide.

"About?"

"About Christopher. You've known him for a long time. Your family knows him as well. Tell me everything, Faye!" I breathed out.

"I-I can't." She shook her head and stood.

I followed her up. "Why not?"

"Because we have a code of silence."

Bullshit.

"Oh, come on," I grabbed her hands. "Please. It's not like I'm going to tell anyone anything you tell me. But I need to know everything, and

I think, there is a lot you're not telling nor is anyone else." I wasn't sure what was *hidden* from me but even thinking about it made my heart pound.

"You can't take it." She turned her eyes away from me and began walking outside of the shop.

"Why not?" I chased her.

"It's—I can't tell you, Bek. It's not my place and whatever I tell you, you'll not be able to take it and it will probably ruin our friendship. And I'll have to go against a code. If anyone finds out I told you, I'll be doomed for eternity!" She stopped and explained, her face full of strange fear that I didn't quite understand.

"Please. I beg you, Faye."

"Bek—"

I stopped her before she began. "I need to know, Faye. I need to know everything because I'm going crazy here. Just a couple of weeks ago, I was perfectly fine in my life until that night at the station and then, it's all just fucked up. I cannot sleep properly, I cannot eat, I fear I'm being followed half of the time and the other times, I believe I'm going to be murdered by the end of the week." I spilled out whatever I had been holding inside and it was a lot.

The wind whistled and the bells at the top of the store tinkled as we moved out and stepped into the street. People passed by us, walking in different directions, while I stood idle against Faye, hoping she would tell me everything she had been hiding.

Her mouth tightened. "Not here..."

"Of course." I gave her a nod.

"Your house?"

"No." My lips turned into a frown when I remembered everything that was happening back at home. "My parents are getting divorced. I don't feel like being home."

"Oh." She was a bit surprised. "Let's go to mine then," she offered and I agreed before following her back to her car.

33

REBEKAH

Faye lived downtown with her parents. They had a cozy three-bedroom apartment on one of the tallest buildings in Laford. We went up a high-speed elevator to the eighteenth floor where her apartment was. I had been at her place a hundred times but this once, it felt unusual.

My heart ran a thousand miles per hour. I could feel the drumming of it against my chest. Nerves in my body twisted and tightened as we went inside Faye's bedroom. There was no one at home except for her dog, Sam. Her parents were out doing chores, but she felt better to have the conversation in her room.

I sat on the bed, one leg underneath my hips while the other leg dangled off the bed. Faye walked in circles before she went to her closet and grabbed a book. I could tell it was hard for her. She had a different panic spread over her features.

She handed me the book and I raised a brow at her. "A picture book?"

"Yes..." she stuttered. "Just look at it."

"Okay." I nodded and turned the pages.

There were family pictures of Faye and her parents. When I turned the plastic pages, I found pictures of her with her cousins, along with that woman, Alicia, and her husband. It seemed like it was all taken a year ago since she wasn't pregnant in the pictures.

I went ahead and turned the page to only find images of... *wolves*. Some of the pictures were taken in the dark in a forest, and some were taken in the morning. I furrowed my brows in confusion but didn't question the pictures yet.

By the time I finished the picture book, I raised my head and my gaze met with Faye's. "What's all that?" I asked.

"I-I don't know how to say this..." She took in a cautious breath before sitting down. Seconds passed, she fiddled with the hem of her shirt and then her nails. "You cannot tell anyone," she warned me, for the fourth time.

"I won't. Promise."

She stayed silent for another long, stretched-out minute and I truly understood nothing. None of my questions had been answered yet. I continued to look at her, her pupils widened, and her gray eyes turned even lighter.

"Well, we—my family and I—we are called *shifters*." She scratched underneath her ear and then looked away. "Or *werewolves*. Anything. Doesn't matter. We occasionally turn into wolves, and we live in packs."

I blinked once and then once more before a smile spread on my face. "Are you joking?"

"No, Bek!" She spoke in a serious tone and whenever there were two lines on her forehead, she was serious.

Oh.

Shit.

"Wait." My lashes fluttered; I stopped her. "What are you saying? I don't understand anything."

"Just listen…" She rose both hands, palms faced against me before she heaved in another long breath. "It's like a gift, like we were gifted with this power to shift into a wolf and carry its strength while we are in our human form. It sounds like bollocks."

"Yeah," I agreed with her.

"But it's not." Her voice turned stern. "We've had a pack of *werewolves* since the beginning of time or since we were born. When I was born, I became a member of the same pack as my parents. I first shifted when I was eight, and I was confused then but my parents told me everything. Shortly after that, I met the leader of our pack, the Alpha—Christopher Delfino."

I wasn't sure if I wanted to laugh or cry. My emotions mixed even further. *Was this a joke or not?* I had known Faye since I was a baby, and I knew everything about her.

"I couldn't tell you this. My parents helped me to form some *lie* to tell you since you were human and then, I told you about the cult my family and I *worship*." She wasn't lying. "I had to hide it from you and everyone else who are normal humans."

"How do you know I'm a normal human?" I asked her while still adjusting to what she had just told me. There was a point that she was correct in. Since the beginning, she'd always told me about these *cult activities* with her parents, sometimes for days and sometimes for months.

I really didn't think about it much then.

It all seemed normal.

"I can smell you. A werewolf has a different scent while a normal human has a diffcrent one…" She trailed off.

"Okay."

"So, yeah, we are *werewolves* and we can turn into a wolf whenever we want to. We move in packs and most werewolves belong to a certain pack. I—" She placed a hand over her chest, and continued, "—belong to the Wolf Creed Pack. We have a hierarchy of an Alpha, the strongest and the leader, a Beta, who's the second in command and after that follows mid-rank wolves and warriors and then omegas, which come in the lower ranks." She moved her hand while mentioning each position.

I nodded my head, listening to her while keeping my own thoughts at bay. Before making assumptions, I had to let her finish. In the twenty years of having Faye as a best friend, she had never joked about something like this, nor she had lied.

There had to be something believable in her speech.

"You wanted to know about the Alpha, Christopher, right?" she asked.

"Yes."

"Laford, this city, it's under his ruling. It has been under the ruling of the Delfino family for over a hundred years. *He* controls the city and everything from going in and out."

I shook my head in denial. "That's not possible."

"It is, Bek. There are humans here, but the population of werewolves is much higher than humans. You have seen him—his strength and his power. He's the strongest and the smartest werewolf of this time, of our time. He controls everything in this city, and he knows everything that happens here." She explained it to me in a way that she *wanted* me to believe her.

But how could I? This all seemed like bollocks.

Werewolves didn't exist. It was all fantasy and lore shit. *How could I believe that?*

"I know you're probably thinking that I'm lying…"

"Are you?" I cocked a brow at her.

She shook her head. "No. Of course not. You have to believe me, Rebekah. It's the only way this can work."

"Can you prove it?"

She blinked hard before color drained from her face just as I expected it to. I rose from the bed, rolling my eyes at her words. This was all bullshit.

"I can, Rebekah," she said from behind me as I approached the door. "But you cannot tell anyone. If *he* learns that I showed you anything, he'll kill me, as I would've broken the code of silence." She rose from the bed and approached me.

"I'll not tell anyone." I straightened my back and turned completely toward her.

What was she going to do? Turn into a werewolf?

She stood in front of me and stretched her arms forward. I lowered my gaze as her eyes pressed shut. She heaved in quick breaths and her pulse quickened before her fingernails stretched and elongated, turning into sharp, bloody *claws*. The bone structure of her hands shifted completely as well. The snapping of her bones made me nauseous, and I gasped before looking away.

"Stop. Stop," I begged her, covering my eyes.

When I looked at her hands again, I found her thick hair fading and the claws returning to fingernails as she turned back into the human she was.

Fuck.

I slapped a hand over my face. My heart pounded in my chest. "Why are you telling me now?" I turned to her and asked. "Why didn't you tell me before? Fuck, Faye, I was your best friend for fucking years, and you never told me anything." Warm tears pooled in my eyes.

I wasn't sure if I was frightened or upset about her reality.

"I wanted to but—I just couldn't." She approached me. "I'm still your friend and I always will be. You don't have to ever be scared of me. I'd never ever hurt you in my life and this, what I am, it's something I can control and something I know. You can trust me. Please?"

I sniffed hard and wiped my tears away from my cheeks. "Of course I fucking trust you."

She smiled and wrapped her arms around me. "I love you."

"Don't pull that shit on me again," I warned her. Whatever it was, it terrified me, and I didn't want to see that again. But I believed her and every word she had said.

There was more to this world, more than I had seen and I had thrown myself into this mess. I needed to accept it now. My best friend was a werewolf and the man I had nearly let fuck me was one as well—probably a worse one.

I swallowed hard.

Faye laughed before pulling away from me. "I won't."

"So…" I moved away from the wall and went back over the bed. My heart eased a little. "Werewolves…" I breathed out, taking in the term. "…are real. What's next?"

"Witches and underground tunnels."

34

REBEKAH

Witches.

It was a known fact that witches lived among us. I believed in witchcraft, and I had read a thousand stories about witches being present between us, casting spells, doing magic—most of it black and harming people, but I hadn't ever encountered one.

"What about witches?" I leaned forward to Faye, my brows collected as I questioned her. The fear washed away, and curiosity settled inside me. "Are they real? Do you know any?"

"A couple. Though, in our world, witches are a threat to us. They perform magic to control us, sometimes to even kill us. We fear witches and whoever practices witchcraft," she explained to me with horror in her eyes.

Oh...

"Are there any here?"

She shook her head. "There is one, but asides from that, we forbid witches to enter the city. Any witch found entering is killed on the spot, if possible, or else they are managed in different ways. That depends on the Alpha." She fluttered her hand in the air and sighed.

The Alpha.

Christopher.

How could I not be surprised? His show of strength and power only meant one thing—he was always in control. In the back of my head, I knew he was a *part* of something big, maybe a gang, but I didn't know that he *ruled* a whole city, the city I had been born in and I had been living in for years.

How could no one know? How could I not know?

"What did you say about the underground tunnels?" I turned my attention back to Faye who didn't hesitate to answer the questions I had for her—and there were still a lot.

"The tunnels were made long before. They were made for werewolves to roam around the city without catching the attention of humans. It's also like a *safe place* for us werewolves to stay if we are ever in danger. The tunnels aren't known to any human here." She paused, taking a breath. Telling everything to me meant threatening herself. Faye was taking a risk. "The tunnels are located underneath the subways—"

"The subways?" I cocked a brow; my mind went back to the day where I found Christopher taking the life of an older man inside the subway. "How is it possible?"

"At every station, there is a technical room that leads into the tunnels, which then will take you to a whole new world."

My lips parted and my jaw hung. *Secret tunnels.* I was intrigued, maybe even more than that. I began to wonder if that was the reason Christopher was there in the station that night. He didn't seem like a man who'd take the subway anywhere.

It made sense now.

"Wow. Can anyone go there?" I asked Faye with a hint of excitement in my voice. The worry subsided. I was curious about how there were tunnels under the city that no one knew about.

"No, only werewolves, Bek." She shook her head and then laughed. "Though, if you want, I can take you."

"Please. What is it like?"

"It's a like whole underground city. You'd love it." Faye hopped up from the bed and headed to the table to grab her phone. Her eyes were glued to the screen before she spoke. "There is party on Halloween and it's going to be a blast. I can sneak you in if you want?"

I drew my lip into my mouth and bit it. My nerves were quivering, but at the same time, I was growing excited. I wanted to go but I had to go with Rose, to her high school Halloween party. I couldn't be in two places at the same time. *And did I want to be surrounded by werewolves?*

I just learned about them today. It could get overwhelming for me.

"What time is the party starting?" I asked her.

"It's starting at ten, ends by sunrise," Faye said, reading from her phone before tucking it away. "You should come. The parties held underground are—*mind-blowing*. Drugs, alcohol, money, everything, and people are wild. You'd enjoy it so much. Plus, you haven't been to a party in a while," she suggested, a smile spread over her face as she waited for me to agree with her.

God, I wanted to go.

But there was a bit of uncertainty inside me. *What if something bad happened? What if another werewolf like Christopher began chasing me?*

"I'll come. But I need to be at Rose's high school party first! Hers is at seven, so I'll be done in no time and then we can go together, and you can show me everything!" I exclaimed with a thrill dancing in my core as I imagined it all.

I couldn't wait.

"Oh, that's amazing. Yay!" She threw her hands in the air. "I promise, you'll love it all."

"But wait—" I stopped her. A scowl spread on my face. "Isn't there going to be a problem if I, a human, comes?"

"Oh, silly, there isn't going to be any problem. You're the Alpha's destined mate. No one can touch you, except for him, of course," she replied. "The only thing you need to worry about is what you're going to wear."

Huh?

I pursed my mouth and looked away while understanding what she had meant. It took me a moment but then I understood it. *All of it.*

35

Rebekah

The costume came out perfectly. I had picked it up from the mall with Faye when we went shopping earlier. She was dressing up as Juliet, from Romeo and Juliet, a white princess hoping to find her prince.

I wore a full-length black suit; it was made of pristine leather that wasn't too harsh on my skin. It was something I had been wanting to wear for a while but couldn't.

Last year, Adam forced me inside a barbie costume while he dressed up as Ken. It was terrible. I barely even took any pictures. Thankfully, this year, I could wear whatever I wanted.

I was single.

"God. You look like a someone who's going to kill!" Rose exclaimed, rushing inside my room. A gasp escaped her throat while she kept her cool. "Wow!"

I turned away from the mirror after combing my blonde hair down. "Thank you." I smiled at her and then saw her costume. She was going as a witch. "And you—you look interesting." She wore a goth dress and a pointy hat that Mom managed to buy for her a couple of days ago.

Her high school party theme was about *witches* and a legend where hundreds of people were killed by them. The more I thought about it and compared it to the reality I had stumbled upon, I realized it could be true.

I needed to ask Faye later, whether witches had killed anyone here.

Rose walked up to me, and we stood near the tall mirror. I placed my hand over her shoulders and said, "We kind of match."

"Yeah, we do." She nodded, fluttering her lashes.

"Great! Let's go say goodbye to Mom and get out before we get any later for your party." I reached over to the table and grabbed my bag, only keeping some necessary things with me.

We showed our costumes to both our parents and received a couple of compliments. For a long while, I hadn't seen Mom and Dad sit together but somehow, today, they were sitting beside each other.

Dad loved decorating the house for Halloween and this was his first one after having cancer cells in his body. He had changed the house completely, even filled up a box outside the door with chocolates and baked brownies and cupcakes for the little kids who were going to pass by.

"Be safe out there, darling!" Mom exclaimed behind me as I just turned to leave.

"I will be, Mom." I looked over my shoulder and gave her a quick smile.

It was hard for both of my parents. They were going to divorce soon, and Dad was moving out. There wasn't much time left. These were the last few memories. My heart was broken but Mom's decision was final and so was Dad's.

The night was still young, filled with children rushing back and forth, collecting chocolates and gifts from their neighbors while everyone else enjoyed the spirit of Halloween—the evil spirit.

I drove Rose to her school and went along with her to meet with some of her classmates and loosen up a little before the actual party I had to attend with Faye. There was still plenty of time left for that.

Horror-themed music played in the background while people played fun Halloween games and danced to gothic, scary music.

I spent a little more time with Rose, meeting her teachers and whoever else I knew at the high school. Just two years ago, I was here, enjoying the same Halloween parties.

Faye arrived at the high school an hour later than I did. She wore a white dress with a pair of wings at the back. The corset on her waist was promised to be tightened once we were going to be off school grounds, as then it would flash her breasts.

"Is this the same thing you got from the mall?" Faye asked, her eyes wide. "It fits you so perfectly. You look like a slut."

My jaw hung. "Don't call me that." I zipped up the jacket I had gotten along with the fit, just to keep everything PG and avoid showing my entire figure to my high school teachers out of respect.

After spending a couple more minutes at the school, we both left together. Mom promised to pick Rose up later in the night, whenever she was done partying with her friends. I, on the other hand, didn't have any intentions of returning home tonight.

It had been a while since I had been wasted and I was prepared for it all tonight.

Faye drove, she began driving from the high school to downtown and then into an abandoned alleyway between some high structures. By the alley, there was a parking lot filled with hundreds of cars and people walking out and entering one of the elite clubs in the city.

The Mellow Club.

I stepped out with her and followed her into the club where showing IDs wasn't a requirement. Faye and I both were underage for any clubs, but we carried a fake ID with us most of the time, but it wasn't necessary here.

"So, a club?" I furrowed my brows while passing through the curtains and entering the club.

"It's not a club."

I stared ahead and found a spacious seating area. She was right. It wasn't a club. It was a *front*.

"Come on. I'll take you underground." She wrapped her hand around mine and shuffled closer to me. "Stick close. We don't want anyone to know that you're a human," she whispered, rubbing her shoulders against mine.

Hmm.

"I thought the tunnels were connected to the station." I grew confused.

"There are a hundred tunnels, Bek. They are connected to every subway line, some certain buildings and even some private residences," she explained while leading me down an escalator.

I turned my head around, noticing every detail. The further we walked, the bright lights faded, and the floorings changed. After descending from an escalator, she pulled me into an elevator and pressed on *Underground Laford*.

The elevator was filled with people, some couples, and some singles, all dressed up in their Halloween costumes. I grew excited but at the same time, afraid. My thoughts ran wild as I realized they were all werewolves.

Fuck.

Shit.

I was going to die.

I grabbed onto Faye's hand tighter, digging my nails into her palm for the next minute or until the elevator came to a halt.

When the metal doors drew open, I held back my gasp upon finding a whole world underneath. My heart thudded.

We walked for several minutes before passing another entrance to a nightclub. *A real one.* This one was different. Neon and bright lights shone at me, nearly blinding me. I lowered my gaze as we went past the gates. My breaths came out slowly. It was a monstrous club; the walls were stretched high to the point where the ceiling couldn't even be seen and the length of it ran for miles and miles.

Hundreds, if not thousands, of people were seen dancing, drinking and partying.

"Holy fuck," I whispered to myself.

Faye didn't even hear it over the music bursting from the speakers. The ground underneath me shook as the bass drummed through the walls. The scent was thick and rich with alcohol. Poker and gambling were taking place.

My eyes widened. I was at a loss for words.

How does such a place even exist?

"Oh, Faye, I hate you so much!" I yelled at her for not bringing me here earlier.

This was the *core* of Laford.

36

REBEKAH

I wasn't scared.

Not even the slightest. When I first thought about Faye's words, I imagined walking into a party full of werewolves, *shifting* and biting each other's heads off while howling under the full moon—but I was wrong. The werewolves weren't even wolves, they were like me, *human*. There was nothing to fear.

My fear washed away the minute I tossed down a shot. After the second one, I began laughing at it all. At the fourth one, I realized I didn't need to be scared of anyone, whether it was a werewolf or Christopher.

I didn't need to fear anyone.

The whole idea of werewolves was still sinking inside me. It had been a few days since Faye told me about it, but I was taking it well. They were just humans that could turn into *animals,* sometimes. There was nothing terribly wrong about that.

"What are you thinking?" Faye screamed as I went in for another shot.

I took the glass of the table and held it with my two fingers while trying hard to remember which shot I was taking. *Probably fifth.* "Would you ever kill me?" I asked her.

"No, why would I do that?" she replied, shaking her head.

She was screaming on the top of her lungs, but I barely heard her over the music and since the alcohol was kicking in, I began hearing something else.

"Don't kill me, please."

"I won't."

"You're going to kill me now?"

"No. I'll kill you tomorrow." She grabbed the shot glass from my hand and rolled her eyes before dragging me away from the lounges and onto the dance floor. "Move your ass in that tight suit."

"It's not even that tight." I ran my hand down my body, feeling the material brush against my skin. Somehow, the costume fitted me perfectly for once.

Different shades of light swirled, sweaty bodies slammed against each other at the beat of the loud song and danced. I shook myself, lightly, in front of Faye before we began dancing with others. There was an energetic crowd here, youngsters enjoying the night and partying. It felt wild and worth every minute. When I began to get a little tipsy, the music became louder in my ears and a buzz spun through my head.

My heart beat quicker, thundering in my chest before a hand was pressed against my hip. I turned, hoping it would be Faye but instead, I found someone better.

A young man.

My smile tightened and I ran my tongue over my lips before dancing along with him. He placed both of his hands over my hips, and I moved my arms to his shoulders, simply enjoying the night before it ended.

I didn't care much.

I savored every moment.

"Taken?" he asked, inching closer to my face.

He was handsome, broad shoulders, strong features and his cologne was intoxicating—or maybe he'd had too many drinks.

A chuckle escaped my throat before I shook my head. "Of course not."

"Mhm, that's always good to know."

I withdrew my arms from his shoulders and trailed my hands down to where his were placed, on my hips. Giving him a light push, I backed away and grinned. "Come back in an hour and we'll talk."

The man returned a warm smile as I faded from his sight and tried to find Faye so she could help me not mingle with men. *It wasn't a good time.* Bodies surrounded me, people danced and screamed as I went past them to leave the dance floor.

I barely made it out when a hand came wrapping around my wrist. A chill ran down my spine and my heart jumped at the *feeling* that spiraled through my body.

"Talk about what?" A strong voice echoed in my ears and for a moment, I only heard those three words even when the music was blasting.

I placed my hand over my chest and turned around to find Christopher standing in front of me. I held back my gasp and replied to him, "Oh—oh, nothing actually." I pulled my hand away from him and quickly changed my tone. "What are you doing here? Stalking me again?"

He took a few steps forward in silence and I backed away, away from the dance floor. "You're in *my* club, *amore*, mingling with *my* men and then you ask me what *I'm* doing here. It's funny because I should be asking you the same." His gaze ran over me before he grabbed my wrist again, holding me in place before I moved any further from him.

"What are you even dressed as? A fucking *gatta*?" he mocked.

I nudged an eyebrow at his comment. "Yes. I'm a cat." I closed my fingers, turning my hand into a fist before pulling it away from him but failed. He pushed his fingers deeper and held it firmly.

"What are you dressed as?" I mimicked his mocking tone, hoping to get it right. When I ran my gaze over him, I realized he was dressed as *nothing* but that didn't stop me. "A *wolf*?"

His mouth lined straight, his grin turned sour, and confusion washed over his face. "What did you say?"

"What you heard."

He stepped forward and I backed away. "Who told you?"

My breath hitched. I dared not mention my friend's name. "No one you need to know about."

"What else do you know?" He moved me further away from the music and the dance floor, cornering me to the bar where it was much quieter. "Tell me."

"Everything."

"Who told you?" he repeated, his eyes darkening. "Don't play with me. Tell me who told you. Was it your friend? Or was it someone else?"

Shit.

I promised not to drag Faye's name into this. She was already scared of spilling the *secret* to me.

"What's the matter? I know, isn't that enough." I tugged my hand away from his hold. "I know everything about you, who you are and what this place is. Now, if you want me to stay silent, you are going to leave me alone," I offered quietly, keeping my mouth shut rather than telling everyone else what I knew.

His expression softened and he chuckled before nearing me. My lower back pressed against one of the empty seats of the bar and I felt myself shrinking in front of him. His hand slid over to my neck, and he wrapped his fingers around my throat before lifting my head. The pressure wasn't enough to restrain my breathing, but I still felt on the verge of dying—or getting killed.

"Who are you going to tell? Who's going to believe you? Oh, that's right, no one. And for the better, since you know *everything,* it will be easier to make you mine. You, Rebekah, belong to me." His breath fanned over my cheek as his body towered over my little frame.

"No."

"Yes. And stop mingling with men. I don't like to share what's mine," he whispered in my ear, tracing his thumb over my lips.

"You can't do anything about it, can you? You cannot hurt me, *Christopher*. I know where your obsession roots from and your brother mentioned a certain bond to me earlier. If you ever want me—" I met with his burning gaze and took a sharp breath. "—you'll have to learn to be nicer, maybe then I'll consider ever dating you. Otherwise, you can forget about me and stop with the threats. I'm not scared of you."

"Nice?" He laughed, shaking his head. "You don't want nice, *amore.* You enjoy this more than you should. Don't lie to yourself."

My nostrils flared. "I don't," I snapped at him.

His hold on my throat tightened and he breathed down my neck. "Really? You don't?"

I shook my head and licked my lips.

I didn't.

Fuck.

Why was I denying it?

I pressed my eyes shut and took a breath. Several emotions tingled inside me. *God.* He was right. I was enjoying this, all of this. When my lashes fluttered open, I looked straight into his eyes, and he read the longing on my face before grabbing my arm once more and dragging me out of the club.

My knees were already weak, and I felt my body burning. "Where are taking me?" I asked him, my heart beating in my stomach.

We walked in the same direction I entered the club with Faye earlier. Instead of heading toward the direction I came in from, Christopher dragged me right and pushed open a door that led us into a restroom.

He locked the door behind and then turned to me. "To make a cat fucking purr."

37

REBEKAH

An intense gaze met with mine. I chewed on the inside of my cheek while my heart drummed endlessly. His fingers tangled in my hair while I became trapped between a reflective mirror and his large body. He wrapped another free hand around my face, lifting my chin and forcing me to meet his eyes.

"I'm going to go insane because of you," he whispered, his mouth only inches away from mine.

My breath faltered. I didn't know what to say. No words left my throat. Flashes from the past crossed my mind. Every nerve in my body froze but then I melted when his lips pressed against mine. He kissed me with such heat and desire that I found myself burning under his kiss.

I pressed my eyes shut and kissed him back without a care in the world. It was exhilarating, kissing him. It always was. It drove *me* insane. The feelings I had been suppressing surfaced and I tried to push them away, hoping they'd go but they didn't.

Not this time.

My body felt like it had been starved for weeks, not for food, but for something else. I had never felt such hunger, such need before, for anyone, not even for my ex—who I enjoyed having sex with even though it was boring.

There was a different attraction here. My mind was denying Christopher, but my body wasn't. I was pooling from within, starving to be touched and fucked. I couldn't get rid of my thoughts from the time he had finger-fucked me in his bedroom. That memory was imprinted in my head.

And now this...

His fingers looped in my hair as he bit down on my lower lip. A chill rushed down my spine. Denial became a struggle. I pressed my body against his, letting his heat delve with mine, consume me.

God.

A sharp pain rose in my head when he tugged on my hair and broke the kiss. A small gasp escaped my throat followed by a few staggered breaths as I looked up at his fiery, domineering eyes.

"Tell me what I want to hear," he rasped, and my nerves tingled.

My teeth clenched as his hold on my hair tightened. "Never," I whispered back, knowing exactly what he wanted to hear.

In the snap of a second, he whirled me around and forced me near the mirror and away from the wall of the restroom we were in. His fingers remained in my hair, holding hard. My back pressed against his chest, and my ass skimmed across his jeans, where I felt him growing behind me.

When I lifted my head, I stared at my reflection ahead of me. The mirror was wide and tall, showing everything inside the restroom. There was no one else here, just *us*.

His free hand drifted over the cat-woman suit I had worn. It was leather—or something similar to it—but the material stuck to my skin, showing every part of my body to anyone who saw me. It contoured my breasts and when his finger slid over my nipples, they instantly hardened, and my spine curved against him.

Desire was thick in the air.

He played with one of my nipples through the suit, pinching it and sending agony across my body before his hand trailed over my stomach and closer to my sex.

A silent moan left my mouth and every fiber in my body quivered in delight.

His warm breath fanned over my ear as his hand pressed against my pussy. My arousal seeped out and I clenched hard as my neck tilted.

He trailed a few kisses across my neck and jaw before his mouth returned to my ear once more. "By the time I'm done with you, you'll be saying everything I want to hear, *amore*."

My eyes fluttered shut and my lips parted when he rubbed his hand over my sex. A primal need washed over me, making me yearn for more.

He snarled under his breath before the ravenous, wild kisses resumed across my neck, trailing all the way down to my collarbone and shoulders. When I looked up at my reflection, I found my nipples hard and stiffening with every passing second and a desire growing in my eyes.

Only then did I realize that I *wanted* this. I couldn't deny it anymore. I stared at myself in the mirror and learned I was indeed craving and fancying Christopher more than I thought.

The desperate look on my face gave everything away.

Christopher groaned in frustration, his chest rumbled as he drew his mouth away from my neck and glanced at me through the mirror. "Get rid of your clothes before I tear them off you," he threatened, his hand now clenching onto the shirt piece of the suit that was tight and barely moveable.

"I'd like to see you try."

Without letting a second pass, he ripped off the shirt, parting it wide open and removing it from my body. Leather—or whatever the material was—couldn't be torn, but somehow, he did.

Heavy breaths escaped my throat as he gripped the fabric of my pants and then ripped them apart as well, leaving me bare with nothing except for my underwear on.

He pushed me back over the counter near the mirror and grabbed my face. "Don't ever dare me again, *amore*," he whispered, inching closer to my lips. "I can do things you could never even imagine. If I choose to be *gentle* with you, it's because I want to, not because I have to."

He kissed me once more, harder, with urgency. I squirmed beneath him. His hand locked around my throat, taking my breath away, leaving me desperate for both air and him. My senses whirled. He lifted me up in a swift movement and pushed me up and over the counter before spreading my legs around him.

His hardness brushed over my underwear. I gripped his arm as adrenaline coursed through my veins. By the time he broke the kiss, my lips were swollen and bruised, yet needing more of him.

He stepped back, unbuckling his pants in front of me as I watched him. My chest rose and dropped as I caught a glimpse of his hardness poking through his underwear.

Lifting his head, he met my lustful gaze. "Touch yourself."

"No." I breathed hard.

"Don't make me fucking repeat myself. I want to see you touch yourself, *amore*. Do as I say." His voice rose, savagery clear in his tone as he spoke with such threat. When I still didn't listen, he wrapped his hand around my throat and pulled me closer to him. "What is it going to take to make you listen to me?" he asked.

The corners of my mouth lifted into a grin. I trailed my finger over his chest and lower to his abdomen, brushing over his cock and giving him his response.

He shook his head. "I'm not going to fuck you until *I* get what *I* want and I want to see you touch yourself." He stayed firm on his words, not changing his intentions, even for a moment.

I drew my finger over his growing length, he was hard—nothing could stop him. "I doubt that," I replied, in the same stance and giving him the same energy.

"Fucking hell." His eyes darkened in anger and he grunted under his breath before tightening his hand over my throat, forbidding me to breathe.

I bit my lower lip, still grinning at him as he curled his fingers around my underwear and ripped it out from between my legs. He parted my legs wider around him and tugged me closer.

I wrapped my hand around his wrist while trying to breathe. I swallowed hard and his hold over my throat loosened but his fingers dug deeper, surely leaving marks.

He hissed over my mouth, and I purred beneath him as he freed his cock and brought himself closer to my soaking entrance.

38

Rebekah

My body trembled in both fear and delight. Before he thrust his cock into me, he pressed two fingers over my sex and a thumb over my aching nub that longed to be touched. I wrapped my legs around him, locking my feet behind him. He pushed me down over the counter with his hand still on my throat, choking me. Breaths barely left my mouth.

He curled his fingers inside me, thrusting them in and out of my soaking pussy. My breasts rose and dropped, my nipples hardening with every second. As the pleasure exploded inside me, I blanked out everything, including the loud music from the club.

Suddenly, I could only hear my own breathing and raspy moans of desire leaving my throat, along with the sounds of his fingers slapping against my skin and my juices, creating such a melody that I wanted to hear forever.

His eyes shifted from my pussy and to my face, where he watched me as I became vulnerable to his touch. The pace of his fingers ramming in and out of me quickened. I drew my brows together and whimpered as I began reaching my climax.

"Fuck." His jaw clenched and his hand tightened around my throat before he buried two fingers inside me and moved them against my G-spot. My hips rose, I squirmed under his hand as every muscle in my body tightened. "Not so fast, *amore*." He withdrew his fingers from my sex before I could finish.

"Christopher!" I moaned, needing more. I was only seconds away, mere seconds. *Fuck.* Something boiled inside me.

"Yes?" He smiled. "If there is something you want, you can tell me." He waited and waited for those specific words to leave my mouth, but I didn't give into any of his games.

"Fuck you."

He pushed my legs apart and held one down to the side with his palm. "I think you meant *fuck me*," he whispered. "Tell me. What do you want, Rebekah? I won't fuck you until I hear those words leave your pretty little mouth." He leaned over me, his hand on side of my head and the other one between my legs while his cock probed forward, sliding across my thigh.

My chest rose and dropped rapidly. My insides twirled and twisted with the heat forming within them. I held my breath back, not wanting to give into him but there was nothing else I could do.

I needed this.

I needed *him*—inside me.

But then it was all going to be real. I wouldn't be able to run away from this. Then, I would have to accept the feelings I have for him. Sex was something near sacred for me, I only had it with those I wanted a relationship with, like Adam.

At the same time, I couldn't resist anymore. The need was growing with every second.

"Tell me." His warm, hot breath trailed down my neck and over my chest. "What do you want?" He pressed himself against my aching sex, rubbing his cock over my pussy and parting my lips.

My legs closed around his hips. "Fuck me."

A wicked smile spread over his face before he forced himself into me. A small shuddering gasp left my throat before my breaths began speeding. My heart jumped and my insides instantly tightened around him as he stretched me wide open. He thrust all the way into me, filling me up in a way I had never been filled before.

I gripped his shoulders as he edged deeper into my soaking wetness. He placed his hands on the sides of my hips before leaning back.

His eyes glowed with content. He moved inside my swollen opening, rubbing himself against my tight muscles, consuming me while his right hand brushed over my clit, rubbing my sensitive nub till my moans and screams became louder in agonizing pleasure. My back arched and I threw my head back while broken breaths left my throat. He barely fucked me, yet I was drowning deep in the pleasure.

"*God*," I groaned, clawing his arms while it became all too intense to hold back anymore. My nipples throbbed, needing to be touched and fondled.

His stroke soon became rough enough. The longer he watched me, the more violent he became, sliding his cock in and out of me, giving me a taste of something I never really thought was possible.

My whole body convulsed.

Delicious sensation spread through my lower body where he pressed his hand down, only increasing the pressure growing inside my pussy.

After a couple more quick thrusts, he pulled himself out of me and probed his cock close to my quivering entrance but didn't slide in. His gaze was fixated on my lower area while I looked at him, watching the lust growing in his eyes as he slowly stretched my pussy with his cock.

"Fuck..." I groaned, fisting my hands, unable to take the slow torture anymore.

Upon hearing me, he lifted his head and met my eyes. Leaning forward, he placed his arms on either side of my head while I felt his cock filling me up once more. His fingers tangled in my hair and his warm breath trailed down my cheek and jaw.

"I enjoy stretching you open with my cock, *amore*," he whispered and I clenched around him while my nails raked down his arms. "Fuck. You're fucking milking me. Do that again and I won't be controlling myself anymore," he groaned in my ear while increasing the pace of his thrusts.

He pushed deep inside me, I tumbled back over the counter, and he pressed one hand over my head, saving me from hitting my head against the mirror behind us as he rocketed inside me.

I raised my legs, spreading them wider and locking them around his lower back. He pinned me down, underneath him and fucked me hard till I writhed and screamed while reaching climax.

My insides shattered and every inch of my body trembled as the warm juices seeped out of me while his cock still sunk deeper into my pussy. Hot, quivering breaths left my throat. I barely kept my eyes open. His teeth grazed my jaw and then lowered to my neck.

"Your body is mine tonight and every other night," he whispered before leaving a little bite over my neck, which promised something else. "Don't forget that."

For the next few minutes, he became stiff inside me as I convulsed around him in fierce pleasure. His pace slowed but his hands on my body and hair tightened, and his breaths quickened in my ear before he pulled himself out of me.

An inhumane, feral growl echoed in my ears. My heart jumped in both fear and surprise. He soon finished, his warmth seeping down and to the sides of my inner thighs.

39

Rebekah

My muscles ached with delicious pain. I glanced at my clothes and then shook my head after finding what state they were. I couldn't wear them again as they had been ripped and I surely couldn't walk out of here naked, with only my underwear on.

"Take my shirt. I'll have someone get you clothes," Christopher said, unbuttoning his black shirt and handing it to me. It was Halloween and he was greatly underdressed, but I doubted he needed a costume—since he already was one.

I took the shirt without any hesitation and buttoned it up, covering at least a few bits of my naked body until I could get something else to wear.

"If only you didn't tear my clothes…" I trailed off, glancing down at the ground where only pieces of it were left.

"Don't act innocent. You wanted me to tear them." He smiled wickedly as he buckled his pants.

I avoided staring at him for a long time, knowing I would fall hard if I did. His chest was muscular, arms thick and flexing. I had seen him naked for the first time while he had already seen me naked a couple of times.

I looked away while tapping my feet on the ground as he placed a call to someone regarding my clothes. I still couldn't walk out of here just wearing *his* shirt, even though it smelled good.

Faye would think of a thousand things, and I didn't want any judgement from her after I had bashed Christopher in front of her. This was just—*sex*. Nothing more. Though, I found myself denying it over and over again.

The door was still locked, and we ignored any knocks that came from girls wanting to go to the restroom. It was ruined, here, inside. Everything was on the ground; the entire room was trashed. Thankfully, the mirror was still intact and so was my head.

"Once you have clothes on, I want you to leave here and don't come here again," Christopher said, stepping toward me after he had looped his belt and covered his legs with his pants.

"No, I'm not leaving," I stated, folding my arms over my chest as a frown spread over my face. "Just because we fucked doesn't mean I'm going to listen to you like some bunny and hop behind you."

In seconds, my back was pressed against the wall, and I was trapped once more. "I know how to bend you to my rules, *amore*. And I know exactly how you're going to listen to me now." He paused to take a breath and then continued, "You're going to leave this party. I don't want you here, not tonight. It's not safe for you. Is that better?"

"Mhm." I nodded my head and looked away.

"Good girl." He traced his finger down my cheek and I slapped his hand away from my face.

"I hate you."

"Keep telling yourself that." He rolled his eyes at me and turned as another knock sounded on the door.

This time, the man on the other end announced his name before Christopher opened the door. He gave him the clothes and I reached forward, taking them from his hands and stepping into one of the cubicles to change.

In the silence, I heard Christopher talking to the man. I had seen him before but had forgotten his name. He was the man who had driven us—me—back to Laford that day when I went to see Adam and he was the same man who had stalked me outside of my house.

It was his driver, maybe even more than that.

When I removed Christopher's shirt from my body, I took a quick inhale of his intoxicating scent before placing it aside. My skin was red and burning. My insides were swollen and aching with desire. I needed more than what had been given to me. The sounds of his flesh hitting mine was pierced into my soul. I could never forget it.

I knew what was coming next.

An obessession.

I didn't want to have sex with Christopher because I feared that I would then have to accept my feelings for him. And now, I had to. There was no such thing as meaningless sex in my dictionary.

"It's not looking good outside. We were able to clear half of the crowd but the rest of it is stern and they aren't leaving. The longer the crowd remains, *they* will attack." I heard someone's tense voice behind me. It belonged to the driver who had gotten the clothes.

My brows furrowed. I dressed quickly with whatever was in the bag and stepped out of the cubicle to find Christopher stressed. He stopped the driver from talking as soon as he realized I was here.

Turning around, his expression changed and stiffened before he said, "Good, you're dressed. Leave now."

"I want to find my friend. I'm not going to leave without her." I pushed the shirt back to Christopher before walking past him and stepping out of the restroom that we had been in for over an hour.

I wondered where Faye disappeared off to. She had my phone with her and my purse since I was planning on getting drunk.

Christopher grabbed my arm before I went any further. "Do you not listen to me? I asked you to leave. Your friend will find her way out. I need you to leave right now." He heaved in a breath and diverted his attention to the man standing behind me. "Take her home, Michael. Don't stop anywhere."

"No!" I exclaimed, pulling myself away from him.

"Yes. Michael, take her."

"Don't touch me, Michael," I warned him before turning my head to Christopher. "I'll go home by myself. Thank you very much for your—concern." I gave him a stiff smile before turning away and leaving the restroom.

It wasn't going to be hard to find my way out of here. I remembered where I came in from, but I wasn't a hundred percent sure. However, I was sober enough to pave my way through these tunnels and find Faye along the way.

But when I stepped out and began walking, I found people rushing away from the club and toward the exits. Some seemed terrified and screams tore through the crowds. My heart jumped at the screams.

I wondered what happened.

When I looked over my shoulders, I found the club behind me emptying. It couldn't be that late. Either way, I didn't go back, even though my curious self wanted to.

Christopher

"Follow her. Make sure she reaches home safely," I told Michael as I buttoned up the shirt Rebekah had just been wearing. Only a few minutes and I could smell her all over me. My senses reeled. I desired to be inside her once more.

If only I could.

Michael nodded his head and left the restroom, following her out of the tunnels. When I first saw her here, I was a bit surprised, but it washed away soon when I realized her friend, Allision's cousin, had told her everything. It became easier for me to have her now. I didn't need to tell her anything.

At least not the unimportant bits about my life.

If I hadn't had something to handle tonight, I would have taken her again, in my bedroom, and would've had her scream my name the entire night. I wouldn't have stopped until I had marked her body, imprinted myself over her soft skin. Her insides were warm, and she clenched around my cock perfectly.

Her pleasure was all mine to take.

Her body was mine.

She was mine.

Nothing could stop me from getting to her. I had her already, most of her, only one thing was left—her stone cold heart but it wasn't going to be long before she'd offer it to me herself.

Then, I'd be completed.

Though I wondered if things would've been different if we hadn't collided with each other at the subway station that evening. Maybe then she'd be less hesitant and more willing. There were a few mistakes I had made along the way, but I couldn't help it.

She brought the worst out of me. There was nothing more I desired than having her burn for me and controlling her.

I stepped out of the restroom and watched the crowd fleeing. Some of them were aware but most of them didn't know why the Halloween party was coming to an end early.

There had been an interruption.

An attack.

I stepped into the club that had now become silent with the scent of alcohol still lingering in the air. The strong neon lights still flashed back and forth across the club as I paved my way into it, nearing the bar where *they* had been spotted. My men crowded the three woman that had barged into the party.

They remained inside the bar, their actions controlled.

Folding my hands against my chest, I leaned against the bar while watching the leader of the three meet my eyes. "You're in my territory, Selene. I think I warned you the last time you were here," I said, my voice threatening.

I didn't like anyone entering my city without my approval and I surely didn't enjoy watching these *witches* barge into my party. It angered me. If it had been any other day, I would've had them attacked but tonight, I was rather calm.

My wolf had been fed, I had been fed. Rebekah's scent was still lingering over me, it kept me in my senses.

"We heard something and we are just here to confirm it." She smiled evilly while pacing back and forth with her two *sisters* behind her, protecting her. "I tried to reach you. However, you were unavailable, so I paid a visit here myself."

"What do you want?" I asked.

"Your mate," she whispered, inching closer to me. Her eyes turned deep red, and her face morphed silently with the newly found information that had *somehow* reached her. My jaw tightened as she continued, "Don't lie to me, Christopher. A little birdy told us about a woman, a human, you've been seeing recently. Where is she?" Selene asked, darting her eyes around the club.

Rebekah was long gone—thankfully. I couldn't have her anywhere near these witches.

My stomach tightened at the sight of Selene standing in front of me. If there was anyone I despised, it was her. The only witch I couldn't kill with my bare hands. The only witch that was stronger than me.

"I don't have a mate," I replied, staying stern on my words. "You've received wrong information."

"I don't think so." She shook her head and frowned. I didn't give her anything, no explanation. I needed her to leave Laford and the quickest way to make her leave was giving her silence. "Fine, Christopher, play your games," she groaned and turned away from me. "But we want your mate and the minute we learn who she is, we'll have her. You have the option to give her to us yourself and I might be able to give you back what I've taken from you."

"I don't want anything from you, Selene. I just need you to get the fuck out of my fucking city." My hands curled into fists. Anger swept through my body, setting every inch of me on fire.

"I'll leave." She raised her hands in the air and a small chuckle escaped her throat before she instructed the women behind her to follow her out of the club. "Have a good night's sleep!"

40

Rebekah

"You're the sweetest, amore. I can taste you in my mouth," he whispered as his hot breath fanned over my sex, over the bundle of my tight nerves. His fingers caressed my inner thighs whilst his mouth devoured me.

I pooled underneath myself as his tongue lapped over my wet pussy once more, sucking and tasting me. I ruffled my fingers through his curly hair and threw my head back before letting out a shuddering moan. Pleasure coursed through my body. I faltered as he assaulted my throbbing clit, driving me out of control. My stomach tightened, I lifted my hips and dug my fingers deeper into his hair before finishing for the third time today.

I had already lost count.

Christopher licked me clean before rising up from between my legs. With a single pull, he positioned himself near my sex. His cock probed toward my entrance, but he didn't plunge in just yet. He lowered his head to my mouth, placing a warm kiss over my lips that drove me senseless.

Everything was different now.

His hands moved my legs and wrapped underneath my head as he leaned over me. His gaze fixated on mine and a smile spread over his face. "Tell me, Rebakah. Am I evil?" he asked.

My thoughts scattered. I wrapped my legs around his torso and trailed my fingers down his chest as heavy breaths left my parted lips. Shaking my head, I told him, "You're not evil. You could never be."

I moaned in glorious pleasure as he drew himself away from me and rubbed his unyielding hardness against my throbbing sex, my stomach coiled in heat and I lifted my hips before he pushed the tip of his cock in, stretching me only a bit. The hair over my skin rose.

He moved slowly, in a teasing motion, forcing me to burn for however long it was going to take to satisfy him. Like a glove, I tightened around him instantly as he drove deeper into my cunt. My wetness glistened over his cock as he drew all the way out and then plunged back in, finally giving me what I needed.

I bit down on my lip, holding back my moans while staring down, watching his entire length disappear into my pussy. When my eyes trailed up to him, I found him looking back at me with a furious expression spread over his face.

My brows furrowed.

"What's wrong?" I asked him while my fingers loosened from the comforter I had been gripping.

He placed his hand over my lower belly before his strokes became rough and cruel. "You're wrong, amore." He breathed hard. "I'm evil, and you know what else? I'm going to take you to fucking hell with me. And you're going to enjoy burning with me because that's what you want—what you need."

"No." I shook my head, a chill running down my spine. "No!"

He thrust into me harder. The walls around me began to close and breaths barely left my throat. A wicked grin spread over his face before he dug his fingers into my thighs. "And don't forget what I can turn into."

Fear spread all over my body. My chest tightened as the pleasure subsided, replaced with terror. His fingernails extended into claws, and I screamed once before they sliced through my flesh.

Then, after seeing blood, I screamed again, louder.

I jolted awake sweating and screaming while gripping the sheets underneath me. After taking a glance around my surroundings, I returned to my senses and realized it was just a dream—*a fucking wet dream*. My bed was soaked, not with sweat but rather with my wetness.

It wasn't the first one I'd had.

"Fuck," I cursed before dragging myself off the bed and grabbing the sheets along with me.

The throbbing in my forehead only lasted for minutes before I drank water and hydrated myself. I tossed the dirty sheets into the laundry bin before running a hand through my hair.

This was the fourth time in a row that I had been having the same wet dream—the same exact one. There was no difference. The same words echoed in my head as I grabbed new sheets from the closet and spread them over the bed before anyone found out I had been having wet dreams.

I wasn't sure what was wrong with me but after Halloween, after the whole sex-in-the-club-restroom, I couldn't stop thinking about Christopher, even in my sleep. He was *branded* in my head, in my thoughts, and I couldn't get rid of him, no matter how hard I tried.

It was almost as if he had fucked me and given me his *morbid* obsession.

I couldn't help myself. Every inch of my body wanted him again while my mind kept denying me from reaching out to him. It had been four long days; I hadn't been disturbed.

But the wet dreams.

God.

The wet dreams always started great, and I enjoyed them up until to the part where I realized he would never change, and neither would my *view*. He was the perfect definition of evil, nothing more.

But the way he took me. It was something I'd never forget.

An hour later and after tidying everything, I headed downstairs to greet my mom and sit with her for some time before she left for work. I found her near the dinner table, opening envelopes and marking something. Only then I remembered my parents were divorcing and before they could divorce, they needed to make sure all loans and debts were settled.

Mom was *making sure* of that.

It was going to be a clean, agreed divorce. Dad would move out in a week or two, and we would live here with only Mom. Rose was off to school, studying, while I spent most of the time at home, searching for a new job and trying to get my head straight.

The Halloween party was four days ago, after that night I hadn't received a single message from Christopher nor been disturbed. I took it as a sign that his obsession over me had died down and I could finally resume doing whatever I was doing *before* him.

Which wasn't much.

"Everything sorted, Mom?" I asked her as I carried a warm cup of coffee while entering the dining room where she was seated.

"Yes, yes, darling." She drew her glasses down and glanced over her shoulder. "I've been meaning to ask you about the money you had gotten from your friend, Faye, right?"

I froze in my steps and then nodded after recalling the *lie* I had told Mom. "Yes. She—her family—they gave it to me."

"We have to eventually return it. I was making adjustments with the expenses after your dad leaves and hopefully by spring of next year, we should be able to manage it all," she explained while pushing her glasses back up.

I blinked and then swallowed hard before sitting beside her. The money did not need to be returned. Christopher gave it to me in exchange for a date with him. It wasn't a *debt*. It was an exchange. I didn't need to give it back.

"No, Mom. It's fine. Faye's family has plenty of money. They won't bother for a while. Don't worry about it," I told her, forming another lie. *What else could I do?* I didn't need Mom to worry about the money.

It was gone, Dad's debts were paid and so was everything else.

A thought crossed my mind and before I could rest my coffee on the dining table, I stood and began approaching the door. "I've to get to some work. But don't worry about the money, Mom!" I told her before taking the stairs back to my room.

I placed the coffee over the side table and leaned underneath the bed to grab the golden box where Christopher had once sent me a dress and—*a thong*. I opened the box and found the burgundy dress still inside.

A smile lifted the corner of my mouth before I grabbed the box from the ground and placed it on the bed.

Probably a good time to return it.

And a good reason to see him.

41

REBEKAH

The silence was killing me.

I was in over my head, driving myself crazy over the past four days while he had been giving me nothing except silence—*after* we'd had sex. I needed to know what it meant. I needed to know if I had only been *used* for sex or if something else was going on.

He looked pretty serious that night, after we had sex and after we were disturbed by his driver. I wasn't sure of the conversation that went down but it sounded unusual. Maybe something was keeping him occupied.

Maybe.

Just maybe.

I had the address to his residence. It was a twenty-minute drive away from my home and the entire time, I chewed on my nails, wondering if this was the right thing. Often, I neared a U-turn to go back home but something stopped me, and I kept driving toward his place.

What if he had found another woman to obsess over? That couldn't be possible. He wouldn't just play with my feelings and toss them aside. But again, it was him, and he was the incarnation of the devil.

"What am I doing?" I whispered to myself while nearing the curved, golden gates of Christopher's residence. The street close to his place was entirely empty. Not a single soul could be seen or heard.

I slammed on the brakes near the gates and waited for someone. A man walked out from the room beside the gate and approached me. Rolling the window down, I brushed away the anxiety growing within me and glanced outside at the guard.

"Yes?" He cocked a brow at me, confused at my presence.

The dress and the box Christopher had given to me rested in the back seat of the car. I had nearly tossed it in, not caring much. It was just an excuse to fulfill my impatience and see him. I had no other option. It wasn't like I was going to approach him and tell him that I had been *dreaming* about him and that maybe we needed to do whatever we did on Halloween once more—just to figure things out.

My heart clenched. *What was wrong with me?*

I opened my mouth, hoping words would fall onto my tongue but none did. After seconds of having an internal battle with myself and my thoughts, I finally said, "I'm here to see Christopher."

"And who are you?" the guard in the front asked, nearing the window.

"Rebekah," I replied, stating my name. "I was here—something like a week ago. I don't really remember but I'm sure he does." I gave the guard a smile.

His mouth lined straight, and he peeked back. "What's in the box?"

"Something to kill him—" I stopped joking when I figured out the guard wasn't taking any of it. "It's just a dress. I was going to return it to him. Like, what else am I supposed to do? Keep it forever? Or something? And the thong was ridiculous. I just want to give it back," I rambled, not even stopping for a breath.

My heart was thudding hard and fast. I grew more nervous each second. Just parked in front of the gates of his residence gave me a full-blown panic attack. All this while, he had been *pursuing* me and now, I was here.

I was here and I truly didn't even know why.

The guard ran his questioning gaze over me before he said, "Leave the vehicle here. You can go inside."

I rolled my eyes and reversed my car back a little before thrusting forward into the empty lot near the gates. Once parked, I killed the engine and stepped out. Sucking in a sharp breath, I pulled my jacket closer and buttoned it up. A shiver raced down my spine. It wasn't the cold. I knew it wasn't.

The guard unlocked the smaller gate and allowed me in. After walking past the gate, I heard his voice behind me once more. "Don't you want to take the dress and the thong?" he asked with a hint of humor.

Smart.

My cheeks turned red with embarrassment. "Maybe another time," I murmured, walking straight ahead and toward the courtyard. Not once did I glance back at the guard whose chuckle still rang in my ears.

The cool afternoon breeze whooshed over me, tangling my perfectly straight hair that I had just combed before leaving the house. While walking, some of the disturbing thoughts in my head calmed, while the others still remained, taking over my conscience. Looking ahead, I found the water fountain without any water and remembered the *date night* I had with Christopher all those weeks ago. Then, I was sure I was never going to see him again.

Not anymore.

I continued to walk across the driveway, glancing at the green lawn and trees surrounding the house. It was quiet here, almost peaceful. The greenery could be seen extending for miles and miles, almost as if it was their own private woodland. I assumed here was where their *wolves* ran—able to turn into their true forms.

A sense of fear washed over me before I strolled past the fountain and found the grand entrance.

Tension tightened inside me, and I suddenly stopped walking when my eyes lowered to the four cobblestone steps near the entrance and over the liquid that ran down the steps. It was dark red, similar to the color of *blood*. I hesitated before lifting my head in horror of what was happening in the doorway of the house.

A small gasp escaped my throat and after that, I held back any more breaths.

The thudding in my chest grew as my eyes trailed over Christopher's hand that was buried in another man's chest—*a dead man's chest*. It was inches deep, probably surrounding his heart. Blood seeped out from different parts of his body and dripped down the stairs, pooling around the doorway and in front of me.

Christopher was leaning over the man, his hair falling over his face as he killed the man underneath him. His shirt was filled with the man's blood along with both hands, one still buried in his chest. His brother stood behind him, watching, along with another familiar man who stood on the opposite side to his brother.

My stomach clenched in disgust and fear.

"Fucking pussy energy," his brother cussed. "Couldn't even stay alive for a minute more." He rolled his eyes before lifting his head from the man's body and fixating his eyes on me. "Oh, *shit*."

My legs took a step back on their own. Suddenly, he stepped away from Christopher and began marching toward me with a surprised expression on his face. All eyes turned to me. The screams in my throat suppressed, no voice or breath left my mouth.

My fingers quivered, my heart beat rapidly. Everything around me closed, suffocating me. My head felt light. Only his brother's footsteps echoed in my ears.

No.

"Don't touch her, Pietro!" Christopher's voice rang in my head. The fear within me only grew from there. "Michael!" He yelled louder—for his *driver.*

I kept moving till my back pressed against the dead fountain. His brother gave me an icy stare, still approaching me. Only then did I snap into my senses and twisted around. While screaming at the top of my lungs, I paved my way away from the fountain, running back toward the gates but before I could go any further, I was blocked.

By the driver.

His large frame forbade me to move an inch. There was no expression on his face—*nothing*. He lifted his hands, pressing them on either side of my head. The atmosphere shifted and the sky changed colors.

It grew dark.

I knew what was coming next.

I had been here before.

"No," I rasped, shaking my head.

"*Morpherous*," he whispered under his breath before closing his eyes.

Another scream spilled from my mouth but was cut in half when I felt every inch of my body weakening, every limb faltering, and my senses slipping from my control. It took only seconds before my eyes fluttered shut and my head struck against the solid ground.

42

REBEKAH

My eyes peeled open, and a gasp left my mouth.

It only took me a second to remember what I had just seen outside in the courtyard and what his driver had done to me, *again*. I didn't move much, only looked around and figured out where I was.

In his bedroom.

I sensed him inside the washroom, cleaning the blood off his hands, which meant it hadn't been a long while, probably just a few minutes or maybe an hour. I didn't know. The water kept running and running. I drew my hand away from the pillow and slowly rose from the bed. I needed to run, as fast as I could, and as far away from him as possible.

I couldn't have him chase me, not again.

Not this time.

My legs fell to the ground and my heart pounded faster in my chest. The door to the washroom was wide open and from a distance, I saw his shadow. The tap water continued to run. He was just cleaning his hands, not showering.

I slowly stood from the bed and my gaze traveled over the room where I found two large windows opposite each other. I didn't care. I wanted to leave him, and it didn't matter if I jumped from a window and broke a few bones rather than dying entirely from his *murderous* hands.

Not only he was evil, but he was a *killer*—a *murderer*.

At the subway station, I wasn't sure if Christopher had killed that man inside the room but now, I was certain he had killed him—and probably many more.

I was next.

The tap water stopped running and it became deadly silent inside the room. I held my breaths back and stood idle beside the bed as he walked out of the washroom with a hand towel in his grip.

"Oh, you're awake." He stepped forward and tossed the towel aside.

I stared at him in disbelief and my gaze ran over the blood spots on his shirt, his pants, and even some on his arms. His hands were clean but the rest of him was soaked in *someone's* blood. I swallowed hard as panic raced through me. My chest pumped furiously, I tried to breathe but it was difficult.

I stood on the other side of the bed, still far away from him. Before he got any closer, I screamed for help and backed away from him. My back pressed against one of the four corners inside the bedroom, and I slowly leaned in and wrapped my hand around the glass vase while killing the screams in my throat.

"Let me get out of here," I said, my voice trembling and bile growing in the back of my throat, making every breath difficult.

"If you keep acting like that, you're definitely not leaving," he replied, frustrated. "I didn't know you were coming or else I would take my *matters* elsewhere. What you think happened is not what happened. I didn't kill that man for no reason. There *was* a reason and I'll tell you that if you can calm yourself," he explained—explained a murder he'd committed—and then stepped forward.

Fear jolted inside me, and I clenched the vase harder before slamming it against the wall and shattering it into a hundred pieces of glass. One big, sharp shard remained in my hand while others spilled on the ground beneath me, creating a loud clatter that echoed for only a few seconds before disappearing.

I didn't know how to fight—I never did learn and there was probably a greater chance of dying here then getting out alive, but I didn't care. I was going to do whatever it took to leave here unharmed.

Christopher stopped in his steps and raised both hands. "I'm not going to fucking hurt you, Rebekah. You know that."

I took a few quick breaths before raising my own hand toward him. "Then let me leave," I whispered.

He didn't *listen,* instead he stepped closer, and I pressed myself against the wall as my chest rose and dropped. Fear engulfed me from all sides. The hair over my skin rose. Terror spread through my body like never before. My heart ached and my body trembled.

"Don't," I snapped, curling my fingers tighter around the top piece of the vase that was in my hands. My pulse quickened as he continued to near me, taking steady steps forward.

"It won't do anything to me. You're only going to hurt yourself." He reminded me of the power and the inhumane strength he held.

I clenched my teeth and said, "Good. You'll have more blood to clean then."

He stepped onto the broken glass, and it crushed underneath his shoes. Before I even had the chance to swing the piece of vase in my hand, he quickly jumped in and grabbed my wrist, pushing it up to the wall while his other hand wrapped around my free one.

"Give it to me," he snapped, his gaze seizing mine while he forced my fingers to unwrap around the piece of the vase. As soon as he got a hold of it, he pulled it away and tossed it on the ground with the rest of the broken glass.

My skin crawled and I swallowed hard. I lowered my gaze while struggling to free myself from him but stopped upon realizing I wouldn't be able to escape, not now, not today, and probably not ever.

"I don't kill for fun, Rebekah. I had a goddamn reason—"

"I don't want to know. I just want to leave." I cut him off while looking away from him. He cornered me with his body and trapped me.

"You're going to *listen*. Look at me." He slipped his fingers underneath my chin, forcing me to turn my face and meet his threatening, murderous eyes. "I *had* to kill that man. I've a fucking city to run and the minute something goes wrong, it's either my head or someone else's. I'd rather it be someone else's than mine." His voice was filled with anger when he spoke, matching his furious expression.

I turned my face away from him and remained silent. I didn't care whatever reason he had to kill someone, it was wrong—terribly wrong—and I didn't want to associate myself with someone who *killed* and then had his *driver* lull me into sleep every time I tried to run away from him.

He watched my face and when I gave him no response, he continued, "I'm sorry you had to see that but you're not stepping out of here until you can fucking talk to me. So, make yourself comfortable." His grip around my wrists loosened and soon, his hands parted, freeing me, even if it was just for a moment.

I stepped aside from the wall and away from the broken glass in the corner. He walked over to the other side of the room and with a grunt, he grabbed his phone and called someone.

I ran my tongue over my lips before pursing my mouth shut.

"Send Claudia up here. There is broken glass." I heard him say to someone on the phone before he cut the call and tossed his phone on the desk. Once he was done, he turned to me and said, "Don't run away from here—from *me*, Rebekah. You'll not make it far. I'll chase you for however long it takes. You came here yourself. You want me. It's better if you accept your destiny with me."

43

Rebekah

It was the third time I'd found myself stranded here. Once more and it would feel like it was meant to be. I no longer could blame my bad decision making for this. If I had any clue Christopher was a murderer, I wouldn't have dared to step into his home but here I was, yet again.

A woman walked inside the bedroom moments later and cleaned up the broken glass before wetting the floor and mopping it. I stood by another wall, my hands folded across my chest as I watched her clean and then leave.

A cry for help wasn't going to exactly help me in this situation.

What would I even say?

Christopher stood on the other side of the room, attending a call, and gawking at me carefully, watching my every move. The door was wide open. I could run but I knew myself, and my legs wouldn't make it that far, especially for the second time.

The last time, his younger brother, Pietro, had helped me out of here and this time, I doubt he would even look at me.

Christopher followed the woman as she left the room. He locked the door behind her and tossed the key into his pocket, where I couldn't reach it—*yet again.*

A disgusted expression remained on my features. It didn't budge. I had seen someone commit a literal murder and the reasonings didn't matter. It was what it was.

I grimaced as he approached me. The corners of his mouth lifted into a smirk as if he was enjoying all of this. I could barely meet his eyes. He lifted his hand, placing his on the wall behind me while he leaned in closer. "Don't look at me like that, *amore.*"

I snapped my head around. "Like a murderer?"

"Like I'm something evil."

There wasn't much difference.

"Well, that's because you are!" I exclaimed in bewilderment. *How could someone kill and not know they were evil?*

"You wouldn't have come here then," he argued back, as if it was going to change the hatred I held for him.

I pushed my head back against the wall and suppressed a groan that nearly escaped my mouth. "I made a mistake," I whispered with my teeth clenched.

His nostrils flared a little, his eyes burning into my soul. He leaned even closer. "You know what I am, Rebekah. You know well. Don't act as if you were clueless. You saw me at the station, you knew what I had done then and yet you came here. You came back, over and over again. And you were quite willing to take that money. What makes you think it wasn't blood money? What makes you think you're innocent? And even after everything you knew, you gave yourself to me. You're not above me or squeaky clean."

In a swift moment, I pushed him away from me and when he didn't budge, I moved myself from the wall. When out of his suffocating trap, I was finally able to breathe.

But even then, his words burned in my head. "I'm not going to stroke your ego—"

"I don't need you to." He turned away from the wall and faced me. "Accept the fact that you knew everything."

"I didn't know you were a murderer!" I exclaimed, my mind running wild. He was right about certain things, about the fact that a part of me knew what he was and what he did—that he was involved in some violence and crime, but not murders.

"I'm not a murderer. I didn't kill in cold blood," he snapped, his eyes darkening as I further fueled his anger. There was a long silence in which he took a deep breath to calm himself. "There was a reason I killed him and you're not going to understand that because you don't live in *my* world."

I snorted at that. "I don't want to either."

I wasn't sure what I even wanted at this point. I was engulfed with both terrible and terrifying thoughts of the man who stood in front of me, yet there wasn't an ounce of fear within me, instead, there was something else, something I felt disgusted about. *How could I still want a man like Christopher? How was it even possible?* I had accepted the fact he was a *werewolf*, a different creature than us humans that could turn into a wolf whenever he wanted, and I'd made peace with it.

It didn't terrify me.

But I couldn't make peace with the fact he was a murderer.

"Halloween night, I told you to leave and I had Michael follow you home. It was abrupt, I didn't want you to leave but if you stayed, you would've been taken as a sacrificial lamb—and not by me." He shot me a tense look.

I drew my brows together, and in unease, lines appeared in my forehead. "Who?"

"A group of witches. They are unrepentant and powerful." He didn't step toward me or invade my space, rather, he kept a distance and continued, "And they want *you*, for a sacrifice probably. I'm not sure about the exact details. But it's my mate they require. On Halloween, they were there, and they would've taken you if I hadn't *forced* you to leave. And that man I had killed was the one who fed those witches information about you."

I lined my lips firm in irritation and then gave my head a light shake. "You're lying."

He scrambled forward, his gaze intense. "Why would I lie to you, Rebakah?" he asked, cocking a brow at me. "If I had let that man live, he would've fed more information to the witches and it wouldn't bring any harm to *me*. The information he had given them was about *you*, your whereabouts, your family, your work, your life—not mine. I was—I am protecting you."

Horror washed over my face. The strangest and darkest thoughts appeared in my head and haunted me as I made sense of his words.

After a moment of silence, anger bit into my thoughts and I stated, "I wouldn't needed protection if it weren't for you!"

"It doesn't matter."

"You put my life at risk and now you're acting as if you're the one saving it," I scoffed and waved a hand in the air. "I'm done playing your game. I don't need your protection or *you*. I'm leaving," I whispered before marching toward the door.

He grimaced. "It's not like that, Rebekah." He grabbed my elbow, dragging me farther away from the locked door. "It doesn't matter if I'm in your life or not, if I had ever found you or not because being mated to me means you're fucked and that's fucking destiny. The witches would've found you either way and they would've used you for one of their sacrifices."

"No," I said firmly.

"Yes." His hand tightened around my elbow and in that moment, I wondered if he was telling me all this to force me to stay or whether it was the actual truth. "You're a human and my mate. To them—to us—that is not *normal*."

"Good. I don't care. I'm still leaving." I ran my fingernails down his hand till it parted from my elbow, and I grew free of his hold. "Your world, your mess—not mine. Handle it and leave me alone."

44

Rebekah

"You came here on your own but you're not leaving until I say so." Christopher spoke behind me before I heard the jangling of the keys in his hand, the key to the bedroom door, the key to my freedom. I turned, facing him as a scowl appeared on my face. Staying here, with him, meant endangering my *own* self and I wasn't stupid.

I inhaled, thinking of everything that was going to let me leave here in one piece. "I-I just need some time to think," I said after a moment of silence. I didn't need any time. I just needed to leave in any way possible.

He closed the key in his fist and said, "I want you. And I'm not stupid enough to believe you need *time*." He grimaced once more before giving me an eye roll. "I don't want you to leave because I know the moment you do, you'll not come back. The witches *will* take you. I'm protecting you for your own benefit."

"And I don't a believe a word you say. You're just covering up for yourself." I folded my hands across my chest while my gaze lingered on his shirt where the blood of the man he had killed still remained. It was turning dark second by second, but his hands were clean.

It was as if my dream was replaying itself in my head. The same thing that I had dreamt about was happening and I wasn't sure which was scarier.

"What if I show you?" he asked.

My brow rose out of curiosity. "What do you mean?"

"If you believe I'm just lying, then let me show you what the witches are capable of." He walked past me and approached the door, unlocking it while I remained confused.

What could he show me?

His hand stretched toward me as the door slightly creaked open. I rolled my eyes at his *welcoming* hand and followed him outside without taking it. We walked past several doors before the spiral staircase came into view. While descending the stairs, I looked around, my heart thudding as I hoped to find another escape route if things didn't turn out well. They weren't going to.

I knew well.

Just at the end of the stairs, I found his younger brother, Pietro, standing idle, a smile spread over his face while his hands were folded around his chest. He didn't say anything until we reached him.

"I thought we were going to bury two bodies today." He pouted at his older brother.

"Yours might be the second one. I don't want you around here, go hide somewhere or leave," Christopher snapped at him before wrapping his hand around my wrist and tugging me along with him.

Pietro laughed and I glanced over my shoulder, finding him still chuckling for the next few seconds. "It's a human, Christy. It's never going to be the same. Your luck is ruined, might as well move on."

My brows furrowed. I didn't think too hard. His words were clear. It was odd in their world to be *mated* with a human and it was problematic. Though, there wasn't much I knew. I only had information from Faye.

We entered another room and my heart jumped at the sight of Michael, the same man who had me drop unconscious in seconds, twice.

"She wants to see what the witches have done. Do you mind showing her?" Christopher asked him while his fingers were still tight around my wrist as if he knew I was going to run from here.

Tension spread over my face. *Wait. What?*

"You said *you'd* show me—"

I was cut off before I could even finish. He turned around and said, "I can't show you, but Michael will." A smile spread over his face before he let my hand go.

My heart raced. I took a long step back away from Michael as he approached me. "This is barely going to hurt," he whispered under his breath.

"No. Wait—" I didn't want to see anything like this—whatever it was. My head whipped around to Christopher, and I stared at him with fear growing in my eyes. "I don't want to see anything." *Not with this man.* I feared him more than anyone else here.

"Show her, Michael. It's not going to hurt." The grin continued to play across his mouth as he folded his arms across his chest and drew farther away from me. "Start with who the witches are," he added, informing his driver, who had to be a witch himself.

Before I could do or say anything more, Michael pressed his hands against my head and closed his eyes before whispering, "*Clariato*."

The world flashed away in seconds. Bright lights nearly blinded me before everything went dark and silent. I no longer saw Christopher or

Michael or the room I was in. Instead, I saw flashes of blood dripping from brown walls and heard the guttural growls of animals screaming—*in pain*. It grew cold, ice cold. Fear crawled down my spine. My head felt heavy.

The screams continued, never faltering.

A sharp pain rose inside me, starting from my feet and drawing all the up to my head. I let out a scream of my own, almost as if I had just been *killed* by some entity.

The witches.

Moments later, I was standing barefoot on wet grounds while a group of women chanted in front of me. The pain split through my body again. Glowing red eyes met mine. I screamed before snapping my eyes wide open.

I held my breath as my gaze raced over the room where I found Michael standing in front of me, his hands now drawn away from my head.

What had I just seen?

"Show her what the witches did to you," I heard Christopher's voice close to me.

My knees weakened, and before I could say anything a pair of hands pressed hard against my head once more, triggering a recollection of a memory that wasn't mine but someone else's.

Michael.

It started again in the similar way; white light blinded me and then grief and betrayal filled my heart as if something had happened to *me*.

I heard countless whispers and murmurs before I saw *someone* pouring scorching hot acid over my hands and burning me. The pain swept through my body. I screamed. Tears poured out of my eyes. The whispers continued. Blisters rose on my hands and my skin melted.

'Don't ever think you're any better than me. I'll always be the strongest. I killed your parents, have no doubt that I won't kill you,' a woman in a black cloak whispered to me.

I couldn't look up; I couldn't see her face. My gaze was fixated on my hands that were burned with acid. There was nothing I felt except for pain.

My eyes struck wide open, returning to *reality*. Sweat trailed down my forehead and back. My chest rose and dropped as I breathed heavily.

Shaking my head, I drew farther away from Michael who remained standing in front of me. "That's all," I rasped, my voice breaking through my rapid breaths. "I can't see anymore." I turned my head to Christopher.

The smile had long disappeared from his face. "No, no, there's more. Don't be scared." He wrapped his hand around my wrist, holding me from running away from whatever this was.

"Please, no," I begged.

The horrific images of the *visions* Michael had shown me were going to haunt me for the rest of my life. I couldn't see anything else. I couldn't bear to handle someone else's pain.

"That's not all, Rebekah. You have barely seen anything." His eyes clicked to Michael, and he motioned for him to show me more. *What else?* "Show her what the witches have done to me."

"No—"

His hands returned to my head before I could argue and then it was too late. The bright flashes split through my vision. I gasped for breath as I slipped through several of Christopher's memories, none of them involving bloodshed until later.

The loud sound of the clock ticking echoed in my head and before it shattered my ears, I placed my hand against them and fell to the ground in pain. Even then, the sound weakened me. An ache rose in my chest, slowly spreading through my body as I lifted my head to find dead bodies spread all around me.

There wasn't just one or two, but hundreds—all of them men and all of them dead. There were some *wolves* lying dead on the ground, blood seeping from their wounds where they had been attacked. None of them moved.

The killer wasn't anywhere to be found. The sky darkened and the sound of the clock ticking picked up, tearing through my ears once more.

I clenched my teeth hard and tried to suppress the loud sound, but it didn't go away.

Suddenly, the clock stopped ticking and it became completely silent. From then, I only heard my own heart thudding in my ears and my heavy breaths as I paved my way across the dead bodies. Before I could make it far, I fell to the ground, losing control of my limbs.

My skin changed color and my hands deformed. *Someone* stood in front of me—the face veiled.

A stabbing pain shot through my body, the burning ache consumed me, and countless screams fled my throat while my fingers dug into the wet ground beneath me. It only took a minute for the pain to spread over my limbs, forcing them to weaken and become numb. Soon enough, I couldn't feel my own body, any part of it.

My soul was empty, as if someone had just ripped it out of me, as if someone had taken the only thing that mattered to me.

I heard a trembling growl, unsure if it came from me.

'*Your curse, Christoph*er,' a woman whispered.

45

Rebekah

"Stop," I screamed, pushing the hands away from my head while my knees scraped against the rough ground I was standing on moments ago. "I've seen enough." I placed my hand on the ground, finding my bones still within my skin and my body perfectly fine. My hair fell over my face, and I swallowed hard.

Michael moved away from me, no longer forcing *memories* into my head.

All the pain I had felt, it was raw and almost real but when I snapped into reality, the pain had gone, and my body was at ease.

I turned my head and asked Christopher, "What did they *do* to you?" I couldn't see all of it. I couldn't see what the witch had done to him—*me*—in the vision because I had escaped from it early.

I couldn't endure the pain he had felt.

The witch had done something, something terrible, but I didn't know what it was. I knew what happened to Michael, his hands were burned, he was betrayed, and his parents were killed by the witches. I assumed the witches were his family once. But Christopher, I couldn't understand.

"You don't want to know." He shook his head, masking his emotions and hiding the truth.

I heaved in a breath and sat up on the ground while recalling it all. He wasn't lying to me. He was telling the truth. The witches, they were even more dangerous and more *powerful* than anything I had ever imagined.

"She's been dreaming about you, Alpha," Michael said behind me, his words ringing in my ears like the clock.

Color drained from my face and my eyes widened as I realized he must've been able to slip into my head while giving me the visions. My neck elongated and I looked up at Christopher whose attention was on Michael. I held back my gasp.

"What?" he asked him.

No.

No.

"Nothing." I quickly rose from the ground, hoping to end it right here, before he said anything more. "I've not been dreaming about anything!" I exclaimed while standing in front of Christopher.

"She has." Michael nodded.

"About?"

My heart raced. "Nothing—" I was cut off.

"They have been rather—*vulgar* dreams," he said before I was able to stop him.

I heaved in a breath and held it back. The atmosphere in the room stiffened. I couldn't breathe. Christopher's gaze clicked to mine and soon, a smile spread over his face before he let out a soft chuckle. "I don't think you're going anywhere anytime soon, *amore*."

My cheeks turned red with embarrassment. "I didn't dream anything!" I exclaimed, hoping to save myself and my dignity along with it.

When I dreamed of Christopher, I *never* expected for him to know about them. They just came to me in a moment of weakness.

"Thank you, Michael. I'll handle this from here." He wrapped his hand back around mine and pulled me out of the room. Blood flushed to my face as we stepped away. He pushed me up against the wall and asked, "Tell me, what have you been dreaming?" His breath fanned over my cheek as I looked away.

My heart jumped in surprise. "I didn't—I didn't dream anything," I whispered.

"Liar." His grin only grew, wider and wider, as his ego stroked itself. "Tell me. I want to know."

To my left, there was a long, dark hallway and to my right, there were three doors, one of which I had just been in. No escape. I looked back, meeting his gaze. My mouth trembled.

"Only about a murderer."

He pressed himself harder against me, invading my space entirely while his hand wrapped around my jaw, just above my neck. He titled my head, and repeated, "Tell me what you have been dreaming about. I'm only curious." His eyes lowered and trailed across my lips. "Did you dream about having me inside you? Or something even better?"

My lips parted and I didn't know what to say.

"Tell me." His lips brushed against my cheek. The slightest touch making me *undone*. Heat spread to my core. My heart pounded roughly in my chest. "I promise I'll take care of it. You won't have to dream ever again." A sinister chuckle escaped his mouth. "Not on my watch."

My eyes drifted shut and I felt my insides clenching with vivid dirty thoughts of the dreams about him, about Christopher. I didn't want to dream, yet I did and here I was now, melting at his touch, submitting to his words as heat grew between my legs.

His trailed his mouth across my neck while his hand slipped underneath the shirt, fingers brushing across my skin. "Did you finish after those dreams, Rebekah?" he asked, my name rolling off his tongue just perfectly.

"Yes." I pressed my head against the wall as a whimper slipped past my lips. "I did."

"Fuck." A growl rumbled from his chest before I felt his *hardness* poking against me. I held back a small gasp. His fingers dug deeper into my back before he drew himself away from me and pulled me toward the door to the far right.

My stomach tightened. He pulled me into the room and slammed the door behind him. A loud thud echoed across the library before I heard the snap of the lock.

46

Rebekah

Thick fingers dug into my throat as Christopher leaned in closer. Whimpering breaths fled my throat and my lips parted while his free hand traveled over my back. The fabric of his shirt pressed against mine. His gaze fell to my face, eyes brimming with sheer, wild desire, only growing with every passing second.

"You're not the saint I thought you were, Rebekah." In silence, *only* his voice filled my ears and echoed through the thick walls of the library he had dragged me into. "All along I felt guilty for wanting you."

"At least you felt something." I spat out without a second thought and then realized I should've sealed my mouth.

His fingers tightened on my throat, forcing me to choke on my breath. "Don't fuck with me." He tugged me forward, closer to his mouth and he remained merely a few inches away.

My chest tightened at his presence. There were things I had *felt*, knowing well I shouldn't have. I drew my eyes away from his mouth and looked up at him, only finding his lust growing. He neared and pressed himself roughly against me as the back of my legs collided with something hard behind me. I didn't dare look back.

"Alright. What do you want me to say? That I have feelings for you? That I dreamed more than once about you? Or that I have been craving your touch." I sucked in a sharp breath, realizing once more I should have kept quiet. "I'm never going to say any of that."

"You just did." He laughed, pressing himself closer. "But that's not what I want to know," he continued, shaking his head while his voice lowered to a warm, tormenting whisper.

My knees weakened and with a little push, I fell back on the couch near a table. He quickly reached over me, his hand still on my throat, holding me before I ran. His hips brushed against mine. The promising heat returned. I clenched my teeth, holding myself together but no matter how hard I tried, my body responded the way it wanted to.

There was no control.

"What then?" My eyes lowered to his chest. His body was hard with arousal and even harder when I trailed my hand under his shirt, closer to his growing thickness. "That I want you." I fed his ears with exactly what he wanted to hear from me. "In more ways than one." My fingers curled at the waistband of his pants. His skin—*he* was warm.

"Yes," he hummed, and then growled under his breath before he swooped in for a rough kiss.

My senses reeled. I wrapped my hand around the back of his neck, pulling him deeper, sucking him in like a succubus in need. He choked me harder, forcing me to part my mouth before his tongue plunged in, tasting me entirely. My pussy throbbed and wetness pooled beneath me.

I drew his pants down, needing him, as he pulled my shirt down, baring my breasts and my chest. My nipples turned into hard pebbles, brushing against his chest as he trailed his mouth to my neck and then my sweet spot where I had been craving him more than usual. Like electricity, it pounded through my veins. My whole world twisted and turned.

His hot breath and the sharpness of his teeth brushed against my neck, sent shivers down my spine. I wasn't sure what it was, but I couldn't get enough of it.

I turned my head, my eyes fluttering shut as he continued to my nip at my skin. His fingers clenched on my hips as I rubbed myself over him.

"Bite me," I moaned, arching my back ever so slightly. My cunt throbbed like never before. A new burning heightened. It was different and it stretched all over my body.

"No." His chest shuddered as he growled before he drew his mouth lower to my chest. A hot tongue lapped against my nipple and the sensation pulsated between my legs. I bit down hard on my lips, moaning and groaning in silence as he twisted and played with my breasts, tormenting me with such pleasure I had only *dreamed* of.

He moved his hand to my pants, ripping them from my body and another hand reached up to my shirt, unbuttoning and baring me before I could even take a breath.

The walls closed around me. I saw nothing and I heard nothing except his heavy breathing against mine. He didn't remove my underwear, instead he pressed his hand against my quivering pussy and watched the white and red cloth turn dark with my wetness.

His fingers teased me, spreading over my pussy, caressing me till I lifted my hips and begged for more.

My arm reached forward, my hand nearly wrapping around his but before I could, he yanked it aside and flattened it over my stomach while something even wilder grew in the back of his eyes.

"What's wrong, *amore*? You want everything *your* way? Tough luck on that. I'll play with you *my* way, whichever way that is," he hissed, rubbing his fingers over my covered pussy even harder.

My insides tightened. I groaned in pleasure and closed my legs, but he drew them even wider over the plush couch. My brows furrowed and my hands clenched the cushion as I watched my own body give up control.

"Oh, just fuck me." I squirmed, reaching the end of my patience.

"Where is the fun in that?" he asked, pressing his index finger against my wet opening. My underwear was soaked, and he enjoyed watching it. "I'd rather have you beg for it."

"Never."

At my response, his eyes darkened, and he slipped his hand inside my underwear, his fingers against my bare clit. Sweet, warm sensations drove me to the edge. I raised my leg over the couch, spreading it wide as my heart burned in my chest.

His large hand clasped my throat. I released a trembling breath along with a stream of moans.

"Beg, *amore*." He pressured me, danger in his voice. I sealed my mouth shut. *Not again.* His fingers quickened, rubbing violently against my clit. My cunt was throbbing, needing to be filled. The hardness of his cock brushed against my thigh. *He* needed me. "Tell me what you want or I swear there will be nothing filling your hole tonight," he warned, turning his attention to my face.

He lowered his mouth to my neck and clamped his mouth once more on the same exact sweet spot. My pussy wept. Countless moans left my throat. My body ached. Every nerve in my body shook.

"Christopher," I breathed, even my voice was tense.

"Yes. Tell me."

He softly pressed his finger at my entrance, teasing me to the edge, knowing I needed more than just a finger.

Fuck.

In no time, I conformed to his demands and found myself breaking through the control. "Fill me up, *please.*" My breaths were ragged. "I want you—please. I don't care about anything you do. *Fuck.* I just *need* you right now."

My legs wrapped around his waist, curling at his back as he removed his fingers from my underwear. He drew back from my neck, and I whined at the remaining sensation. My head grew hot and heavy.

"That wasn't hard, was it?" An evil smile spread across his face as he ran his hands over my body. His predatory gaze fell over me.

A gentle knock fell on the door, catching me in surprise. I quickly sat up and covered my breasts while Christopher's head turned. His nostrils flared as he sensed *someone.* Another knock, and then another one, getting rougher.

"Fuck," Christopher whispered, shaking his head and lifting himself off me.

I had barely finished.

No.

"Who is it?" I glanced at him; eyes wide.

"It's my brother and he's not going to leave me alone," he growled and grabbed my clothes, handing them to me.

My face flushed red, and I stood before putting my clothes on. At my acceptance, I was denied. *Great.* This was going to be a long day of torment.

47

REBEKAH

"Come with me." His hand stretched as I fastened the last button of my shirt. His brother was still outside, waiting for us to leave the library but I assumed Christopher had different intentions.

I took his hand, and he led me up the stairs. The smell of books, paper and wood crawled up to my nose. It was a great sight. The library was massive, bigger than any other I had ever seen, and it was filled with knowledge. There was barely any dust on the covers or the shelves, which meant it was being well kept.

"Where are you taking me?" I asked, my voice hoarse. Just moments ago, I was going to get what I wanted—not anymore. My desires heightened uncontrollably. The heat in my sex only grew while something within me became frustrated with the fact that we were interrupted. "Why don't you ask your brother to just go away?" I chewed on my lower lip, waiting for his response in the silence.

"Because he won't," Christopher replied seconds later.

"Why?" I furrowed my brows in confusion.

"Because I've done the same to him more than once. He's not forgiving and I've no energy to deal with him right now." His fingers tightened around my wrist.

He led me deeper into the library before coming to a halt in front of an old wooden door. With a slight push, he opened the door and there was nothing except for darkness ahead.

My chest clenched. *Was he going to kill me now?*

I followed him inside. A sliver of light appeared, showing another descending staircase, going even deeper than where we were now. *Underground?*

I swallowed hard and continued walking. The walls were tight, solid, but a few roaches and cobwebs could be spotted. I tried not to think too much. Once we were down the stairs, he took me across a long *tunnel* before stopping by another door.

"What is this place?" My eyes were wide, swarming everywhere.

"Tunnels," he responded, unlocking the door in front of me with a key from his pocket. "My grandfather built them. They spread through the whole city."

I remembered Faye's words then. She had told me about them and had even taken me to one of them. It was still a confusing sight.

"Why would he build them?"

We walked through the door and appeared in an old office room that had been untouched. There was a small bookshelf in the corner, a leather chair, and a wide wooden table with several papers scattered across the surface.

"More than a hundred years ago, werewolves weren't safe. They were getting killed left and right by the witches that took it upon themselves to kill everyone that had *sin* in their blood, the shifters," he explained, his back faced to me while his hand reached for the bookshelf, finding something.

I winced at his words, remembering my little sister. She had told me something exactly the same. It was the Halloween theme of her high school party, and it was based on lore.

It wasn't *lore*.

"But why? Why would the witches kill your kind?"

"Long story short, they enjoy it—" He turned around. The bookshelf moved forward, opening like a door. "Just as much as I'm going to enjoy you in my room." I caught a glimpse of his wicked tongue as he smiled and grabbed me, taking me up the stairs and straight into his bedroom.

It hadn't been long since I had left here.

And I was back again.

Wrinkles appeared in my head in confusion. *How was it even possible?* Just a minute ago, we were in the library that was on the ground floor of the place and now, we were back here.

"What about your brother?" I glanced at Christopher as he drew the curtains shut, blocking out any moonlight.

"He's not allowed in my wing. Someone will stop him."

I folded my arms across my chest. "You hate your brother, don't you?"

"Yes." Christopher nodded, agreeing with me. A small frown curled on his lips as he returned to me.

"Why?"

"You're asking too many questions."

"Because I want to know—" I paused, thinking once more before the words left my throat. "About you."

His gaze fell over mine and he grinned in satisfaction. Hands rose to my shoulders where he brushed away my hair. "Watching you accept your feelings for me delights me."

"I'm not accepting." *Maybe I was.*

"Yes, you are, and you did."

The images of the visions Michael had shown me were still in my head, reappearing each second. I couldn't brush them away. The hair over my skin rose in fear from the witches. I had known nothing about them until those glimpses.

"What did the witches do to you?"

Christopher frowned, and his gaze tore away from mine. A hint of discomfort appeared when I asked another question. I was curious. "Nothing," he said in a low whisper before turning away from me. I lifted a brow, waiting for more, but there was nothing except for silence.

"Tell me." I neared him.

I still wasn't sure what the need was to force those visions into my head, but he wanted to show me something.

"What did I see?" I asked, not stopping anytime soon. If he didn't want me to know, he shouldn't have shown it to me. "Did they take something from you? Is that why you're scared of them?" I asked slowly, eyebrows furrowing at his silence.

"I'm not scared of them," he scoffed, shaking his head while clear fear grew behind his voice.

I folded my arms over my chest once more and gave a stare till he told me the truth. He knew *everything* about me, and I didn't have to tell him anything since he had his people informing him day and night. I didn't know anything about him asides from the fact he was a werewolf.

He turned back to me, his eyes dark.

"They took my wolf," he responded after another long moment of silence.

I grew confused as I tried to make sense of it. I had been here long enough to know what that meant. "So, you're not a werewolf?"

"I am," he rumbled, inching closer to me. His tall frame hovered over mine. I swallowed hard. If there was something that could make Christopher quake, then it was definitely going to terrify me. "It's just that I cannot shift any more. The witches stole my wolf, they have locked him away from making any connection with me simply because I was tired of their people running in my city. So, when I killed their witches, they took my wolf in return," he explained, and I understood a part of it.

"Oh…" I trailed off, my eyes wide. "That's bad?"

"Yes, but it's been a while since *it* happened. While the loss of my wolf still hurts me, I know he's somewhere still inside and I know something that's going to trigger him to surface." By now, he was standing only an inch away from me, his body heat meddling with mine.

I swallowed hard in fear of what he was about to say—I knew it wasn't going to be good.

Faye had told me most of the things about werewolves and the way they were connected to their gifted wolf. In the wild, they could shift, run, and attack whenever they wanted and that was their strength.

But if Christopher didn't have any connection with his wolf, it meant he didn't have enough strength either.

He was *weak*.

His eyes flicked to me, lust returning to the depths of them as the corner of his mouth curled into a mischievous grin. I knew from the bottom of my heart this wasn't going to be good.

"Don't tell me I'm going to be the reason that you're going break through some curse the witches put on you." My heart was thudding. I knew he could get anything he wanted.

He got *me*.

"Well, you got it right, *amore*." His eyes glinted with delight. I lined my lips straight, waiting to know if I needed to be *killed* in order to break his curse. "Although, I'm not entirely sure, but you could be a loophole to breaking the witches curse."

"Are you going to kill me?" I lifted my head.

He chuckled in response. "Of course not. I wouldn't dare even harm you." His warm hand returned to my face, pressing against the side of my cheek.

"You already did—many times," I reminded him.

"Those were—" He looked up, taking a moment to think. "Just a few instances. I'm trying to be a better person—" I gave him another stare and cocked my brow at his own remarks. "At least for you."

"You killed someone."

"It wasn't you. Why are you getting worried?" he snapped back.

I sighed, lowering my head, and shaking it. I guess I had to now lie in the grave I dug for myself.

His hands lifted to my shoulders, and he leaned inward. The taut expression on his face softened as he met my eyes. "I'm not going to hurt you, *amore*. I promise." For a moment, he sounded as if he was everything I had ever wished for, the man of my dreams—the man *in* my dreams.

I stiffened and took a deep breath. "What do you think *I* have to do to break your curse?" I changed back to the topic we were talking about earlier.

"Nothing." He shook his head and leaned closer, brushing his lips over my cheek. The pounding in my heart grew. "All I have to do is bite you and mate with you."

"What?" My eyes grew wide, and I stopped breathing.

"It's nothing bad, *amore*. Just a little bite to claim you. It would complete the mating bond. My scent would linger over you at all times.

No one would be able to touch you or come near you," he explained, his tone possessive.

"Mating bond?" I blinked. I knew what it was—Faye had told me and so had his little brother, but I didn't know that I would have to *seal* my fate with someone forever—someone like Christopher. It was terrifying in its own way to even think of it.

"You're my mate. I'll claim you one day or another. The earlier, the better." He slipped his hand behind my neck and tucked away the hair from my shoulder to my back before his mouth trailed down to my neck, back to the sweet spot that needed to be touched. "Just here."

"Oh." I breathed out while my eyes fluttered shut.

"I *need* to," he whispered, his hot breath fanning my neck. "I'd bite you and you'd bear my knot, completing the mating. You'd become just mine. No one would ever touch you or dare to bat an eye at you. All of you—" His hands raced across my waist and lower to my hips. "—would be mine then. And I'd be *yours*."

"Your knot?" I furrowed my brows.

"It's going to be the greatest pleasure you've ever felt, *amore*."

It was a sweet melody to my ears.

48

Rebekah

Raw heat grew inside me. It settled between my legs and didn't disappear, even when my house came into view. My legs remained closed and every muscle in my body tightened.

I didn't want to know what he had meant earlier but I was dying to open a dictionary and find the meaning of it or even worse, going onto the web and finding lucid details about it.

About knotting.

"Stay home for as long as you can." He parked the car at the back of my house and turned off the bright headlights. It was dark and the next day was only minutes away.

"Why do I have to stay home?" I glanced at him while holding my thoughts aside for the moment.

"Because it's not safe for you to wander around outside without anyone. And I don't want to send Michael to stalk you repeatedly. It's better if you stay indoors or with your friends," he explained, and I tried not to focus on the moment we had shared earlier.

He was so close to taking me to his bed and railing me till I was out of breath. But something stopped him, and it was the urge to claim me right then and there. I still needed time to understand what he wanted to do with me—*all the things he wanted to do to me.*

"I'll try," I said honestly.

His lips pursed. "If I see you out of your home without any reason, trust me, I'll chain you to my bed and the next time you'll be seeing your family will be on New Year's Eve and even then for five minutes," he warned, frustration tinging his tone.

I grinned to myself and turned to the door, unlocking it. "I might as well do exactly that," I whispered to him while stepping out of the car.

"Stay home," he repeated once more. "And if you find anyone odd lingering, it's a witch. Call me."

"Alright, Dad." I slammed the car door shut. A cold breeze brushed over my body, and I shivered involuntarily.

He rolled down the window of his car. His left hand remained on the steering wheel while his eyes swarmed over me, desire hidden behind his controlling self. "I'll be coming to claim what's mine. *Soon.* You have your time. I better not hear anything I don't want to hear," he said, his tone rough and his expression stiff.

I pressed my thighs closer, brushing off any images of him with me, naked, and earlier in the library. "Don't try to get yourself killed."

His surprised gaze followed me. "I didn't hear that. Could you repeat yourself, *amore*? Did I just hear *concern*?" he teased me.

"Goodnight," I mumbled, turning around and walking farther away from his car while his taunting chuckles rang in my ears all the way till I reached the back door to my house. Only then did I hear his car engine running and drifting out of the block.

I sighed with relief and stepped inside my house.

A couple of tears streamed down my face, but I brushed them away before my parents caught a glimpse of it. I watched my little sister, Rose, listen to my parents as they tried to explain to her why they were parting from each other. She was still young, unable to understand they were going to part forever instead of just a couple of weeks or months.

Dad had his bags packed. They were three suitcases set in the corner, near the door, waiting to leave. He was going to catch the flight tomorrow, in the morning, that would take him to his hometown where he'd spend some time with his extended family.

The papers were finalized—I was holding onto them.

My parents were divorced.

There was a lump growing in my throat, taking away my breaths and my voice. My chest felt tight with tension and fear of the unknown. I had spent my whole life seeing my parents together, loving each other and now, they were probably not going to see each other for a very long time.

"When will I be able to see you?" Rose asked Dad, her eyes filled with tears that were gushing down her cheeks as she tried to understand.

"Anytime, baby. Whenever you want to. I'm not going to be far, just a three-hour drive away and I'll come by every weekend just to see you," he said, picking her up from the ground and placing her on the seat beside him. "Nothing will change between us. I'll be still here for you, just a little bit farther away."

There had been a lot of tears and arguments. I had fought with my parents over the past few days, ever since I'd found the signed divorce papers delivered in the mail. Since then, my thoughts were consumed, and I was furious.

It wasn't my place to be, but I still was.

I wished Dad didn't have to leave. We barely had spent any time with him after his sickness and now he was going to live hundreds of miles away from us, somewhere where we couldn't even reach him.

"I'll miss you tons!" She hugged him for a long minute before Mom suggested Dad sleep with her before his flight tomorrow morning.

It was going to be a hard night for Rose.

Mom switched off the lights in the living room when Dad walked upstairs with Rose, putting her to sleep. I sighed and glanced away from the divorce papers. *What even went wrong? Who stopped loving here?*

"It's going to be alright. Don't worry. Wake up early." She placed her hand on my shoulder and my heart ached just a little more.

"Of course, Mom." I nodded.

She walked back into her room and soon, there was nothing in the house asides from silence. Tomorrow was going to be worse. We wouldn't be able to listen to Dad and his loud television. He was still here, alive, but he wasn't going to be *here* anymore.

The silence crept into my ears and invaded my thoughts. I tried to think of anything else but couldn't. I felt worse for Dad since Mom no longer wanted him, even when he still loved her.

It was just too much for Mom to handle.

She wanted a new start.

My phone buzzed on the table beside the papers, catching my attention. I picked up Faye's call. "Hey," I whispered, wiping my cheeks dry.

"How did it go?" she asked, concerned.

"Terrible. Rose is devastated."

"What about you?"

"I think I'll be fine." I pressed my hand against my head, hoping to fall asleep soon and wake up early to drop Dad at the airport but at the same time, I couldn't stop thinking about how happy my parents were before everything happened.

"Sure?"

"No." I shook my head, changing my words. "I don't think I can sleep alone tonight or even here. Can I come to yours?" The moment I thought about going to my bed and falling asleep, the hair over my skin rose and I grew even more worried.

"Yeah, of course!"

I stood up from my seat and hunched over the cabinet beside the kitchen. Grabbing a bottle of wine, I tucked it inside my bag and said, "I should warn you. I've had a couple of drinks."

"Oh." She was surprised. "Do you want me to come pick you up?"

"No. I'll call a cab. That's alright," I whispered before heading out quietly from the front door and stepping in the cold.

"See you in ten!"

I placed my phone inside the bag with the wine and locked the door from outside. It was half past ten and it was cold but leaving the house allowed me to breathe finally. Just as I turned around and walked down the street, I found something better than a cab waiting for me.

"Well, well, the devil never stops working..." I trailed off, reaching the passenger door of the car. "Were you here the whole evening?" I asked him while buckling my belt.

"No. Just since ten," Michael replied. "The Alpha wants to make sure you fall asleep without having any witches surrounding you—"

I stopped him before he could continue. "And since you're a witch, you can sense when one is around, can't you?" From the corner of my eyes, I caught a glimpse of his burned hand wrapped around the steering wheel under the moonlight.

The witches had *tortured* him.

"Yes." He smiled sharply.

"I want to go to my friends. Please, take me?"

I couldn't think about Christopher right now, not after finding and learning about the wicked details about what the mating bond was and what it required to complete it in the werewolf world. Most of the details were in a small werewolf handbook Faye had given me last week, which was also when I last saw him.

After marking me, he would knot—*inside* me and breed me, completing the mating bond, which may help his wolf come to the surface.

I still wasn't sure.

He gave me time—plenty of it—and space to let me make my decision. He was waiting for me to accept *him* as *my* mate as only then could he mark me. Before that, he vowed not to touch me or seduce me in any way.

It was all up to me now and I didn't know what to do.

49

REBEKAH

Michael dropped me straight to Faye's house without any questions asked. "You can go back to Christopher. I'll be fine here. Her parents are home as well," I told him while stepping out of the car.

He agreed and drove off, cutting his stalking shift short for tonight. I mean, there wasn't much threat here for me. No one asides from Christopher and his own people had stalked or approached me. If I needed protection, it was from him.

I placed my hand over my head and quickly walked into the building before the rain got any heavier. Some parts of my hair got wet while the rest of me was still dry. I entered the floor and headed up to Faye's apartment. She lived with her parents, like the most of us, but she was planning to move out soon, just as she was done getting her law degree.

I was greeted with her parents, Mr. and Mrs. Leonard who were still awake. They were watching television when I let myself in through the front door as I had the key to it at all times.

Before I could say more, Faye rushed out of her bedroom and dragged me back to hers. I'd had a couple drinks before coming here and neither of her parents were aware.

"Are you drunk?" she asked, eyeing me from top to bottom.

"No!" I exclaimed, shaking my head, and resting my bag on her bed. "Why would you think that?" I felt a bit tipsy but that was all. A few drinks couldn't get me drunk.

"Your eyes are red."

"My parents got divorced, Faye. Of course my eyes are going to be red," I reminded her with a faint chuckle. Slowly, this all was turning into a bag bad joke.

"Oh, shit, yeah. You feeling okay?" She was concerned to say the least.

"Yes, I'm going to be fine. I just don't want to talk about my parents or their divorce. Tell me something else—anything else. Are you dating someone? How's law school? When are you going to graduate?" I quickly asked while slumping down on the couch beside her bed.

I just didn't want to think about my parents, at least for one night.

Her eyes followed me. "Soon. How did you get here? Didn't you just leave like five minutes ago?" She folded her arms across her chest, wondering what speed got me here.

"I didn't drive!" I exclaimed, throwing my hands in the air. "It was Michael, he was outside my home and I told him to give me a ride here. He drives very well."

"Why was he outside?"

"To-to make sure I don't—" My brows closed as I tried to think of a reason why Michael was outside my home. "I don't know exactly but I think he was there to protect me. It's a long story. You don't want to hear it. I don't even want to hear it again."

I didn't want to think of Christopher either. He rose different emotions within me, and it was difficult. He just held all this influence over me, and it was hard to break through it. With my previous relationship with Adam, I didn't really have to think much about everything—what lipstick I was wearing, what underwear I had on, did I shower, and all those silly little things.

It was *easy* with Adam and after he cheated on me, it was even easier. I could just go to him whenever I wanted to whine, eat, or have sex and he wouldn't have a problem.

With Christopher, everything was hard. I had to be cautious with everything *I* did, even though he was the evil one here.

It was like I craved his attention—*him*.

"This is some good fucking cookies and cream," I mumbled while letting the ice cream melt in my mouth.

Faye watched me as I shoved another spoonful of ice cream down my throat. "That's the second tub, Bek. You're going to get diabetes if you continue at this pace," she joked, taking some of the ice cream on her little spoon.

"So are you," I smiled at her and swallowed the cold ice cream.

It was the only thing that rested my mind, asides from the series Faye played on the television. We had been in here, cooped up with each other for more than just a few hours. She had found my wine bottle and replaced it with an ice cream shake, forbidding me to drink on a weekday or get drunk.

"I'm going to go check on Mom and Dad and find something else to eat asides from ice cream." She jumped off the bed and wandered outside the room.

I remained on the bed, the blanket draped over my legs and chest while I had a bucket of ice cream resting on my stomach.

The phone on the side of the bed rang. I stopped shoving ice cream down my throat and quickly jumped up when I saw the caller ID flashing on my screen.

"Fuck. Now?" It was the middle of the night. *What did he want with me now?* He knew I had to be sleeping at this point.

I wiped my mouth clean and waited for a few more rings. I grew more hesitant to pick up the call but just before it got missed, I picked it up and said, "Hello."

"Took you a while to pick up," Christopher said, his voice dreamy and doing all the wrong things to my body.

I cleared my throat and replied, "I was eating."

"Is that so?" He knew whenever I lied or had any kind of bluff in my voice. "I spoke with Michael. Is something happening with your family? He told me you seemed upset, *amore*," he asked, concern lacing his voice.

"Yeah, my parents got divorced," I instantly responded without even giving it a thought. It was only after that I realized I shouldn't have said that.

"Oh, that's terrible. Are you alright?"

"I am—now." I nodded to myself while looking outside the slightly opened door. Faye was going to walk in any second with food and I needed to cut the call by then.

"Good girl. You'll be okay," he said, sounding a bit soft. It was hard to believe he'd have any concern for me without a reason, but he did. "Let me know if you need anything."

Yes, you.

"I'll be fine." I leaned back on the bed with only his deep voice ringing in my ears. Only if I could be with him, pour my heart out and forget everything. But I didn't want to act desperate or needy. I did once and I found him killing someone in his courtyard.

It was starting to make a lot more sense about his reasonings—why he needed to kill and what he did behind the curtains. Those visions helped, a lot.

I still needed a little more time and he was waiting for that—for me to accept him, to let him in, to let him mark me. Without my acceptance, he wasn't even going to get close to me, and this past week had been a torture alone.

I guess I did enjoy all those times he'd kidnapped me.

"I'll be going to sleep soon," I whispered, pressing my legs together and forgetting about all the things he *could* do with me if I wanted him to.

"I could fuck you on that bed you're lying on."

Suddenly, all those thoughts returned, and I sighed, closing my eyes. "I'm at my friends," I told him as my brows furrowed in disgust with the image of Christopher taking me on Faye's bed.

"Don't care. I'll still fuck you on her bed, *amore*," he said, his voice so intense it rose the feelings I had been trying to bury.

"All words, no game," I replied with a smile playing over my lips.

"All you have to do is tell me what I want to hear. I wouldn't even hesitate. You know that," he continued, without taking a breath or letting me take one.

I ran my fingers through my hair and asked, "If I don't tell you what you want to hear, what then?"

He growled in warning; it was deep and low before I heard silence from him. I let out a soft breath while still waiting for his response.

A growl wasn't one.

"Then goodnight."

50

REBEKAH

"Alicia just had her baby. Oh my God!" Faye exclaimed at the top of her lungs, thrusting herself inside her room. Her cousin, Alicia, had been pregnant for a very long time and she had finally given birth.

I drew my attention from the room and looked up at her. Excitement displayed all over her face. "Really? She has?" My eyes widened a little.

"Yes! Get up and get ready, there is a celebration this afternoon."

I yawned once more. It was early in the morning, and I couldn't find myself getting away from Faye's bed. I had been crashing at her parents' apartment for more than three days. I hadn't found the courage to go back home ever since Dad left. Rose and I had dropped him off at the airport and said our goodbyes to him.

Going back home to find it partly empty was heartbreaking. I didn't want to step inside Dad's room and find all his belongings gone. He had reached his hometown a few days ago and had been texting us all day and night, yet that wasn't enough.

I missed him terribly; I missed my whole family.

"Do I need to go?" I asked Faye while burying myself deeper under her sheets.

"Shut up and get your ass off the bed. I'm not going to be depressed with you and I'm not going to let you be depressed for another moment. You're going to go back home, make amends with your Mom, and live there," she scolded me while dragging the sheets off my body.

I pouted and shook my head. "I'm not ready yet."

"You're never going to be ready. Your Dad is just a couple of hours away from here. Stop acting as if he dumped you or something. And your Mom also needs you. You're not a child. I'm done babying you!" She sounded a bit more than frustrated at my current situation.

I hadn't done anything these past three days expect for drinking the wine I had stolen from my mom's cabinet before leaving and watching old videos of my parents and photos of when they had gotten married. Never in my whole life did I think they would ever separate.

Now they had.

I somewhat felt guilty about it. If I hadn't given the money to Mom to clear Dad's debts, maybe they would have still been together. The debts would've tied them for a couple of years more. Mom wouldn't have asked for a divorce, and we would all be living together.

"Alright. Fine! It was just a few days." I lined my lips straight and stood up from the bed before all of Faye's excitement wore off. "Did you get any pictures of the baby?" I asked her, changing the topic.

"Yes." She grinned and pulled out her phone, showing me the newborn's pictures her cousin had sent her.

"Oh, it's beautiful," I whispered. "How's Alicia?"

"She's doing perfect. Werewolves heal a lot quicker than—humans."

I tried to not act surprised. "Wow." I swiped to another photo where the baby boy was found perfectly healthy and in his mom's arms. "Isn't it too early to throw a welcoming party for the baby? I mean—I doubt Alicia can even walk right now."

"There is nothing too early. And she can walk, Bek! It's not anything big. Just a small party with her close family and friends to see the baby." Faye squealed in excitement while fisting her hands. "I can't wait!"

"Close family and friends. I don't need to go." I flashed a mischievous smile at her while repeating her own words.

"Shut up. If I'm going, so are you, so go home, talk to your mom, change out of your pajamas and take a shower for God's sake. I'll pick you up by one and we'll go from there," she explained while taking a whiff of my terrible scent. "Oh, the Alpha hosts these parties at his residence so you can see your *boyfriend* there and maybe come back to your senses."

Oh. That was certainly piquing my interest.

"Christopher is not my boyfriend," I lowered my voice to almost a whisper.

"Mhm." She rolled her eyes and turned away from me.

"What was that?" My lips parted and my jaw hung at her response. "Did you just roll your eyes at me?"

"One o'clock, Bek!"

The afternoon came too soon. One blink, I was home and another one, I was in Faye's car, being driven to Christopher's house downtown. Today was going to be real difficult.

"I didn't see you on the list, *amore*." Just as I took a sip of the orange juice, I heard his voice behind me and his soft breathing trailing down my neck.

I turned to him and offered him a smile, more than what he could do. "I came with Faye. I hope you don't mind."

He lowered his gaze to the long slit going down my chest. I had worn a floral dress; it was the only thing I could come up with at last minute. The sleeves were short, but the neckline was a bit too long.

Just perfect.

"I don't."

"I didn't know you were so into having welcoming parties of babies," I said, creeping closer to him till there was barely any distance left.

It was a fairly small, quiet gathering just as Faye had told me. Alicia was with her baby boy who still had to be named. People were giving gifts to the newborn, eating cake, and then leaving. Meanwhile, I was waiting till *someone* had spotted me and he did.

"I don't. She my cousin's wife, therefore, I suggested this."

I didn't hear anything he'd said. My mind was blurred. I could only feel and hear my heart racing in his presence. It had been more than a week. He left me that night wanting more, and I still hadn't gotten anything—neither had he. His answer was pending.

I was still unsure if I wanted to live with this man forever.

"How are you feeling now? I heard you haven't been home in days," Christopher asked, walking with me. His hands were neatly behind his back and nowhere near my body.

It frustrated me how he could keep such distance. "I haven't."

"Why is that, *amore*?"

I shrugged, not knowing the true answer to it. "I don't know."

I watched the newborn's parents seated with the baby with Faye sitting beside Alicia and playing with the barely one-day-old child. It was a beautiful sight. The baby had just been born and he had been receiving love from everyone.

My view was obstructed by a large body. Raising my head, I glanced up at Christopher who had a questioning expression on his face. "Is there something you want to tell me?" he asked.

I sighed. "Yes." My lips parted, my eyes flickered back and forth before I continued, "I want to tell you something but not here. Maybe somewhere else."

He gave me a quiet stare for a moment before nodding and heading outside the room. We walked up the grand staircase, walking past a few random strangers before he took me straight into his room. The hallway to his room was dark and empty. I felt my own breaths echoing in my ears as I followed him into his bedroom.

He closed the door behind me and the lump in my throat grew.

"Tell me now." He stood in front of me, tall and awaiting.

My pulse spiked. My thoughts scattered everywhere. I had no clue what I even wanted to tell him, but I couldn't resist being alone with him after spending this past week without him.

When I didn't say anything, he asked, "Did you make your decision?"

"No," I quickly replied before clicking my eyes to him. "Why do you need me to agree to this *thing*? Why can't we just get along and see where it goes, instead of making a decision that could be changed anytime? People change their minds day and night. What if you wake up and decide you're obsessed with someone else who isn't me?"

What Christopher had asked from me was something I *couldn't* agree to. From everything that I've learned, mating was tying souls, it was even deeper than marriage in his world. I couldn't understand why he wanted to *only* mate with me. *What's the worst that could happened if we just explored instead of making a life-and-death commitment?*

"Because it matters to me. There has been a part of me waiting for my mate for years and years. I was cursed by the witches in one way, and I assumed, somehow, they might've taken away my ability to find a mate as well." He heaved in a breath and stepped forward. His brows collected and the expression on his face tightened. I swallowed hard, welcoming the foreseeable rage. "Everything changed when I found you and it didn't matter how vicious you got those days, I only wanted you. And when I had you, I was fulfilled until last week, till I realized it will only take moments for you to flee from me. I don't want you to run, not without a real reason—"

I cut him off. "Killing is a reason."

"I'll stop killing if that's what you want, Rebekah." He neared me, and with every step I backed up till I was against the wall again. "Tell me if that's what you want and I'll stop this instant. You'll not find blood on my hands after today, if that convinces you how much I *need* you." His voice was rough but clear in my head.

My nerves tightened and a sinister chill ran down my spine while knowing what was coming next.

"I'm not telling you to love me," he rasped. "*Let me.*"

51

Rebekah

At his vulnerability, I found myself melting. Unspoken words found their way to my ears. I heard everything I *wanted* to hear. He groaned into my mouth, grasping my hips, and pulling me closer to him. I wrapped myself around him, my fingers slipped into his hair and his teeth dug into my lower lip.

My breathing became uneven, staggered. My eyes remained closed. My dress rose up to my thighs and my legs folded beside his. Sweat built at the back of my neck. My chest rose heavily and dropped. The slick, sloppy kisses lasted longer than I thought they would. When out of breath, I pulled my mouth away from his and found his golden eyes burning deep into mine.

Suddenly, there was nothing more I wanted except to live in this moment, over and over again. The pull was strong, and it finally made sense why I was being dragged to him repeatedly.

I drew my hand away from his hair. Heavy breaths escaped my parted lips. Blood pumped in my ears as my heartbeat quickened.

"How many people have you killed?" I asked, rasping, and eager to know.

His fingers dug into my back, he forced me forward, over him. "More than you can imagine, *amore*." He didn't give me an exact answer. "Doesn't matter anymore." He paused, slipping one hand into my hair, and pulling back a fist of it. My neck stretched. "You're willingly sitting over my dick. I don't think you want to know anything I've done but only what I'm going to do to you."

He pulled aside the collar of my dress, exposing my barely covered chest and nuzzled into my neck. His bristled jaw brushed against my neck before I found his mouth kissing my sensitive flesh. A terrible, frustrating ache spread through my body like a wildfire. My nerves tightened. He pulled me forward and restrained me over his lap.

My underwear brushed through his pants; my sex drenched now. I rode him and felt his cock stiffen in his pants. I moaned at the rising tension in my body. For more than a week, I had been craving his touch and now, he was here, *touching* me. The pressure between my legs only rose.

He closed his mouth around my nipple while wrapping his hand around the other one. I bit down on my lip, arching my back as my sex pressed against his roughly, nearing a release. His sharp teeth pricked at my nub, and I whimpered while my entire body trembled in pleasure.

Golden eyes met mine. "Tell me you're mine, tell me what I want to hear." He parted his mouth from my breast while rubbing them gently with his hands and occasionally pinching my nipples. He lowered his mouth to the middle of my chest and placed wet kisses all over my neck, driving me crazy.

I pursed my lips shut and my eyes rolled to the back of my head. When he received no response, he dug his fingers into my hips and gripped me roughly.

"Tell me what I want to hear." His voice grew wild, different.

My heart jumped as he stood from the couch and tossed me onto the bed. The mattress bounced underneath me while my sex clenched hard.

His large body frame came over mine and his hand went straight over my throat, fingers wrapping tightly around it, constricting my breathing. His eyes flashed red. Every muscle in my body quivered as I looked up at him.

"Tell me, Rebekah, or I swear you'll watch me as I fuck someone else in front of you." He lowered himself to me and pushed my legs apart. "I have been patient enough. A fucking week was more than enough. Wasn't it?"

"Yes," I choked out.

His grip on my throat loosened. "Good—"

"I'm *yours*."

The expression over his face changed in the span of a few seconds. The gold in his irises returned and the red disappeared as if it was never there. A grin spread over his face, and before my eyes, I saw him entirely change—everything about him.

He looped his arm underneath my head and his mouth neared mine. "I want to hear that again." He waited, a different excitement in his voice.

My legs trembled lightly under him. "I'm yours, Christopher," I whispered, accepting him and losing myself.

My body was on fire—I was on fire, and I could not keep running away from something that was already written in my fate. I wanted him, no matter how many times I had been denying the ever-growing feelings I had for him.

His thumb ran across my lower lip while his eyes darkened as I repeated the words he had been *dying* to hear. "Fuck." Before placing his lips against mine, he mumbled under his breath. "You've no idea what you've done to me."

As he kissed me, I slipped my hands under his shirt and closed my eyes. Muffled moans of pleasure vibrated through my throat. There was nothing more beyond him. My legs curled around his waist. He kissed me with delight and gently, as if he was savoring every taste and touch before he began spreading bites over my lips and then lower to my chest.

Needy, I thrust my hips toward his, wanting him inside me instantly, needing a release. Heat rushed straight into my core and settled there, aching.

He pulled the sleeves of the dress down and pushed the hem of the dress up to my waist before pulling my underwear down to my ankles. He squeezed my breast in his hand and I moaned when his mouth fell between my legs, nearing my drenched pussy.

"Just fuck me, Christopher," I begged, arching while gripping his shirt roughly.

"Shh," he whispered while running a finger down my slit while his hand remained tight around my breast, flicking my nipple. "I need to make sure you can bear me, my knot. I want your pussy fucking dripping." His tongue lapped against my sensitive folds, and my toes curled.

Without a warning, he pushed in his large fingers at once, curling them inside, stroking my sweet spot and forcing me to scream for him. My muscles tightened instantly around his fingers. He sucked on my swollen clit violently while drawing his fingers in and out of my throbbing pussy. The pleasure heightened, growing in my belly even more, wanting to explode.

"Oh, I'm going to come," I rasped, drawing my knees together, hoping to hold it for longer.

He pushed my legs apart and looked up. His mouth glistened with my wetness and his eyes filled with rage. "Close your legs again and I'll tie them up, *amore*," he warned before diving back in, eating my pussy as if he had been starved for months and months while it had only been a week.

I threw my head back, staring up at the ceiling while shocks of pleasure pulsed out of me. Wave after wave, I finished, exploding in his mouth and over his fingers uncontrollably as he didn't stop.

When he pulled out his fingers, my wetness pooled out along with them. He raised himself up from between my legs and dropped his mouth over my mine, letting me taste my juices. His tongue ravished my mouth just as it had ravished my pussy a few moments ago. Everything became a blur. I couldn't think of anything but the awaiting pleasure, him, his mark, his knot.

My body was already numb, and my pussy swollen.

He parted his mouth from mine and traced his wet fingers over my lower lip. "Taste yourself, the last of yourself, because after today, all of you will be mine."

I almost finished again.

52

Rebekah

I sucked on his fingers, swallowing my wetness as he played with my mouth and trailed his fingers down my chin, leaving a wet trail, before his mouth lowered to mine for another kiss. The tension eased a little within me.

Breathing heavily, I kissed him while wrapping my hands around the back of his head. He tensed above me, only growing larger. His erection brushed across my stomach as he positioned himself between my legs and removed his pants. My eyes remained closed, my chest rising and dropping in need.

Hot pressure built in my belly, wanting to explode, over and over again.

God. I was insane for doing all of this, for even wanting this—but I couldn't stop.

My nails dug into his shoulders as I curled my legs around him. The tip of his cock rubbed against my sex, drenched in my wetness. The tingles and the fire returned. A quiver fluttered down my body as he placed his hands on my hips and pulled me lower, farther away from the pillow that kept my head high.

His hand wrapped around my throat, and he pushed me back, breaking from the kiss. His eyes brimmed with desire, almost as if he was intoxicated with it. His body was warm, warmer than I had ever felt him before.

It was different.

This was different.

My eyes lowered to his cock as he fisted it between my thighs and rose it to my lower stomach. My nerves twisted and turned, yearning for the pleasure.

He pressed his fingers a bit harder on my throat, taking my breaths while his gaze collided with mine. "This is how *hard* you make me, *amore*," he growled, parting my legs and applying firm pressure over my pussy.

I drew my lower lip into my mouth, but the room filled with the sounds of my pleasure and need. "Let me feel it inside," I breathed, lifting my hips, rubbing my aching clit against his throbbing thickness.

Heat spread further. I dug my fingernails into his wrist as he tightened his hand around my throat and slid the tip of his cock over my wetness. It glided against it with ease. He repeated it. *Thrice.* I grew needy, desperate, even more than desperate. Every second felt like torture, torture he had pushed me into.

God.

My breathing quickened. His cock teased my opening, slipping in and out as I held onto his shirt, urging him to hasten it all. I slid down, letting his length further inside. He retorted, pulling himself out and only teasing me. My back arched, wanting him all.

"*Please*," I begged, tears on the brim of spilling out of my eyes.

It burned, everything burned—I was on fire. He teased my entrance, pushing his hips back and forth, giving me a taste of the pleasure and then taking it away from me without ever filling me up. The muscles in my thighs tightened. I didn't move. He loosened his grip on my neck while pressing another inch of his cock inside.

Not full.

My teeth gritted. I closed my hands around the sheets. The intensity only rose from there before he plunged all of him inside me. His entire length disappeared between my legs. I gasped at the surprising sensation. My muscles clenched tightly around his cock, sucking him in.

"Fuck," he groaned and I whimpered.

He lowered himself to me, his chest against mine but his clothed and covered with a shirt he didn't dare remove. I slipped my hand under his shirt, feeling his skin as his cock thrust all the way inside of me once more.

Filled.

He remained deep inside me for a few seconds before emptying me and driving back in while his warm breaths fanned in my ear. My pussy tightened around him once more and he grabbed my hair in response.

"Do that once more and I'll be fucking you in another form," he threatened, his voice deep and dark.

My teeth clenched while my body eased to his thrusts, my insides stretching and opening for him while I feared his knot at the same time. I could only imagine the pleasure it was going to bring.

He ran his tongue down my throat, licking and kissing me while I raked my nails over his shoulders, leaving marks of my own. His pace was slow—I was still adjusting. When I did, he quickened, ramming into me wildly. The sounds of his skin slapping against my wet pussy filled the room. His growls vibrated through my ear and across my body.

I felt him within me.

Inside me.

My clit pulsed against his thrust, leading me to another orgasm that soon flooded out of me. Just as one passed, another one built inside. He roughly rammed into me with force while his hand fisted around my hair, holding it tight. My scalp burned in pain, but it was barely anything compared to the intensity of the pleasure.

I felt his growing further inside me, stretching my walls, filling me to the brim. The tip of his head rubbed against my G-spot and my pussy tightened around him.

"What did I tell you, *amore*?" he growled, restraining me to the bed with his weight while his hand tightened in my hair, pulling it harder. "Don't make finish until I want to."

A throaty moan escaped my mouth. I barely controlled myself under his wrath. Pleasure twisted and turned inside me. Wetness dripped from my pussy, covering his cock. His length seared back into me in another forceful thrust, and I threw my head back, moaning and screaming.

He grabbed my hair, tugging my neck to the side before I felt his tongue lapping over my sensitive flesh, threatening to mark me. The hair over my body rose. Short, quick breaths fled my throat.

I closed my eyes as I felt him growing *bigger,* his knot.

His lips brushed over mine. "Take it like a good girl. You wanted this," he whispered, slowing his thrusts while his cock expanded my walls.

"Yes," I whimpered, nodding.

His lips were almost against mine, but he quickly drew back and sunk his teeth into my neck. Under him, I couldn't move an inch.

My insides tightened around his cock. It was painful but soon became bearable when he began moving inside me. Pleasure returned and exploded out of me in seconds.

"Fuck," I cried, scratching his arm as his sharp teeth went inches deep into my neck.

I had never felt as full as this before. *Never.*

His fingers brushed against my scalp, and he closed his hand before drawing his mouth away from my neck. Growling in my ear, he gave me a last rough thrust before his warmth flooded deep inside me. Slowly, he pulled his throbbing member out of my pussy and my insides quivered in delight at the rawness and the emptiness I was left with.

It didn't matter if he stopped.

He had marked me; he was *within* me now and I wasn't sure of how strong the ties were going to be, but I knew it was going to be forever. There was no turning back now.

Not that I wanted to.

With heavy breaths fleeing his throat, he pressed his hand against my jaw and looked me in the eyes. I swallowed hard, looking back. A smile spread over my face. His hand moved up to my cheek. I played with the back of his hair while his mouth lowered to mine for a sweet, soft kiss.

"You don't know how crazy I am about you, Rebekah." His voice grew intense as he rubbed his finger over my cheek. "You make me want to become a man I've never been."

"Will you?" I ran my tongue over my lip.

"For you, I'll be anything you want me to be." His eyes filled with heavy desire, and I melted in them.

53

Rebekah

My heart beat hard and fast in my chest. I tried to breathe normally, but I couldn't. Christopher's hand came around mine, his fingers closing. He smiled at me; I smiled back at him. There was a new, strange, welcoming feeling growing inside me as if something *powerful* had happened.

The mark on my neck throbbed and whenever I touched it, I felt my blood pumping through my entire body.

It somewhat terrified me.

A month ago, I knew nothing about this world, and now, I was here, a part of it. If someone had told me everything would change in a few minutes for me in that subway station, I wouldn't have believed them.

Faye was shocked when she learned what had happened at her cousin's sister's newborn party. We had just been gone for an hour. I left the party without any scent over my body and now, Christopher was all over me. I smelled like him from top to bottom. It was strong, diving back into my nose repeatedly.

"Congratulations," Alicia's husband said, shaking my hand first and then Christopher's. I assumed this was the only *family* he had along with his brother, Pietro, who was nowhere to be found. "I wish you two a great journey ahead!" He raised his glass and offered us a smile.

My legs were sore, there was an ache between my thighs and my neck. Something was at unease—I was. I wasn't sure why. My hands parted from Christopher. I whispered to him that I'm going to talk with Faye and Alicia before they left the place. The newborn was asleep in another room.

I walked inside the room. The lights were dim, it was silent. A couple of whispers rose from Faye as she waved her hand at me.

Approaching the cradle, I found a baby asleep, at peace without any worry in the world. My face filled with awe, and I smiled at Alicia.

"It's a beautiful boy."

"Thank you." Alicia lowered her gaze to the cradle and rocked it slowly. "It's going to be a long, hectic life from now."

I laughed at her words. "I wish you good luck then!"

She lifted her head and met my eyes. "You too." I didn't think much of it. I suppose she meant *good luck* with Christopher as now I had been tied to him for the rest of my little life. "Well, I'm going to go get some pumping done and some food. I'm sure you will both take care of him?"

I nodded. "Of course."

"Yeah, don't worry," Faye whispered while getting even closer to the newborn. She was completely in love with him and wouldn't stop cradling and playing with him.

I sat on Alicia's seat as she left the room and closed the door behind. For a few silent minutes, we both gawked at the sleeping newborn, wondering what was going to happen once he would wake up. It was going to be hectic.

In the silence, I glanced at Faye and asked, "You don't seem so happy about Christopher marking me?" I could sense her disagreement from far away when I told her what had happened earlier, while I was gone with him.

She immediately shut down and didn't say anything. "Are you happy?" she asked me instead while caressing the newborn in the cradle.

I blinked before giving her a nod. "Yes. I am. I don't believe I've done anything wrong and this, it eventually had to happen. I like him, Faye, I really do," I whispered to her. It was the first time I had told someone my feelings for Christopher.

"That—that's good." She looked away from me once more, uncertainty clear in her eyes. "Then I'm happy for you."

"No, you aren't." I shook my head, catching her in a lie. "Just this morning you were forcing me to come here and see my *boyfriend* and now, you're acting differently. Why? Did I do something wrong? Did I make a mistake?" My heart raced at the thought.

Every part of me was in comfort. I *knew* that by letting Christopher mark me, I had done the right thing. I had spent the past couple of days in torture, away from him, trying to understand my feelings, but I didn't need to anymore. I was his and he was mine.

And now, I felt *complete*. I was warm everywhere, knowing I had done right by myself and there was no other way I would've wanted this—*him*.

"No, no, you didn't," she whispered before her gaze swept over me. Her eyes fixated on the throbbing mark on my neck. "I'm happy for you, Bek, really, I am and I wish you all the best."

My hand stretched and I placed it over hers while my lips lined straight. "Are you hiding something from me?" I asked her, my mind overthinking once more.

"No."

"Don't lie to me." I furrowed my brows, forcing her to tell me whatever she was hiding from me, and I knew from the bottom of my heart there was something. "I really like Christopher and you know that. I know I'm still new to this world—your world—and some things still terrify me. But if there is something you're keeping from me, about Christopher, don't. I'll be on edge all over again and I'm scared of going there." My throat closed a little.

"There is nothing for you to worry about. He's a good man and eventually, he'll become a better one with you," she replied with barely any emotion in her voice.

My heart thudded hard and fast in my chest and my palms grew sweaty. I didn't believe her. I had been friends with Faye for over a decade and I could tell when she was lying to me.

"My parents just got divorced, Faye," I reminded her. "And when I think of them now, I don't believe they ever loved each other and that since the beginning, they were only compromising for their children. I don't want that. I don't want to compromise with someone for my entire life, so if there is anything, please tell me before I'm in a place where I have to compromise with Christopher."

The rays of sunshine from behind the curtains began getting dim The room got even darker as the sun started setting. I heard a few sounds from the outside of the room, people and staff shuffling around. There was still plenty of time before Alicia was going to return and before that, I needed to know why Faye wasn't happy for me.

"When you left, earlier, I was with Alicia here and we were putting him to sleep." She glanced at the newborn. "I asked her about—" She hesitated to say his name. "—Christopher and what she thought about him since she's married into his family."

"What did she say?"

"She told me he was a good man and that he really wants you, he'd do anything to have you. She then mentioned an interaction she had with him a while earlier after the whole wallet mishap." I watched Faye's fingers as they intertwined with each other at the hem of her dress. She was worrying. "There's something I haven't told you about our world."

"What?" I asked her, my tone low and filled with fear.

"When a werewolf comes from a bloodline of Alphas, they possess a certain power to turn humans into werewolves. It's an uncommon practice, no one does it anymore." My stomach twisted. I waited for her to continue. "A simple bite from an Alpha on a new moon can turn you into one. Christopher intended on turning you during that time, without your knowledge."

I held back my gasp and shifted my legs over one another. Something tightened inside me and suddenly, I felt trapped.

54

REBEKAH

I panicked instantly. My hands went to my hips as I paced back and forth inside the room. Sweat beaded down my forehead. *What did I do? What had I done with myself?* I knew it wasn't going to be long before I would begin regretting my decision.

"But he didn't. That's a good thing, Rebekah," Faye whispered, jolting up from her seat as she walked to me, confused. "He would've if he wanted to but he didn't do it. He didn't turn you in one of us."

"But he *wanted* to. Why would he even think of it?" I threw my hands in the air, sounding more than just frustrated. "What made him even think I'd ever want to become—a werewolf?" My thoughts raced, I scurried to where my bag was kept and searched for my phone.

"It's not a new moon tonight, if that's what you're thinking." Faye came behind me.

I pressed my eyes shut and sighed in relief. Some of the tightness in my stomach uncurled itself. He had bitten me today and if the new moon rose—I'd be an animal. My face scrunched in disgust, and I stepped out of the room, unable to hold in the rage furling inside me.

I searched the house till my eyes met with Christopher's. There was still a bit of a crowd but most of them had left. Everything became a blur around him. My mind was in a haze I couldn't break from. Countless doubts and questions fell into my head.

Did he still want me to become like him? Like the people inside this house? A werewolf?

As much as I was getting comfortable with the fact that werewolves existed, I was never going to become one or let anyone turn me into one.

"What's wrong, *amore*?" He stepped closer to me, acting as if he had no clue about anything.

"Were you—are you planning to turn me into an animal like yourself?" I asked him, quickly changing the words to learn about what he intended on doing with me.

"What?" Christopher furrowed his brows. "Who told you?" he asked after pausing for a moment.

"So you did want to?" I folded my arms across my chest while heaving in a breath. My tone became bitter and loud.

He averted his gaze from me, glancing around at all the people surrounding him before his hand came around my elbow. I shrugged him off, hitting his hand away before following him inside another room.

In the silence, he came closer to me, and his expression relaxed before he asked, "What's wrong with if I want you to?" My head boiled. I let him continue. He had to finish, and I needed to hear him. "Yes, I would've done it earlier but I stopped myself and waited. I don't see a problem here, Rebekah."

A grimace spread over my face. "I don't want to!"

"Not now—"

"Not ever!" I cut him off and finished it myself.

He scoffed, shaking his head before nearing me. His hand returned to my elbow, not holding it, just lightly touching it with his cold fingers. "Eventually, you'll turn. It might not be tonight or this month, but you will."

Something clicked in my head and then I barely controlled myself. "I don't want to turn into a fucking animal!" I exclaimed, my voice hoarse.

"Your *wants* will change." He remained calm and it threw me off.

My blood ran cold, and I spat out, "No they will not. What makes you think I'd ever want to become one of you? I don't and I never will. If you wanted someone like yourself, you should've found someone like yourself."

He shot me a piercing gaze and the edges of his eyes grew dark at my words. He took a threatening step forward. The emotion on his face was dark, yet somewhat warm. I wanted to confide in it and at the same time, I wanted to run away from it.

"You're mine whether you like it or not. I didn't turn you, not yet, so don't paint me as if I'm the devil. And even if I do turn you, what are you going to do about it, Rebekah?" he asked, a threat in his tone now. "Tell me. *You* let me mark you. Do you think you can run? Think again. Wherever you go, you'll always come back. Don't find a fucking reason to leave now."

My eyes burned into his. "You think I'm your property now?" He didn't respond and his silence gave me the answer I had been looking for. "I'm not your property, you don't own me and you never will. I'm not going to let you turn me into a werewolf so respect my choice and don't ever try to control me again."

I stepped back, away from him, and walked past him. As I reached the door, I expected him to change his words, to tell me he wouldn't *turn* me into a werewolf any time he wanted to and that he would rather wait for me, but he didn't say any of it. There was nothing except silence from him.

I didn't understand why he didn't agree with me.

So what if I remained human? How would it affect him? Nothing would've changed. I accepted all the terrible parts of him and overlooked all the bad qualities. Being a human wasn't a bad quality, it was who I was, and I couldn't change it, I didn't want to.

I didn't want to turn into a werewolf.

I grabbed my belongings from the other room and zipped my bag shut before throwing my hair into a ponytail and leaving. From the corner of my eyes, I found Faye approaching me with a questioning look on her face.

"What happened?"

I didn't stop walking. "I'm going home."

"Why? What happened, Bek?" She picked up her pace and followed me. "Did you fight with him? Oh, god. Just wait two minutes, I'll get my keys."

I slowed down a little bit and shook my head. "It's alright. I'll take an Uber home. You stay here and spend time with your family. I'll see you later." I placed my hand on her arm and gave her a little squeeze before leaving.

Faye tried to follow me, but I didn't let her. I didn't want to take her away from the party even though it was ending. I stepped out on my own and booked an Uber home. It was a bit far, but it was time I went back to my own broken family instead of meddling with others.

It was nearing six in the evening. The skies above changed colors and the weather became violent as night approached. I strolled over to the next street where the Uber was parked. He couldn't come around Christopher's residence due to restrictions, so I walked on my own instead, searching for the white sedan.

My whole body was in pain. I didn't want to leave, not after everything we'd shared earlier but at the same time, I couldn't bend to his every demand and turn into a werewolf when I never wanted to become one.

God. Everything was going perfectly.

A hand pressed against my back. I gasped at the unwanted touch and turned around to find a strange woman standing behind me.

"Poor little girl. Such a terrible life you have," she whispered.

I swallowed hard. "Excuse me?"

"You'll never get the love you want. Not in these wealthy neighborhoods or among these werewolves."

"What do you mean?" My brows collected at her words. It was a complete stranger standing in front of me and talking to me as if she knew me.

The corner of her mouth lifted into a smile. "*Morpherous*," she whispered under her breath and in those few seconds, I realized it was not just any stranger.

It was a witch.

55

REBEKAH

The sickening yet sweet, homely scent of tons of candles and herbs drifted to my nose and my face scrunched in disgust. I didn't like it. Twisting around, I rolled over the uncomfortable tiny space before reaching the end. My arm dangled down along with my right leg. When I realized I was inches away from falling onto the ground, my eyes snapped open, and I instantly sat up on an unknown couch.

My eyes wandered and I froze when I caught a woman staring back at me.

She stood a small distance away. There was purple around her mouth and her skin was as pale as ice. Her fingers were stained black, and her hair seemed like it hadn't been combed in months.

I quickly gasped before pulling my legs to myself. It took me a second to understand the woman who was looking at me—a witch. It had to be.

Another woman appeared from the room behind the witch. They looked similar. The only difference was the shape of their noses and their foreheads. Everything else was similar.

I'd been *kidnapped* by the cruel witches.

Tension creased on my face, and I snapped my head around to the open window where I heard wind rustling and several howls of animals from a distance. Moonlight flooded into the house that was only lit with candles and no other light.

"I don't think we've met," one of them said, the one with the purple mouth stepped forward, nearing me.

"I don't think I want to meet you." I gave her a terrorizing stare while backing farther away from her. Michael had shown me enough visions, which made me believe witches were not good.

When she came closer, I got a clearer view of her. She had light gray eyes, almost white with wrinkles underneath them. She stretched her arm out, her hand opening in front of me. "I'm Selene," she whispered.

"And I'm not going to touch you." I gawked carefully at the black stain around her fingers and then shuddered while shaking my head. "What do you want from me?" I asked, lifting my head.

"Don't be scared. I'm not going to hurt you, Rebekah. We only harm those that have sin in their blood, and you don't," she clarified, sounding quite familiar.

I scoffed, "You sound like my little sister." I remembered Rose before Halloween. She spoke the same way when talking about the witches.

The irony of it all.

My legs rolled down to the ground, but I kept the blanket over me. It was warm in here even with the window wide open. It was surprising that for a kidnapping such as this, I wasn't shackled or locked up in a room. The main door of the house was just behind the couch, the windows were open and there was a clear passage to escape.

I doubt they were going to let me escape. *And what was I going to do by escaping? Turn into the animal Christopher wanted me to become?* I hadn't forgotten anything, though I wish I had.

"It was quite hard to get a hold of you with all those werewolves surrounding you day and night. I'll repeat again, Rebekah, we wish no harm on you. I hope we can be civil about this," Selene continued and the woman behind her remained quiet, her dark eyes on the ground.

"What do you want from me?"

"Whatever you *can* give us."

I cocked a brow at her in confusion. "What could I possibly give you?"

"A lot." She heaved in a breath and moved toward the furnace that provided heat. "You're paired with an Alpha. A human and a werewolf, that's certainly something special."

"I don't think so." My foothold on the ground steadied in case I needed to run from here, which I assumed was going to be soon. I wasn't drowning in fear until I recalled the visions Michael had given me, then I was at the edge of my seat, only wanting to run. "Why would I help you? I've seen what you've done, with Christopher and with others."

The woman near the furnace tossed in some more wood and it quickly burned with a strong fire. She then stood and turned. Something changed in her face. I couldn't tell what it was.

"What *I* had done with Christopher needed to be done. He had to be stopped and I found it convenient to take away his wolf and let him live in misery instead of taking away his life, which would've been a lot easier for me." She reached closer and moved her hand underneath my chin, tilting my head till I looked into her terrifying eyes. "Haven't you seen what he has done?"

"No." I shook my head.

"Then you're in luck." The sides of her mouth curled, and a shiver crawled down my spine. "If you knew him all those years ago, you wouldn't have dared to even speak to him again."

"Why?"

I had seen parts of Christopher, and while he was cruel, he hadn't harmed me in any way or any of those he cared for. There were reasons for all the killings he had done, as he had told me earlier.

"He was a monster, darling. By taking away his wolf, I tamed him," she whispered and my stomach turned at her words.

I bit the inside of my cheek while the woman behind Selene came forward. A confused expression tightened on her face before she stated, "She's been marked."

Selene's grin instantly disappeared and turned into a frown. She moved her hand from my chin and pushed away the pieces of my hair dangling over my shoulder, exposing the mark on my neck. I doubt it had disappeared since I was aware I hadn't been *out* for long.

"No," Selene murmured to herself, her eyes wide. She took a deep breath and walked away from me.

"She's useless to us now," the woman added, her hawk-like eyes on me.

I wasn't sure what they *thought* they were going to get from me. It didn't make sense. *What were they planning on doing?*

"But he's not," Selene said, and then reached for something inside the shelf before handing the object over to the other woman. "Take her blood while I think of what needs to be done now that she's been marked by Christopher."

The woman reached me and grabbed my arm. She pulled out the knife Selene had handed to her. It was a sharp blade.

I quickly panicked. "No!" Her grip on my wrist tightened. I tried to pull away, but her hold was strong, like iron. "No. You said you wouldn't hurt me!" I screamed at Selene who stood meters away from me.

"It's not going to be painful. We aren't going to drain you, Rebekah. Cooperate with us and we will not hurt you." Selene came behind and her hands drifted to my shoulders. I knew what was coming next. "She's only going to nick you. That's all," she whispered.

I swallowed hard, agreeing. If I didn't, she would've used the force of magic over me, and I didn't want that. The woman in front pushed the tip of the knife against my palm and the blade cut my skin easily, without any force. Blood seeped out from the small cut and the woman slipped a glass underneath my hand, letting the blood fall into it.

My mind ached with countless terrifying thoughts. I tried not to panic, not unless there was a reason to. The blood continued to pour out of my palm and into the glass, filling it up. My chest tightened in fear. I needed to get out of here.

"Why are you doing this to me?" I asked Selene as my right hand began turning numb from the loss of blood. "What are you going to do with my blood? You just told me, I'm useless to you now."

"There was something special about you when you were destined to become Christopher's mate, but when he marked you, he consumed that part of you. To our luck, it won't be difficult to get him to us." She paced back and forth in front of me while the other woman watched the blood drip into the glass. "After all, we do have *you* and your blood, we might just require it for the ritual."

Ritual? What ritual? I didn't even want to think about it.

When the glass was filled, the woman took it away and disappeared into another room. I closed my fist and pressed my fingers against the wound, hoping it would close. I moved my eyes across the small, packed house. My heart pounded inside my chest. Christopher was never going to find me after the argument we'd had, nor was he going to send Michael to *check* on me—not until after a few days of silence. My family were aware that I was spending time at Faye's.

No one was going to come for me.

Or save me.

"It's time for you to sleep, darling," Selene whispered, leaning behind me while her hands returned to my head.

"No, please—"

Before I could reach for her hands, she had already mumbled the word that weakened my body and then my mind. The walls closed around me, everything became foggy before I felt my head hitting the soft couch I sat on.

56

CHRISTOPHER

My fingers grazed against the glass of wine before I sipped on it in the complete dark. It was quiet, but not in my mind. I placed my legs over the table before leaning back against the seat while watching the breeze outside. Every time my thoughts went to Rebekah, I sucked in a breath and wiped her memory from my mind, but no matter how hard I tried, I couldn't get rid of her scent that had soaked into my flesh.

Only if I hadn't marked her.

It was too quick. She wasn't ready—for anything. I should've known that.

A shadow appeared in the doorway and moments later, Pietro walked in. "Seems like it wasn't a good day for someone." He grinned at my miserable state and enjoyed every moment of it. "Let me guess what might've happened. She found out the list of women you've slept with and left?"

I didn't respond. Any interaction with him was only going to infuriate me.

"Or did she realize that someone so repulsive might just kill her anytime," he continued, forcing a reaction out of me.

I still didn't give him one.

I had sacrificed parts of myself for Rebekah, I had promised her not to kill anyone, I had changed myself for her, I had turn *warm* for her, only to find out she couldn't make one sacrifice for me in return.

It wasn't like I wanted her to turn into a werewolf tomorrow, but it was a part of a longer conversation. Eventually, as an Alpha, I was going to need her to become a werewolf, to be equal to me.

Pietro clicked his fingers in front of me and after a few seconds, I glanced up at him, no longer furious. I needed for this night to be over. I didn't want to think about Rebekah or anything else. I had chased her enough for a lifetime.

"Well, goodnight to you. I'm going to pass out. Get some sleep soon." He waved his hand at me and then walked out of the door, leaving me alone in the dark, just where I needed to be.

It had been more than just a few hours and I hadn't heard anything from her, but I kept wondering what she was doing, whether she had eaten anything or even slept.

The screen of my phone lit up, and I turned my head around, finding an unknown call. My brows furrowed. I rested the glass on the table and grabbed my phone to attend to the call.

"Christopher." It was a woman.

My eyes rolled to the back of my head when I recognized the familiar voice. It belonged to none other than the witch I despised the most. "Great. I've to change my number now that you've gotten it." I suppressed a growl and asked, "Are you going to return my wolf or what?"

"I suppose by now you must've gotten him back. After all, you did mark your mate, but it could take a couple of days for the curse to fully break."

I leaned forward, my eyes opening and the numbness from my body draining away. I wasn't wrong. The curse was going to be broken—it already *had been*. Which meant my wolf was going return to me.

But something else clicked in my head and in horror, I stood up.

"How do you know I marked her?" I questioned as tension filled me. I hadn't told anyone aside from the people who were at the party this morning and all those were trustworthy enough to know they wouldn't share the information with the witches.

"Because I'm looking at the mark right now..." she trailed off with an evil chuckle.

My fingers tightened around my phone. *No.* It couldn't be possible. My voice strained as I said, "You're bluffing."

"Where is your mate, then?" she asked. "I knew it wasn't going to be long before you took your eyes off her and when you did, earlier this morning, we took her and the best part is, no one was there to save her."

My eyes dashed back and forth in the darkness as I tried to make sense of it. *How could it be possible?* She was supposed to be *home*.

I became blind with rage. "If you dare even touch her—"

"I'm not going to do anything to her, Christopher. She's useless to us now you've marked her. We don't need her, but we do need you. A fair exchange, isn't it?"

I moved the phone away from my ears. My teeth bared and a growl ripped through my chest. *How did I not know?* I blamed myself entirely for it, for letting her leave without anyone following her, without having Michael stalk her or at least update me on whether she had reached home or not. She had been gone for hours, taken by the witches and I hadn't been aware of any of it.

My hand rolled into a fist and my blood boiled in anger.

"Meet me outside the city at midnight and we'll deliver your mate back to her home. But if you use any of your tricks on me, rest assured I'll kill her and I'll not hesitate," she continued, her words threatening enough to shake fear inside me.

Selene was a powerful witch, the only one. No one could defeat her no matter how hard they tried but I wasn't going to let anyone take my mate away from me.

Nothing other than Rebekah mattered.

If I had to sacrifice my life, so be it.

57

Rebekah

"Mom's telling you to wake up and that it's pretty late for you to sleep for another minute," my little sister's voice rang in my ears before I felt her small hands on my legs, shaking them back and forth and forcing me up.

I jolted up with a gasp and glanced at my surroundings. It was my room. *How?* My brows furrowed, I turned around and looked at Rose, who stood beside my bed with a wide smile on her face.

"I missed you!" She wrapped her arms around me. "Don't go away again, please. And if you're going, take me to Faye's as well."

I closed my eyes, giving my mind a moment to think of what had happened. The witches had taken me, and Selene—she had taken my blood before she knocked me unconscious with her magic. I had no memory after that. I had no clue how I was in my bedroom or when I returned.

Air filled my lungs, and I breathed out before opening my eyes. "I'm not going anywhere, Rose. Now, run along, I need a shower," I stated, hopping off the bed while she still clung onto my leg.

"Promise?"

"Promise."

She rushed out of the room and went back to hers. I reached my door and stared outside at the staircase and the window beside it. Sunlight blinded me and I squinted away before slamming the door shut.

Did Selene just let me go? It was the next day, twenty-four hours since I'd left Christopher's residence and since I was kidnapped by a witch. *Was it over? Was that all?* Selene hadn't hurt me aside from taking my blood. *Was that all she wanted from me?*

I let out a sigh of relief, believing it was over and that I didn't need to worry about anything in regard to the witches.

I stopped close to my phone and hesitated before picking it up. There were a couple of calls from Faye but none from Christopher, not even a single message. He hadn't even bothered. Not a call or a message. My jaw clenched as anger engulfed me.

I had been taken by the witches, kept hostage for hours, and he didn't *care*.

I heaved in a breath and tossed my phone back on the bed. There was no use calling him or messaging him when he hadn't bothered to in the first place. I didn't find any reason to tell him about the witches or the fact that they had taken my blood.

He wouldn't care.

And neither would I.

It suddenly felt like I had made a mistake with Christopher and hurried into things when I didn't even know much about him. *What if he had just used me to get his wolf back? Or maybe even something else?* Selene told me he was a different man before she took his wolf. I had no clue about it.

The only thing we shared was the heaps amount of pride. For as long as he wasn't going to reach out, I wasn't going to either.

After a shower and lunch with my family, I checked my phone once more and Faye began calling me repeatedly. Last night's ordeal had scared me. I needed a moment away from her world. My head was going to tear into pieces.

I placed the phone on its screen on the table and spent time with Mom before she headed for her work. Rose and I agreed to go over to my dad's at the end of the month, by ourselves, and see his new place.

Silence.

Eight long days had passed and there was nothing but silence that surrounded me. It was killing me. I hated it from every nerve in body, but something held me back from reaching out to Christopher.

I stepped out of the interview after hearing the same words three words I had been hearing all week: *We'll call you.* My eyes rolled to the back of my head, and I scoffed before taking the lift to the lobby and stepping out of the building. It was a P.A job, but I believed I was blacklisted throughout Laford.

I needed a distraction from Christopher and even then, I couldn't find one.

I stepped back on the ice-cold streets of downtown Laford, it was the end of November and the beginning of the coldest month in the year. Winters were surely going to be unforgiving this year.

My boots kicked against the ground as I paved my way to the nearest subway station while trying not to remember what went on under the ground of this city. A strong breeze brushed against my face, knotting my hair from my sides. I pushed the strands behind my ears and tightened my quivering fingers around the bag.

A black car pulled to the side of the road, slowing down beside me. I didn't look. The high beams flashed at me. I still didn't look.

"*Principessa*," I heard the thick Italian accent and turned around to find Christopher's little brother waving his hand at me. "Need a ride?" The car came to a complete halt in the middle of the traffic.

"No, I don't." A scowl instantly appeared on my face. "Thank you very much."

His mouth lined straight. "Come here or we'll have Michael grab you in the middle of this crowd and that won't be a pretty scene." He glanced ahead at the driver's seat, and he was found driving the car.

People walked past me without a worry in their minds. None of them glanced at me once, even though there was a car stopped inches away from me, forcing me inside.

I sighed and looped my arm out of my bag before Pietro opened the door for me. Slipping inside, I sat down and moments later, the car left the busy road.

"Did Christopher send you?" I asked his brother while my brows furrowed. *Was it going to be hard if he came by himself?* It had been more than a week and all I'd received from him was complete silence, as if he didn't care about me at all.

"No." Pietro shook his head. "He didn't."

"Then?" *Now, I was terrified.*

Michael drove out of the busy roads and into the residential area where he entered the community where Christopher lived with his brother. The entire five-minute ride, Pietro didn't say anything. I grew concerned. *Were they taking me to him? What was this? An intervention?* I didn't want to talk to him until he agreed with me and respected that I didn't want to turn into a werewolf.

Tension coiled in my skin when the car entered the driveway and stopped by the front of the house. I swallowed hard and stepped out before Pietro guided me inside.

My hands folded underneath my chest. "Where is he?"

Pietro scratched the back of his head before turning around with a confused expression on his face. "Yeah, that's the problem. No one has seen Christopher in over a week."

I stilled. "What?"

"I thought he'd be with you but when I sent Michael over to yours, he confirmed that Christopher wasn't with you." Pietro cleared his throat and closed his hands behind his back. "Has he contacted you?"

"No. He hasn't."

Knowing Christopher, it was surely something he was doing to get my attention but at the same time, I wondered where he had been if he hadn't been here over the past week. *Was there something wrong?* A shuddering breath escaped my throat as I glanced over to Michael who stood a small distance away from me with uncertainty and worry in his eyes.

"Well, I've asked all his sources and he hasn't been seen with anyone, which makes me assume either he has fled after whatever you did with him—"

"I didn't do anything." I cut him off as a frown appeared on my face.

"He was upset that night."

I scoffed. "So was I."

Pietro paused and took a deep breath. A quiet minute passed. My throat grew thick in the silence. *Where was Christopher?* All these days I thought he was here, making the best of his life and doing whatever he did before me. But it wasn't true. *Had he met someone else? Did he run away?*

This was *his* city; he couldn't run away.

So, where was he?

58

REBEKAH

"I need to know where Christopher is. He hasn't been here in days and there are a few issues he needs to handle. I cannot reach him through his phone and the only way I can find out his location is through *you*," Pietro started while circling me.

I gave him an odd stare while shaking my head. "How?" Suddenly, my mildly tranquil expression wore off as I came to the realization of what he wanted from me.

"Michael here has a little trick up his sleeve." Pietro placed both hands on my shoulders while grinning behind me. "Don't worry, it's only going to hurt a little."

My lips lined straight. "You're not serious?" I turned around.

A few moments later, Michael walked through the front door, all prepared to set my brain on fire. *Was it even possible?* I didn't know Christopher's location. Nor did I have any clue of where he'd be. I was just as clueless as everyone else.

"I'm serious." Pietro turned me to face Michael once more. "You share a bond with Christy and now that you two have mated and wrecked the sheets, your souls are tied, meaning Michael can tap into the bond to find out if he's alive or dead. That's all I really want to know." He shrugged with only minimal tension on his face.

"Why do you think he'd be dead?" My eyes widened a little.

"Just guessing..."

I didn't think too much about it. My eyes fluttered shut and as much as the past week had been agonizing, it was much worse to know that Christopher had been missing all this time while I was cursing at him for not contacting me.

Now, I felt *terrible*.

Michael planted his hands on either side of my head while Pietro tightened his hold over my shoulders. Just then, I became aware of the pain that was going to tear through me.

"You'll be unconscious for a couple of minutes. Don't try to wake up and don't panic at all. It's the only way I'll be able to tap into the mating bond," Michael said above me, his voice deep and terrifying.

I squirmed a little as the tips of his fingers spread through my scalp before he murmured something to himself. I couldn't hear what it was. The words, the language, it was hard to understand.

Just as he finished, my body dropped to the ground. Immense pain split my head in half. My throat became constricted. Everything within me painfully burned as if I was set on fire. It was gruesome but only last for barely a minute.

I rose from the ground, gasping for air. My chest rose and dropped as I looked up at Michael who had found out Christopher's whereabouts and so had I. It appeared like flashes in my mind, of him and of the witch that had taken me earlier. He wasn't hurt in any way, but something was wrong.

"He's with the witches," Michael announced.

"What witches?" Pietro was fuming at the information. "Selene? Why would he be with her? He despises her. Is that where he has been?"

I shuffled back and forth, my heart racing.

"I think someone's missed out a few details..." Michael trailed off, his questioning glare on me.

"What details?"

Words barely escaped my throat. This was because of *me*. Christopher had been gone ever since the witches had returned me. Something happened while I was there, something I wasn't aware of. All this while, I thought the witches had just tossed me home because they got what they needed—my blood—and deemed me useless after it.

But I was wrong.

In the silence, Michael explained what he'd seen in my thoughts. "Selene took her first. Last week, after the party, the witches took her, and they took her blood as well."

Pietro turned his attention to me, and his brows furrowed. "Why didn't you tell anyone?"

"I-I didn't think it was significant. They just took my blood and let me go and it made me believe that was all they wanted. I didn't want to poke the bear, so I didn't tell anyone." I ran my hands through my burning head while realizing the stupid mistake I had made. "I put him in trouble, didn't I?" Worry creased all over my face.

"Dammit." Pietro pulled out his phone while his eyes darkened. My thoughts raced. "Christopher must've exchanged himself in return for you. They sent you home because they got exactly what they wanted—the Alpha," he growled to himself while dialing a number on his phone. "The witches had taken him once and everyone knows how that turned out. It's not happening again."

From the vision Michael had shown me, the witches had taken away Christopher's wolf brutally all those years ago. *What could they possibly take from him now?*

"I need the exact coordinates of the witches," he said to Michael before his eyes snapped to mine. "And for your safety, you're not leaving this place."

I nodded, agreeing with him before he got on a call with someone named Walter. It was a familiar name, but I couldn't pinpoint where I had heard it.

Hours passed by quickly. I was surrounded with books from the library in the residence and while some of my thoughts diverted, I couldn't entirely stop thinking about Christopher. There hadn't been an update yet. It kept me on edge. Upon calling him, the call went straight to voicemail. Any message I dropped to him; he didn't respond, even when he'd received it.

It was odd.

My mind was spinning with a hundred questions. *What were the witches going to do with him? And if they were planning to do something, why hadn't they done it?* From the vision Michael forced me to see, Christopher was unharmed. He wasn't in any sort of pain, which relieved me in a way.

But if they weren't hurting him, what were they doing?

I tossed the book aside when I heard someone enter the library. Turning around, I found Pietro walking in with a familiar man I had seen with Christopher once, outside of the town.

"Do you have any information to where the witches had taken you?" the man questioned me, stepping forward.

"This is Walter, Christopher's second in command and he's a little sharper on these matters," Pietro said, standing tall above me as I remained seated on the couch. "The coordinates led nowhere. It's a dead end. Michael couldn't get any more information, therefore he suggested we come to you since you were taken by the witches earlier."

I forced myself to revisit the day the witches had taken me. The entire journey was a blur—I was surely unconscious, but I did remember where I woke up.

"It was a lodge—or maybe a cabin in the woods. There were two witches, both similar and one of them was named Selene. I can't remember anything else," I responded with a shrug. I had barely been conscious for more than thirty minutes there. It was all I could tell.

"That could be something. We'll have someone scour the area for any cabins," he said, turning to the man beside him.

In the distance, we all heard a voice, an engine roaring. A slow breath escaped my throat. My brows furrowed as I stood up straight. "I don't think you need to look anywhere," I whispered as the loud sound of the car engine tore across the silence inside the library.

59

Rebekah

Something crawled over my skin.

Pietro bolted outside along with the other man, both of them confused. I stood near the doorway, behind the shades, watching as the car rolled into the driveway of the house. The wrought iron gates began closing from behind as the car came to a complete halt at the front.

Knots appeared in my stomach, even when I knew it was Christopher who was inside the car, completely fine. He stepped out, shades covering his eyes from the gleaming sun before he stepped away from the car and tossed the key over to the man standing nearby.

"Where have you been?" Pietro asked. "Did the fucking witches take you?" The tension in his voice was clear, even when he spoke in a whisper while trying to refrain from getting the attention of the others surrounding us.

It made sense.

There weren't many people here who had knowledge about the witches. It seemed like all this while, Christopher was protecting his pack from them.

"They didn't take me. I went, willingly," Christopher responded, his voice different, *rougher*. He drew the shades down from his eyes and leaned closer to his brother. "Stop whatever you were trying to do and stop acting as if you care. We both know the truth," he whispered close to his ear before walking away from him and approaching the doorway.

There was no expression on his face, even when I tried to search for it.

Nothing.

He reached closer to me. My heart was pounding hard in my chest. I felt the pulsations of my racing beat under my fingertips. Suddenly, my throat and tongue were dry.

"Christo—"

"Shh." He placed his finger over my lips and the hair on the back of my neck stood as fear washed over me. I tried to remain calm, but something felt wrong, even though he was right here, standing in front of me.

He drew his finger away from my mouth and slipped his hand behind my hair before closing in and kissing me. I kissed him back instantly. It was rough. He bared his teeth, nipping at my lower lip while his hand tightened in my hair. *God.* I'd missed him.

A deep growl rumbled from his chest. The sound was strong, it piqued my attention. I planted my hand on his shoulder and broke the kiss. Taking in a few shallow breaths, I opened my mouth to question what had happened, but he didn't let me.

"We can talk later. I *need* you right now." He looped his arm around my waist, grabbing me closer. My cheeks turned red in shame as I found others, including his younger brother, staring at him in confusion. "All to myself."

"But—"

Lifting his eyes, he planted his hand over my mouth while shaking his head. With hesitation, I followed him as he headed up the stairs and into his room. Often, I glanced over my shoulder as something gripped me. *Fear?* I wasn't sure. *What was there to be afraid of?* I bit the inside of my cheek as we went into his bedroom that had been untouched this whole time he was gone.

He closed the door behind me and turned to me.

"What happened?" I asked immediately without giving my thoughts another minute to run wild. "What were the witches doing to you? That woman—she took my blood, and I don't know what's happening, but I want to know," my voice was brimming with panic as I spoke to him.

His jaw tightened and his hand returned to my hair. The color of his eyes changed from expressionless golden eyes to predatory, unflinching. He drew me closer to him and said, "I told you—" His fingers raced down my cheek and brushed over my neck. "I don't want to talk about it, Rebekah. Not right now," he whispered, his mouth nearing mine.

He hushed me once more with an aggressive kiss while growling at the same time. I tasted the hint of alcohol in his mouth. It wasn't too much, which made me assume he'd had something to drink before coming here. My thoughts only ran wild from there. He drew my bottom lip into his mouth, sucking and nibbling while his hands pushed me toward the bed behind him.

I had gone days without him. The need was there—*still alive.* My core grew warm at his hostile touches. He grabbed my hips, pushing them against the sheets before pulling my pants down and my underwear along with it.

My head grew hot and heavy. I wrapped my arms around his neck and the kiss deepened, turning into something we both wanted.

I didn't resist.

He closed his hands around the bottom of my shirt before pulling his mouth away from mine and removing all my clothes. I was bare in seconds. His lustful gaze ran over body. My legs wrapped around his torso. Heavy breaths escaped my throat.

He lowered himself over me while removing his pants. There was something different. He didn't say anything about being gone for days, he didn't question me nor give me any answers.

My mouth danced over his once more and the worries lifted off my shoulders for a moment as if nothing had happened, as if everything was right. His throbbing erection pressed between my legs. I spread them wider in need, only growing hotter.

"*This.*" He grabbed my hips once more, holding them tightly while his mouth drew away from mine. "This is what I want."

"You have it."

"No. No, I don't." He shook his head as his eyes fell over my body. He pushed me further back against the bed and wrapped his hand around my breast while the other one held my hip painfully tight. "That doesn't matter anymore anyway. You're *mine*, Rebekah," he growled, his voice different, deeper than before, almost as if it was his *wolf*.

Did it mean—

"I'm yours."

"Fuck, yes." He sank his head into my neck, inhaling deeply before dragging his tongue over the mark he had given me.

He pushed my legs apart, spreading them wider so he could enter me. The tip of his cock pressed against my opening. Wetness pooled between my legs. I closed my eyes and swallowed a gasp, containing my craving as his hand moved to the back of my head, grabbing a fistful of my hair. I began throbbing under his savagery, liking it—*enjoying it*.

He thrust into my tightness, and I hissed at the sudden movement. His arms wrapped tightly around me; he didn't let me move an inch while he filled me up. My toes curled forward as he repeated, ramming inches of himself inside me, parting my lower lips, sliding in and out till my insides adjusted to him and to his length.

His cock twitched inside me, and I moaned as I felt my core on fire. Warmth spilled out of me. I raked my nails down his back and moaned as he lifted himself off me and drove deeper at the same time.

Pleasure twisted inside me in a way I hadn't felt before. It was greater than before. I barely restrained it.

His hand remained around my neck. Choked breaths made their way out of my throat. He moved his hips back and forth in a *punishing* pace, slamming in harder each time and forcing a throaty gasp out of me.

I took every inch of him and whenever I finished, he quickened his pace, ramming his cock into my pulsing entrance as if it was the last time he was ever going to fuck me.

He was ruthless.

With a wild growl, he turned me around to my stomach and lifted my ass to him while pressing my head down to the bed. His fingers tightly wrapped around my hair as he entered my pussy once more, this time from a different angle. I fisted the sheets as the uncontrolled sounds of pleasure rolled from my throat.

His cock delved into my depths and he began pounding roughly. The sound of his hips slapping against my ass echoed through the walls of the room. Every nerve in my body trembled as tears threatened to escape my eyes.

"Fuck." My legs buckled as another orgasm streamed out of me.

He forced my legs apart and pulled onto my hair, dragging me up toward him. "Do you want me to be merciful?" he asked, his mouth against my ear as he drew my skin between his teeth.

I shook my head. "No."

"Good." He pushed me back down over the bed. "I wasn't going to be either way."

60

REBEKAH

I stared at the ceiling above me, still breathing heavily and adjusting. With every movement I made on the bed, my insides became sorer. I turned to Christopher, finding him asleep on the left side of the bed. He remained near me, only a few inches away, while his arm was dropped over my chest.

He had fallen asleep in seconds after finishing inside me. Hours had passed. He hadn't given me any answers. I didn't ask. It wasn't the right time.

Taking in a deep breath, I lifted his arm over my body and rose from the bed. Every nerve in my body tingled in pain as I made my way to the washroom while limping on my legs. I barely had any strength left, he'd made sure to take it all away.

After cleaning myself, I put on my clothes and stepped outside the bedroom. My eyes darted back and forth. There was no one in the hallways. I walked for a few long minutes, heading to the other portion of the house before knocking on Pietro's door.

He opened moments later and ran his gaze over me. "Were you attacked?"

I stared back at him in horror. "By your brother? Yes." I stepped inside his room, and he closed the door behind him. "I think something happened. I don't know what it is but there's something wrong with Christopher and he's not telling me."

Pietro folded his arms across his chest. "I can tell."

Creases of worry appeared on my forehead as I recalled the past few hours I had spent with him. It made my skin crawl. He spoke differently, he acted differently, and he even fucked me in a way he had never done before.

Mercilessly.

"Did the witches hex him or what?" It was the only thing I could think of.

"No, they didn't." Pietro shook his head and spoke slowly as if he was thinking hard. After a moment of silence, he came to a conclusion and shared it with me. "They didn't do anything. He got his wolf back."

"What?" I furrowed my brows.

"Christopher is a different man without his wolf and a different one with his wolf. The part of him you've seen is without his wolf—weak, humane and somewhat sympathetic." He heaved in a breath and walked away from me. "There is another part of him that's *cruel*. With his wolf, he's powerful and fierce," he explained with a hint of horror in his eyes.

I stepped back, blinking slowly. "But then why would he want his wolf back if he knew he'd change into something like that?" It didn't make sense.

Christopher *wanted* to be a different person. He'd told me himself he wanted to change, for me. He wanted to become better. I couldn't understand why he craved for *his wolf* if he knew he'd become cruel.

"Why not?" Pietro turned to me and shrugged. "He's an Alpha. Not having a wolf threatens his title, Rebekah."

I blew out a breath and asked, "So you're telling me his wolf is back?"

"Yes. He marked you, that triggered his wolf to return and for the curse to break. The curse was placed over him because the witches believed he—"

"He was a monster and by taking his wolf, they tamed him," I finished, remembering Selene's words and what she had told me that evening. I felt the color draining from my face as the rest of her words echoed in my head.

She had taken his wolf for a reason.

This was it.

Pietro nodded before he let out a sigh and walked into another room. When he came back out, he had a suitcase and tossed it on the ground.

"What are you doing?" I cocked a brow at him.

"Packing my shit and leaving," he said without any hint of sarcasm. *Fuck.* He couldn't be serious. "I've dealt with my brother in his *unforgiving* phase, and I don't want to do it again. I'd rather leave and wait for some miracle to happen than have my own brother kill me in spite—which he'll surely do." He unzipped the suitcase and pushed it open.

I ran my fingers through my hair while my breathing quickened. "You can't leave!"

"Yes, I can, and I will. And a suggestion, you should too. This is just the beginning. You're going to see faces of him you've never seen before…" His voice faded as he went into the other room and grabbed his clothes. When he returned, he continued, "With his wolf, he's a different man. You've only seen the tip of the iceberg."

"What are you talking about?" I grumbled in frustration while fear filled my voice.

He shoved his things inside the suitcase and began packing. "Years ago, when Christopher had his wolf, he killed wolves left and right. If anyone dared him, he'd kill them. If anyone threatened him, he'd kill them. If anyone irritated him, he'd kill them," he grumbled while rolling his eyes. "There was a time where he nearly killed me. His own blood. What makes you think you're safe here?"

"But I'm his mate," I reminded him. "He wouldn't hurt me." I knew it. He promised me he wouldn't ever. I believed him.

"Good luck with that theory."

Pietro ran back and forth, packing his things before Christopher woke up. Panic set deep inside my heart as I watched him. He was *terrified* of his own brother. In just a few minutes from the conversation to the packing, he practically ran out of the residence, taking only his things and told me to tell his brother he's going for very long vacation.

I had only known Christopher for a couple of months and those were far more than enough to believe he wouldn't hurt me.

But was I sure about it?

I swallowed hard and twisted the door handle to his room, pushing his door open and walking inside.

My heart skipped a beat when I found him awake.

"I've been waiting for you, Rebekah."

61

Rebekah

"Why do you keep running away as if I'm going to do something terrible to you?" Christopher asked as he looped his arm around my waist and pulled me closer to him. "Haven't you missed me even a bit?" His finger traced the side of my cheek, close to my hairline.

I shuddered in complete fear and my heart raced. "I did—I do." I nodded. It was the truth. I did *miss* him, and I wondered where he had been all these days. "I just thought you were busy. I didn't think you were with the witches. Why were you with them? Did they offer an exchange?" My brows furrowed as the questions fell from my mouth by themselves.

The corner of his mouth curled into a smile. His eyes raced over my face, gleaming from within as if this was something to enjoy. "Your life for mine?" He cupped my face and his arm tightened around me. "Yes, they did offer me that. Of course, I couldn't let any harm come to you."

"Are you okay?"

"Do you believe I'm not?"

"I don't know. Pietro told me—" I wanted to tell him about the countless thoughts running in my head but before I could, he cut me off.

A frown appeared on his face. "Pietro says a lot of things. Since when did you start listening to him? He's full of shit." He paused to take a breath and unwrap his arm from me. "*Nothing* happened. I had been occupied by the witches for the past week and that's all I can tell you. They gave me what I wanted, and I'll give them what they need. Asides from that, don't be concerned because that's the last thing I want for you."

"But—"

Christopher placed his finger over my mouth, silencing me before I could question anything at all. "I don't want to talk about anything. You're well and alive, so am I. I don't see a problem here. Don't make one."

"I don't want to."

"Good." He heaved in a breath and turned, heading toward the washroom. "Go home. I've things to finish," he abruptly said before slamming the door behind him.

There was a storm twirling above him when he spoke, and he couldn't see it himself. I froze where I stood, and my heart continued to thud deeply in my chest. Pietro fled for a reason. There was something wrong. *Why couldn't Christopher see it?* He was different in every way. *Had he lost his humanity? Was he going to turn back into the cruel monster he once was?*

I left the bedroom when I heard the shower running. He didn't want to tell me anything and clearly, something was wrong. Taking the stairs, I headed down and searched for Michael. Pietro was long gone and there was no one else here asides from the servants.

"Michael." I knocked on the door of his room or at least where I last remembered he stayed. "Are you inside?" I whispered, knocking again, but there was no response.

I pursed my lips and wrapped my hand around the doorknob. It was open. The door slightly creaked as I opened it and looked inside. My mouth went dry when I found Michael standing near the window, hands spread and his eyes completely gray. There was no color within them.

My heart began beating fast at the sight of him. It was terrifying but at the same time, I knew he was trying to do *something*.

Complete silence crept into my ears, and I shuddered while reaching closer to him. He was in a deep trance, frozen in place. I couldn't hear the sound of his breathing, but his burnt fingers twitched every few seconds while he remained absent.

It took him a moment before he snapped into reality and breathed heavily. His eyes changed color, returning to the shade of dark brown and meeting mine.

"What did you see?" I questioned him, knowing he had the answer.

"A wolf—the Alpha's wolf," he responded, his voice shaking in fear. "It controls him now. The curse is broken. The witches didn't do anything to him asides from feeding and mending his wolf as he returned to surface. That's why they wanted him. They knew the curse had been broken when they saw the mark on you."

"What do they plan on doing? It must be something. The woman, Selene, she spoke about a ritual they were doing and they took my blood for it. You must know what the ritual is about." I eyed him with curiosity while fiddling with my fingers and recalling last week with the witches.

If only I hadn't left...

"Something. I can't tell—I don't know about it. There are only a few things I can sense and understand. This was all." He walked away from the window where the blazing sun fell over his face.

I turned as he did and watched the dust particles feather through in front of the bright rays. Even more dust flew as he walked. The wood underneath him creaked. I caught a glimpse of the room, the large bookshelf and the old furniture, along with the essence of witchcraft and herbs that flooded through my nostrils.

"It's going to get worse from here, isn't it?" I asked, my words trembling.

"It could." He neared the shelf besides the bookshelf and lit a candle. The room lit even more. "The Alpha has to be in control of himself and his wolf. Selene wouldn't dare curse him again as she finds him beneficial with his wolf. Without the curse, the Alpha will remain violent."

"What can I do?"

Michael shrugged with an idle expression on his face. "I don't know, Rebekah."

"Can't you take his wolf? Like the same way the witches had done it before?" There had to be a way around this.

Michael was a witch, just like Selene and the other one. If they could curse him, he could as well. He could take away his wolf, let Christopher be in control of himself. It would stop all of this.

He laughed at my suggestion and turned to me while shaking his head. "I cannot defy him, not even if he himself wants me to."

I groaned and ran my fingers through my partly wet hair. Gathering air in my lungs, I let out another long sigh while my body grew tight with tension and sore from Christopher's wrath he had displayed earlier, in bed.

"But I can and I'm certainly going to." My lips twisted in rage, and I headed to the door to face him again.

I wasn't afraid of him.

"I wouldn't advise you to, Rebekah." I heard Michael behind me but ignored him while leaving the room.

Just as I did, he began following me while uncertain noises filled the silence inside the house. My brows furrowed in confusion. *Was somebody here?* I was unsure. Before Christopher left for a shower, he told me had *things* to take care of.

I followed the voices into the large seating area across the hall and close to the dining area. The doors were closed, yet some voices from inside fled and echoed through the house.

"Don't go inside." Michael stopped in front of me, blocking the door.

"Why not?"

Fear flashed over his face and his eyes turned light once more. "You don't want to."

"I certainly do."

I walked past him and thrust open the door to confront Christopher and force him back to being the man he was a week ago but to my surprise, my gaze collided with the female witch that had kidnapped me.

Selene.

62

REBEKAH

"What is she doing here?" I demanded. My hands folded across my chest as I snapped my head around to Christopher who *sat* with the witches, as if they were slowly becoming his buddies. "She literally kidnapped me and now you're befriending her? Is that why you wanted me to leave?" My eyes burned into his.

He stepped away from the witches and approached me. "What are you doing here?" he asked, his voice low against mine.

I rolled my eyes. "What is *she* doing here? What are *they* doing here?" My finger directed toward the witches. It wasn't just Selene, but rather two more witches, one I had seen with her earlier in that cottage and one more I didn't recognize.

"Nothing." Christopher wrapped his hand around my elbow and began taking me away from them. "I've work to attend to. You should go home," he suggested, nothing but a chill in his voice.

I tore myself away from him. "I'm not going home while you begin tying friendship bracelets with the same people who hexed you, kidnapped me and taken my blood. Something is wrong with you if you've invited them into your home." I looked up at him with my brows furrowed and anger clear on my face.

I couldn't believe they were here right now, when all this time Christopher told me how much he had hated them. *Where did that hatred go? What had they done to him?*

"It's none of your business, Rebekah." A storm appeared in his eyes before his hand returned around my elbow, pulling me away from the witches who sat quietly a distance away.

Upon glancing over his shoulder, I found Selene grinning in silence. *She had done all of this.* I wasn't going to let her enjoy it—not on my watch.

"Let go of my hand." I fought back against Christopher, but he didn't stop. "I'll go!" I exclaimed, pushing him off at last.

"You'd better."

Heat filled my face as I dusted off my clothes and stood still for a moment, catching my breath. I brushed my hair off my face and turned toward the door. Michael wasn't there as he knew the witches were here. He must've sensed them and tried to stop me from going inside but I still did.

While everyone here had to bow to Christopher as their Alpha, I didn't, and I was never going to. Defying him ran through my blood and I was going to take every chance at it.

I was his equal. *What could he possibly do to me?* Nothing.

My heart skipped a beat as I grabbed onto the antique show piece placed over the small wooden table and threw it in the air, aiming it toward Selene. Christopher grabbed my hand, but it was already too late by the time he did so. The brass piece nearly collided with her scrawny head, but she got up quickly. Gasps rose in the silence as the piece fell onto the ground and split into several pieces.

If only it had gone through her head.

I gritted my teeth in anger. "Next time, you're not even going to know where it came from. Bitch!" I snapped at her and for a moment, I saw the fear in her eyes, which was soon replaced with fury.

Christopher's hand tightened on my wrist, and he dragged me out of the sitting room while closing the large door behind him. "What is wrong with you? Do you not see I'm in the middle of something?"

"Actually, I don't see it, just like you can't see what you're doing."

"I know well enough what I'm doing, Rebekah," he yelled as his fingers dug into my flesh. "And I don't need you interrupting me. I'll do whatever I wish to do and you're not going to do anything about it. Do you understand that?"

"No."

"Fuck it. What is your problem?" he growled deeply.

"You. What are you doing inviting her and her posse here? Do you not know what they did with me? And what they did with you? I can't even recognize you anymore." My voice lowered and softened as sorrow and guilt curled in my stomach. I blamed myself partly for letting the witches have me and for not reaching out to Christopher to check on him.

Maybe if I had reached him earlier, he would have still been himself.

"They did not do anything to me," he repeated once more. "Am I hurt? Am I in pain?" he asked before taking a step back and splaying his arms open. There wasn't any injury on him. "No. I'm not, so leave it alone. This is my fucking city and I'm going to do whatever I want to do with it."

I took a step forward and whispered, "What are you doing to do?" *What was he planning to do? Why had he mentioned Laford in all of this? Was this all bigger than I and everyone thought?*

"Nothing you need to know. You're *merely* my mate, Rebekah. You don't need to overstep, so go home like you gladly did that afternoon.

I'll do as I wish and if you've a problem with that, deal with it—yourself," he said rudely and with a hint of anger behind his words.

A scowl appeared on my face as I realized he was angry about what happened before I was taken by the witches. We had been in an argument when I told him I didn't want to become a werewolf and he stayed stern on *turning* me one day. He had promised me he wouldn't kill anyone, but I doubted he was going to keep his promise after all this.

"Did you just wanted to mark me so you could get your fucking wolf back?" I asked with surprise.

"Think whatever you want." He scoffed and turned, returning to the sitting room where the witches still were. He closed the door on his way in and the loud slam echoed in my head for the rest of the day.

A small tear of grief trailed down my cheek, but I quickly wiped it away while walking across the hallway. On the other end, I found Michael standing there, listening to everything that had happened.

"He's only pushing you away because he doesn't want to reconnect with his feelings. Once he does, his wolf will lose the control," he said to me, halfheartedly. "Don't leave right now."

"I don't want to," I whispered, shaking my head. "But he wants me to."

"He doesn't. He *needs* you." Michael approached me and we walked further away from the sitting room where Christopher was seated with the witches, planning something I didn't know "From what I've heard, the witches could possibly be planning for another *massacre*. A similar one happened more than a hundred years ago. It was when the witches killed werewolves to end their kind. It didn't work."

I froze in my steps when I heard the same exact words that I had heard from my young sister once and from Christopher just a while ago. The massacre was true. It had already happened once.

"Is that it?" I turned to him with my eyes wide and full of terror.

"I believe so. They must've promised something to the Alpha, to not harm him or those he doesn't want dead. That must've been the ritual they were planning on doing here, in one of the only cities where werewolves live freely," he further explained.

I released a breath and my lips parted in surprise. "That would be cruel." Hundreds and thousands of werewolves dead—it was *vicious*.

Why would Christopher ever agree to it? Or was he forced to?

63

REBEKAH

My leg folded across the other one as the door flung open. A warm smile spread over my face as I raised my head and saw Christopher.

"What are you still doing here?" he grunted while stepping in and unbuttoning the first few buttons of his tight shirt. "I thought you would've left by now." He seemed irritated by my presence but that was exactly why I was here.

"Oops, must've left my mind." I shrugged as he continued to glare at me from the corner of his eyes.

As some of buttons came undone, he turned and leaned over me, planting his hands on either side of my head and inching closer and closer till there was no distance left between us. "What do you want?"

I placed my hand on his chest, brushing my fingers against his bareness. "*You*. Is that bad to want?" I pouted and looked up into his scorching eyes where I still didn't find the man I had been looking for. He couldn't be just *gone*. "I don't care what you do, Christopher, as long as you're okay, and I know you're not right now. I care for you, and I don't want you to make mistakes you shouldn't be making."

"That's good to know." He smiled at me. "But you should go home. I'm going to be occupied for some time and I don't want you pulling the scene you just pulled each hour. It's better if you head home."

Whenever my mind went to witches, I grew enraged. They were going to pay for whatever they had done.

"What are you planning on doing?" I questioned him, changing the topic.

Michael had given me a possible hint of what was happening but if it was the truth, I needed to hear it from Christopher. He couldn't be in his right mind to help the witches kill werewolves and conducting a massacre.

"Nothing you need to know."

Before he leaned back, I grabbed his arms and pulled him toward me. "Tell me." His skin was hot against mine, *searing*. I loosened my hold instantly.

"Nothing," he repeated, tearing himself from me before he could *feel* anything. Michael wasn't wrong when he told me he was suppressing his feelings. "You're wasting your time here and mine. Go home, I'll see you later."

I nodded and stood up, this time leaving him alone. There wasn't much I could do if he was pushing me away. His gaze slipped away when I reached the door. He didn't turn to stop me or even give me a goodbye kiss. *Nothing*. I unlocked the door and headed back downstairs. The witches were gone when I scoured through the sitting room. Christopher had been with them for nearly an hour.

What were they discussing?

Michael drove me back home. My head throbbed on the entire way back. I couldn't stop thinking about Christopher. *God.* I just wanted him. But I wasn't sure anymore if he wanted me. After all, he did get what he wanted the most—his *wolf*.

"Keep me updated. I might leave town for a day but if anything happens, please tell me, and if you do manage to get inside his fat head and figure out what's wrong, tell me," I said to Michael while adding my phone number into his phone.

I intended on leaving the town for a day to see Dad over the weekend with my little sister but after everything that happened today, I was exhausted and needed an escape earlier than later. And I needed someone to talk to—someone who understood me.

"Mom!" I called while walking into my house and searching for her. The scent of warm, fresh pasta trailed up to my nose and my stomach grumbled in hunger. "That smells so good," I whispered, slipping into the kitchen.

She twisted away from the stove and smiled at me. "It's not done yet. Going to take a bit more time. How was your day?" she asked while clutching the large wooden spoon that had been dipped into the sauce.

"Alright..." I trailed off. "I'm planning to head to Dad's and staying with him tonight. I'll be back tomorrow. Is that fine with you, Mom?" I asked her before making up my mind.

Surprise washed over her face. With raised eyebrows, she turned to the stove and circled the spoon in the pasta. "I thought you weren't going until the weekend."

I had thought that too. It was a last-minute plan. I wanted to escape from here and unwind just for a night. It broke my heart today when I saw Christopher and his second demeanor, one I hadn't seen before. He had never been rude before but today, he was. I needed a moment to adjust to it. The upcoming days, even weeks, were going to be me chasing him as the witches tried to control him and conduct a massacre.

"Plan changed. I miss him a lot so I thought it would be better if I headed there now. I can take Rose with me later at the weekend, so she won't miss school," I suggested to Mom while biting my lower lip.

"Of course. Leave before it gets dark, it's a long ride there."

A smile spread over my face. "Thanks, Mom."

"Eat before you leave."

"I will!"

My fingers traced down my wet hair as I detangled them while holding the phone with my other hand. The loud rings continued in my ear and at the fourth ring, Christopher finally picked up my call. I had called him four times earlier and either he was too busy or dead.

"Why are you bothering me, Rebekah? Let me have a moment of peace." He sounded tired, as if he'd had a long day of battling with himself.

I paused, holding back my words, the words I wanted to share with him. My tongue ran across my lower lip, and I swallowed hard before responding to him. "I just wanted to tell you I'm going to my dad's, and I'll be back tomorrow."

"Great to know!"

My lips lined straight as I heard the excitement in his voice. He was barely bothered. *How strange?* The scowl on my face disappeared and I took a deep breath. "Fine. Talk to you later."

"Goodbye."

The line went dead after that. I held the phone to my chest for a few minutes, adjusting to what had happened. Even if I wanted to, I couldn't be angry at him for something he wasn't in control of.

I ran my hand over my cheeks, brushing away the involuntary tears that fell on my face. The ache remained in my chest. I combed my hair once more before switching off the light in my washroom and tossing the pregnancy test into the bin.

I wasn't sure.

The lines were clear, but I didn't know if it was right.

I slipped into my car and started the engine. It hadn't been long since I had left Christopher's—barely an hour. Something kept bothering me and the rational part of me forced me to take the test. It was positive and it wasn't the *only* one I had taken. I just hoped Mom wouldn't go through the bin inside my washroom until I came back.

Pushing my hair behind my ear, I rolled out of the parking lot and began driving out of Laford, heading to the small town where my dad had moved to.

64

Rebekah

I stared out of the window with a warm cup of coffee wrapped around my fingers. The view from this side of my dad's house was breathtaking. I hadn't had the chance to view it in the morning, but I knew I was going to be surprised when the sun began rising.

"How is it here?" I turned to him and asked as he walked in.

It was a small cozy room with a fireplace on the other wall by the window. I had gone through the house and according to Dad, it was an old family home where he sometimes spent time with his brothers when they were all younger. A lot of memories surfaced when he came here. There were dozens of pictures of him and his brothers inside the house.

"It's wonderful." The smile never washed off his face. He took a seat beside me and sat down. "I believe this was all I needed after everything. The city life was too quick for an old man like me."

I pouted. "You're not old, Dad."

"I'm certainly getting there." He trailed off with a chuckle and we both looked outside.

It was quiet here, serene, peaceful compared to where I had just come from. The pain in my head had finally gone after hours and hours. My thoughts came to a halt when I reached here. There was no time to ponder—not yet.

"How's Rose doing?"

"Oh, she's doing good. She really wanted to come but school and the classes after that. It would've been a lot of trouble if I had bought her along with me," I continued while turning my head to him and catching a glimpse of the unhappiness in his eyes. "Don't worry, Dad. I'll get her on the weekend, and we can all spend time together."

It was difficult being alone. Dad did have his brothers, my uncles, but even then, a part of him missed *us*—all of us. He had spent half of his adult life in the city, with Mom and us before he was driven to bed because of cancer. Just as he'd healed, he became all alone and went far away.

"It's alright. I'm just happy you're here. Nothing else matters." He looped his arm around my shoulder and pulled me into his tight embrace.

I clutched the coffee with my dear life, hoping it wouldn't spill. My lungs begged for air. A sudden urge rose in my throat, and I quickly moved away from my dad. Standing up, I placed the cup on the table and rushed into the nearest bathroom. The pain in my stomach spread. I pushed my hair back over my shoulders and gagged before spilling the meal I'd eaten earlier into the sink.

I coughed a few times while the running water cleared the sink.

"*Fuck*," I whispered to myself as the back of my hand wiped my mouth clean.

Just when I thought everything was getting better. It was getting worse, and it wasn't something I could keep to myself.

I grabbed the towel from the back of the door and dried my mouth before heading back outside. Dad had shifted his position and concern spread all over his face as he rose a questioning brow at me.

"Everything okay? Are you sick?"

I shook my head and sat back down. The sickening taste remained in my mouth for a long minute until I washed it away with coffee, which made it somewhat better.

"Yes. It's just my stomach. Must've eaten something bad when I was out earlier." My voice cracked a little as I responded.

"Are you sure?" he repeated, placing his hand on my shoulder.

I nodded and leaned in to take another sip of the coffee while my thoughts raced. I had seen the results of the test. I was certainly pregnant. *But who could I tell?* I couldn't tell Christopher as he was unbothered with anything in regard to me and he had his own agenda to deal with. Anyone else, Dad and Mom, they were both uninformed about my relationship with a werewolf. Telling them anything was going to raise flags.

Unless...

Dad and I stepped out of the house and sat on the porch as it got a bit too warm inside. I sat on the wooden swing, which seemed as if it was going to break into two at any time and Dad crouched close to the sectional white sofa near the door. The fairy lights hung from the walls and flickered above me while the trees wavered along with the wind.

I barely took notice of the time as it passed. It was a three-hour drive down here but felt like none. Once I was here, I was relieved from all the tension I had left back at Laford until the minute I had puked over the sink inside the guest bathroom.

Now, I returned to being worried.

I wrapped my hands tightly around the ropes of the swing that was fixated to the roof and said, "I need some advice, Dad."

"Tell me." He waited, leaning forward with his hands closed. "You know you can tell me anything, Bek?"

"Yes, I know." I blew out a breath and my eyes raced around before returning back to Dad's.

"It's about a boy, isn't it?"

My lips parted. "How did you know?"

He shuffled back against the seat and chuckled. "We've only had two serious conversations in our life. The first one was when Adam broke up with you and you came to me, sobbing and screaming. The second one was when the doctors found the tumor in my chest."

A smiled lifted across my mouth as I recalled both forgotten moments. It was all well and different now. Time had passed quickly.

"What is it now? Don't tell me Adam broke your heart again because I'll not be able to hear that," he said with a hint of sarcasm.

I shook my head and laughed. "It isn't him. We haven't spoken in a long while—not since—" I held my words back before everything came spilling out.

The last time I recalled seeing Adam Chase was at his new apartment out of the city, when he was so afraid that he had to run away in fear of Christopher killing him.

"Doesn't matter. It's not about him, Dad. It's about someone else, someone new who I had met a while ago." I paused to take in a breath while the swing moved slightly beneath my weight. "He's a nice man but there's a part of him that I can't seem to *accept*."

"And what part is that?"

"I cannot tell you."

I couldn't tell my Dad about the shifter world that was beneath the city, deep inside the tunnels of Laford. I couldn't tell him that pure magic ran through the city and that werewolves, part humans and part wolves, lived among us—or we lived among them.

He wouldn't be able to bear it even if I told him.

"It's just something about his world that terrifies me and every day I discover something new that makes me want to leave his world and never return," I continued, a trickle of fear in my voice. "But at the same time, I want him with all my heart. I want him, Dad, but I don't want his world. I *hate* it. I despise it and everything that comes along with it."

Just as I finished, I felt an intense twinge in my chest as I finally came to understand myself and my emotions.

"That's not fair. Is it, Rebekah?" Dad gave his head a shake while his eyes lowered. "Acceptance is love. If you want him so deeply, you'll have to accept everything that comes with his world and it's challenging, but it's important. It's either everything or nothing. You cannot half-love anybody."

65

REBEKAH

Love.

My body shuddered at the sound of that word. I rolled over the bed as my phone rang twice. There were two notifications from Michael, and it was barely morning. The sun was still hidden behind the clouds when I rubbed my eyes and checked the messages.

'The witches have gathered in the tunnels and parts of the tunnels have been cleared out by the Alpha. I paid a visit to where they were and found them preparing for something. It has to be the ritual they mentioned to you. Unfortunately, that was all the information I could get.'

The second message was a picture of an unknown place. It seemed underground and somewhere close to one of the subway stations. Witches were scattered all around the area. I recognized them from their cloaks and the bluish skin around their fingers, which probably meant something.

What was Christopher even trying to do?

God.

I rose from the bed and dialed his number. After four rings, it went straight to voicemail. I called him again and he didn't pick up. My head grew hot.

I called again.

"Hard for you to talk to me now?" I questioned with a frown on my face and my voice full of irritation as I had just woken up.

"I'm busy."

"Doing what?" I cocked a brow. "Settling the homeless witches you have gotten?" It was the only thing I could imagine after the message Michael had sent me.

"Mind your business, Rebekah," he scolded, suddenly changing his tone before realizing what he had done. He switched to a different subject and asked, "Did your reach your dad?"

"Yes. I did."

"Good." His tone was stiff, and it worsened.

"I'm going to leave in a couple of hours and return," I told him while staring at the bland ceiling above me.

"Okay."

That was all. I ended the call after that as it became unbearable to hear his straightforward replies. A quiver ran down my spine as I closed my phone and tossed it aside. My head pressed against the pillow, and I sank into the bed while wondering if I had done anything wrong.

What if he had changed after that day when I told him I wouldn't want to turn into a wolf? What if I was the one who had hurt him?

It would make sense.

By midday, I was on my way back to Laford after saying my goodbyes to my dad and leaving him with a freshly home-cooked meal that he loved. My dad's words remained in my head. I couldn't half-love anyone. It was either all or nothing. It was either Christopher's whole world or nothing.

Two hours into the drive, I intended on going back home and changing before going to Christopher's to speak with him. Hopefully by that evening. But before I could make my mind up, I received a call from Michael who had found the details of the witch's plan.

"It's true. I could get some information from Walter as the Alpha had spoken to him earlier. The witches are promising him and his chosen pack of wolves protection and in return, the Alpha is letting them proceed with the ritual on his land—in the city, inside the tunnels," Michael explained on the phone, his voice sounding heavy and rough.

"What kind of ritual?" I stared at the empty road in front of me, which was taking me to Laford.

"A werewolf massacre."

"Why?" My eyes bulged. "What benefit would Christopher get from this? All this time, I thought he loved *all* of his wolves."

"They probably brainwashed him into believing that the weak werewolves in the pack mean nothing. It would make sense. They are cleaning the city by killing the weaker werewolves and letting the stronger ones live—for the time being."

Deep lines appeared on my forehead. "What do you mean for the time being?"

"It's witches, Rebekah. They despise werewolves. This is just beginning. If their ritual works and if they manage to kill the weaker werewolves in the city, they'll strengthen themselves and begin dropping the stronger werewolves, including the Alpha and his warriors," he further explained.

One thing still didn't make sense.

"Why Laford? Why here? Aren't there more packs to attack? Or other werewolves to kill?"

"When the massacre happened all those years ago, the city was painted red with blood. The tunnels are crucial for the witches to hold the ritual. Without it, they wouldn't be able to do anything."

Hmm.

I ran my tongue across my mouth before pushing down on the accelerator, speeding up just a little bit to reach Laford quicker.

"So, all we have to do is throw the witches out of the tunnels?" I asked Michael, just to confirm the theory.

"Yes. The Alpha never allowed them into the tunnels as he was aware of what they could do," he responded.

My lips parted, and my fingers closed around the steering wheel. Whatever spell Christopher was under, it needed to be broken, and I didn't care what it took.

"I'll go to him now. Just keep your eyes on the witches, Michael. Make sure they don't begin with the ritual or anything. I've got a plan, but I need Pietro, so call him." I heaved in a breath and turned toward the exit that began approaching from the right. "And get my blood back too. I'm not comfortable with the idea that a bunch of lousy witches have it."

"Noted!"

66

Rebekah

"**C**hristopher!"
I screamed his name through the house while searching for him. Shoving every door open, I still couldn't find him. He had to be somewhere around here. Just as I stepped out of the kitchen, I heard several groans echoing in the silence.

My eyes clicked to the closed library down the hall where the voice had come from. Opening the large doors, I invited myself into the library and held back my gasp when I saw Christopher standing above a man whose blood was smeared on the wooden flooring beneath.

"I thought you promised me you wouldn't kill anyone." My hands folded across my chest as I took a step forward.

He tore his eyes away from the injured man and glanced at me. "Aren't you early?" The taut expression on his face explained everything and it wasn't a surprise anymore.

There was something threatening about his demeanor today as he shifted above the man whose hands were splayed as he bled further. I couldn't see the wounds on his body as he was clothed but there was a deep wound on his neck, almost resembling claw marks.

God.

I looked away instantly and my eyes searched for Christopher's as I reached closer to him. "You're breaking a promise."

"And you're disturbing me. Go home," he whispered while wiping his bloody hands down his shirt and trying to clean them. He was so focused on the man beneath him that he barely even looked at me.

I furrowed my brows and blocked his view by standing in front of him. "Can you take care of this later?" I asked, and he straightened himself. "I've missed you."

As soon as he heard the words leaving my mouth, his expression changed. Eyes hooked into mine. A chill ran down my spine as he smiled.

"Is that so?"

"Yes." I let his arms snake around my waist while my hand pressed against his chest. My gaze lowered to his lips and my skin tinged. "I've missed you the whole night and I couldn't bear another minute away from you."

All his attention parted from the wounded man who continued to bleed just beside us. I tried not to think of him, either. Christopher smiled even more while his fingers dug into my back. My lips parted as I reached closer to his mouth and ran my hand through his hair, ruffling it a little bit.

"Would it be a stretch if I asked for you to kill this *one* later?" I asked in a low whisper while battling with my own desires that formed upon seeing him. I felt something deep for Christopher, and no matter what I did or where I went, it wasn't going to go away.

"Anything for you."

My fingers trembled around his hair as he leaned in, covering his mouth with mine. His big, warm hand wrapped around my face. The tension between us grew tight. My heart raced as I pulled him away from the library and took him upstairs while nearly forgetting about the man he had *almost* killed.

He groaned behind us as we left him bleeding. There was truly nothing more I could do than this. I couldn't interfere with Christopher's work.

"If I knew you were going to miss me this much, I wouldn't have let you go." The corner of his mouth lifted into a grin as I pushed him back into the chair next to the window inside his room.

There was something I couldn't understand. The sudden switch in his behavior. It was the same yesterday morning when he was yearning for me. He spoke to Pietro as if he felt threatened by his own brother's presence.

But to me, he wasn't.

Which meant, he had never stopped *wanting* me.

His wolf was succumbed to me. The mating bond. He could control everything in this world, but he couldn't control that—*us*.

"You shouldn't have let me go, Christopher." I pressed my hands against his chest, pushing him back into the chair before sitting on top of him. My hair fell over my face as I bent down to trace my lips against his. "Everything aside, I don't want to be far from you ever and I don't want to lose you."

"You will not." He shook his head, eyes brimming with desire while his hands raced across my hips. He surrendered to the slightest temptation.

I weakened him, his heart, his soul, his wolf—all of him.

"I know," I whispered, placing my fingers over his mouth. His lips brushed against my fingertips and I felt my insides clench. "There's something I want to do to you..."

"What is it?" He was entirely and completely caved in.

"Just something. Can I do it?"

His eyes fluttered shut as he trailed his nose down my cheek, taking in my scent and intoxicating himself with it. "Yes. You can do anything to me, Rebekah," he said in a low whisper that barely reached my ears. "Anything."

I slipped my hands into my shoulder bag that I'd dropped beside the chair. Fiddling through the numerous objects, I finally wrapped my fingers around the metal cuffs and pulled them out. Christopher was unfazed as they came into light, not knowing what I was going to do with him.

"Have you brought those for yourself?" he asked, grinning and holding me harder over his lap.

"No," I shook my head and pulled his hand away from my ass. "I bought them for *you*."

It took me a moment to seal the cuff to his hand and the arm of the chair. He remained clueless. It was easier than I thought it would be. I believed he was going struggle and toss me off, but he didn't. He didn't do anything. When I cuffed the other hand to the chair, I turned back to him and found him perplexed.

My lips fell into a smile, and I wrapped my arms around his neck while a small giggle escaped my throat. "I thought you'd fight me."

"Why would I?"

"Because..." I moved my hand from his neck and slipped into his pocket where I found his phone. "You've been a bad boy and it's time you sit down."

I stood up and away from him and quickly backed further away before he had any chance to grab me. The expression over his face stiffened and his eyes darkened as he began to realize that he had been played.

I didn't want to, but I had to.

"What are you doing, Rebekah?" he questioned, jaw clenched, his hands turning into fists.

I kept his phone to myself and neared the bedroom door to lock it. No one was going to leave here, and no one was going to come in. Christopher remained calm but confused as I reached for my phone and switched it on.

The last messaged displayed over my screen and it was from Pietro: *'Use metal cuffs and don't let him shift.'*

I called Michael from my phone, informing him of what had to be done next while Christopher glared at me from a distance.

"Rebekah—"

I looked away from him and said on the call, "I'll send a message from his phone but in the meantime, you and Pietro should get closer to the witches and force them to leave."

"It will not work," Michael responded, panic in his voice after I told him what I did with his Alpha.

"It will. Just try," I persisted before dropping the call and turning my attention to the other phone in my hand.

Using Christopher's phone, I dropped a message to Walter—the second in command— and disguised myself as his Alpha while telling him to clear the witches from the tunnels. It was a direct command from the Alpha—it had to be listened to.

Another odd moment passed by before Christopher got clued in to what was happening and he was no longer calm. "Remove this,

Rebekah. I won't repeat myself again," he whispered with a threat in his voice and a scowl over his features.

67

Rebekah

I reached closer to Christopher and stood between his legs. His untamed fury raced through the air as he closed his blood-stained hands from the man he had planned to kill earlier—just a few moments ago.

"Don't worry. It won't be long. You just need to stay put for an hour. I'll handle everything for you. The witches will be gone, and all will be well. They won't have the tunnels to do any kind of ritual and it may take a while, but I believe you'll return into your usual form in just a few days."

He growled when I told him what I was doing. Anger stormed into his eyes as they changed colors. I swallowed hard and took a hesitant step back from him. He pulled on the cuffs at once. They didn't break as they were made of metal, but the arm of the chair creaked, forming a crack beneath where he had pulled from.

Fuck.

"You don't know what you're doing," he said, his gaze meeting mine.

I quivered under his scrutiny. "Better than what you were trying to do."

He inhaled sharply and looked away, his gaze faltering to the cuffs. He stopped moving his hands and using his energy. "Remove this."

"No."

"Rebekah!"

My heart skipped a beat. I stepped back while my fingers tightened around the phone I was holding. I might have miscalculated the power he held. The metals cuffs weren't going to keep him restrained for long.

His eyes flashed bright red in warning before I heard a small creak from the wooden chair. A shudder crawled down my spine before I backed away, nearing the wall behind me. I had miscalculated more than just a little.

His fingernails stretched, elongating into claws. My heart dropped at the sight of it. *He was shifting*.

"What are you doing?" I asked, my eyes widening while my lips parted. I didn't think he'd actually do something.

The cuffs tightened even more around his wrist as his flesh became thicker and pitch-black hair came into view. Breaths barely left my throat. I jumped back at the sound of the chair snapping while the rest of his body shifted into a wolf. Dread covered my face and closed my throat. His face morphed into an animal I had never seen before. Splinters of the wood flew across the air as he became a wolf.

"Christopher?" I stuttered.

He growled and fell on all fours, nothing holding him back anymore. It was a seven-foot male wolf, bigger than any other wolves I had ever seen. His fur was all black but there was a white imprint on the top of his head. His piercing red eyes were staring back at my soul. His lips were tight, mouth dripping in hunger and fury.

Everything fell into silence when he stopped growling. Then, I only heard his raspy breathing and my own heart thudding in my chest out of complete fear.

I moved away from the wall and close to the door—*his escape*.

He reached closer toward the door himself, hoping to rip it open with his bare, sharp claws that had extended onto the plush carpet beneath the bed.

"No." I shook my head, my lower lip quivered. "I can't let you leave."

I couldn't believe what I was doing or what risk I was putting myself in but this was the only way. If Christopher left, he'd be willing to let the witches settle in the tunnels and take over the city while killing hundreds of innocent werewolves who weren't involved in this.

His tongue brushed against his sharp canines before he moved from me, quietly. I rushed behind him, threatening my own life, as he reached for the closed window across the other end of the room.

His phone remained wrapped around my fingers and so did mine. Both of them buzzed. Michael should've managed something now. After all, it had been a while since I dropped a message to Walter.

Something should've happened.

"I can't let you leave, Christopher," I whispered, breathing heavily. My hair fell over my shoulders and tangled.

Not yet.

This time, an ear-splitting growl thundered in my ears before he leaned close, forcing me to move from his path. But I couldn't let him. This was the only chance. There was nothing more if I had lost him.

He was vulnerable, locked up in a room with no option but to harm me if he wanted to leave, and I knew he wouldn't do that.

The window opened slightly as I backed up to it. He cornered me once more. The fury in his face didn't weaken.

He lunged at me—beside me. I didn't know. I scurried to the bed, heart racing as my feet knocked something on the ground. My back fell against the mattress. His wolf strangled above me. I didn't move an inch. My eyes trailed over his large body. It was surprising and terrifying at the same time.

He shifted back in moments. The sound of his bones cracking and his flesh shifting creating a sickening sound. My body tensed as I planted my hands on the mattress and began sliding away.

That was until he grabbed me.

He was bare now. His face was the same, brimming with anger while his body was warm, slick, and pressing against mine.

"Give the phone, Rebekah," he said, jaw twitching.

I stretched my arm and pushed it all the way back to the end of the bed while he held my empty hand and reached for it.

"No," I slid back, pushing him at the same time, but before I could get off the bed entirely and run from the room, he grabbed onto my ankles and pulled me. "I can't let you have it."

"I'm going to have it either way." He forced me closer to him. I clutched onto the phone with my entire life but no matter how much I tried, he was stronger than me and he got it.

"Please." I grabbed his arm before he left the bed. "Don't leave."

"Why not?" he growled, turning to me. His jaw clenched in frustration. "This is my fucking city, I will do whatever the hell I want to do with it. I want to ruin it, so I will. Give me a good fucking reason why I shouldn't leave, Rebekah? You wanted to. *Every time*. You wanted to leave!"

This wasn't about his wolf or the witches controlling him.

It was about me.

"Christopher." My breath hitched. "I love you."

68

CHRISTOPHER

"I love you," she said, and it was the first time I had ever heard those words. Those words that contained something to weaken me. Those words I had never heard before, never heard coming from a woman, coming from Rebekah.

My heartbeat slowed. I pursed my lips and waited for her to continue.

"And I know this isn't you. You're a man with pride and violence but you're also a man with devotion—to me, to your family, to your people. You would never want to betray anyone, and I know that." She pressed her hand against my chest, fingers splayed as I listened to her. "I rebelled, you chased, but you *won*. I'm yours. I accept every form of you, every part of you. If you want to become cruel, so be it, but don't turn away from me."

I cleared my throat and turned my head away, tearing away from the forceful gaze I held with hers. "You don't know what you're saying," I whispered, under my breath.

She placed her hand on the side of my cheek, turning me back to her. I saw nothing other than than honesty and truth in her eyes when she uttered the same three words again.

"I know what I'm saying, Christopher. I love you and that's not going to change. *Never.*" She pulled me closer to her and like a succubus, I delved into her charm.

A smile curled on my face.

She loved me—she loved us.

What more could I ever want?

Her confession was more than enough to rattle me. It was everything I had ever dreamt of—her acceptance. *Her.*

"If you still want to continue with your plan with Selene, so be it. Do it. It's not going to change my feelings." She trailed her hand down over my neck and to my chest where my heart thudded at her words.

For the first time, I was at loss, confused. I didn't know what to say. No woman had ever claimed to love me. I hadn't been this close to a woman before.

I admired her for a long moment. Tucking the pieces of hair away from her face, I leaned closer and pressed my mouth against hers. She was warm, *loving*. I needed her. I had her. Nothing was going to change that. Her words repeated in my head like a sweet melody.

I melted.

She kissed me back, softly and gently. I felt her warmth. Her body melting into mine, her heart pounding roughly against mine. I felt all of her in those few seconds.

When my lips parted, I knew what needed to be done.

"Stay here." I jumped back to my feet. "Don't go anywhere. Wait for me. I'll come back." I grabbed a shirt and buttoned it up quickly before clothing the rest of me and leaving the room.

Just before I left, I stopped in my tracks and turned around, glancing at her one last time. She sat against the headboard, a smile on her face, a smile I didn't want to dare play with.

I needed her just like this.

With a sense of urgency, I pulled the door closed behind me, leaving the house in haste. I had to locate Selene and her witchy cohorts. I had to drive them away. It was a fleeting moment of vulnerability that had allowed them to stay here and in the tunnels. Had I been in control, it never would have happened.

But now, control was mine.

"You won't have to look far," Pietro announced, stepping out of the car and blocking my exit from the driveway. He cast a shadow over the multiple vehicles parked there, their windows shrouded in darkness. *My cars.* The cars I had given to the witches—to Selene and her sisters. She emerged from one of them, a familiar figure in tow.

"Christopher, I thought we had an agreement," she complained, standing a hair's breadth away. "But your wolves drove us out of the tunnels, and it was anything but pleasant."

Taking a deep breath, I glanced at my brother, anticipating something. Standing with him were Michael, my second-in-command Walter, and a handful of other pack wolves. They awaited my signal.

The entire city yearned for my leadership, willingly submitting. And I had been on the verge of sacrificing it all for a false sense of security and power offered by the witches.

"No deal exists between us," I declared, taking a step forward. "I don't need your protection, nor do I crave the power you've promised. I have plenty on my own."

"You've gone mad, Christopher. Again," she snarled, her nails darkening as she looked up at me.

"I haven't lost anything, but you need to get out of my city. You've no idea what I can do now that I have my wolf—"

"A wolf you can't control! A wolf with a mind of its own. You need me, Christopher!" she interrupted, her teeth bared.

I shook my head. "A wolf that *submits* to his mate."

"That can't be true," she scoffed, her eyes widening in disbelief as the reality of my words sank in. Her face lost its color. "That's not true."

"It is." I crossed my arms. "Now, you need to leave. I have my wolf, my mate, and my pack. Do you have any idea how I could annihilate your existence if you don't leave my land? There are hundreds of ways. I'd rather not go into the gory details."

"This isn't over, Christopher. I'll be back. Your wolf will be mine!" she threatened, clenching her fists before departing with the other witches.

As she disappeared down the driveway, Pietro approached me, arms outstretched as if he were about to embrace me.

"I knew you'd come back, Brother!"

I recoiled, dodging his embrace. "Get out of my face," I spat through clenched teeth. There was nothing in this world that could make me like my younger brother.

Nothing.

I hurried back upstairs, aware that I had kept Rebekah waiting far too long. If there was one thing I knew about her, it was her disdain for waiting.

For her, it was now or never.

Mia Kerr is a paranormal erotic writer with over 35+ million views on Wattpad and Inkitt. Believes in everything fictional and adores felines. When she isn't writing, she's managing her cats and their charades and when she is writing, it's all about dominant alphas taking control of their kinky shifters.

You can read more of her works through various platforms including Wattpad and Patreon.

To stay updated you can join **Midnight Lust Pack** (Facebook group)"

Patreon

Website

Blood Moon Series
Red Riding The Alpha
Red Loving The Alpha
Red Saving The Alpha

The Pack Duology
The Omega's Dominant
The Alpha's Submissive

The New World Order Series
Bloodbath
Bloodlines
Bloodlust

Hell and Him

Devil's Plaything

Standalones

The Alpha King's Hunt
The Scarred Beast
The Alpha's Desire
Railed By The Alpha
Submitting To The Bully
The Billionaire's Pup
The Alpha's Dungeon

Get a free short erotic book by signing up for my newsletter!

http://miakerrbooks.com/newsletter/

Printed in Great Britain
by Amazon